OMNI VIOLENCE

#BORNTOSLAY

SCREENPLAY BY RYAN JACKSON
AVAILABLE ON REQUEST

Rights: Italia Gandolfo

Gandolfo Helin & Fountain Literary Management

italia@ghliterary.com

UNCORRECTED DRAFT
ADVANCE READER COPY

OMNI VIOLENCE

JONES WORTHINGTON

Omniviolence

This is a work of fiction. Names, characters, places, and incidents either are the product of the author's imagination or are used fictitiously. Any resemblance to actual persons, living or dead, events or locales is entirely coincidental.

ISBN: 978-1-64548-065-5

VESUVIAN BOOKS

Published by Vesuvian Books
www.vesuvianbooks.com

Printed in the United States of America
10 9 8 7 6 5 4 3 2 1

For our phenomenal editor Christopher Brooks.
Thank you for elevating our work to a whole new level.

Acknowledgments

A big thanks to all those who were brave enough to join us on this journey.
Particular shout out to our publisher, Vesuvian Books, and our agents, Italia Gandolfo and Reneé C. Fountain, for letting us run loose with this one.

Preface

While this is a work of fiction designed to thrill and amuse, the seed for this story is inspired by the sociopolitical work of Dr. Daniel H. Deudney, who, at the time of writing, teaches political science, international relations, and political theory at Johns Hopkins University, USA. In the book *The Limits of Constitutional Democracy*, edited by Jeffrey K. Tulis and Stephen Macedo and published by Princeton University Press, Daniel lays out one possible near future for humanity—a state of "omniviolence." In the essay, omniviolence is considered as the leakage of nuclear weapons capability into the hands of non-state actors (think a terrorist group versus Uncle Sam). But this idea has grown to encompass violence of all forms committed by everyone against everyone—and for such widespread violence to be socially acceptable.

Importantly, the democratization of technology and declining faith in both government and state-controlled currency means that this latter definition of omniviolence is increasingly possible. Once upon a time, to inflict population-level violence, one required an army. However, it is now possible for a single person to control millions of small quadcopters, each carrying a small, shaped explosive charge. Theoretically, these drones can be programmed to target anything or anyone—perhaps blond-haired men without mustaches—then fly into a major urban area and kill anyone fitting the description. Now imagine that payments for such services can be completed via cryptocurrencies on the dark web and combine this idea with a complete lack of government to uphold the law or defend country borders against foreign agents. Finally, factor in our increasingly politically divided society, where canceling your opponents is commonplace and viciousness on both sides of the aisle is increasing.

How long will it be until we reach a state of omniviolence?

PROLOGUE

Lying on his belly on the scratchy living room rug the color of long-spoiled milk, nine-year-old Jackson Cross stared at the words under his most recent SlipStak post. In his photo, his dark, chubby face contrasted against the skinny porcelain tone of his mom, slathered in green eye shadow. Jackson analyzed TubaniTucan44's every word and, though the full meaning escaped him, the message somehow burned into his chest. The stink of the carpet clawed at Jackson's nostrils, so he wriggled up and sat with his back against the stained thrift-store couch. He tucked his knees against his chest and worked his toes into the clotted yellow fibers littered with chip packets and the occasional disfigured kids-meal toy.

Jackson thumbed the profile button of TubaniTucan44, real name Komo Tubani, a twelve-year-old who lived at the end of Jackson's block. Herc Royer said Komo's dad sold drugs and that's why their place was nicer and why they drove fancy cars. Jackson didn't know one way or the other. What he did know was Komo wasn't any fun to be around. Komo slapped Jackson at the bus stop, pulled on his afro at the co-op's run-down playground, and yelled *half-breed* down the street.

Yesterday, Komo had one-armed a basketball so hard into Jackson's stomach that it knocked the wind out of him. Jackson had tried not to cry. He'd run home through the snow and told his mom about it, then watched her march up the block and bang on the Tubani's ornate front door. Nothing ever came of it that Jackson saw.

What was a *half-breed,* anyway?

Jackson re-read Tubani's comment over and over. His skin prickled hot and his belly soured. In the gloom his eyes burned, fixated on the bright three-by-eight-inch screen clutched in his hands. He scrolled the other comments.

> *Louise Earnest: Hahaha. half-breed! Good one.*
> *MikeyMike6: Don't listen to them. You do you.*
> *Luan Va: Get right or get even!*

Jackson fingered the screen again and zipped back up to Tubani's main comment. He typed out a feeble response, deleted it, and watched the replies mount.

> *Damshady132: Hahaha!!! Half breed. Burn in hell!*
> *Proppitt: Don't stoop! Chest out, chin up. Respect must be earned.*
> *AceMcgee99: Do what it takes to prove him wrong!*
> *DeadDuck00: Bwahahahahaha!!!!*

Jackson wished Dad was still around. Tubani wouldn't be so tough, then.

Jackson's eyes welled.

No. No crying. He wiped a sleeve across his face and scratched at his matted afro.

Another unrestricted browser window clicked open at the touch of his hand. He tapped at the screen, his large eyes reflected in the hypnotic glow. He scrolled the reels—fails, pranks, fights, and a gang of girls in G-strings. His finger reached out for the video of the girls. Their bare butts jiggled. He felt warm inside.

The familiar scratch of metal on metal. Jackson closed out the unrestricted browser as his mom opened the front door and bumbled into the living room ahead of a wall of cold air. Keys clattered on the sideboard, and she clicked the door closed.

"Jackson, baby, you hungry?" she wheezed. "I got you Yippee's."

"I ate that yesterday. Twice," he said without looking up.

Jackson's dad had always taken him to Yippie Burger. It didn't taste as good now.

His mom didn't say anything, so Jackson pulled his gaze from the screen. She hovered there, her expression worn and sad, still wearing her nail salon uniform under her tattered down jacket, the Yippee bag in one hand.

"I'm sorry, baby. I got no excuse. What would you like?"

"You not hungry?" he asked, noting the lack of a second bag.

She set the greasy brown bag on the couch and smoothed her hands over the little paunch under the uniform's belt. "No, baby, I'm fine."

The meaty scent steamed up Jackson's nose and made his stomach rumble. He frowned, wondering if he'd had lunch or not. He remembered the inside of the fridge, the grimy bare shelves, a pack of American cheese slices, a carton of OJ with a swallow in it, and a case of tropical wine coolers. He'd eaten two slices of cheese, then stepped back onto a belly-up cockroach.

The memory of peeling the body off his bare foot, then having to pick each crisp, dried leg one by one from his skin, sent a chill through him. His notifications dinged again. He looked down at the screen. Fifty-six replies, now, to Tubani's comment. And climbing.

"You should turn that off now," his mom said. "Been on it for hours."

"I'm talking to my friends," he whined.

"Oh, new friends?" His mom pulled off her shoes and winced, rubbing the soles of her feet. "Which ones?"

Jackson forced a smile.

A familiar, lonely expression returned to his mom's face. "Okay, twenty minutes," she said, then forced another weak smile and sauntered into the kitchen, probably to fetch a wine cooler.

Jackson peeled the brown paper bag open and peered inside. The hot steam bathed his face. Another car toy, as part of the kid's meal. He hadn't played with cars in years. His stomach rumbled, but he closed the bag and tossed it to the manky carpet. His mom could have the burger later.

Seventy-four comments, now.

> Gogodawg: Hahaha half breed faggots.
> KikoSam: Get a life peeps. Leave the half-breed alone.
> Hooman4: Revenge. Pure and simple.

The sourness in Jackson's stomach deepened. How many people would see this? He'd definitely hear about it at the school co-op tomorrow.

His mom walked back through the kitchen in sweatpants and a tube top that pushed her boobs up. She leaned against the wall, making kissy lips, and took a selfie. She'd post it to her stack alongside many others just like it. Jackson screwed up his face and considered unfriending her, but she had even fewer followers than he did.

He slid his phone under his thigh. "Mom?"

"Mmm hmm?" She took another picture from a higher angle.

"What's a half-breed?"

"What?" she snapped.

"Half-breed?" Jackson asked.

His mom dropped the phone to her side, her duck face now a scowl. "Did someone say that to you?"

Jackson shook his head. "Just heard it."

"Jackson." She raised her voice. "I'm serious."

"I just heard it, Mom." He studied an action figure he'd pulled the arms off, lying on the rug.

"It's rude, is what it is." She huffed and stormed up the stairs to her bedroom.

Jackson scrolled down his feed. Maybe throwing up would make him feel better. He rubbed his feet on the grimy carpet and scrolled past a video titled *U.S. President Pro Tempore Bunker Hit!* by some kid who thought herself a journalist. He scrolled back only long enough to see a billow of white smoke and men in black suits running around like ants. He scrolled on.

Jackson's phone dinged, and an inbox notification lit up. He clicked on it.

DeadKillerSlim: U gon let that kid talk to u like that?

Jackson read the message again.

JC4Sho: I guess.
DeadkillerSlim: Wanna teach that dick licker a lesson?

Jackson conjured up all the times Tubani had made fun of him or punched him in the face. A prickle of heat danced across his scalp.

JC4Sho: Yea.
DeadKillerSlim: Whats his house number?
JC4Sho: ?

DeadKillerSlim: His address. Where he stay at.
JC4Sho: S Morgan St Chicago. Why?
DeadKillerSlim: Number lil bro.
JC4Sho: 6431.
DeadKillerSlim: R u sure?
JC4Sho: Positive.
DeadKillerSlim: Cool. The Tubanis look home?

Jackson got up and crossed to the living room window clouded with frost. He squinted down the darkened street at the house with the fancy door glowing at the end of the block, two cars in the driveway.

JC4Sho: Lights on. His dad's car is there.
DeadKillerSlim: Perfect. Gimme a min.

Jackson's mom trundled down the stairs wearing a neon green halter top. She leaned back dramatically in the doorway to the kitchen, flipped her hair just right, and took more pictures. Jackson switched from SlipStak to a video platform app and streamed one of his favorite movies, *Big City Ninja*. His mom fussed when she caught him watching movies with a lot of blood.

The DM notification pinged on Jackson's phone. He slid back to SlipStak.

DeadKillerSlim: Walk to the front window, young buck.

Jackson stared at the screen.

DeadKillerSlim: Anytime u ready ... u tell me.

A tingle of realization crawled over Jackson. Did this guy see him? Know where he was? Down the street, a plastic bag flapped on a bent fence spike and a mangy stray dog pissed a yellow hole in a drift of ice-crusted snow. Jackson's breath fogged the glass. He wiped it with his sleeve and looked back at the screen.

DeadKillerSlim: U Ready? Say the word.

Jackson licked his lips, chapped and peeling.

JC4Sho: Ready.
DeadKillerSlim: hehe.

The brilliant flash of fire blinded him for a moment. He ducked his head as the blast wave rolled down the street like thunder and set off every car alarm in its path. He pulled himself back up to the windowpane, heart hammering in his chest.

"Jackson!" his mother screamed as she blundered across the room, one hand pressing her halter top in place. "What the hell was that?" She clutched him against her body as she stared out the icy glass, then raised her phone and recorded the house engulfed in orange flames and thick black smoke, the cars shredded by debris. "Oh, God," she hooted, "it's the Tubani's place!"

Jackson looked down at the smooth cream of his mother's skin, mashed against the mocha of his own. Pinned to his chest, the screen of his device glowed into his Lycra T-shirt. He thumbed the power button, and the glow vanished.

"Baby, stay here," she said. "I'm going to get a better shot!" His mother threw on an overcoat and flung the front door open. A razor of icy wind cut through Jackson, hanging in the air when his mom slammed the door.

He watched her stumble out toward the sidewalk, hugging herself with one arm, her phone held up to record the fire. Flames gushed from every open port of the Tubani's residence. Their big door with the diamond windows shattered and smoldered in a dirt patch yard across the street. Everyone on the block poured outside as the nicest house on the street turned into an absolute inferno. All the kids who'd laughed when Jackson cried, and their parents—everybody but the Tubanis.

Jackson looked down at his reflection on the black screen of his device. A brace of nausea swirled up into the back of his mouth. He touched the power button and the screen blinked on.

> *DeadKillerSlim: Boom! Everything those drug dealing shitbags deserved.*

Jackson flipped to his SlipStak feed, now showing one-hundred-four replies to Tubani's comment. The last one, a high-angle video of flames gushing from the Tubani's place.

> *DeadKillerSlim: @TubaniTucan44 Another scum of the earth racist bites the dust. Anyone else wanna call lil homie a half-breed? I din fuckin think so.*

Jackson gazed at the screen. Not a single comment followed. Not one.

Outside, his mom waved and shouted into her phone. The civilian fire brigade scrambled around down the street, spilling more water than they managed to get from the hydrants onto the flaming hell.

Jackson swallowed and looked back at his screen. He flipped to his messages.

> JC4Sho: You totally killed them.
> DeadKillerSlim: U needed some justice and I needed to pull a job on his dad. Two birds an all. U want something in life? Respect, money, power? U gotta take it.

A message in sparkling letters popped up in Jackson's SlipStak inbox: *DKSlim wants to send you 500 Giltcoin. Do you have a wallet?*

> DeadKillerSlim: Here's ur cut lil homie. Thanks for being my eyes on the ground. More where that came from if interested.

Jackson's face glowed in the artificial golden light, and a powerful urge stirred in his chest.

CHAPTER ONE
SIX YEARS LATER
Jackson

T he unmarked delivery drone dropped from the sky and came to a near-perfect stop just above Mrs. Evesham's walkway. It hovered there, quad rotors humming, level with her chin. The barrel of a suppressed micro pistol flashed. The old woman's head exploded in a mess of permed purple hair, bone, and brain. She slumped to the concrete walkway, legs spasming. The drone auto-stabilized, then screamed off into the clouds, a thin wisp of gun smoke trailing behind.

"Shit," Jackson said, more at his over-poured bowl of crunchy loops than the assassination he'd just witnessed. "Old bat must've pissed somebody off," he muttered and swept the spilled loops to the linoleum beneath his sock-covered feet. Morbid curiosity forced just one more look at his neighbor's corpse. Her body twitched in a growing pool of blood right beside a long row of pink and purple mailbox pansies.

"Typical Genial."

To Jackson, Gen X, Millennials, and Zoomers—Genials for short—were one amorphous swath of adults. They were caught in that weird period between paper and electronic worlds before everyone stumbled into the next level of social consciousness. They'd set up camp on static social media platforms and felt safe saying whatever they wanted. Their parents had taught them freedom of speech absolutism, which they believed in. Even the Zoomers, the cancel-culture generation, thought their righteous calls for justice could never be silenced. Now, running your stupid mouth from behind your keyboard had consequences.

Mrs. Evesham probably reprimanded some kid in Korea for his sissy-hypno-porn post, not realizing that if that same kid possessed a smartphone and half an ounce of tech know-how, he could smoke her ass from across the globe.

Why? Because he's worth it—the unrelenting mantra every generation fed to their kids and their kids' kids. *You're special. Just go for it. You deserve it. No one can stop you from doing what's right for you.* A never-ending social anthem of *Fuck everyone else if they think differently.*

So that's what people did.

Fucked everyone else.

Jackson's generation didn't bother trying to understand how humanity ended up here, or how the Collapse had come about. On the other hand, Jackson liked to think of himself as smarter than his idiotic peers. He knew how they had arrived at this dog-eat-dog nightmare, and he embraced it.

Jackson scarfed down the last spoonful of cereal, picked up the bowl, and drained the sweetened milk into his mouth. He tossed the spoon into the sink and clacked the floral-pattern ceramic bowl on the side of the basin, then sauntered off toward the basement door.

"In the dishwasher, Jackson!" The shrill voice of his mom could penetrate any wall.

"Just do it when you're cleaning up!" he yelled back.

His mom screamed something so high-pitched only dogs could make sense of it.

Jackson scratched his ass through a hole in the seam of his shorts and peered into the optical scanner fixed to the wall. The ten-gauge steel door popped open, and he stepped through. Old yellow bulbs flickered on, then the heavy door clunked shut and auto-locked behind him.

Still half asleep, he let out a long yawn as he stumbled down the wooden stairs and into his very own base of operations. The leather chair, well-molded to Jackson's narrow shape, hugged the edges of his shoulders. He swiveled the seat around to the ten-foot-long console, rubbed his hands together, and pulled up the nearest keyboard. A few taps, and he was in.

Eight high-end monitors winked to life.

One screen always had the crypto market up. Jackson's skin prickled as he watched the dramatic wax and wane of coin value. With a few more clicks, he checked his balance. Up nearly four hundred and seventy-nine thousand in Kitcoin today.

A first-person shooter game stood paused on one screen. On another, a movie played on a streaming service while talking heads traded barbs on a twenty-four-hour news channel on yet another. Not actually news with an anchor, but a user platform where influencers and self-proclaimed truth seekers got paid in crypto to upload footage of breaking incidents from around the world, or scream insults at each other over trivial agendas. The videos with the most views got paid more. Users like Jackson had to filter the garbage—cat videos and amateur porn. He only focused on a few reliable sources.

A public service announcement popped up from Anja Kuhn, her glottal Germanic accent harsh in Jackson's ears. "The kill-kill ratio has spiraled in the last five years," she began, "with one remote murderer now slaying an average of four hundred innocent civilians per action. Humanity cannot sustain—"

Jackson muted the channel and rolled his eyes. "Again, with this shit. Life sucks. Get over it, stake." He turned to his second favorite monitor, filled with the giant breasts of some chick being drilled by a dude in a unicorn mask. His fingers groped at the bulge in his shorts, but before he could get things going, the news channel cut to a live feed from Hellcat_59.

Hellcat. Always at the right—or wrong—place at the right time. Jackson turned the volume back up.

Shot gonzo, with a smartphone, it looked like New York, perhaps Madison Square Garden. The glass walls and billboard out front gave it away. Hellcat pinged the location, confirming Jackson's suspicion. A huge crowd spilled across the intersection, stopping all traffic. Placards bobbed up and down that read *Stop Sylcoin!* and *Sylcoin will kill us all*, or *Sylcoin = Sly-coin.*

"The protest was today?" Jackson blurted out, then scrambled to read his emails.

Nothing. No rejection letter.

"Come on!" he yelled. "Fuck!"

Traffic around the arena ground to its usual halt. The doors of three self-drive yellow cabs opened simultaneously. Jackson cranked up the volume. A swarm of single-rotor drones poured out of the cabs, and a monotonous hum filled the streets. Each tiny helicopter carried something like a coiled rope flat to their bellies. They fanned out into concentric circles and held their position a few feet above the crowd.

Jackson stood and clutched the keyboard. "You motherfu—*really*?"

Under the net of drones, the crowd screamed, then fractured in all directions.

The outermost ring of drones detonated first.

People crumpled to the concrete, their bodies transformed into pulped hunks of meat. Those who survived fled inward to the center of the drones' formation to escape the ring of fire. A second wave of drones exploded and continued the spiraled domino effect, wiping out more of the wailing throng. The firestorm pushed from the sidewalks to the middle of the street, leaving behind a cluttered war zone of dismembered bodies, black smoke, and drone fragments.

Hundreds dead in less than a minute.

He slammed the keyboard into the monitor. "That was *my job*!" The screen shattered in a spray of sparks. "Don't they know I'm the best of the best? CyberRonin81, bitch!"

Lungs heaving, the broken keyboard dangling from his hands, Jackson wracked his brain. Drone fragments could be traced. Tons of collateral damage. The target was only that one programmer for Sylcoin. But the killer went and took out half a city block.

Jackson's stomach roiled. The thrill of the unexpected rattled up his spine and settled at the base of his neck. The idea of killing so many to get to one. Amazing. Disgusting. Jackson respected it.

The alarm on Jackson's crypto trading site blared.

He wheeled his chair back to the desk, plugged in a new keyboard and monitor, and logged into his crypto platforms. By the last keystroke, Sylcoin had halved in trade value. With a scream, Jackson stood bolt upright, grabbed the new keyboard, and cocked it over his shoulder, ready to swing.

He sucked in a deep breath and pinched his lips. He'd lost a job to an amateur, as well as half his Sylcoin savings. "That's what you get for keeping your coin on the exchange, dumbass," he muttered under his

JONES WORTHINGTON

breath. But then again, squirreling all his coin away in offline wallets, even digital wallets, would mean he couldn't instantaneously take advantage of market shifts. "Still holding my Giltcoin, though."

Gilbert Flint Coin—or Giltcoin, named after its inventor—was Jackson's preferred stable currency. It propped up some of the leading network chains on the planet. While decentralized chains and currency effectively removed power from governments, sheeple had started the same capitalistic exercise all over again. Giltcoin had become as powerful as the old dollar.

"Be cool, man." Jackson sat back down and cracked his neck. "You're a cryptokiller, and we don't bitch. We get even, stake."

He smirked. Drop the word *cryptokiller* into any search engine, and reams of web pages, blog posts, and videos popped up, all whispering about the cyber assassins'—*his*—exploits. Sure, any moron could attempt to 3D print a drone or a gun to slay someone who cut them off in traffic, but many were too chicken—or just shit at it and blew off their own faces. Even DKSlim got ended a couple years back with nothing more than a pipe bomb.

Jackson was a pro and slayed people for a price. Pissed-off housewives, husbands who couldn't stop gambling, and irked sports fans provided a lot of business. Jackson once programmed a smart fridge to explode to kill a cheating boyfriend in some shitty part of Birmingham, England. Dude ended up with ham and pineapple cocktail sticks blown through the back of his head.

The real coin, though, flowed in on contracts to take out the owners of fledgling network chains that posed a threat to post-capitalistic crypto empires. A couple of years ago, he'd paid a kid in Africa fragments of a token to letter-bomb the CEO of Mzeecoin in his Nairobi high-rise office. That gig had earned Jackson close to a million Giltcoin. Easy money, near zero effort.

For a 146-pound teenager from Chicago, it was a fucking wet dream.

Unlimited power.

A teenage millionaire assassin.

The coolest kid alive.

CHAPTER TWO

Joe

The blood clotted and ran together in little intersecting rivulets that pooled in the shallow depressions of the pan. There it congealed, an oily film cast across its lumpy surface. Another job well done.

Not blood.

Joseph Carboni screwed up his face and winked one eye closed.

Not blood, Joe. Marinara.

He closed the other eye and crossed himself, forehead to sternum and both shoulders. Joe gave a slump-shouldered sigh and sat the empty lasagna pan by the oversized metal basin. Scalding hot water hissed from the tap and splattered into the sink, rinsing away bits of cheese and noodle. A meat-sauce-scented steam rose in waves from the basin and tickled his face. Over his shoulder, a damp gray dish towel hung limp.

Joe twisted off the water and leaned on the edge of the basin. The heavy muscles of his tired old arms flexed.

"Joseph!"

He straightened at the voice and forced a smile that cracked the weathered crevices of his face. Joe wiped his hands on the dish towel. "Everything okay?" He tried hard to mask the exhaustion deep inside.

"*Okay?*" the little bespectacled man said and waddled closer. "Squisito!" He kissed bunched fingertips.

Joe waved him off. "Sure, sure, Micky."

The little man's eyes widened behind fishbowl lenses. "I mean it! Everyone loves Joe's lasagna. They look forward to every other Thursday. A real treat, I tell ya." He placed pale, delicate fingers on Joe's shoulder.

"Well," Joe said. "Least I can do."

"It means a lot that you care, the way things are these days. The world is in the crapper, I tell ya." Micky squeezed Joe's shoulder. His eyes bulged again. "Hey, look at you! Still hitting the weights at your age?"

Joe shrugged. "Gotta do somethin'." He squinted. "Whadya mean, *at my age?*"

"Ahh, you know what I mean." Micky waved him off. "That stuff is hard on the body, and we ain't getting any younger."

"Better than wastin' away." Joe stacked the reusable aluminum lasagna pans, unrolled his wrinkled shirtsleeves, and eased back into a rumpled suit coat.

"Touché." Micky rubbed his paunch. "We'll see ya in a couple weeks, then?"

"You got it, Micky." Joe turned for the kitchen's rear exit. Red paint had faded on an old metal sign riveted to the top of the door, the words *Emergency Exit Alarm Will Sound* barely legible.

"Hey, Joe." Micky tilted his head back toward the common area. "Come this way for me, will ya?"

Joe looked to the rear door again—a door that didn't actually have an alarm hooked up to it. He shrugged. "Easier to slip out this way."

Micky gestured to the front of the place again. "Just want to show ya somethin'. It'll only take a minute."

Joe hesitated, then lumbered through the simple, outdated kitchen, still warm with steam and the heat from the ovens. He nudged the swing door open with his shoulder and backed through, scowling at Micky, who followed. Joe turned and froze. The room erupted in applause.

"Thank you, Joseph!" a chorus of little voices called out.

The sudden noise almost made him reach for the snub-nosed revolver tucked in his waistband. Almost. He stood there, mouth open, staring at a large white banner adorned with clowns and balloons that read, *Happy Birthday, Joseph!*

The common area full of children, many of whom sat in wheelchairs or lay saddled with oxygen, continued their applause. A young boy, hair-thin from chemo treatments, clapped his bony hands and offered a skeletal smile.

"Sonofa …" Joe swallowed.

Micky patted him on the back. "You do so much for us. When I got the social notification about your birthday, I knew we had to celebrate you. Happy birthday, Joe."

"Good grief, Micky. I hate surprises." Joe scanned the unadorned cream-colored walls for a way out as the kids kept up the racket. The last thing he needed was too much attention on a fake birthday.

Micky motioned for the twenty or so folks in the room to quiet down. In the back, Teresa emerged from the admin office and gave Joe a wink and a little wave. Micky held up his hands, and the applause died down.

"Thank you, Joe, for the time you've donated here at Faithful Shepherd. Your generosity, your friendship." Micky waved at the empty, red-sauced plates around the room. "And your lasagna—are a gift to us!"

A young boy, perhaps five years old, screamed his approval from an old wheelchair. The applause swelled again. Joe felt the heat in his cheeks deepen. The prickle of nervous sweat beneath his shirt. He didn't deserve this. Didn't want it.

"That's why the staff all pitched in," Micky said, "and got you something."

Joe's guts tightened. All those bright little eyes on him. Little minds thinking he was some sort of saint. "I can't accept—"

Micky extended a business card-sized envelope. "A small token of our gratitude."

Joe took it in his hand the way one might accept a sleeping baby. His lips pressed into a line.

"Go on," Micky urged. "Open it."

Joe slid out the clear plastic card, the edge lit with micro OLED technology. On its face, shimmering coins danced in a shower of confetti. *This card entitles the bearer to 0.05 Giltcoin. Scan now to add to wallet.*

Micky's eyes seemed to shine with the act of giving. The room felt too warm, overstuffed with wide eyes and the energy of human expectation.

Joe thought he might be sick.

The cheap flip phone in his pocket buzzed and played a three-note chime.

Joe stammered as his eyes darted to the sick children's faces and then back to Micky. "Sorry. I gotta go. Thanks."

As Micky walked Joe to the entrance, the daily murmur and

movement of the sick and infirm returned. He shoved the brace bar up, then cracked the blast-proof metal door. "Don't gotta rush off, ya know."

"Yeah," Joe grunted. "I do. Got a lot going on."

"Okay, then. Take care, Joseph. And don't let that warehouse work you too hard, all right?"

"Sure, Micky." Joe waved to the little man. "See ya next time."

The door clicked shut behind him, followed by a louder clunk as the brace bar dropped into place on the other side. Joe stood on the stone stairs, facing the busy street. He twisted back to look up at the dingy, bulletproof glass shrouded by burglar bars. A gust of city air, warmer than it should be for early spring, buffeted his clothes and pinned his trousers to his legs. He took a deep swallow from the wind, savoring the city's familiar, if not clean, smell.

Joe worked the card over in his hands, his mind filled with old regrets. He crossed to the bottom of the stairs and stopped before the donation kiosk in front of the facility, where he slipped the card into the slot. A message flashed on the screen.

Donate 0.05 Giltcoin to Faithful Shepherd Home for Children?

Joe tabbed the yes icon on the screen.

A fanfare of music cascaded from the machine, accompanied by flashing lights and an excited buzz. "Congratulate this human on their selflessness!" a voice from the black box bellowed over the sound of the traffic. "Would you like to connect this courageous act to your social media?" it asked. "Let your friends know just how big your heart is!"

Joe shrunk into the collar of his coat and kept walking.

That black box didn't know him. Hell, Micky and the rest didn't know him. Not the real him. The guy they knew was a line worker at the district dropship facility on the other side of town. A simple man with a charitable heart. A far cry from the real Joe Carboni.

If the big boss knew Joe had taken risks with his identity in public, he'd have him filleted and put on display as a warning to the boys. *Maybe that's what you deserve*, Joe thought.

The phone in his pocket buzzed again.

"Must be important." Joe fished out the old flip phone, the kind they didn't even make anymore. People rarely called, but messages meant it was time to go to work. He flipped the device open.

Go to the intersection of Central Pk Av + West Lk St, the little gray screen read. *Face N and pull to curb. 1:45 p.m. Pkg sent secure to your veh.*

Joe checked the cheap analog watch strapped to his wrist. Only twenty minutes to get in position. He spun and trudged for the car two blocks down. Stepping from the curb, he popped the trunk of the clean but well-used rental, a fully blacked-out Chrysler 300.

The scream of a buzzsaw echoed off the brickwork and ran the length of the street. Joe ducked and fell, half-crouched, against the side of the car. A jolt of electrical adrenaline stung the nape of his neck, and his sweaty palm closed on the snubby at his waist.

A hit.

A large disc-shaped drone, rotors chopping with an ungainly AK-47 swingarm attached to its underside, dove past his head and into a sea of honking traffic. Joe gritted his teeth and braced. *A hit not meant for me.* A twisted mess of gratitude and regret soured in his chest.

The drone swept through the traffic, drew pace alongside a driverless yellow cab, and opened fire. A stream of bullets ripped from the AK-47's upper receiver. Gleaming brass flipped in the air like thrown coins. The rounds raked across the cab, exploding glass and turning the sidewall into Swiss cheese. Blood sprayed the windows. Tires spun. Cars smashed against each other a block past Joe, swerved onto the sidewalk, and mowed down pedestrians. A pudgy woman by the edge of the neighborhood park sat gut-shot and glassy-eyed, blood-soaked fingers pressed against her belly.

The yellow cab, nearly torn in half, rolled to a stop against a light pole. Inside, two passengers lay in bloody heaps. The drone pivoted left and right, then—with a little *pop*—a shower of tiny paper ribbons exploded from a hatch in its lid. With a high-pitched whine, the drone shot skyward and was gone.

A restless Chicago wind gusted again and brought with it moans of agony, the burnt smell of cordite, and a few tumbling strips of hand-cut paper. Joe held his breath, waiting for the sirens—the boys in blue coming to get the perp, the fire medics rushing to deliver aid.

They don't come anymore, Joe.

"Not after everything that made sense in the world came tumbling down," he mumbled. *Now, it's every man for himself.*

Joe bent and plucked a paper ribbon from the gutter.

Dickface in the yellow cab wanted to argue that the Bears are better than the Raiders, it read in a tiny sans serif font. *He's DEAD wrong. HAHAHAHA!* The note was signed, *MarcoDarko69.*

"Hail Mary, full of grace …" Joe rubbed his face, palm raking over the grayed stubble of his chin. He pushed off the side wall of his rented Chrysler, eyes lingering a little too long on the carnage: the slack, lifeless expression of the gut-shot woman by the park and the broken bodies of pedestrians run down as other drivers fled. So much senseless collateral just to snuff one or two.

Joe pushed the trunk open and extracted a slender hardcase the color of port with the words *Diora Brass* inlaid in golden script. He shut the trunk, entered the Chrysler, and set the hard case on the passenger seat beside him. He pulled the door to him, the quiet interior shutting out the cries of the wounded and the dying. Used to be Joe, and men like him, were the only ones with moxie enough to go out into the world and shut people's eyes. Now, any idiot with half a brain and a little tech could call himself an assassin. But there was no art, no precision to what they did. No rules. No respect. What those clowns perpetrated was madness, pure and simple. What Joe did was something else entirely.

The phone chimed again.

He didn't need to read the countdown timer. "Yeah, yeah, clock's ticking." If Joe wanted to survive in this hell, he'd have to go on playing the part of the devil's marionette.

And right now, it was time to dance.

CHAPTER THREE

Jackson

J ackson checked his mobile device: 13:03. He leaned back in his chair and rubbed at his eyes. Four hours straight, trying to track down leads on the original contract for the Madison massacre. No luck. Of course, that was the point of dark-web network chains—anonymity—but many of the scythers, cryptokillers, and contract providers often added a little signature. Just a small digital calling card because humans are dumb and want to be famous, or perhaps infamous. The real pros, though—people like Jackson—kept a low profile.

He climbed from his chair and poked at his belly. Time to get some grub. Jackson picked up his Mark 3 Lenser and fingered its sapphire crystal surface. Chicago had over twenty-five thousand cameras on its streets, a remnant from the old government. These, of course, got scythed, re-scythed, and scythed again. A handy way to follow your enemies, stalk an ex, or see if that quiet kid down the street is porch-pirating your drone deliveries. Jackson's Lenser remained a tool to keep him off the grid.

His stomach complained again. "Yeah, I hear ya."

Jackson pulled on a pair of well-worn jeans, then slipped into some dingy white sneakers and a charcoal hoodie with no cinch strings. He stuffed his phone into his ripped pocket. No need to flash the hoard of crypto hiding in his accounts. Not enough yet to get him and his mom out of Chicago to that private island off the coast of Mexico. His dream—stupid perhaps, but with enough coin, totally possible. Still, no matter how full his digital wallet, he never felt it was enough.

And perhaps, just perhaps, he liked his job too much.

Jackson slid the Lenser mask over his face, then flipped up the hood of his sweatshirt. He peered through the groove-free eye areas of the sapphire glass to check his reflection in a smudged mirror, then climbed the stairs. One sneaker *popped* from a loose sole. The bolted door at the top unlocked as the motion sensor activated. He pushed through, then shoved the door closed again with his shoulder.

"I'm going out, Ma," Jackson yelled as he left the house without waiting for a response. Stepping onto the porch, he peered over the chain-link fence to see his neighbor's body still on the sidewalk, blood now congealed around her busted head.

A quick tug on the front of his hood, Jackson marched off toward the shrimp joint around the corner. Halfway down the block, a small mob of young teenage boys across the street—right in front of the still-burned-out Tubani place—jumped a podgy Genial who carried a sack of groceries. The boys worked the middle-aged porker over with short lengths of rebar. The porcine Genial took his beating without a fight. The boys fled, hooting and hollering as they redistributed their loot. The bludgeoned pig-man lay curled up on the sidewalk, arms clutched to his chest, blood streaming from a busted nose and a split forehead.

"Fight back, at least …" Jackson mumbled, then shook his head and trudged on.

Englewood was a shithole. Always had been. Now no one even pretended to care about the crappy neighborhoods. No county commission to petition, no city council or senator to pitch for funds. No corrupt mayors or dirty cops to at least make a show of keeping order and decency. If your local crypto-riche self-appointed tsar wasn't feeling altruistic, then your little slice of hell just rotted away. Anyone who made any real amount of coin left the 'hood as fast as they could.

Everyone except Jackson.

No one would suspect a fifteen-year-old crypto-millionaire assassin would stay in Englewood. The only thing he'd paid out for was a better net connection. Otherwise, Jackson's whole life's savings remained secret, spread across trading platforms and digital wallets.

Two men in matching gray jogging suits, hoods up, bowled toward Jackson. Each wore a child's party mask that looked like a lizard. "The Gecko Brothers," Jackson whispered to himself. Well known in the 'hood, but harmless. And at least they weren't stupid enough to wear the silicon masks 3D printed by some chump who sold his face for coin. Just last week, a wave of Frank Gallaghers from Minnesota had robbed an old lady, killed a hobo, and kidnapped someone's Chihuahua.

"Ronin," the Geckos said in unison, with a nod, as they passed.

"Boys," Jackson replied in a sonorous tone from the sonic modulator he'd installed in his Lenser.

The manufactured voice didn't sound like some twentieth-century vox machine, but perfectly human. Which meant these days, not only could someone steal your appearance, they could steal your voice, too. Since network chains meant hacking bank accounts had become infinitely harder, ID theft had morphed into a way to destroy someone's social life.

Cheryl Madison had found that out the hard way.

When Jackson was twelve, Cheryl told everyone on his block he was a mongrel with a black drug-addict dad who'd abandoned him and a white-trash mom who could barely read her own name. Cheryl had moved onto the block a couple of years after the Tubani place was hit. Jackson could have smoked her, too, but even at that age, he knew drawing attention to himself wasn't clever. And Jackson liked being clever.

Unfortunately for Cheryl, her own dad had been selling her face for a few extra coins, and Jackson knew it. An easy steal. So Cheryl found herself plastered all over the internet, a phallus in one hand, spouting filth that would make most German porn stars blush. She and her family moved away that same week.

Jackson rounded the corner and found the entrance to the shrimp joint hidden beneath a huge mat of broad, heart-shaped leaves. "Shit's everywhere," he grumbled. His mom reckoned it was kudzu, some kind of invasive plant from China that had already taken over half of the southern United States before the Collapse. Now no one bothered to tame the growing carpet. He teased back a curtain of leaves and pushed through the door to the shop.

The deep-fried shrimp smell made his mouth fill with saliva. He'd paid up front via an app, so a quick code punch at the automated checkout, and a plastic drawer popped open. He fished out the paper bag and opened it. Steam rose in a puff across his face. The shrimp were pink, fresh, and hot. He pinched the mouth of the bag tight, then fought his way back through the kudzu curtain. He quickened his step around the weed-covered building, hopped a short fence, and took a seat on a bald patch in an undeveloped lot otherwise consumed by grass six feet high.

Jackson scanned his surroundings. Nothing but swaying yellow blades. Satisfied with his concealment, he pulled his mask up onto his forehead and popped a delicious shrimpy morsel into his mouth. Jackson grunted his approval. Just enough seasoning to not overpower the cocktail sauce. He wolfed down the whole bag and kicked back in the dirt, eyes fixed on the wool-gray sky. The grass wafted back and forth as he studied the thick clouds.

Why the hell did the contract go to someone else? He'd been negotiating for days. Even came down on his fee because he'd get a massive upside as soon as Sylcoin slid in value and his altcoins shot up. *Total bullshit.*

Jackson pulled out his smartphone, ensured the encryption app was running, then opened his main social platform, VidSkid. He, of course, used a fake persona and not even his usual Ronin moniker. A reel of a girl not much older than Jackson flashed up. She danced and gyrated in a run-down living room, giving off vibes that told Jackson she'd been around the block more than once. She flaunted what was under her skirt, turned, and winked at the camera. Jackson smashed the love icon and skimmed on.

The latest video from MurderBot22, a cryptokiller wannabe, popped up. "Always good for a laugh," Jackson said, and thumbed the play icon.

"This Genial wants to *at* me over my custom piece," MurderBot22 said, and waved a janky-looking Glock with an ill-fitting slide crammed onto a busted frame. "Motherfucker don't know who he's messing with. Don't fuckin' *at* me if you can't take my truth, because my temper, baby—it goes from zero to death row in a nanosecond!"

"Yeah, right," Jackson said, chomping on breaded shrimp.

MurderBot22 lifted the Frankenstein pistol, the muzzle pointed down in his best gangster pose, and pulled the trigger. The gun exploded like a handheld grenade. The weapon's slide flew back and smashed its user in the face, splitting the bridge of his nose. The speakers squealed with MurderBot22's wails of pain, and Jackson guffawed as he rolled around on his back.

"What a dumbass," Jackson said, and wiped tears of pure joy from his face.

He scrolled on a little further, then sighed at the lack of attractive females and switched to his mail app. "Okay, there's gotta be something in here. Something I missed." His thumb moved in a practiced blur and the messages zipped up and off screen. "Nothing," he said. "Whatever, bruh," he mumbled. Another swipe through the authentication protocols logged him into his crypto platforms. "Fuck yeah. Giltcoin up three hundred percent. Two hundred on Shubcoin," he said around a mouthful. "Madison Square made me some moolah, at least."

Jackson flicked over to his image gallery and keyed up the only photo in the folder. Azure water and golden beaches with tall palms lit up his phone. Across the idyllic scene, scrolled text read *IslandLife*. The dark-web company sold small atolls—a way for people to live off the grid. The dream. His dream. IslandLife only accepted certain coins, like Giltcoin, and most importantly, reserved applications for people who'd stayed off the grid in the first place.

Jackson's phone pinged.

A message via his encrypted service. He frowned and opened the digital note.

Heat swarmed across his face. "What the ...?" He shifted back and forth and looked over the dry stalks of yellowed grass to scan the grime-caked windows of the dilapidated brown-brick, kudzu-covered buildings that rose on all sides. Nothing.

He turned back to the message.

> HELLCAT_59: Heads up, Jackson, you've been made.

"What? Hellcat doesn't know me." He jerked the Lenser mask back over his face and scrambled to crouch in the dirt. "Shouldn't know ..." Jackson corrected himself, his shrimp-filled belly tense.

The yellowed grasses rustled as something pushed through the lot in his direction. Jackson tapped at his Lenser screen to activate the heads-up display. His heart raced and the shrimp threatened to make an unwelcome return as he selected an enhanced microphone and augmented vision with two more rapid taps against the mask. Drones were easy to hear coming, even the small ones, and the software in his mask analyzed the motion of the grass to identify any discernible pattern, such as the turning of wheels or treads.

No threats detected. A luminous green square flashed up, indicating movement low to the ground. Too low for a person, but not consistent with a drone. The system suggested a rat.

"A rat?" Jackson gave a nervous chuckle. "No one would use a stupid …" His eyes widened, locked on the swaying grass.

A gray blur lurched from within the tall, dry blades. It struck Jackson in the chest and sent him reeling. He dropped his phone into the dirt and fell back, a desperate scream in his throat. In the wild melee of Jackson's scrawny arms and legs, the thing jumped and hit the cracked mud with a flat *thud*. Jackson scrambled to stand, stumbled over his own scuffed white sneakers, and fell again, square on his butt.

He sat there, lungs laboring, eyes pinched shut.

Something pushed at his right sneaker. Once. Twice.

Jackson unscrewed his eyes and peered down. A small, floppy-eared stray ran around in circles and chomped at its own tail just inches out of reach. It careened into his foot, shook off the impact, then resumed its pointless game. The dog stopped when it met Jackson's eyes, its tongue lolling from its little sharp-toothed mouth, big eyes wet.

Jackson blew out a nervous sigh and shook his head. "Damn dog." He scrambled to his haunches and searched for his phone. Another message ping and Jackson found the device nestled between stalks of grass. He grabbed up the phone and shooed away the puppy that whined and chewed at its own belly.

Another message from Hellcat.

HELLCAT_59: Woof, woof, BOOM!

Jackson's attention snapped to the dog, which licked a line of stitches along its stomach. He seized the pup—perhaps a little hard, because it yelped—and hurled it as far as he could, high above the tall grass and across the lot.

The stray's yelp cut short with a wet *bang*.

Chunks of strawberry-colored Jell-O sprayed over the dried-up field. Bits of gray fur caught the wind and drifted lazily across the street. Somewhere down the block, a car alarm went off.

"Muuutherfu—" Shoulders hunched, Jackson pulled his fingers from his ears.

His phone pinged again.

HELLCAT_59: Time to go.

Jackson scrambled along through the grass and back out toward the main street. He scaled the chest-high chain-link fence, swung his leg over, and dropped to the other side. Mask down and hood up, Jackson skulked along the garbage-filled, kudzu-burdened streets and passed by Ryan Harris Memorial Park, headed for the old Englewood High School. He slipped between the rusted gates and booked it for the main entrance, which hadn't been locked in decades. Jackson shoved through the ancient double doors, then closed them behind him. He rested there for a moment, collected himself, then headed to room twelve on the second floor—his hideout. On the way, he stopped by locker 112 and retrieved an old-school rucksack.

Safely inside the old geography classroom, dusty and adorned with dingy maps and rows of buckled chairs, Jackson sat on the teacher's desk and yanked off his mask. He fumbled with the rucksack zipper a second before whipping it open. He grabbed a can of room-temperature BrainStorm, popped it, and took three big gulps. A massive belch later, his blood swarming with triple caffeine and a bucket load of refined sugar, he felt ready to mull over his situation.

"First I get dropped from a contract, and now some asshole wants to slay me," he mumbled. "And Hellcat saved me."

Jackson pulled the smartphone from his pocket and went straight to the cryptic blogger's dedicated channel. The famous street reporter now had over one hundred million followers. *Beyond insane. All those people, and I've been singled out.* He scrolled through the uploaded videos, looking for any clues in the titles. Today's massacre at Madison Square sat high in the upvoted videos, having just live-streamed to the whole damn world. 1.5 million views already, and people had started posting GIFs and memes of the carnage.

Jackson watched as two new videos popped up. *Scarlett Moon: Trouble with the Wife?* and *Funny Dog.* He clicked on the first. Onscreen, in a dimly lit, water-stained brick room, a man and a woman exchanged quips. Jackson cocked his head to match the odd angle of the recording, which cut the bickering couple's faces off at the nose.

The woman stepped into frame, her face now fully visible.

"Anja fucking Kuhn." Jackson belched and wiped his forearm across his mouth.

The fanatical woman led Scarlett Moon, an organization in Switzerland. Their mission? To re-establish governmental control across the globe. Normally, Jackson wouldn't bother himself with politics or do-gooders like Anja, but a while back he'd lost a 500,000 Shubcoin deal because the contractor had suddenly chickened out—under the influence of Scarlett Moon. So Jackson decided to learn as much as he could about this radical nut-bag and her organization.

According to what he could find on both the dark and sheeple net, Scarlett Moon, an offshoot of the old Red Cross and Red Crescent aid organizations, had a web of offices embedded in almost every country. The organization had signaled a desire to use their network to re-establish some provision of aid, both within Switzerland and across the world. Anja and her lackeys helped an ailing Swiss government hell bent on keeping its pre-Collapse government. That quickly morphed into local administrative dominance and a worldwide mission to end what Scarlett Moon called *omniviolence*——the current state of the world without government protection, where anyone could murder anyone, even killing whole groups of people from across the globe for minor infractions.

Jackson screwed up his nose. "How the hell did Hellcat get a camera inside Scarlett Moon?" From the angle, it looked like a miniature lens mounted to a bug drone.

"It will work, Marcel," Anja said in that odd glottal Swiss-German accent. "I promise you. You just need to give me time." The waif-thin woman's short blond hair fell about her face.

"Your plan sucks," Marcel said, his accent neutral. Even with half his face off camera, his muscled bulk eclipsed everything onscreen but Anja. "What I'm doing is real. Action *means something.*"

"The world doesn't need your kind of action." Anja headed for a steel door.

"But it needs yours?" Marcel snapped back.

Anja hovered in the doorway. "This madness can't be allowed to continue, Marcel. We have to end omniviolence."

"Humans have been violent since the dawn of time." Marcel gave a dismissive wave. "Can't fight what we are, but we can *use* it."

She shook her head. "But you can't use my own argument against me. You'll see I'm right," Anja said, then gave a thin condescending smile and left the damp stone room.

Marcel turned toward the camera, the bottom half of his face in shot. The grainy feed stopped.

Jackson's eyes widened. He tilted the can of BrainStorm, emptied the rest of the contents into his mouth, and studied Marcel—the lines of the man's lips and the mole on the edge of the square chin.

Jackson threw the can aside and it clattered across the desk and onto broken floor tiles. "What?" he said. "Not even possible."

He fished out an empty, frayed pack of cigarettes from his rucksack and opened it. A single photo lay inside. Keeping images of himself or his mom online was bad form. No way—not if he wanted zero digital footprint.

He pawed at the photo of his mom and his dad outside the shrimp joint.

Jackson held the picture up beside the phone screen. The chins of the people in the images were nearly identical, as were the lips. Both had curly dark hair and onyx-colored skin. But, the kicker? That mole.

"Dad?" The word hissed across Jackson's lips. But his father's name was James, not Marcel. "Did he … did he change his name? Does he work for Scarlett Moon?" He huffed and jumped down from the desk. "Fuck him. He left. Why would I care?" Heat tingled across Jackson's face and neck. He stuffed the photo into the rucksack.

What else did Hellcat have? Jackson tapped the *Funny Dog* video and a wash of ice slipped between his shoulder blades. Onscreen, Jackson saw himself—shot from above the field in which he had been sitting, mask perched atop his head. In the video, Jackson shrieked as the puppy burst from the grass. After a moment of both Jackson and the dog spinning in circles, Jackson seized the tiny ball of hair and launched it with a pitch worthy of the Cubs. The stray exploded in a flash of fire and blood. The moment hitched and replayed, the dog detonating over and over to the old-school track "Boom Boom Boom" by the Black-Eyed Peas.

Jackson swallowed. "I'm on the grid."

Nowhere safe, now. He needed to get home and use every resource at his disposal to find this Hellcat. Whoever they were, they knew who Jackson was—and, perhaps, why someone wanted him dead. He zipped up his rucksack and fled for the door, bumped into a child's school desk that clattered against the dust and leaf-strewn tile, then bolted down the corridor.

CHAPTER FOUR

Joe

J oe buckled his seatbelt and the car chimed to life. On the inner windshield vid screen, a sun set with a flash behind a brilliant cityscape. "Welcome to the future of driving. Welcome to the Chrysler experience," the automated voice said. Joe adjusted the climate control to his liking.

"We must stop the madness of omniviolence." The radio returned to full volume. "Humanity will pull itself apart if we don't—"

"Damn." Joe turned the satellite radio off. "More PSAs than music, these days." He touched the car's navigation icon and waited for the faint *blip*. "Take me to Central Park Avenue and West Lake Street. Park on the street," Joe said. "Maintain full dark."

"Destination confirmed," the Chrysler's AI said. "Full dark engaged. Enjoy the ride."

The already near-black windows on all sides turned the color of pitch. Across the inner display, an ultra-high definition, zero-delay video reproduction of what a driver might see—if they were driving—faded in. The automated electric car eased from the curb and entered the flow of traffic.

Joe's fingers tingled with the need to grab the steering wheel. What had happened to the good old days, when people had to drive their own cars and a guy could feel the rumble of a real gasoline engine beneath him? Still, the future had come with a few perks—fully bulletproof glass and ceramic rifle-resistant inserts in the doors, as well as the full-dark blackout feature which maintained complete anonymity while traveling, most definitely sweetened the ride in Joe's line of work.

He didn't keep a smartphone and refused to have a personal computer in his no-frills apartment. The boys, Lorenzo, Richter, and Frank, ribbed him about him being a fossil. They weren't wrong, of course, but an almost imperceptible side-eye from Joe reminded the pups with whom they were fucking. Besides, just because the kids were happy to scarf a smorgasbord of digital banking, robotic laundry services, and suites of on-demand streaming services—all washed down with a glass of *This sparkly new thing will save you so much time*—Joe didn't have to do the same. For him, the need to navigate strange new platforms and wade through instruction manuals, all while struggling to remember fifty logins, left even less time for the things that really mattered—like family. Not *The Family*. Joe's family.

He tapped the console and scrolled through his contacts until he found her. Sheila.

Place vid call? the screen prompted. Joe tapped the *yes* command.

It didn't even ring. The screen filled with the large toothy grin of a teenage boy. "Uncle Joe!"

"Hey, Charley," Joe said. The corners of his mouth twitched up. "How ya doin', Champ? You just answer your mom's phone now?" Joe gave him a scolding look.

"I was expecting a call, sir …" Charley said.

Joe's brow creased.

The kid blushed and fidgeted.

Joe winked at his nephew. "Hey-ya, ya little rogue. Going with all the ladies, now?"

Charley smiled. "Just one, Uncle Joe."

"Good man. Treat her with respect. Be the consummate gentleman, like I showed ya." Joe jabbed his finger at the screen. "Your mother there?" he asked.

The boy's eyes widened. "The sink's dripping again. You really don't want to talk to her right now."

"Charley!" Sheila, Joe's sister, shouted in the background. "Get down here and help me with this!"

Charley circled a finger at his temple and flashed the whites of his eyes. "Crazy," he whispered.

Joe chuckled. "Go easy on her. She's doing the best she can."

"You can take a look at the sink if you come for dinner tomorrow?" the boy said, a hopeful gleam in his eye.

"Whadya mean, *if*? I wouldn't miss it!"

"Charles Edward!" Sheila shouted again.

Charley tapped a cringe emoji that briefly filled the screen.

"Hey, you'd better go help. She threw down the middle name," Joe said. He glanced up as the car turned onto West Lake, crammed with a swarm of honking traffic. "Look, I gotta get back to work, kid. Tell your mom I'll call later."

"Okay, Uncle Joe. Be safe," Charley said.

"You too, buddy."

The screen blinked dark. Joe let out a long sigh. Fourteen years old and Charley still had the heart of a child, unlike most rotten kids these days. Such a good boy. Hopeful and bright. A glimpse of the good that might still blossom in the corpse of humanity.

Joe knew his own record. He wasn't a great man. Hell, he wasn't even a good man. But he was there, and he cared.

Sometimes, that's enough, Joe told himself.

He watched through the vid-screen windshield as the car eased to the curb between a high-end Mercedes—one of the models with a suite of defensive options—and a first-generation Ford on blocks, its valuable wheels and chrome parts stripped long ago.

Joe checked the clock. Just in time, though a schedule was more of a guideline than a rule. The game changed. It always did. Targets lived their lives with plenty of irregularity. No reason to get all hitched up over something like a timeline. Joe crossed his arms and waited.

The vehicle chimed. *Incoming message …*

The file appeared onscreen—just a small blue folder like the ones Joe remembered from the desktop computers of his youth. He touched the icon. It unfolded, and pages spread out across the display. In the corner of the screen, a series of characters danced beside the words *Encrypted by Bombproof Digital*.

Joe touched the first image, a picture of a man Joe knew well. A chill formed between his shoulder blades.

So, this is what it's come to.

The car phone rang with a soft trill.

Joe tapped the emerald answer button onscreen. "Yeah," he said, and wiped at the corners of his mouth.

"Confirm you have the package," the refined voice on the other end said, little more than a ghost's whisper in an ancient brownstone.

Svanire. The squid. Joe wiped his mouth again. *Fuckin' orphan.*

"I got it," Joe said. "Look, you can't be for real with this—"

"Stop talking, old man," Svanire said, voice now low and saccharine sweet. "Your target is Rocco Vitale."

"Just like that?" Joe spat the words out. "We're cannibalizing our own, now?"

"Vitale stepped on his crank one time too many," Svanire said. "Thinks he calls the shots. Boss says it's time for him to take a nap."

How does the underboss over Chicago's Nueva Cosa Nostra outlive his usefulness? Joe thought. *What sort of heat is this gonna bring down on me?*

"The plan is to hit him with a hot drone delivery," Svanire said. "Send a message to the rest of the organization."

Joe shook his head. "He has a drone shield. The package'll detonate before it ever gets to him."

"That's where you come in, Joseph."

Sonofabitch never calls me Bones, Joe thought. "You want me to do him."

"Not quite." The sound of Svanire drumming his fingers rattled the car speaker. "On Thursdays, he enjoys lunch at the park. He owns the park, and his security detail will be tight."

Joe swallowed. "Vitale has been with this family for more than thirty years. Doesn't he deserve more than that?"

"Let the big boss decide what he deserves," Svanire said. "Vitale isn't your target. His shield operator is."

Joe touched the next onscreen photo, which depicted a round man in sunglasses with a head of slick black hair.

"Take out his shield operator and we'll send in the package," Svanire said.

Killing had always been Joe's business. But right here, right now, a sickness grew in his stomach. "You're gonna bomb a whole bunch of our own fuckin' guys just to do him?" Joe rubbed at the back of his stiffening neck.

"Do him *right*," Svanire said.

"Just let me take the shot on Vitale," Joe pleaded. "It'll be clean. It'll send the same message. Everyone gets in line."

"No," Svanire cooed. "Your job is to be a good soldier and follow orders. That's all. Besides, you're old and tired, Jojo. Your time was then. This is now. The boss knows it. He just has an affinity for old relics." Svanire cackled, a sound that belonged amongst the smoldering fires of hell.

"Asshole," Joe said under his breath. He let the silence build. Refused to dignify such paltry disrespect. *It's like you two are back in that fuckin' alley again, Joe.*

"Did I hurt your feelings, Joseph?" Svanire said, each word drawn out.

If you'd only been a little faster back then, Joe. Held on to the little orphan sonofabitch a little tighter. He wouldn't be a capo today.

"No," Joe said, clipped. *A capo who never acknowledges the name that you worked so hard to forge.*

"Then do your job."

The line clicked. On the dash, the words *Call Terminated* flashed.

Joe's thick lips pressed into a thin line. He could do the job, or he could find his own head on a pike. He canceled out the notification onscreen, selected the file again, then leafed through the pages to familiarize himself with the location, time, and target. He synched his watch to the vehicle and plugged in a secondary address on the touch screen. Satisfied, he grabbed the Diora Brass hardcase on the seat next to him and exited the solitude of the parked Chrysler.

Wind gusted through the empty park and leaf-strewn street as the AI pulled the driver's door closed. Joe popped the rear door open and took a step back. The smooth sole of his dress shoe slipped. "Ah, shit," he muttered. He eyed the bottom of the shoe, now smeared with some pinkish sludge, then the row of purple-black pods hidden in a green carpet that clogged half the sidewalk. "Not enough that it took over the entire South ... now this junk has to have Chicago, too?"

Another breeze ruffled Joe's jacket and stood the collar up. He grunted and scraped his shoe on the curb, then took off his suit jacket, folded it, and placed it in the back seat of the car. From a zipped bag, Joe retrieved a long coat the color of rubbed charcoal, along with a matching fedora. He laid the case on the back seat, slipped into the hat and overcoat, and entered the old-fashioned wheel-lock combination. The mechanism clicked and the lid cracked. Out of habit, more than need Joe checked the street. Few pedestrians, and only light traffic.

With a gentleness that bordered on affection, he eased the lid open. Inside, a gleaming trumpet sat in a mold of crushed black velvet. The instrument had belonged to his father, and could the old man make it sing. Joe, however—and much to Father's disappointment—never had any talent for music. But that didn't mean he didn't *love* music. Joe took a moment to admire the trumpet's shining brass perfection, then lifted the insert, trumpet and all, from the case.

In the bottom of the Diora Brass case sat what appeared to be matte-black pieces of a cleaning kit, each nestled in its own slot. Joe slipped the stamped metal parts from their grooves and dropped them into specially sewn pouches in his long coat. He replaced the trumpet, shut the case, activated the car's defensive measures, and stepped onto the sidewalk, careful not to tangle his feet up in the overgrowth.

A shrill meow stopped him short. Joe searched the hedgerow for the source of the cry. He ducked to take a quick look under the car. When a second meow came, he found the bugger bunched up in a corner by the stairs to a two-story walk-up. Joe looked in the direction of the park, swore, then nudged the Chrysler driver's side door back open. He retrieved the last pop-top can of cat food from the stash in the glove box and re-secured the car.

Joe stepped onto the sidewalk and popped the tin's lid. "Hey, buddy. Psst, psst, psst."

The cat, black and gray with eyes that flared with wild hunger, shrunk back and hissed.

"Yeah, okay, okay. You don't trust nobody. I get it. Here ya go." He placed the tin on the sidewalk. The metal squealed on the concrete as he pushed the tin toward the stairs. Joe stood slowly and eased the tin closer with the polished toe of his shoe.

The cat, still hunched, didn't blink once.

Joe checked his watch. "Yeah, okay," he said with a sigh, and made for the park. With a final glance, he noted the shy tom already at the tin gobbling down the cheap meat. "Bon appétit." A little smile pulled at the corners of Joe's mouth and he straightened his hat.

The short two-block walk to the metro's Conservatory Station entrance afforded Joe a moment with his thoughts. What in God's name could Rocco Vitale have done to make The Family kill him? The underboss of La Nueva Cosa Nostra in Chicago doesn't just get marked for no reason. *On top of that*, Joe thought, *they want me to kill a bunch of my own guys. For what?*

Joe felt eyes on him, and caught the stare of a trio of bums crouched along the covered stairs to the metro. Bums weren't much of a threat, but if one had a smart device, they could capture his image and sell it on the open market in the aftermath of what was to come. Joe popped his collar again and tucked down his chin.

"Where ya headed?" said the scraggly bum with dark skin and a full beard.

"Yeah, whatchu got in dat coat?" the second said, his voice tinny as he grunted his words through a mangled nose.

Joe slowed at the mouth of the stairs when the dark-bearded beggar stuck his foot across the entrance.

"Looks fancy," added the third bum with a face the color of skim milk.

"Gotta pay the toll if you want up." Dark Beard grinned a mess of brown teeth.

Joe scanned the hands of the bums. No weapons. No phones. He'd seen it all before. Strong-arming people who wanted to ride the privately-run metro system.

Joe came to a full stop, cleared his throat, then checked his watch.

"Got somewhere to be, mista?" Dark Beard asked with a twinkle in his eye.

The others laughed.

The homeless were a double-edged sword. On the one hand, they could be pushy and, on occasion, downright dangerous if they got desperate enough. On the other, they ensured all the would-be lookie-loos avoided the metro, giving Joe room to conduct his business.

Joe kept his chin down, fedora covering the top two-thirds of his face. With his right hand, he reached down and drew back the edge of his coat to reveal the snubbie revolver tucked in his belt. "If you boys aren't out of my way in five seconds …" Joe paused and locked eyes with Dark Beard. "Imma shoot a hole in *your* face."

Dark Beard's grin faded.

Joe looked to Mangled Nose. "Then you." He flicked his eyes to Milk Face. "Then you."

The trio of bums squirmed at Joe's toneless words.

Joe looked at his watch again. His fingers closed around the snubbie.

"It's okay, mista," Dark Beard said, collecting his belongings and shuffling from the covered stairwell. "Everythin's okay."

Joe waited as the bums grabbed their things and cleared out. Without another word, he mounted the stairs to the elevated platform. A quick scan left and right. Finally, alone. He made a hard right and lumbered along the shadowed edge of the walkway to the end of the platform on the conservatory side. There he leaned against the platform railing, then pulled a small can of wasp spray from his coat. Without raising his face, he lifted the can and shot a stream of off-white gunk against the lens of the overhead camera. Greasy foam dripped from it in globs.

Never know who's hacking what.

He stowed the can and climbed over the outer rail with greater ease than a man his size should be able, then slunk behind the unused handicapped elevator. He slipped around the side and found another rail, this one short and likely only decorative.

Joe sat on the cold concrete, then removed the pipe, cylinder, and springs of the trumpet cleaning kit from his coat. The hunks of molded plastic and stamped metal followed. With methodical precision, Joe clipped, screwed, and mated the parts together in a ritual he could perform in his sleep. In less than thirty seconds, a trumpet cleaning kit had become a sixteen-inch micro bullpup rifle.

Joe removed a small case from his jacket and popped it open. Inside laid a one-by-nine power scope with a self-illuminating reticle. He snapped it into place on the upper receiver of the bullpup and fished out the final piece—a Whisperlite sub-compact sound suppressor. With a twist, he ratcheted it into place over the muzzle of the weapon.

A quick watch check. The target and his entourage would arrive any time, now.

"God have mercy on us." Joe crossed himself.

He licked the tip of his finger, then held it up to test the wind. From inside his coat, he produced a small notebook. Inside the thin cardboard flip-top cover, he'd scrawled, in nearly illegible script, a series of set distances and windages in a graph-like scale. Joe consulted it, his lips pursed.

Tires bumped and suspensions squeaked as a trio of all-black sedans entered the parking lot from Central Park Avenue. Joe looked up long enough to take note of the standard VIP formation. "Vitale, you poor bastard," he whispered.

Joe re-checked the dope chart on the notebook's flip top and unscrewed the adjustment caps on the rifle scope. *Elevation's correct for a shot just beyond one hundred yards.* He gave the windage a series of clicks to accommodate the steady city breeze that flapped his collar against his neck. Satisfied, Joe replaced the adjustment dial caps, snugged the bullpup rifle into his shoulder, propped it on the low railing, and waited.

In unison, every door of the sedans popped open. Men in dark suits exited and faced out from the cars, eyes concealed behind dark sunglasses.

Joe scanned the faces of the security detail. None matched the image of the drone-shield operator. *Because he's not in the detail, you idiot,* Joe thought. *He's forward reconnaissance.* Joe swung the rifle scope to the tree line by the park, the lot, and the other cars. A man in a floppy tweed cap and a light tan jacket sat on a bench at the entrance to the park. With methodical slowness, Joe raised his hand to the scope and adjusted the power to full zoom. He watched Floppy Cap toss a handful of feed to a group of hungry pigeons. The man's other hand, concealed in his jacket pocket, shifted.

A remote. It's the guy.

The detail leader by Vitale's car touched his ear and nodded to the others. He stepped over to the rear passenger side of the middle sedan and opened the door. Another nod and a few words spoken into the back seat.

Joe wet his lips and took aim at Floppy Cap. The amber triangle in

Joe's scope centered on the bridge of the man's nose, then swung the scope back to Vitale's sedan.

Rocco Vitale stepped from the vehicle and gave an appraising look around. He turned back to the open door and offered his hand, which filled with plump little fingers. A child, no more than nine, wearing a unicorn sweatshirt, jeans, and little white sneakers, climbed from the back seat.

"Dear Jesus God in Heaven ..." Joe groaned from behind the scope's glass. A kid. Svanire had said nothing about a kid. He rubbed his eyes. *This can't be what my life has become.* Joe felt an acidic tingle in the back of his throat.

Svanire's voice echoed in his head. *You let us decide what he deserves.* Joe shook his head. The boss wouldn't order this.

Joe centered back on Floppy Cap and closed his finger on the trigger. Despite the chill, a single bead of sweat rolled from his hairline and slowed at the corner of his eye. A fake tear from a man with no tears of his own.

Murderer. Child killer. Monster. Joe's finger flexed and pulled flush against the smooth curve of the trigger. He let out a half breath and held the rest.

Joe swung the rifle down. The weapon bucked against his shoulder with little more than a *snap*. A necked-down 7.62 case bounced off the wall and rolled to a stop at his heel.

Rocco Vitale's head opened like an emerging flower bud, red and gray and white spraying in all directions. The child screamed and clutched at the underboss's legs as he fell. The security detail jolted to life. Some crouched, others took cover, and all of them produced guns. They jittered and scrambled, shouting and searching.

Murderer, yes. But not a monster yet, Joe. Not yet.

Joe covered the glass of his scope to conceal any glint of sunlight they might see from the parking lot.

The kid would live. Traumatized for life—but life, nonetheless.

A second *snap* cracked across the lot. Floppy Cap toppled from the bench, sending dozens of pigeons bursting into the air.

"No—" The plea scraped from Joe's throat.

A half-dozen stealth drones descended from the sky, rotors whirring. Joe's mouth opened and something like a moan came out. He focused on the girl, her eyes large and white, little fingers clinging to her dead father.

The first drone exploded, followed by a second. Joe clenched his eyes shut and willed the concussions to stop. The blast waves rocked the parking lot one after the other, shattering the sedan's windows and flinging broken bodies in all directions. Glass scattered on the blacktop and car alarms went off for two blocks.

The sounds of the explosions faded, but Joe's ears hummed. He ground his molars against one another until they hurt, until he tasted blood. The hot flesh of his face quivered. He crossed himself, hand shaking, and drew a slow breath. Joe looked down upon the blackened parking lot. The mangled bodies of the security detail and other hapless patrons of the park lay tumbled and torn. Drone fragments smoked. Somewhere in the smoke came a wail. Joe opened his mouth. No words came.

Surveillance drones from wannabe investigative journalists swarmed like flies to filth.

Joe had to go. Now.

His hands moved fast, disassembling the rifle and inserting the pieces back into the pouches in his coat. Joe grabbed the spent brass casing at his heel and stuck it in his pocket. With only a fleeting look at the tiny twisted black corpse in a bloodied unicorn sweatshirt, he hopped the rail.

Joe dropped onto the empty metro track and crossed the platform. On the street below sat the Chrysler. The car's automated assistant must have followed his direction and waited at the curb. Joe vaulted another railing, rifle parts clinking inside the coat. He grabbed a support pole and slid, fireman-style, to the street. The car's auto-defense system disengaged with a chime and the driver's door opened. Joe ducked in and pulled the door shut.

"Go," he said. "Drive."

"What destination would you like?" the automated assistant said.

"Across town," Joe said, breathless.

"What destination?"

"Give me control, you silly sonofabitch." Joe grabbed the wheel, a tickle of sweat on his brow.

"That is not advisable. It is safer if—"

"Right fuckin' now!" Joe shouted, spittle on his lips.

A blip sounded. The words *Manual Drive Control Activated* flashed on the screen.

Joe swung the blacked-out Chrysler into traffic and headed south.

"Slow down, you idiot," Joe muttered. "Blend in." He angled for the 290 Interstate, his fingers gripped tight on the wheel.

Then the car phone trilled.

Joe eyed the number, marked as *Anonymous*. He swore under his breath but answered it. For an instant, Joe thought the call hadn't connected, but an openness came from the dash speaker, the sound of deliberate silence in an empty room.

A strange fear, so unfamiliar to a man like Joe, pinched at the nape of his neck. "What the hell was that all about?" he said.

The silence deepened. Something shifted in the background of the call. Such a small sound, little more than the flitting of a restless specter across a moonlit graveyard.

"I know you're there, Squiddy, playin' your fuckin' games as usual," Joe said, a snarl on his lips. Joe was out of line. He knew it. The Family could have his balls for talking like that to a capo. But the image of that little girl's body, black and misshapen in a bloodied unicorn sweatshirt, filled his mind's eye.

A disinterested sigh. "Ol' Jojo had to do things his own way, didn't he?" Svanire's chuckle, low and dark, filled the car. "Just like Vitale ..."

"You did this," Joe blurted out.

"No." Svanire's voice took on a scolding tone. "You did this. Just like I knew you would."

Joe rolled his shoulders. *Orphan sonofabitch. Should have killed him all those years ago.*

"The boss ain't happy, Joseph. Says he can't have soldiers who won't obey his orders," Svanire said. "It's time for you to come in."

Joe swallowed, and a feeling deeper and colder than the darkness of space grew inside him.

CHAPTER FIVE
Anja

Anja Kuhn leaned on the crumbling outer wall, which ran the length of the main road that wound around the mountainside up to the lower guardhouse. The sheer rock face stretched hundreds of feet below her, where it disappeared into an evergreen tree line. Behind sat Castle Tarasp—sturdy and squat, save the tall square palace with its pointed roof and defunct bell tower which reached into the cloudless sky. In this very fortress, once upon a time, the human venture to rule united with the colossal wilderness of the Upper Engadine.

For Anja, Tarasp—Switzerland, for that matter—seemed a fitting place from which to orchestrate the rebuilding of civilization. Who better than the Swiss, orderly and focused on the needs of their neighbors as much as themselves, to set the example? And where better than an impenetrable stronghold, hidden away from the digital world?

A cold wind bit at Anja's face, forcing her away from the wall. She wrapped a silk scarf around her thin neck and stole one last look over the edge. The grassy plain, scattered hamlets, and small finger of a lake, while choked with a green mat of creeping vines and leaves, still exuded tranquility. Few would suspect the surface-to-air missiles and twin-barreled 7.62mm miniguns, poised to blast intruders from the sky, hidden amongst the chlorophyll and thatched roofs.

Anja shook her head. A necessary evil.

She walked at a clip back along the wall toward the guardhouse. Once, there would have been soldiers clad in armor wielding bows and pikes and rifles to greet her. And while she did indeed employ a contingent of armed security, cameras monitored the entrance on a closed network that utilized facial, spatial, voice, and thermo-sensing technology to determine who could pass. Any unauthorized person attempting access now would receive a healthy electrical blast to short-circuit their brain and render them unconscious and likely covered in their own urine. Even Anja had lost count of the concessions she'd made in the name of peace.

Painted on the sand-colored wall, a large, faded, double-headed eagle crest presided over a set of red and white striped doors to the lower gate. Two cameras, housed in metallic boxes on either side of the passage, eyed her while a single wall-mounted machine gun slept. Anja's skin prickled each time she passed through this outer barrier.

An audible sigh of relief escaped her as she pushed through the doors without incident. She meandered down the path toward the main palace, but instead of heading straight to the nerve center of Scarlett Moon, Anja found herself in one of the many bathrooms, staring at her own reflection. Two curled candelabra holders fitted with white plastic stick light bulbs flanked the ornate mirror, which returned the visage of a cold and calculating woman. Anja's steel blue eyes, angular jaw line, and harsh blond bob all spoke of efficiency over decoration.

How was it, then, that her own flesh and blood, a brother whose features were so similar, could fall so far from the Kuhn family tree? Ralph looked like her, talked like her, yet he'd turned away from their safe cocoon in Zurich to explore a world on fire.

Anja sat on the lip of a bathtub covered in white porcelain tiles painted with cobalt blue landscapes. She studied the cracks and missing pieces in the opulent restroom. The artwork was old and failing, but it remained. From a time when the world's people learned from one another. She curled her slender fingers around the lip of the bath. The striking blue-on-white tile art, made so popular in Europe in the seventeenth century, came direct from China, where artisans had found a way to decorate their beloved kaolin.

As far as she could tell, no one learned from each other anymore.

The world had spiraled into tribalism where self-important, virtue-signaling morons fought to abolish individual opinions, thoughts, or the sharing of cultures. The self-righteous shouted buzz words such as *micro-aggression*, *bias*, and *cultural appropriation*, to support their theses. Of course, the irony being those who abhorred these taboos themselves engaged in defamation and destruction.

"Agree with me," Anja said under her breath, "or suffer the

consequences."

She freed her foldable phone from her pocket and opened it. With a few flicks of her delicate index finger, she switched to Ralph's BingOn profile. His picture still smiled, all these months later, accompanied by a rainbow emoji. His last post sat at the top of his feed, a selfie by a street sign in New York. "Wall Street is over," Anja said, reading the picture's caption aloud.

Just below Ralph's toothy smile and righteous slogan, a slew of hateful words littered the comments section.

How dare you, one person had written.

How stupid do you have to be? wrote another. *No one posts pictures of that place. We don't even mention its name.*

Anja scrolled down, though she knew each mean response by heart.

Iluvfr33dom wrote, *Wall Street was built as a defense against attack from Native American tribes, you asshat.*

*Not to mention, it was New York's first slave market. R*cist, sl*very-loving pig*, added Momblo88er2010.

Anja's heart pounded as her thumb hovered over Fightracism671's comment *I will find you.*

She pressed on the commenter's profile link.

A twenty-something angsty white male with a mop of black hair peered out from the screen. Fightracism671—or Tim to his 6,745 online friends. Nearly four hundred new followers and a few extra whiskers about his round chin since the last time she'd visited. Tim had been pretty active in the last months, so this time it took a little longer for Anja to scroll through to the specific post. But she knew the image all too well. A photo of Ralph lying in a pool of blood outside the Waldorf-Astoria. *Successful removal of another Nazi from the world*, Tim wrote underneath. He'd even tagged Ralph's account.

The image had nearly three thousand likes.

Anja snapped her phone closed, wiped away the tear before it could fall, then got to her feet beside the tub. She smoothed down her hair and marched from the bathroom down the wood-paneled corridor and into the main palace—her command center.

As she pushed through the heavy wooden doors, a clamor filled her ears. Her team shouted over each other and banged on keyboards. A massive monitor on the rear wall blared a map of the world. In the middle of the space, some of her team gathered like baby hogs and snuffled around a log table piled with fruit, chocolate, and bags of chips in yellow packets.

Anja squinted to mute the sensory onslaught.

"Ah, Ms. Kuhn, I mean, Anja!" said a young woman with bright orange hair and a prominent nose. She held a tablet. "There's an issue with supply—someone hit the facility in Brazil!"

"What?" Anja took the device from the woman and marched toward the balcony doors. "Why would someone do that, Tabea?"

On the tablet screen, thick black smoke billowed from the ruins of a one-story concrete building. With no private fire department in Porto Alegre, the locals ran to and fro with buckets of water that sloshed too much.

Tabea shook her head. "Security says whoever it was believed it to be a cocaine distribution operation."

"Cocaine?" Anja stopped short of the exit to the balcony. The desire to be outside again, away from the chaos, clawed at her brain. She blew out a puff of air and handed back the tablet. "What's the impact?"

"Well," Tabea said, bringing up projections on the tablet, "our offices in Cape Town, Kuala Lumpur, and Istanbul all report that they're on track, but it's difficult to tell—you know how it is in those places. Only as reliable as the value of your coin."

"Sylcoin just took a massive hit, right?" Anja said, then started back to a console on the other side of the command center.

Tabea nodded and followed Anja. "Which will, for sure, make KL unhappy. I guarantee they'll ask for more coin, since the value just bottomed out."

"Or, maybe an altcoin?" Anja took a seat at the console and logged in.

"Maybe, but we're not mining or earning enough, and can't buy any more." Tabea swiped a curl of fiery hair from her face. "We've tapped out anyone who accepts the Swiss franc. It's on its last legs, even within our borders."

"Damn," Anja said under her breath. The Swiss franc had been the last bastion of FIAT worth a damn to anyone. The dollar, the euro, the ruble, and all other currencies were pretty much worthless, now. Money only ever had power because the people gave it value. Ralph had compared the switch from cash to crypto as the village bank that had hoarded seashells until, one day, everyone decided seashells were shit, and they wanted to be paid in frogs. The banks and fisherman? Dead broke. Anyone with a pond in their backyard? A millionaire.

"That's how crypto works," Ralph had said. "Anyone can create a coin and give it value based on the chain functionality." And so they did. Private healthcare companies decentralized medical records. HR departments removed the need to pay middlemen and lawyers with secure contracts. You name it, there was a network chain for it. And for each chain, a crypto coin or token of value given to those who mined or hosted the network.

A special little token as unique as the little human snowflakes who used them.

"Anja?" Tabea pressed.

"We have to wait," Anja said, snapping her attention back to Tabea. "We've been working up to this point for years. Cutting ourselves short now would be pointless." They'd come so close. "See if one of the other facilities can increase production."

Anja leaned back in the chair and played with her scarf, stare fixed on the ornate ceiling and brick buttresses. *A week won't matter, will it? Do it right, or not at all.* Her plan had to touch seventy-eight percent of the global population, or it wouldn't work.

"Heard your site in Porto Alegre got hit," a voice said in a dull American accent, though Anja couldn't discern between State's dialects.

She twisted the chair to face Marcel. He loomed in the entrance, dressed head to toe in camouflage fatigues, a giant greasy hamburger clutched in one of his equally massive hands. He raised his bushy eyebrows expectantly over shark-black eyes.

Tabea recoiled, her large nose seemingly able to smell the medium rare beef from across the command center. "Sure, Ms. K—ah, Anja," Tabea said, then clutched the tablet to her chest and marched back to one of the many computer-laden desks.

"Still trying to play nice with the employees?" Marcel said, then took a big bite of his burger and stomped over in boots that clunked against the stone.

"It's not about employer and employee," Anja said, shifting upright. "It's about a vision."

Marcel swallowed his mouthful. "Sure. Anyway, Brazil?"

"Do you know anything about it?" Anja asked.

Marcel shrugged. "Why would I know?" He stuffed the last of the burger into his mouth. "Hat off to the chef, by the way," he said around the mouthful.

Anja pulled her scarf tight like a garrote between her hands. "I think you know what I'm saying."

Marcel held up a finger and closed his eyes, then slowed his chewing. A full thirty seconds of mastication later, he swallowed, then fixed his onyx eyes on Anja. "Nothing to do with me." He plonked himself in the opposite chair, his military green jacket bunching up around his chin. "Jay did that shit, and look where it got him."

Anja cleared her throat. "I've turned a blind eye, Marcel. Up until now. You've worked in some pretty difficult environments and had to leverage less savory support, but—"

Marcel hacked a laugh, then licked the grease from his fingers. "Less savory? Is that fancy Swiss talk for guerilla warfare?"

Anja eyed Marcel, her focus drifting to the mole on his chin. One of the oldest members of Scarlett Moon, Marcel had been loyal and effective. He and his contacts had re-installed small government-like organizations across the world—first in places that traditionally followed dictatorships, like Asia, where the people were somehow lost without one all-powerful god-king to tell them how to live their lives. The trick had been not to install tyrants, but truly democratic leadership. Until recently, Marcel had been successful, but the number of potential enclaves to be converted back to sanity had dwindled, leaving only those larger monstrosities—the U.S.A., China, Russia—to conquer. Africa remained a mess no one wanted to detangle. Besides, wrangling nations of hundreds of millions of people, fragmented into just as many factions, had become an unmanageable task—though Marcel would never admit it.

"Groups with enough influence to remove criminal leadership," Anja said, and tugged at her scarf again. "And since you're not an advocate of The Solution, it's suspect that one of my major facilities was hit on the pretext of some do-gooder destroying a cocaine distribution center."

Marcel narrowed his dark eyes. "Look, if you're going to accuse me, just do it. I'm telling you, it has nothing to do with me. And as for The Solution, you need me to execute it. So don't hold your breath."

"Fine," Anja said, then stood.

"Ms. Kuhn, we need you over here." A short, raven-haired technician scowled at his console.

Anja sighed. "What is it, Hans?"

"Korea," Hans said, eyes glued to his monitor, sweat beading on his forehead. "I don't know how long we can hold the site. The North is making advances. We knew this was going to happen—"

Anja turned back to Marcel. "Can you—"

"Nope," Marcel said, resting his heavy boots on the seat Anja had just sat in.

"Why?" she said.

"Bitcoin City is unstable," Marcel said, then kicked the chair away and jumped to his feet. "Another gang has moved in, La22. El Salvador, I can deal with. I can be in and out easily. Korea's a whole other mess. Which reminds me, I need coin to round up some of that *less savory* support."

"The old Despliegue Nacional?" Anja asked.

He nodded.

"I thought they'd disbanded?" She folded her arms across her pigeon chest. "After we took over."

"They did, but now we're in a shitty place," Marcel said, his dark stare hard and cold. "La22 are brutal. They took out a school yesterday. Forty-three kids dead. They mean business."

"Damn," Anja whispered.

Bitcoin City, or B.C., got set up back in 2022 by the El Salvadoran government. A forward-thinking president had legalized cryptocurrency and built an entire city at the edge of the Conchagua volcano to leverage its geothermal energy, powering Bitcoin mining. Residential areas, commercial areas, services, museums, entertainment, bars, restaurants, airport, port, rail—everything had been purpose-built to run on Bitcoin. The president had even seen fit to abolish income taxes in the city. Combined with a heavily armed federal police force to keep out the gangs, B.C. had been considered the city of the future. Scarlett Moon, even in its infancy, had the foresight to partner with the El Salvadoran government. In the end, the regime became one of the last few national administrations standing after the Collapse—and Anja's first finger hold for The Solution.

"I need coin," Marcel said. "The Despliegue Nacional won't work for free. Giltcoin isn't minting any more tokens, so we can't give away what we have—too expensive. And Sylcoin just tanked."

"I'll work on it," Anja said. "We need to find a better way to gather coins. Jay—"

"Ain't here," Marcel said, and jerked a thumb over his shoulder. "So, get one of your financial wizards in there to find me some coin. Or we're going to lose B.C. and El Salvador. Your gateway between the U.S. and Latin America."

"You don't have to tell me."

"Ms. Kuhn?" Hans pressed.

"In a minute," she snapped back.

"Find the coin, Anja," Marcel said, marching away. "I've got a plane to catch."

Anja watched Marcel march out. He could go to El Salvador. He could put out another fire and keep hold of the crumbling alliance of small governments he'd propped up across the globe, but it would never be enough. She'd tried that route for years. Only her final plan, The Solution, could end the sweeping tide of omniviolence.

And she couldn't let Marcel get in her way.

CHAPTER SIX

Joe

A sit-down, they called it. Joe hated sit-downs. He pressed his teeth together as he steered the Chrysler onto West Chicago Avenue toward Lake Michigan and the Belvedere. Sit-downs were designed to throw a person off, take them out of their comfort zone, or get their guard down. Unpredictable meetings, with no way to prepare. You might be in for a nice conversation and a friendly handshake. Or an icepick in the brain. Or a friendly handshake, then the icepick in the brain. The Family had conducted these meetings in person for most of Joe's long service. Then the Collapse changed all that. Allowed people to still meet, while hiding behind computer screens on video calls. So, The Family adjusted again, finding something in the middle that gave them the upper hand.

At the river bridge just outside the now defunct *Chicago Tribune*, a fat man in a ripped T-shirt—a Romanian clan member, by the look of the blue, gold, and red sash that hung from his jeans pocket—dragged a woman to the sidewalk by her tangled black weave. The guy's fist smacked the woman's bruised face with vicious repetition. A small crowd stood around and filmed the incident. Some leered and encouraged the woman to fight back. She didn't.

Joe drove between the steel gray bridge supports, tires bumping over the junction. Overhead, on the corner of an office tower, a tattered American flag fluttered, A sad but authentic symbol of the country he once loved. A pin in a map his ancestors fought and died for.

Block after block crept past the high-rise max-security hotels along the waterfront, stretching to the clouds. Joe slowed as he reached Loyola University, its windows dark and reinforced with steel cages. He wondered if anyone even bothered going to college anymore, when a preteen vlogger could make millions just by posting reels of themselves playing violent video games. He eased the car to a stop at North Michigan and waited for the toll light. The sound of coins tinkled over the car speakers as the money auto-debited from his rental vehicle account.

A disheveled twenty-something man standing on the corner spat on the hood of Joe's car. He thrust out a white sign with dripping red letters that read *Slaughter the Capitalist Scum!*

"What's your excuse, man?" shouted Disheveled. "Your own car? Really? Capitalism takes from the mouths of the poor and lines the pockets of the rich! You want to align yourself with that? Down with the capitalist pigs!"

Twenty years ago, Joe would have engaged. Fed the silly asshole his teeth. Now, it just didn't seem to matter anymore.

"What are you going to do about it, bitch?" Disheveled screamed, and spat again. "I dare you to park your fancy car and tell me I'm wrong!"

The light changed, and Joe drove on.

He pulled into the Belvedere's private parking deck and lowered the window. A gust of wind off the lake blustered in, and dragged with it the pungent aroma of piss and rotting trash. The attendant ducked his head to look in the Chrysler's open window.

"Mista Bones. How are you today, sir?" he said with a grin.

"I'm doin' okay, Elmore," Joe said. "You?"

Elmore's grin widened. "Just another day in paradise, Mista Bones." He touched the screen of his tablet. "I've got you right here, sir. You know where to go."

The barrier into the garage lowered.

Joe thanked him and eased the Chrysler through. Up a four-level spiraling ramp, tires squealing like something from an old Steve McQueen chase scene, Joe found the visitor spaces marked in yellow. The Chicago branch of La Nueva Cosa Nostra owned the entire building and the adjoining garage, but that didn't mean he could park wherever he wanted. There were rules.

But what about the rule where we don't assassinate kids? Joe cracked his knuckles.

He exited the blacked-out Chrysler, removed the Colt snubbie from his waistband, and hid it under the seat. From his trouser pocket, he pulled a seven-round Beretta Tomcat .32 caliber semi-auto. Old and janky, it still did the job. Just like him. He pulled up his pant leg and folded down his dress sock over a concealed stiletto. He slid the knife and the Beretta under the seat with the Colt. He then took off his overcoat and removed all the rifle pieces from the pockets. A chilly gust against his sweat-dampened shirt prompted him back into the overcoat. With a methodical slowness, he reset the trumpet case and cast one last look at the beautiful instrument. He locked the case and placed it in the trunk. Joe straightened his coat and suit, then put on his hat and checked his appearance in the dark glass of the rental car before heading inside.

A slow clap greeted him as he crossed the concrete landing toward the fourth-floor entrance to the Belvedere. Two doormen flanked the wooden double doors, both wearing shoulder holsters, both with frames that would make a defensive lineman feel insecure. Joe knew Lorenzo, a wise guy—wannabe made guy—with a big mouth. The other doorman was new and, upon closer inspection, young. Maybe learning the ropes.

"Look who it is." Lorenzo stopped clapping and worked a toothpick between his teeth. "Ol' Bones."

Joe nodded.

"Bones?" the younger man asked.

Lorenzo turned to his counterpart. "Shit, Billy, you never heard of Bones Carboni?"

Billy shrugged.

Lorenzo sneered. "Notorious. Legendary. Guy was the fuckin' grim reaper." He waved his hand in front of his face. "I mean, back in the day. Long time ago."

"Not anymore?" Billy swallowed.

"He's still on the payroll, but I mean, look at him." Lorenzo bit the toothpick between his molars and snickered. "Even the reaper gets old."

Joe raised his arms. "You gonna keep running your mouth, or you gonna do your job?"

Lorenzo laughed it off, pulled the toothpick from his mouth, and motioned to Billy.

The new guy bent to pat Joe down. Ankles to groin, around the waistband and chest, up in the armpits, and down his arms, Billy searched with the eagerness of a new recruit.

Lorenzo seemed to sober. "You hear about Flavio?"

Joe shook his head. "What about him?"

Lorenzo touched the point of the toothpick in his mouth and leaned forward. "Not five minutes—*five minutes* after Vitale went down—delivery guy shows up at Flavio Barbone's door. When Flavio goes to sign for the package, the delivery guy sticks him in the throat. Right in the carotid. I heard he sprayed like a slaughtered pig."

"That's the world we live in," Joe said with a shrug.

"Nah, man." Lorenzo eyed new-guy Billy's search-in-progress. "Not five minutes after. It's a shark tank, and there's blood in the water. My bet? All the leadership will be dead in two days. All but the one who seizes control." He grinned and replaced the toothpick.

"Stay in your lane, Lorenzo," Joe grumbled.

"He's good," Billy said.

"I guess you're good," Lorenzo said, and waved at the entrance. "I mean, unless you can't get the old bone to stand up anymore." He pumped his forearm. "Whadya say, Soft Bone?"

Joe's eyes smoldered under a heavy brow. "I'm done wit' you talkin' to me like that."

"Okay, yeah. Of course." Lorenzo laughed it off. "No disrespect."

Joe glared at Lorenzo.

"I'm fuckin' with ya, Bones. Go ahead," Lorenzo said, a slight blush reddening his cheeks. "Holy shit. Relax or somethin'."

Billy pulled open the double hardwood doors, and Joe headed for the elevator.

"Fuckin' mamaluke needs to get laid." Lorenzo laughed, and shoulder-punched Billy. "If he still can!"

Joe entered the Belvedere and crossed the lobby. Huge, brightly colored portraits that his nephew could have painted better adorned the walls, while pointlessly small tables offered tall vases that could have been antiques—or, perhaps knock-offs bought from a Triad stooge down in Chinatown. The gaudy décor, of course, was just smoke and mirrors to conceal a myriad of defensive measures, from blast- and bulletproof windows to steel-drop shutters that could isolate an intruder in seconds. The boss didn't take chances.

Joe touched the elevator call button and waited.

The doors pinged and opened. A tuxedoed elevator operator stepped forward.

"Well, if it isn't Bones Carboni," the operator said.

"Clem." Joe took a step back and raised his arms.

"Gotta pat you down again, sir. You know how it is."

Joe nodded.

Clem finished his pat down and radioed ahead. He collected Joe's hat and overcoat and waved him into the compartment. Joe stepped to the back corner as the elevator operator produced a key card from his jacket, swiped it, and punched the button for the top floor. The doors rolled shut. Inside, speakers concealed overhead played Puccini's aria "Nessun Dorma," from an opera about a brutal tyrant and her murderous reign of terror. Joe never much cared for the piece, but here, in The Family's well-dressed fortress of murder and mayhem, it fit.

The numbered floors lit up as the elevator rose.

La Cosa Nostra, the *old* Cosa Nostra, died after its heyday in the twentieth century. The coalition of Sicilian families, though they only ever referred to themselves as *The Family*, had been forced to change to survive the modern age. After the Collapse, the coalition reformed into La Nueva Cosa Nostra and turned to even darker trades like human trafficking, regional population control, and dark-web crypto supremacy. They had a stranglehold on Chicago and Manhattan and a significant presence in many other cities, but that didn't stop the wars with the Triads, the Yakuza, and any other organized crime outfit that wanted a slice of the pie.

Though The Family's name and some of their tactics had changed, some things stayed the same. First, respect mattered. Maybe it mattered to Joe more than it did to others, but respect was still the rule if you wanted to keep what you had. Second, you followed orders to the letter. No exceptions. The boss gave the word, the underboss set it in motion, and the captains saw it was done. Deviations got a person put on ice and buried six feet under.

The exact position Joe had put himself in.

Except now, with Vitale dead, no underboss could mediate the orders on Joe's behalf. *Lorenzo, the little prick, was right,* Joe thought. All the captains, greedy for more power, would set their sights on the newly vacant position. Another step up the ladder. A recipe for upheaval if Joe ever saw it.

The elevator pinged as it came to rest on the top floor. Joe took a breath, nodded to Clem, and walked out into the foyer of the grand suite, a penthouse that filled the entire top floor of the Belvedere with a spectacular view of Lake Michigan.

Joe's worn but polished shoes clicked against a floor of gleaming white marble. He slowed to admire an original Picasso, *La Rêve,* hanging on the wall by a portal flanked by family soldiers in dark suits. One had scarred hands, burned by fire. The other, a cleft in his chin. Both stood at ease with their hands clasped before them.

"The boss will see you momentarily, Bones," Cleft Chin said, and gestured to the next room.

"In person?" Joe asked.

"Just have a seat, please," Scarred Hands said.

A frown deepened the craggy lines on Joe's face. *When was the last time you saw the boss in person, Joe? Two years ago? More?* Soldiers, even good, loyal soldiers like Joe, weren't often granted access to the man at the top. No one, not even your best people, could always be trusted.

Joe had known the old man for decades. The boss always treated him with respect and fairness. He understood Joe was cut from the old cloth. Don Giordano liked having Joe around to remind him how family, loyalty, and respect mattered, even in a world where they didn't seem to anymore. Why would he level a hit knowing a kid would die?

Doesn't matter, Joe. He smoothed the lapels of his jacket. *He had his reasons, and you fucked up and went against his orders.* Joe'd take his licks with hat in hand and resolve to do better. If the old man meted it out, Joe trusted him, and that was the end of it.

Joe stepped into the study. Dark hardwood bookcases lined the walls and framed a massive, polished desk. A hint of pipe smoke and expensive bourbon hung in the air. A grandfather clock clunked away whatever time Joe had remaining. He paused when his shoe crinkled on clear plastic sheeting spread beneath two rich leather chairs and over an expensive oriental rug.

So you don't bleed on it, Joe.

His stomach soured. He took a seat in one of the chairs facing the empty desk and smoothed the front of his shirt and jacket again.

The shades in the room auto-dimmed, and the expansive view of the lake darkened. A 3D projection flickered and the form of Don Giordano appeared, as though sitting behind the desk.

"Ciao, Joe." The ghost-thin figure coughed, produced a handkerchief, and coughed again.

"Don Giordano." Joe stood from his chair. The plastic sheet crackled.

"Sit down, Bones." The Don wiped his mouth and pocketed the handkerchief. "We've known each other too long for all the formalities."

"Sure, Boss." Joe looked for his seat, then sat. After a beat, the two soldiers followed him into the study and shut the door.

"Joe Carboni, one of my very best. How long's it been?" Don Giordano said, his voice frail with age.

"It's been too long, Boss." Joe felt the heat rise beneath the collar of his shirt. He hated the small talk when they had business to discuss. No, not just business. A reprimand. "Much too long," he said.

The Don nodded. "I'm sorry we couldn't do this in person, but ..." His voice trailed off. "Well, you know how the world is."

Joe fidgeted and swallowed. "Plastic, Boss?" Joe flashed a nervous smile. "Doesn't make me feel too good."

"That's not for you." The Don waved it away. "Do you know how many people I see a day? Never hurts to make sure they understand their position." He offered a thin smile.

Joe all but squirmed in the chair. "Sure, Boss. If it's all the same to you, I know why I'm here. I'd like to get out in front of it with the truth, sir."

The Don made a gesture of concession and folded his hands. "What happened today? I need assurances, Bones. Why would you make my life more difficult?"

Joe felt, more than saw, the two soldiers at the door close in behind him. The soft leather bucket of the chair cradled his shoulders like the padded interior of a coffin. He struggled against the urge to look over his shoulder. "Boss, I—"

"Don't you think," the Don interrupted, "that it's important that my people follow orders? Don't you think I designed it this way for a reason? Or did you think about it at all before you just did things your way?"

Joe lowered his gaze. "Yes, sir. I thought about it."

"And?"

Joe steeled himself. He cleared his throat and raised his eyes. "Boss, we just blew up the second in command, along with twelve of our own guys. Twelve. Men loyal to this family." Joe tried to keep his voice even, but still it rose. He jabbed a finger into his palm. "And," he paused, almost choking on the words. "And we murdered—" Joe stood from his chair. He shouldn't stand, but he did, and the plastic beneath his shoes creased.

Behind Joe, Scarred Hands and Cleft Chin took a step forward.

"No, not just murdered," Joe continued, "*eviscerated* a little girl in that attack. For what, Boss? Killing Vitale wasn't enough? This is not how this Family does business."

"Sit down," Scarred Hands said.

"No. It's never been how we do things," Joe said. "I know it's Svanire. He's twisted you. If we're gonna kill kids, then you should have let me start with that little squiddy bastard the day he picked your pocket—"

"Close your mouth." The Don seemed to eye his own withered hands.

Joe swallowed back the words in his throat and sucked in a breath.

"Svanire isn't your business," the Don said after a long moment. "He's a capo. What he does isn't your concern. It's *above you*. Understand that?"

The words stung like the crack of a bullwhip. "Yes, Boss." Joe ducked his head.

The projection of the Don sat silent as death, unmoving. Joe felt Scarred Hands and Cleft Chin close behind him now, so close, he could hear their breath and the slight rustle of expensive Italian suits.

Joe focused on the old grandfather clock along the wall, clunking away the remaining seconds of his life. His passion exercised, it seemed to bleed away from him. In its wake, a terrible icy void spread. He pinched his mouth into a line. His legs wavered and he almost tipped back into his seat. He'd either made his point, or he was a dead man. Or both.

The Don raised a hand again, and a burn-scarred hand touched Joe's shoulder. It felt heavy with the weight of the Don's authority.

"Sit down," Scarred Hands said behind him. "Now."

Joe's hefty frame sank back into the soft leather.

"What happened to you, Joe?" the Don almost whispered. "What made you go all soft like this? It ain't you, and you wear it like a bad suit." The Don leaned on the desk, his fingers tenting. "Nobody's innocent, Joe. Not really. You, more than anyone, know that.

"We might be kings in our own game, but we're all pawns in someone else's," he said. "Even the children."

Joe looked at the polished tips of his shoes, sporting only a scuff or two, and shook his head. "I didn't get soft … I just …"

"You thought," the Don said in a clipped tone, any touch of frailty gone. "But I don't need my people to think. I need them to move when I say. Nothing more. Nothing less. If I can't rely on you to do that, then I can't rely on you."

Joe wrapped thick fingers around his knees, his spine straight. "Don Giordano, I was wrong. I see that now. If you're going to do me, please just get it over with. I'm ready."

"*Do* you?" The Don's likeness laughed. "Joe, if I wanted you dead, you'd have been a corpse long ago. Why even talk?"

Joe took a deep breath in, held it for a beat, then let the air push over his thick lips.

"No," the Don said, "no, I'm not going to kill one of my most loyal rooks. You had a little slip, that's all. I *know* you're going to make it up to me."

Joe cleared his throat. "Make it up to you, sir?"

The Don nodded. "Got another job for you. Cryptokiller. Bastard interfered with our business for the last time. But he'll see a drone hit coming from a mile away, so it needs to be in person. Cakewalk, for someone of your caliber."

"You have the info?" Joe asked.

"We'll send the address tomorrow morning, then when you get close to the target location, the full packet. Gotta keep it under wraps, as it's very important this one is done *right*, Joe."

Joe cringed. He managed a nod.

"For now, go home and get some rest. Think about what it means to serve The Family." The Don's projected eyes seemed to cut through him. He offered a thin smile. "I still trust your loyalty, Bones. But you got to prove it to me one more time." The image flickered, then vanished.

Joe sat staring at the empty desk and the unoccupied chair, as if waiting further instruction.

"You can go now," Cleft Chin said behind him.

Joe said nothing. He rose and retraced his steps across clean plastic that rumpled beneath each step and didn't give so much as a look at the two soldiers who, with one word from the Don, would have put him in a casket.

Joe's wheels turned in dark, ever-widening circles. He'd been so sure this was it for him, the sweet release of death so close. Now, in its passing, he felt numb.

More people would die before he got his turn.

Joe passed through the neo-modern foyer, reclaimed his overcoat and hat, and rode the elevator down in silence. The elevator man, Clem, stared at the floor call buttons, silent. Joe stepped off into the lower lobby, with its dark hardwood antiques, and made for the parking garage.

Lorenzo laughed at some vulgarity, slapping the new guy's arm as Joe approached.

"Hey, whadya know?" Lorenzo nodded at Joe. "Lookie who's back so soon."

Joe put on his fedora and tugged the brim down, and focused straight ahead as he approached the two doormen.

Lorenzo waggled his thumb as Joe passed, and winked at the new guy. "See ya later, *Soft Bone*. Next time, try following orders—"

Joe spun and snatched Lorenzo's pistol from his shoulder rig beneath his coat. He brought the pistol's heel crashing down against the thick doorman's face. Lorenzo's nose folded flat and a jet of blood shot down his shirt front.

He faltered on wobbly knees, eyes flaring. "You muddafu—"

Lorenzo screamed as Joe seized him by the hair and bent him back. The pistol landed a second time with a vicious *thunk*. A snarl crossed Joe's face. He slapped away Lorenzo's flailing arms and hit him again and again. By the fifth blow, Lorenzo's ocular cavity gave way, the bones of his face deformed.

Billy stepped forward, his eyes giant white orbs. He splayed his fingers and cried an awkward plea for Joe to stop. Joe swung the gory pistol on him, but stopped inches from the kid's face.

"You want in on this life?" Madness swam in Joe's eyes. "Here's your first lesson." He pushed the dripping red barrel in the new guy's face. "Mind your own fuckin' business."

Billy's head twitched.

"Lesson number two," Joe said. He hoisted Lorenzo to his feet. Slick black hair poked between Joe's clenched knuckles. Lorenzo's jaw swung loose, his blood-smeared face sunken, head jiggling beneath Joe's hand like a psycho's puppet. "Show some *fuckin' respect!*" Joe shook Lorenzo's head in time with the words.

Billy nodded and backed away, hands raised.

Joe held Lorenzo close and listened to his gargled breaths. He leaned into the beaten man's ear and tapped the barrel of the pistol against his temple. "Tell me again how soft it is, Lorenzo," Joe whispered. "Tell me again."

Lorenzo groaned. Blood gurgled in his throat.

Joe let go of Lorenzo's hair and let him slump to the concrete. Ol' Bones Carboni bent and wiped his hands on the beaten man's jacket, and left the new-guy Billy, gawking like an idiot.

As Joe neared the Chrysler, it blipped and the driver's side door popped open. Joe tossed the bloodied pistol over the rail of the garage and heard it clatter on the street below.

Joe took off his overcoat, folded it neatly, and placed it on the back seat with his fedora on top. One breath at a time, the red cleared from the edges of his vision and Joe regained composure. He needed some clarity—the sort that only came from sitting alone and listening to a little Rossini or Morricone with a glass of Porto Valduro in hand. He needed to put this day behind him.

Joe smoothed the front of his blood-flecked shirt, retrieved his weapons from beneath the seat, and, with one last look at new-guy Billy fumbling at Lorenzo's pulse, set the Chrysler's destination for home.

CHAPTER SEVEN

Svanire

A message flashed on the console, *Incoming Video Call*, and a trill filled the room. Svanire ignored the call and stretched a spidery finger to caress a framed photograph on the large mahogany bureau.

The video call warbled again.

Svanire stood at the oversized desk, index finger outstretched, until the caller gave up. With half-closed eyes, he inhaled the coppery musky scent of the study. He knew this room better than any other, better than even his own home. It was here that he had completed his metamorphosis, where he'd emerged from his chrysalis a beautiful and deadly monster.

Whispers of Svanire's name still made the citizens of Little Italy shrink back and clutch their children close. A smile teased at his lips. He twirled the large leather chair on its base and took a seat. Lendsey Wentzel Parisi, the name given to him by his idiot parents, had never struck such fear in anyone's heart. That name had needed to die.

The news anchors—when those jobs still existed—had said the inferno engulfed an entire block of Chicago's upscale River North district and kept two fire battalions fighting overnight. The blaze had reached temperatures in excess of fifteen hundred degrees and held for almost fourteen hours, according to the reports. More than enough to disintegrate tooth and bone, it consumed the bodies of his parents, little brother, and the charred corpse presumed to be Lendsey Parisi.

Svanire danced his fingers through the air as if they were those very flames.

The death of an entire family of millionaire socialites might have made the news, once, but twenty years ago, when he'd gone through with it, the country had already spiraled toward collapse. Hatred for old money and family wealth meant the Parisis were just more dead rich people. Even the police investigation lacked any substance.

He rose from the leather chair and his tall, ghastly frame swayed under the weight of the thick black Italian wool suit. His limbs moved adagio as he slid like a wraith along a wall of old sepia photographs, stroking golden frames with a pale index finger as he passed. He stepped into a beam of light that knifed between the velvet curtains and basked in the warmth like a reptile enjoying the desert sun.

The heat on his skin ignited more memories.

The fire that day had set him free. Unshackled from society's rules and no longer held back by the expectations of egocentric parents, he could finally embrace his true identity. Technically, that person embodied a cluster B personality disorder—at least, that's what the shrink who had come to that ill-fated River North home three times a week had written. *Antisocial personality disorder with psychopathic, narcissistic tendencies.* Dear ol' Doc had shot Lendsey full of mind-altering drugs. Expected that to fix what his self-important parents had most certainly found to be a problem.

A lurid smirk spread across Svanire's porcelain face.

The drugs hadn't stopped him from killing everything he could put his spider-like hands on long before the River North inferno. Rats and mice at first. He'd experimented with matches. But snapping little necks between his fingers had satisfied him far more than watching a little fire do the work. It hadn't taken long to graduate to stray dogs and cats, which came willingly to a tin of food. His parents never suspected a thing. Once he'd trapped other people's pets, he'd relished taking his time to enjoy the fear in their eyes. Loved the exquisite feeling as the animals squirmed in his fists.

After the River North fire and the death of the old him, of Lendsey Wentzel Parisi, he'd lived on the street for a few years, one of the city's nameless urchins, able to hone his death-dealing skill. As law and order faded from the community, no one gave a damn about the dead bums that the boy left in his wake or the rich assholes he pickpocketed.

Svanire turned from the window and tip-toed without sound across the plush green carpet to the long black body bag laid in front of a Chesterfield couch. He pliéd to the floor, and stared through the zipped opening at the face inside.

"And all that death led me to you, didn't it?" he said to the body in the cream-colored double-breasted suit. Svanire traced a wire-thin mark in the fleshy neck and admired the bright red stain that soaked through the otherwise crisp white shirt. "My fingers weren't quite light enough to pinch your pocket, were they?" He stroked the bloodless face of Don Giordano, then pressed his fingertips together in a quick flourish. "No sooner had they closed on your wallet, your goons had me," he cooed.

His lithe frame had allowed him to slip from their grasp and disappear into the night. The legend went that the Don had just laughed. "È svanito," he'd said. *He vanished.* The Don's bodyguards had tracked the GPS chip in the wallet and found the feral street urchin pawing through its contents in an alley behind the Bang Bang Thai noodle shop. The boy had fought back, of course, with a shiv made of sharpened tin.

Svanire rubbed at his sharp jaw, nursing the memory of old wounds. "You let your goons put the boots in, though, didn't you? But, the looks on their faces when I sliced them, one by one." He giggled. Such a shock, that a boy could maim and kill so many. The mirth faded from Svanire's features. "Until nobody stood in that alley but me and the one who caught me pinching your wallet—your favored son, Joseph Carboni."

The Don had strolled toward them, unfazed by his dead bodyguards sprawled in pools of blood across the alley. He'd ordered his hitman with his revolver, and the street orphan with his tin shiv, to stand down. He'd said the boy had moxie, and called him Svanire for the first time, then he gave him some coin and offered him the one thing he wanted more than anything: absolute power.

Kill for me, boy, and I'll make you unstoppable.

Bones Carboni had argued, spat, and swore. Vowed he'd never work with the *orphan.* But, from that day, Svanire was Don Giordano's protégé. A young man to be feared and respected by everyone except Carboni, who gave him the nickname Svanire the Squid. It drew a laugh from anyone in earshot.

"Everyone except you," Svanire said.

He leaned into the Don and enjoyed the metallic scent of initial decay as the organs broke down and blood pooled internally along the corpse's back and buttocks. "There was a time I thought you might even love me," he whispered into Don Giordano's ear. "But love is for children and old men, and fathers only exist to fail you." With a flick of his wrist, Svanire zipped the thick black body bag shut.

He rose in near relevé, then stepped past the computer's tangled network of multi-lensed cameras and cables. A *New Video Message* alert strobed on the screen. He eased the leather chair back and sat down at the desk, his back ramrod straight. He exhaled and, though it felt unnatural, slumped his posture and rounded his spine. He picked up the milk-white mask and pressed it to his face. The silicone molded to the contours of his jaw and brow—even his lips and his nose.

He clicked the message and, without listening to it, tapped the icon that resembled an old-fashioned handset. The line trilled twice.

"Don Giordano, so nice of you to return my call," said a heavy-jowled man with olive skin. A few strands of slicked-over black hair covered a balding pate.

"Don Rigoletti, I'm a busy man," Svanire said. "I'm sure you are, as well, keeping Manhattan in order for us." Svanire heard his own voice, but the replicator software morphed his words into a flawless mimic of the late Don Giordano. A little window in the monitor displayed what Rigoletti could see, the tech transformed the ghostly rubber mask into a perfect image of the boss who lay in the body bag.

"Yes, of course, Don Giordano," Rigoletti said. "I just …" The balding man dabbed at his glistening forehead with an embroidered white handkerchief, then cleared his throat. "There's been a lot of … changes." He fidgeted. "What assurances can you give me that our relationship will continue?"

Svanire grinned and opened his hands, which the cloaking software also disguised. "Leo," he said, "does my loyalty to you and the Rigoletti family mean nothing? Business is booming. There's nothing to fear."

"But there is, Don Giordano." Rigoletti shook his head and seemed to swallow back bile. "Our people kill each other in the streets. Blood fills the gutters. *Italian blood.*" Rigoletti's eyes glared out of the monitor as he chose his next words with care. "And it all started when you blasted Rocco Vitale to kibble. He was your number two. How does that even happen? Now, I don't mean to overstep." He shook his fat head. "But this can't go on."

Rigoletti prattled on with his complaint, but Svanire didn't need to hang on every word. The game was too easy to win. All too simple to dominate the other players on the board. They played checkers while Svanire played chess—working the long game. A killer of kings. Taking Don Giordano off the board had only been the first step. The organization heads would fall next, and many others would feel his wrath before it was all over.

Not the least of whom was Joe Carboni. A dying pawn who had seen his day—but first, some fun. Carboni cared about what the Don thought. Cared about respect. More than that, he *worried* about it, the old fool. Just seeing the deflated hitman on the other side of that video call, fearing the consequences of the boss's disappointment, had given Svanire a thrill. He couldn't wait to stick that knife in deep and give it a good twist.

As Don Rigoletti whined on about *disturbing recent events*, Svanire activated another monitor off to the side. He gave the Don a serious nod. "I certainly understand," Svanire said. "But you have my word, Leo— our arrangement will continue, as agreed upon. Why don't you bring your people for a sit-down? You and me and the others. We'll get it all straightened out."

As Rigoletti resumed whining, a disinterested Svanire fingered through several video feeds until he found the microdrone that had followed old Joe Carboni to his residence. Paying only enough attention to note pauses in Rigoletti's complaints, he watched Joe's slump-shouldered bulk ascend the stairs to his apartment.

Find the boy, Jojo, Svanire thought. *Don't fail me.* A cold, almost sexual pleasure radiated in Svanire's chest as Carboni stopped to feed a gaggle of stray cats.

CHAPTER EIGHT

Jackson

A cold gust snapped at Jackson as he jogged, vaulting deep fissures and potholes in the street. Black iron fences, draped with torn plastic grocery bags and other bits of windblown trash ran the length of the kudzu-covered street. Every yard and house a clone of the one next to it. Broken strollers and ruined deck chairs rotted in small brown gardens, while every red brick two-up-two-down abode had at least one boarded-up window. He'd swear that, at one time, his own house had all its windows, and his mom had tended to flowers in the garden. Probably a vape-fueled dream.

"Could use a hit of Strawberry Fields right now," Jackson said aloud.

He pulled his hood tighter, adjusted his rucksack, and quickened his pace.

A lanky figure in a long coat, head down, shuffled along in the opposite direction on the other side of the street. Jackson averted his gaze as the two passed one another. The jittery specter's head snapped up and fixed a stare on Jackson.

"Shit," Jackson said.

Without checking for traffic, the ghoul squeezed between a burned-out sedan and a black Chrysler and skittered across the road. Jackson froze to the spot, breath fogging the inside of his Lenser mask. The thin man stepped into Jackson's path on the sidewalk and rubbed at the pockets of his grubby trench coat.

Jackson raised his hands. A fucking tweaker.

"What chu need?" the tweaker asked, his words slurred.

Jackson unclenched and lowered his hands. "Nah, man," he said, voice transformed into a resonant baritone. "I got a plug. I never buy off the street." He tried to sidestep the tweaker.

"You heard me, dawg," Tweaker said. His chapped lips curled back over purple gums and five brown-yellow teeth. "You got dat fancy mask. So, I know you got coin." He jabbed a finger against Jackson's mask. "Hook me up."

"Get lost." Jackson took a step back.

"Aye, man. I'm serious." Tweaker pulled at the crotch of his pants. "I know you got it. And none dat shit coin, either. Real tokens, dawg." He scratched his neck, his arm, then his face. "Talkin' Giltcoin. Sell you whatever. I got it all. Ice, rock, snow, boy, funk, green—you name it."

No one liked buying from tweakers. Doctors were thin, on the ground, and most had decided to cash in on the scarcity, which put their trade beyond the financial reach of street-level folk. Most tweakers were so strung out, they couldn't form a sentence, let alone a fist.

"Look, geekbag," Jackson said, straightening his spine and puffing himself up to his full five foot ten inches. "Go force your shit on someone else."

The tweaker shoved Jackson in the chest with a bony hand, knocking him to the cold concrete.

"Don't jack with me, dawg!" Tweaker reached his other hand into his long coat. "I'll fuckin' slay you!" He pulled out the upper receiver of a shattered sniper drone, complete with a match rifle barrel and a jerry-rigged trigger.

"Whoa, take it … take it easy." Jackson pushed one trembling hand out. His stomach tightened and his bladder tingled.

"Make the trade, man," Tweaker said, and clawed his neck. "I want dem coins." He pulled out a digital wallet device.

Jackson stared up at the tweaker's simple crypto wallet. He fumbled in his own pocket and pulled out his phone. Jackson thumbed the security panel and held the phone up to enable a near-field connection.

The tweaker, eyes greedy, lurched down to tap his device against Jackson's phone.

Jackson released his thumb and his device unleashed its six-hundred-and-fifty-thousand-volt charge into the tweaker's bony hand.

The drug-addled geekbag shrieked, then fell, stiff as a board, to the sidewalk. His jerry-rigged gun clattered into the gutter and fired. The round zinged off the curb. As the tweaker thrashed, the front of his pants stained dark with piss.

Jackson sprang to his feet and twirled his phone like a Wild West gunslinger. "Yeah, bitch, that's what you get!" he shouted. "No idea who you messin' with, do ya? I'm—" The word *CyberRonin* almost slipped from Jackson's lips. He swallowed it down.

Tweaker groaned, already squirming back to his knees.

Jackson turned and ran. "Don't let me see you again!" he called over his shoulder.

He sprinted a few blocks until he hit a T-intersection, then doubled back on the next street over. He hopped a fence and ripped through the neighbor's yard to the sound of their Rottweiler chained to a drainpipe, barking and chomping with slobbering jaws. Jackson, out of breath, scaled the crumbling stone wall and dropped down the other side into tall grass. Lungs on fire, he blasted into his mom's kitchen through the back door and slammed it closed. He slid down to the linoleum floor and pulled his knees close, gulping at the air, then yanked his Lenser mask off to suck in even larger breaths.

"Dude's crazy," he wheezed, then kissed the still-warm stun gun case that enveloped his phone. "Best coin I ever spent."

"Jackson?" his mom called from the hallway. "That you?" She emerged with a cautious step into the kitchen, one slipper on, the other held high—ready to slap the shit out of a would-be invader.

"Watcha doin', Ma?" Jackson said, climbing to his feet. "You ain't ghetto enough to be dangerous with that thing."

"I can still give you a thick ear," she said, and cocked the slipper back.

"We gotta get out of here," he said with a shake of his head, and shoved his phone back into his pocket.

His mom lowered her fluffy weapon. "You in trouble *again*?"

Jackson peeked out the window, kicked off his sneakers, then backed away to the door to his basement lair. "You gotta go pack. Right now." He didn't have as much coin as he had hoped to make it to the islands—especially with Sylcoin tanking—but it would have to be enough. "We're going to that place I told you about, okay?"

"The place with the beach?" his mom asked, eyes wide.

Jackson slid his rucksack off into one hand and shooed his mom away. "Go pack!"

She spun on her heel and, despite her bad hip, dashed off with an excited spring in her step.

Jackson scanned his iris, heaved open the ten-gauge steel door, then jumped down the stairs two at a time. With a few key taps, he woke his system, then checked his crypto platforms.

"Please, please, please," he whispered.

Zeros. All zeros.

Jackson's mind whirled. "No, no, no ..."

He refreshed the screens over and over, but still his accounts were bare. Platforms, wallets—all empty. Not even fragments of coins left. "How is that even possible!" he screamed, then picked up his roller chair and launched it across the room, where it clattered against the wall.

"Fuck!" he yelled into the air, fists balled.

"Okay, breathe. Just breathe. Someone scythed you." How, though? "My setup is ironclad." State of the art, with identity and passkeys scattered over so many chains, it would take a thousand years to find all the fragments and piece them together. He paced the room, rubbing at his head.

Only I have the algorithm key ... don't I?

"Shit!"

"Language!" his mom shouted from upstairs.

Jackson looked up the stairs to the door. "Mom ..." he said under his breath.

Without his coin, they wouldn't be going anywhere. No IslandLife. No safe haven. He'd spent the last two years slaying motherfuckers to amass a fortune, only for some prick to steal it. And, of course, who could forget dog-bomb? Someone had it in for him, but who? He ran everything dark web. Even though the dark web comprised ninety-six percent of the entire internet, most people didn't have the first clue how to access it, let alone scythe someone like Jackson. They were too busy buying and selling NFTs, digital properties, and pixelated prostitutes in one of the many virtual reality ecosystems. Chumps who buried themselves so deep in cyberspace forgot the real world.

"Focus, Jackson," he said, and tapped on his head. Had to be an insider—a client, perhaps. Someone had to know something. Jackson dumped his rucksack, as if relieving himself of the load would help his brain.

He snapped his fingers and grabbed the chair he'd launched across the room earlier. One wheel hung off at an angle, but it still seemed functional. Jackson plonked the chair down and sat, then rolled up to his keyboard. He logged into his Raptor dark-web browser account and navigated to the chat titled *Insurgent Information,* where he'd often find Hellcat. He bit his nails as the chatroom loaded, which always took a damn age.

The chatroom pinged up onscreen. Jackson scrolled endless single lines of text chat, all without emojis or any fancy formatting. Users gossiped about the Sylcoin massacre that morning and gave each other tips on possible newsworthy events coming up.

TibetanTrekker13 had posted a link to the Tea Horse Road trading network, which had just put up for sale a large contingent of ex-military drones and Det Flex explosives.

"Selling, or suggesting we follow the sale to a good story?" Jackson muttered. He skimmed a few more side conversations. Nothing, and no way to see if Hellcat was online. "Perhaps do a little fishing ..." He tapped out a message and hit return.

> CyberRonin: What's up, guys? Any rumors of a big scythe? A crypto heist?
> Gotgunz: nah man, not herd nuthin. You got a lead?

This asshole. Spelled worse than a three-year-old.

> CyberRonin: Perhaps, could be a big story.
> ReppinFemScythers: you wanna sell the tip? I can spare a few Giltcoin

Pointless. These jokers lived in here, not in the real world. About as useful as a chocolate fireguard.

> CyberRonin: Actually, promised this one to Hellcat. Anyone seen him?
> Cryohead26: Him? Lolz
> Fuckdyogranny: not since this morn cuz.

ReppinFemScythers: what's a girl gotta do to earn some coin?
Cryohead26: I got sum ideas ...
Fuckdyogranny: Nothing you can give in a VRE haha
ReppingFemScythers: like you could handle me when you be
fucking grannies
Gotgunz: can range sum compny fresh batch of yung stok just
in from Romaynya

Jackson leaned back in his chair and rubbed at his face. "Oh my god," he said. "This is going nowhere."

A teal-colored box flashed up: *Private chat from HELLCAT_59.*

"Hell yeah," Jackson said, then hovered his cursor over the link and clicked it.

The screen cut to black. Jackson wiggled his mouse. "Shit, it died."

A young woman's voice emanated from the computer speakers. "No time to type, Jackson," she said.

"Hellcat?" Jackson spluttered.

"The one and only," she said. The alto of her voice suggested a teenager. Perhaps even younger than Jackson. "Look, you're outta time," she said. "Someone is gunnin' for you."

"I know!" Jackson grabbed his monitor with both hands. "What the hell is going on—who are you? How do you know who I am?"

"Too many questions," Hellcat said. "Your details got leaked onto a very exclusive slaysite. I got a tip."

"Slaysite?" Slaysites only listed top kills. "What do I do?" he rasped.

"Well, I hope you're as smart as you are cute," Hellcat said.

Jackson slammed his hand over the pin-hole camera in his monitor. "She can see me," he whispered.

A giggle. "Not anymore," Hellcat said, "but I can still *hear* you, stupid."

"Fuck," Jackson blurted out, then gobbed on his finger and smeared the spit over the camera hole.

"Too late for that, love. I've already got the mental image I need," Hellcat said. "Tick tock, Jackson. Better get moving if you want to keep your head."

He stood and paced his cellar. "Right, think ... gotta get out of here. Need coin, and fast."

"And burn that place to the ground," Hellcat added. "No trail."

"Right, right, that's a good idea." Jackson stopped pacing. "Why should I trust you?"

"You'd already be dead without me," Hellcat said. "I'm your guardian angel. What are you waiting for, dumbass?" The speakers vibrated with her raised voice.

"Okay, I'm a ghost," Jackson said, and chewed his finger. Damn, he needed a vape.

"Oh, and ditch your phone, dummy."

"No need," Jackson said. "My setup is secure."

"You sure?" Hellcat laughed. "I'll throw you a new one just in case. Your usual spot."

"You know my throw sites? Why are you helping me? How will I find you?" Jackson stared at the black screen, but no reply came. "Hello?"

He rifled through a drawer, fished out his off-grid smartwatch, and strapped it to his wrist. "Okay, gotta go," he said. "Gotta go. Where? Where do I go? Somewhere Mom can go, too. Need coin. The only place *to* go." He reached for his phone, but just glared at it as though it had betrayed him. He left it on the desk, then grabbed his rucksack and launched up the rickety stairs.

CHAPTER NINE

Joe

L ow clouds swollen with precipitation scattered across the steel-gray Chicago sky. A lone red oak swayed in the wind, covered in vines and planted in a four-foot-square patch of dirt in a sea of concrete sidewalk. Bits of paper trash stood on edge and danced.

Inside the blacked-out Chrysler parked at the curb, Joe sniffed, then plucked a handkerchief from his suit jacket and dabbed it beneath his nose. He folded the faded cream square, embroidered with someone else's initials, and replaced it. He blew out an impatient whistle.

None of his nightly rituals had brought him any peace in the wake of his meeting with the Don—not the glass of port, and not the sweeping melodies of Morricone. He'd barely slept, his dreams haunted by the charred body of a little girl.

"Send the package already," Joe mumbled.

The Family had a way of doing business … a formula. Systematic processes, checks and assurances that always felt familiar and soothed any anxieties that might precede a job. The past few days had none of those things, as if the boss and his people had forgotten how things were done. "Or … maybe the boss isn't the one running things anymore," Joe murmured. He shook off the thought. "Just do the job," he said to the empty Chrysler, eyes on the red oak whipping in the wind.

Joe pushed the back of his hand against his freshly shaved chin and surveyed the weed-choked block. A wood-paneled shed riddled with bullet holes, its roof sunken, rotted beside brick houses, decayed and neglected. The black iron fences that ringed the block hadn't kept squatters from boarding up an ancient two-story fortress made of once-beautiful stone blocks, now in deep disrepair.

Did a high-profile cryptokiller really live in a place like Englewood? Why the hell would they do that? Anonymity?

Joe shook his head. "Doesn't matter," he said under his breath.

Someone found him anyway. "Can't hide from your sins."

An elderly woman shuffled past the Chrysler, bony fingers fumbling with a thin canvas bag stretched into the shape of canned goods. She stopped and looked at Joe's car, her curious old eyes probing a bit too long. She couldn't see into the vehicle while in full dark, but Joe leaned back anyway. The elderly woman secured the bag strap over her knobby shoulder and continued shuffling.

She neared two hungry-looking neighborhood enforcers, one in red with a pistol shoved in his waistband and the other in black, an AK-47 slung over his shoulder. They leaned against a wall striped with orange and black graffiti. She waved politely at them. The young enforcers nodded back. In the absence of a local police force, these hooligans kept the peace, for better or worse, though peace these days meant brutish enforcement by local warlords. In an age of total chaos, people took what they could get. These two looked like Balkan Boys, Eastern European thugs who filled the niches with which Nuevo Costa Nostra didn't bother.

A can fell from the old woman's bag and rolled into the street. One of the thugs, a squat guy in a fire-engine-red leather jacket, pointed to it and elbowed his buddy. The old woman stopped and looked at the can as it stopped against a sewer cap.

Joe tapped the steering wheel and activated the Chrysler's external microphone. With a *blip*, the sounds of the street filtered through the speakers of the car.

"You need hand?" Red Jacket said, his *H* glottal and his grammar poor—even by wise-guy standards. The two enforcers glanced at each other and pushed off the wall. Red Jacket produced a tablet from his coat. "Miss …?"

"Cates. Morlanda Cates," the old woman said.

Red Jacket typed on his tablet. "6559 South Green Street?"

The old woman clutched at her bag and gave a little nod.

"She's good," Red Jacket said to his buddy, all dressed in black joggers. "Protection paid up till the end of the month."

A smile spread over the face of Black Joggers. "Let me help you." He stepped into the street to retrieve the rogue can. Without asking, he took her canvas bag and rummaged through it. The young enforcer plucked two cans of Beanie Weenies, a can of corn, and a can of tomatoes from the sack and tossed them one at a time to Red Jacket. The woman's bag sagged in one spot where two or three cans remained.

Joe squirmed in his seat. "These pricks."

Black Joggers slung the old woman's lightened bag over his shoulder. "I walk you home."

Morlanda's Velcro shoes scraped the concrete. "I think I can … I can manage now."

"No, no." Red Jacket smiled wider. "We insist. Kilo Rikki takes pride in making neighborhood safe place."

A pained look crossed the old woman's face. "Tell Ms. Rikki I appreciate her …" she swallowed, "… generosity."

The two youths escorted Morlanda to the end of the block, then turned with her out of sight.

Joe shook his head. They'd shake her down again when they got to her place. "Bastards."

As much as having no cops around made his own life a hell of a lot easier, defunding and eliminating the police hadn't been everything that people had hoped—at least, not for the poor and impoverished, the people with no way out and no money for private security.

The screen on the dash lit up.

Data Package Received.

Joe looked at his watch and grunted. "So much for punctuality."

A blue folder, same as the last, blinked in, then grew larger on the Chrysler's screen. Joe leaned forward and touched the glass. The digital contents spilled out, unfolding along creases like paper. Several pictures separated from the bulk of the intelligence. Joe tabbed an image labeled *Jackson Cross.* The photo snapped open. A caramel-colored face with a tuft of short black hair popped onto the screen, an angsty-looking kid.

Joe's brow creased. There had to be some mistake. He opened the second image and stared at a plain, gaunt white woman with thin hair and haunted eyes.

Chrystal Cross: Target's Mother.

"A kid," Joe mumbled. "Like Charley." Perspiration prickled Joe's forehead. He yanked on his silk tie to loosen it. "Mary, Mother of God."

Joe's phone trilled. He ran a hand over his thinning hair, smoothing it down, then cleared his throat and accepted the call.

"Confirm receipt of the package," Svanire said.

Joe pinched the bridge of his nose. "I told you, I don't—"

"You don't what …?" Svanire laughed in his ear. "Kill kids? You would have killed me without a second thought all those years ago … if you *could have*."

A reckless heat bloomed in Joe's chest. "That was different."

"Is that what you'd like me to tell the boss, then?" Svanire asked. "After all the grace he extended to you yesterday?"

"No, listen, it's just—"

"Do the job," Svanire said, his voice low, "or the next target will be on your back, Joseph."

The phone clicked.

Joe sat in silence, eyes closed.

All he'd ever wanted was to be somebody. To be the guy the boss could count on. To be respected. All of that, everything for which he'd worked so hard, would vanish if he couldn't do this one damn job.

He opened his eyes and stared at the image of Jackson Cross. "Some stupid kid who's in over his head." Joe exited the Chrysler and checked the snubbie revolver in his waistband.

A kid who'd be dead in fifteen minutes.

CHAPTER TEN
Jackson

Jackson burst into the kitchen and skidded to a dead stop next to a wicker basket filled with jumbled shoes. He rummaged through the pile and tossed a worn pair of his mom's sandals aside with a curse. He secured a pair of dingy whites with a blue swoosh on the ankle. He stuffed a foot into one, but froze as a *bump* sounded from somewhere in the house.

Jackson straightened. "Mom?"

"I'm not ready yet! Don't rush me," his mother called back, her voice muted between the floors.

Jackson scanned the back windows. "Stop being so damn jittery, man." He shoved his other foot into a sneaker.

He pushed off the linoleum to stand, but locked rigid.

In the kitchen, a gorilla-shaped brute, draped in a long overcoat with a fedora crammed onto his square head, filled the doorway to the living room. Jackson's heart jackhammered and his fingers and toes tingled.

The brute lifted his head just enough to allow cold eyes to meet Jackson's panicked stare.

Jackson bolted, tripped over his own feet, and crashed into a cupboard. The brute lumbered forward. Holding onto the strap of his rucksack, Jackson spun like a running back dodging the tackle and careened out of control past the gorilla into the living room. He pitched, fell, and ate it face-first into the carpet. Rug burn blazed on his chin. He scrambled up, made for his dad's desk, and ransacked its drawers. A framed photo of his dad and mom holding Jackson as a baby clattered to the carpet. Jackson tore out papers, matches, cigarettes, and used-up batteries until his fingers finally found it.

He jerked his dad's old Smith & Wesson 626 revolver from the drawer.

A hard slap knocked the bulky chrome firearm from Jackson's hands and sent it tumbling across the carpet. "Hey, man, don't do it," Jackson stammered as he searched for an escape route.

The brute stepped closer, his craggy face more visible in the natural light of the living room. He sucked at his teeth and rolled his shoulders.

Jackson sprinted to the side, but the old man's leathery hand caught him across the jaw. Jackson cried out and tumbled into a wall. Glass shattered as old photo frames crashed to the floor.

The old man shambled over.

Jackson's mom rounded the bend in the staircase. "What in God's name—?"

"Ma, no!" Jackson yelled, and held out one bloodied hand.

"Who the hell are *you?*" his mom yelled, then grabbed the slipper from her foot and leaped down the last three steps onto the intruder. "Asshole in *my* living room—attacking *my* son!" She pelted the brute across the ear with the fluffy weapon.

The gorilla frowned and covered his head.

Jackson could only stare, slack-jawed, as his mom doled out her moccasin-powered punishment.

"Lady, you wanna knock that off?" the gorilla grumbled, then snatched the slipper and threw it away. "I'm not here to—"

The living room window and the wall beneath it exploded. Jackson shrunk back and covered his face, eyes wide under the bend in his elbow. Powdered brick and mortar covered an enormous capsule-shaped projectile as it smashed through the living room, skimmed past the brute, and slammed into Jackson's mom with a sickening crunch.

Jackson screamed, scrambled to his feet, then climbed over debris to his mom, trapped between the living room wall and the car. "Mom? Mom …?"

Her head lolled to the side, blood streaming from her mouth. She gurgled something, then slumped onto the cab's hood. The synthetic voice of the self-drive AI called out, drowning a golden oldie from the eighties still playing on the internal digital radio: "You have arrived at your destination … you have arrived at your destination … you have arrived at your …"

"Mom, wake up," Jackson pleaded. Tears welled in his eyes. "Wake up." He gave her arm a shake. Her head drooped against her chest.

A meaty paw grabbed Jackson by the shoulder.

He snatched away and sniffed back a bubble of snot. "Get away from me!" Jackson said.

The gorilla in the dusty overcoat bent down with a groan and put two thick fingers to Jackson's mom's neck.

The AI quit its whining, but the radio jammed on with its bouncy beat.

"Sorry, kid, she's gone," the gorilla said, tone cold.

"Get your hands off her, asshole!" Jackson yelled.

"We don't have time for this." The brute touched Jackson's shoulder. "We gotta get outta here." He motioned his large head in the direction of the hole in the wall where the window used to be.

Jackson eyed the gorilla-shaped man whose heavy, slumped shoulders and thinning hair showed him to be just another Genial.

"Get away from me, you crusty old prick!" Jackson slapped away the gorilla's trunk-like arm. "I'll kill you, stake!"

"Steak?" The brute screwed up his already furrowed face. "Like, meat?"

"No, you fucking Genial," Jackson fired back. "Like, stakes—like putting down a bet," he stammered. "Like … like I fucking mean it!"

"You need to chill out."

"This is your fault!" Jackson stumbled back and fell on his butt in the swirling dust.

"Nah, this wasn't me. But I know who did it." The gorilla locked Jackson down with knowing eyes. "And if *you* wanna know, you'll get up and come with me."

"I ain't going anywhere with you, man!" Jackson clamored back to his mother's lifeless body.

"Stay here, and you're dead," the gorilla said. "*We're* dead. They got it out for both of us, now."

Jackson's eyes stung, tear ducts caked with powdered brick. "Who are you?"

"Bones."

"What kind of shit name is that?" Jackson's knuckles scraped against broken rubble as he reached under his mother's fractured ribcage.

Bones grunted. "The kind I worked hard for, and it's a whole lot less shit than CyberRonin Two Thousand or whatever the fuck you call yourself."

"Who's *they*?" Jackson pulled his mom closer. Her legs remained stuck under the car, but her flaccid torso stretched thin and her head flopped into his lap. "Who's trying to kill me? Who killed my mom?" He ran his forearm over his snot-covered nose, which only smeared the mucus across his top lip.

"That's what I'm trying to *tell you*," Bones said through a locked jaw. "Bad people—one in particular. You're from this city, you know who the Giordano family is."

Jackson cupped his mom's face but pulled away when her jawbone jutted through her cheek. With two shaking fingers, he pushed her eyelids closed.

"Kid," Bones pressed.

Jackson lifted his head and sniffed again. "The *mafia*? They want me dead?"

Bones shrugged. "Looks that way."

"Why?"

"I *don't know*," Bones said. "Maybe you blew away someone you shouldn't have." He put out a hand to help Jackson up. "Doesn't even matter. You—*we*—gotta get out of the city, like now."

Jackson stared at the old man's enormous hand.

A new oldie about some "Highway to the Danger Zone" started on the car radio.

"They sent me to *do you*. Get it?" Bones said. "An' I'm not gonna do it. So, they're gonna send everything they got until it's done. Until we're *both* done. Capiche?"

Bones stood tall with that one hand outstretched.

Jackson stroked his mom's forehead. Every curse, irritated snap, and veiled insult he'd ever thrown at her rattled around in his head. "Mom," he mumbled.

Thick fingers encircled Jackson's skinny biceps and he found himself hoisted to his feet, though his rubbery legs did little to offer support. His mom's head hit the carpet with a hollow thud.

"Watch it, geekbag!" Jackson yelled.

"It's a sad thing, kid," Bones said, "but it's done."

Jackson wanted to collapse and hold his mom, but his mind swarmed.

The mafia had now tried to kill him three times. They'd punched through his layers of online encryption, beat his hi-tech disguises to send a bomb-toting dog, and scythed a self-drive car to go on a kamikaze run.

And they'd killed his mom.

The song on the car radio faded, and in its place a woman near shouted in a harsh, familiar Germanic accent.

"Omniviolence is the enemy of progress," said the pre-recorded message from Anja Kuhn. "We have devolved to the medieval Dark Ages—only we have technology, now. We must resist the urge to retaliate against perceived slights. Do not take an eye for an eye. Humanity must be better than that—"

Jackson looked the Genial in the eyes, searching for a fingerhold in this new hell. "The mafia will keep coming?"

Bones nodded. "You need to come with me." He took a limped step toward the hole in the wall.

Jackson swayed on his feet and wiped his nose across his hoodie sleeve. "I know where I'm going," he said. "And it doesn't involve you, stake."

Bones raised a gray eyebrow. "Oh yeah? Where's that?"

"El Salvador." Jackson puffed out his chest.

Bones' face creased up like origami and he hacked out a laugh. "Bitcoin City. Aren't you supposed to be some kinda wiz-kid cryptokiller?"

"What's your point?" Jackson fired back.

"You have any idea how far away Bitcoin City is?" Bones shook his head. "Ever been that far from home? No—better yet, have you ever even left this crappy neighborhood?"

"Fuck off, man." Jackson took a last glance at his mom, then pushed off the car and stomped over broken brick and a crushed sofa toward the hole in the wall. "I kill twenty Genials like you while you're rubbing one out before breakfast." He tripped on a jagged hunk of brick, then scrambled up again. A quick feel behind confirmed the rucksack still sat on his back.

"B.C. is *days'* worth of driving. Why there?" Bones demanded.

"Because," Jackson shouted, "my accounts got drained and I have coin on an off-grid device, but I can't get it drone-dropped, now, can I? I'm on a fucking slaysite, on the grid. Gotta keep moving." He flipped Bones the bird.

Bones shook his jug-head. "You'll never make it, kid."

"I don't need your help."

"The hell you don't," Bones said, starting after Jackson. "I just got myself in a whole heap of shit for not ending you." He jabbed Jackson in the chest with a meaty finger. "So, we both gotta get out of town and figure out why a punk like you is even on The Family's kill list."

Jackson threw up his hands and started back into the living room. "I need my fucking Lenser."

A shockwave of debris and heat lifted both Jackson and Bones from the rubble and flung them through the hole in the wall, the front of the house following them out in splinters. Jackson hit the concrete hard, the skin on his knobby knees and elbows scraped bloody. Head ringing and unable to suck in a whole lungful of air, Jackson pawed about the sidewalk, feeling his way through brick and smoke.

His fingers grazed a body.

"Sweet Mary," Bones wheezed, rolling away from Jackson's touch. "Svanire isn't messing around …"

Jackson peered back into his house, the burning car and his mom now only well-cooked remains on the living room carpet.

Bones coughed as he pulled himself to his feet. He winced and touched the back of his calf. The pants were torn, his flesh marred by a black tire mark. "Shit," he muttered. "Ran me over, an' I didn't even feel it."

Through the smoke, a hunched figure in a frayed wool coat hobbled up the garden path. Dirty clothing hung in ribbons on his skinny frame, little more than rags. A sweat-soaked blue bandana stuck to his receding hairline. The hobo grinned, flashing a few broken-off teeth. He stopped just paces away from Jackson and worked the pump on a sawed-off Remington 870. "Time to die, bitches!"

Jackson raised his hands.

"We ain't got time for this." Bones cleared his throat and pointed at the shotgun. "You gonna take the safety off first?"

The hobo's confidence faltered. He looked down at the rusty shotgun.

Bones jerked the snubbie revolver from his waistband and fired.

Jackson winced at the sharp *crack* and the jet of flame that pushed from the short barrel.

The hobo's head whip-sawed back. His eyes rolled up, and a hole like a third eye in the center of his forehead dribbled a stream of blood. He toppled backward and fell flat against the withered grass. The shotgun clattered beside his convulsing limbs.

Bones cleared his throat and secured the snubbie in his waistband. His old face creased as he bent and picked up the shotgun.

Jackson looked from Bones to the dead hobo and back again. "Was the safety on?" he stammered.

"Hell no," Bones said. He extended a meaty paw toward Jackson. "You comin' or not?"

CHAPTER ELEVEN
Svanire

A ping chimed in the Don's sun-strafed office of warm, rich mahogany balanced with accents of cherrywood and ash. A feeling of time-tested ritual inhabited the space, comfortable yet businesslike, an ageless tradition of meetings, requests, favors, and shaken hands. A place where things got done.

Svanire, chin to his chest, hands clasped at his waist, waited as two attendants—one oval-shaped and another who might blow away in a stiff wind—hoisted the body bag from in front of the Chesterfield couch.

"Careful," Svanire said without looking up.

The attendants glanced at him, then at each other, and eased the Don's body onto a stretcher. "Eh, sir ..." said the oval man with dark circles under his eyes. "You want it ... eh ... him to go ...?"

"Straight to Sanctuary Animal Hospital," Svanire said, not missing a beat. "I have people who will meet you there."

"The animal hospital?" asked the skinny attendant, sporting a pencil-thin brown mustache over wet lips. "Why are we taking him to a—"

"The furnace, you idiot," the oval-shaped man spat.

Svanire lifted a single finger and the attendants froze. He raised his cold eyes to meet theirs. "Go straight there. Do not talk to anyone. Do not deviate." Svanire clasped his hands. "I'll be watching."

Oval shook himself from the grip of Svanire's stare. "Yes, sir. You got it." He glared at Mustache and hissed, "Come on, already."

The attendants wheeled the gurney this way and that, squeaking across the space until they disappeared into the hall. A moment later, the elevator doors dinged closed.

Svanire released a whistle of breath. The end of an era. The beginning of something even greater. He turned to the desk and took a seat, careful not to wrinkle the perfect creases of his suit pants. With a wave of his hand, he activated the screens. Windows stacked upon windows in an orderly fashion across the monitors. Some tracked the rapid rise and fall of the crypto markets or featured surveillance feeds and independent news updates from bloggers all over the world. Dark web live streams filled others with young, naked flesh, writhing and moaning.

He turned his attention to the microdrone feed hovering over Joe Carboni and the Cross kid as they pulled themselves from the wreckage left by Svanire's self-drive car attack. It had obliterated a pathetic little shack and left a hole in the brick that looked like a bomb had gone off.

A new notification pinged in the top right of the closest screen, but Svanire ignored it.

"Zoom in," he commanded.

The image shimmered as the microdrone focused. Carboni helped Cross to his feet, their lips moving in pantomime. If only Svanire could hear their exchange, feel the tension, the fear in their voices as they acknowledged their scrape with death. But, sacrifices had to be made with a surveillance drone the size of an old dime.

Another *ping*. Svanire glanced at the second notification.

Target kill rank twenty-seven, it read. Svanire's brow creased. A sharp uptick, even under the circumstances. A few taps at the keyboard, then he waited, adjusting his pristine gold and onyx cufflinks, as the slaysite Hunter's Dominion loaded. He could reference other sites, but Dominion was, without question, top dog. Everybody used it to find the most valuable targets of the day, and though many well-recognized hunters combed the rankings hourly, the site was also home to scores of hacks—talent-devoid idiots looking to make a quick coin with little more than Grandpa's old double-barrel, some janky hardware, and too much time on their hands.

Ping. The hit on Carboni and the kid jumped up the rankings to number fourteen.

"Level out." The words hissed through Svanire's teeth. He double-clicked on the hit profile.

His slay order on Carboni and the kid had picked up piggybackers, and the bastards were crowd-funding it. Two boosters, HeroGator13 and 4July4eva, battled to see who could up the ante the fastest. They'd even switched to a high-profile coin. Svanire stood from the rich mahogany of the Don's desk, his body rigid. He watched the curved display. The muscles of his back cinched. The hit ranking on Carboni and Cross jumped again, this time to position number two.

Svanire's jaw flexed and held.

"Always have to make it interesting, don't you?" he whispered to himself.

He smoothed the front of his suit, pulled his phone from his jacket, and allowed facial recognition to activate. The phone's home screen slipped open. Svanire accessed his hot list and touched the third name down.

The phone rang thirteen times. So long that Svanire thought it might trigger the recorded message. Then came the sound of a phone sliding beneath dreadlocks.

"Whatchoo want? I'm very busy," a man said in a powerful Afrikaans accent.

"I need a favor, Lekan. You owe me," Svanire said.

"I owe you?" Lekan coughed a dry laugh. "After the last crypto sell-off stunt you pulled? Come to think of it, Svanire, you are right. I *do* owe you. A bullet to the brain."

The game. How Svanire loved the game. He licked his lips. "How could you say that after all the money I've made you?"

"You fucked up my operations, bru," Lekan snapped. "When those diamonds got snapped. Lost ten soldiers getting them back. You owe me ten lives."

"Had to steal them to make them worth even more. And according to my calculations, you made over twelve million in a stable coin," Svanire said.

"Whatchoo want, eh, bru?"

Oh, to slide a knife between your ribs and watch the light in your eyes dim. Svanire drew a breath, long and slow. "I want," Svanire took his time forming the words, "you to remember your little brother's life. I want you to remember that I am not some dirty-footed child soldier who needs your approval. When the hit went out on Saleem, I neutralized his would-be killers with a snap of my fingers. I want you to remember that, *and* I want you to *return the favor.*"

Breath huffed on the other end of the line. "I remember. Now. What. Do. You. Want?"

"Ahh, see? So much easier to communicate when you are willing to play nice," Svanire said. "What I want is simple. Two things, actually."

"Eh, bru, you said one favor."

"It *is* one, just in two parts, Lekan." Svanire allowed his lips to caress the receiver.

Lekan's breathing rattled the phone's speaker.

"Get all your independent contractors, your café boys, and have them create some noise on Hunter's Dominion," Svanire said. "I need to muddy the waters."

"You want real hits or noise?" Lekan asked.

"It has to be real, but the details are irrelevant. Make them legitimate and put some coin behind it. I'll fund what you need and pad your pocket in the process. Everyone wins."

"Too simple. What else, eh?"

"You Hard Living boys still have a stable alliance with the Twenty-Eights, correct?"

"Stable enough," Lekan said. "Why?"

"Get everyone together and wait for my signal to make a hit overseas. I'll provide the transport."

"A hit? On who?"

"Need-to-know basis, Lekan," Svanire said. "And you don't."

Lekan huffed. "One million in Zag Coin, bru."

"No one uses Zag but you, Lekan. This is why you can't hold onto your money."

"One million," Lekan said.

Svanire checked his manicure. "Three fifty."

A sound like a small balloon wheezing out its final breath buzzed from the phone. "Three fifty? Don't waste my time—"

"Remember little brother, Lekan." Svanire wagged a slender finger. "Xiu still wants his head on a stake, and I might be able to tell the mad Chinaman exactly where to find him."

The sound of hurried men hummed on the phone line, boots

squishing in mud, followed by the chugging of an antique diesel truck. "Five hundred," Lekan said. "And no more favors. We're even."

"Four," Svanire said, and grinned. "And, Lekan—you and I—we'll never be even." He terminated the call, made the crypto transfer in Zag Coin, and slipped the phone back into his jacket.

On the monitor, new well-funded hits began climbing the ranks, bumping the job on Joe and the kid from the top spot. An excellent distraction, for now. Svanire rubbed the cool flesh of his hands together and set the desktop to sleep.

He twirled with unnatural grace across the study, an eager spring in his step.

His phone chimed like an old doorbell to a picket-fenced house in the suburbs. The chime sent a wave of excitement through his spectral body. That sound, that perfect sound, only came from one app. He pushed his hand into his pocket and stroked the phone as he freed it. He checked the message, which made his heart beat just a little faster.

"A fresh batch," the message said. "New ones have arrived."

Svanire stepped into the hall with a cool purpose, his polished charcoal-over-black wingtips snapping against the ivory marble of the foyer. He reached the elevator, pressed the button, and checked the platinum face of his watch. A more regimented man might complete all his tasks before taking a foray into any personal indulgence, but Svanire felt his skin tingle with anticipation. He needed it.

There's always time for my loves.

The door slid back and the elevator operator nodded to him.

"Mr. Svanire," Clem said.

"B three," Svanire said.

An almost imperceptible shudder passed through the operator. "Yes, sir." He turned away and pressed the button for the lowest level.

Another *ding* and the sound of sliding doors, and Svanire emerged into an ancient corridor of damp concrete block. Old halogen lights buzzed above, somewhere water dripped, and Svanire's polished shoes clacked as he walked the length of the hall. At the end, he slowed and made eye contact with a slick-haired man.

"I think the room is finally the way you wanted it, sir," Slick said.

"Everything you asked for. I mean …" He wrung his hands together. "You, ah … ready for another one?"

Svanire offered a slow nod and reached for the steel door.

"Any, ah …" Slick's throat moved, "preference?"

Svanire shooed him with his fingertips and Slick scurried away.

Svanire inhaled deeply. The steel door creaked in protest. He took a step inside, then another, and savored the smell of fear and pain and humiliation. Warm and sickly sweet. With another flick of his hand the lights rose, dim and yellow.

He removed his jacket, folded it once, and laid it over the back of an ornate red velvet couch. Along the wall he walked, hand outstretched to the various implements and devices, some sharp and metallic, others blunt and rubbery or made of braided leather. He touched the large wooden rack with its dials, wheels, and gears, and stepped beneath a series of hanging chains bolted into the poured concrete ceiling above.

At the end of the room stood a plush bed freshly made with a silky plum comforter frilled in gold over eggshell-colored sheets. By contrast, the concrete floor beneath his shoes was stark, cold, and damp from a recent rinse. In the corner, blood-tinged rings lingered around the rim of a drain.

The steel door creaked.

Svanire turned and clasped his pale spidery fingers, a dramatic grin peeling across his face. "Welcome."

Slick ushered in a boy whose ribs showed through bare skin like brittle digits. The boy worked his mouth, chewing the skin of his lip, and his throat, as smooth as a girl's, swallowed once. The child pinched his arms across a bony chest and shuffled his feet, eyes downturned.

Svanire danced across the room, his whole body electric with anticipation.

"Another orphan off the street, just like you said." Slick wiped at the sweat on his forehead. "No one's looking for him."

"And no one should," Svanire cooed, "for now, he is home." He waved dramatically.

Slick coughed, then rubbed at his nose. "Anything else?"

"Get out," Svanire said, eyes fixed on the boy.

The doorman stammered. "I'll be, uh ... down the hall if you need—"

"Get. Out," Svanire said.

Slick coughed again. "Right." He pulled the heavy steel door closed as he left.

The boy watched, hollow-eyed, as Svanire locked three deadbolts set into the steel door, top to bottom. *Click. Click. Click.*

A sob escaped the boy and he trembled where he stood. "I don't like it here ..."

"Shhhh," Svanire said, turning back to him with a syrupy smile. "There, there, now. I'll take good care of you, my love." He bent and stroked the boy's tear-streaked face.

CHAPTER TWELVE
Joe

Joe popped the driver's side rear door on the blacked-out Chrysler, threw the rust-eaten shotgun on the floorboard, and slammed the door shut again. "Get in."

Jackson hovered in the street on the other side of the vehicle. "I was always taught never to get into cars with strange old men."

"Just get in." Joe touched his remote and popped the front doors. The display winked to life. "Welcome to the future of driving," the AI said. "Welcome to the Chrysler experience."

"How do I know you're not some perv, huh?" Jackson persisted from the street. "How do I know if I get in your pervert-mobile, you're not going to molest me or sell me into slavery or—"

"Hey," Joe barked. "Were you around for what just happened? Stop acting like a jackass and get in the car."

With a put-on look of disgust, Jackson stooped to look inside the car. "If you try to touch my pee-pee, I'm gonna Taser you."

Joe removed his fedora and sank into the driver's seat. "This is gonna be a long damn day." He clenched his teeth as he pulled in his injured leg.

Jackson peered around the interior, sniffed it, then reached down to swipe a bit of lint from the seat.

Joe stared at him.

"I'm checking to see if it's clean," Jackson said.

"Clean?" Joe choked on the word. "After that shit hole you call a home?"

Jackson plopped down and slammed the door behind him. "Don't talk about my mom's place like that, Genial."

"Clean," Joe repeated. "I should worry about *you* being clean, if we're gonna talk about clean."

Jackson folded his arms. "You're just saying that because I'm Black.

Racist."

Joe's mouth fell open.

A wry smile spread across Jackson's face.

"You're mom's white," Joe said.

The smile slipped away. "Was."

A torrent of quips and apologies sat on Joe's tongue, but in the end he just pulled the Chrysler away from the curb.

Cracked streets filled with potholes, leafy vines, and abandoned junk marked the end of one neighborhood and the beginning of the next. An old Buick hybrid careened through the stop sign ahead and tagged a stumpy smartcar in the rear end. The Buick swerved, bumped over the sidewalk, and drove away. The smartcar driver exited, waving his arms and shouting curses to no avail.

Jackson shook his head at the navigation tracking along the display. He gave a huff. "You're dumb. You know that, right?" He thumbed at the display. "Using navigation when everyone wants us dead? Mad easy to scythe and track. Why don't you paint a bullseye on the car?"

Joe grunted and switched off the display.

Jackson chuckled. "Stupid Genials. Turning the screen off doesn't disable it."

"Won't matter," Joe said. "You've got a smartphone in your pocket. They're tracking that, too."

Jackson shook his head. "I dumped my phone. And the watch is encrypted and off-grid until I say I want to connect it." He waved a black smartwatch with a large bezel in Joe's face. "And I can smoke anyone I want, or scythe any system with this—as long as I get a link up."

"So, you wanna do something about it?" Joe glared. "Or are you planning to save us by running your mouth, Mister Computer Wizard?"

"Cryptokiller," Jackson said, with a smug look of superiority. "Information technology ain't my department, Genial. If it doesn't involve killing, you're on your own."

"Then stop complaining."

"Haven't you heard?" Jackson looked offended. "Complaining is all my generation does."

Joe chewed the inside of his cheek. He pulled his phone from his pocket and flipped it open.

Jackson's face lit up. "Grandpa with the old-school flip! I see you." He pointed and covered a laugh. "Day-um. Not even, like, smart flip … like, *ancient* flip."

Joe ignored the kid, his face hard. He thumbed the numbers on the keypad. "Come on. Pick up, Sheila."

"Who you calling?" Jackson asked.

"My sister." Joe's foot mashed on the pedal and the electric Chrysler lurched forward. "I gotta get her and my nephew somewhere safe before we—"

"The subscriber you are trying to reach cannot be located," the scripted message said.

"Dammit," Joe said. He snapped the phone closed and slipped it back into his pocket. On the dashboard display screen, he initiated a vid call. It rang twice and disconnected. Joe swore again and pressed his foot harder onto the accelerator.

"That flip is outrageous, dude. Don't know when I last saw one of those." Jackson laughed again. "Perhaps a damn age ago when my mom used to use one …" His laugh faded. The kid swallowed, rubbed at his face, and turned to look out the window.

"Attention," the Chrysler's AI chimed, "current roadway conditions are unpredictable. Independent news sources report a food kiosk riot in the area of Brighton Park. This is along your route. Would you like me to drive?"

Joe grunted. "No."

"It would be safer if I—," the AI said.

"Just let it drive," Jackson added, turning away again as he wiped a tear.

"Shut up," Joe said.

"I cannot shut up," the AI said. "It is my duty to—"

"I do not want you to drive." Joe over-enunciated the words.

Jackson smirked.

Joe navigated the Chrysler beneath an overpass where a homeless man, pants around his ankles, urinated directly into the street. He gave them the finger as they passed. They hit the on-ramp to I-90, navigated around a stripped Tesla up on blocks, and accelerated north. Jackson grabbed for the hood of his sweatshirt and pulled it over his head. They spent the rest of the short trip in silence.

The closer to his sister's house they got, the tighter Joe's grip on the steering wheel became.

What if you're too late, Joe? What if Svanire did something crazy? No, Don Giordano wouldn't allow that. Not my family. There are still rules … aren't there? The Chrysler swerved down the exit ramp to Elgin.

"Okay, bro, chill." Jackson peeked out from around his phone. "You're driving like a maniac."

A red battery indicator lit up on the car's display with the words *Power levels below 15%. Please locate your nearest Zap station.*

Joe ignored Jackson and the car's warning. He dabbed the perspiration from his forehead with the sleeve of his shirt. "God-forsaken electric junk." He whipped the car from the off-ramp and swerved into the street, tires squalling in protest.

"Hey, I'm serious, man," Jackson said, fingers clutching at his armrest.

"Almost there," Joe said.

A barricade of yellow and black painted wood on casters stretched across the road. At one end, a large fence ran out of sight. A stiff-backed man walked a German shepherd along the fence, and members of the safety militia dressed in forest-green fatigues with rifles in their hands tensed at the fast approach of the Chrysler. A well-fed and heavily armed woman on the road stepped in front of the car and raised a flat palm.

Jackson hunched down in the seat. "Slow down, dude. Slow down. You're gonna get us slayed."

"They know me," Joe said.

Jackson swore and slid further down into the bucket seat.

Joe slowed the car and lowered his window as the Chrysler inched closer to the barrier.

The heavy female captain on duty approached, rifle raised.

"Hmmm," Joe muttered. "Never seen her before …"

"This is the territory of Moc Aziz Ali. State your purpose," Heavy Duty said.

"Visiting Sheila Carboni. It's an emergency," Joe said.

"What sort of emergency?"

Joe twisted his fingers around the steering wheel. "Ah, the personal sort."

"Explain yourself," Heavy Duty snapped.

Joe shrugged and opened his mouth when Jackson spoke. "She's sick. We're gonna run her to Mount Mercy to get checked out."

"Sick with what?" Heavy Duty asked.

Joe gave her a look. "Isn't that why you go to the doc? To find out?"

Heavy Duty continued as if she didn't hear. "If allowed entrance, do you solemnly swear to adhere to the rules and laws as set forth by Moc Aziz Ali and the Divine Order?" she asked. "And if you fail to adhere, do you agree to submit yourself to the judgment and discipline of the Order?"

"Yeah," Joe said.

"So, you agree to—"

"I know the rules. I'm really in a hurry," Joe said.

The heavy woman eyed Jackson, then Joe. "ID?" she said.

Joe produced a holographic e-dentity card with his picture under the name *Leonardo Musso Jr.*

Heavy Duty eyed Joe's ID and looked hard at Jackson.

"Please," Joe said. "She's really sick." He dabbed at his brow.

Heavy Duty took a step back and waved at the barricade, and the militia wheeled it open. Joe accelerated through and turned into the warren of protected streets.

Immediately, a shift occurred in the landscape. The crumbling, trash-filled streets and fractured neighborhoods that they'd just come through gave way to fresh pavement and small, well-kept houses. A couple walked hand in hand down the sidewalk. A boy and his puppy played with a red ball as a sprinkler watered a lush green lawn next door.

"I'd heard about Ali enclaves," Jackson said. "That they were different. But this is something else …"

"Yeah. It's nice," Joe said. "A slice of old-fashioned Americana. If you're willing to put up with the rules and laws." He turned to Jackson and swirled his finger at his temple. "Wackadoo."

From a sunlit street corner, a militiaman in green fatigues nodded, rifle slung over his shoulder and hands clasped at this belt buckle.

Jackson waved, and the man waved back with a smile. "Weird," Jackson said.

Another block down, Joe brought the Chrysler to a stop before a red brick house. "We're here. Stay in the car."

"Sure, whatever, man." Jackson checked his phone.

Joe secured his fedora, reached for the door release, and stepped out.

"Uncle Joe!" The shrill voice of Joe's nephew cut through the early morning quiet. "Mom got me a kitten!"

"Yeah?" Joe called back from the street.

"Yes, sir," Charley said. "A lady two streets over had kittens, and I got one!"

Joe limped away from the Chrysler to see Charley at the screen door of the simple, one-story brick home facing the street. Freshly painted cream-colored Masonite planks covered the sides and framed an aged but well-kept roof. The boy had something in his hands.

Charley, all knees and elbows, gave a huge smile. "You got someone with you?"

Joe waved Jackson over from the car. "Hey, get your mother and come down here, champ."

"Mom! Uncle Joe is here!" Charley called to the house, then continued down the front steps to his uncle. "But, Uncle Joe. Look. Kitten!" He held up a squirming, skinny ball of black and white fur. Thing was probably a couple of weeks old.

A restless tension grew in Joe's gut. That sick sensation he always had when a hit was about to go sideways. A gust of wind picked up and prickled the hair on his neck. "Charley," he said, "come on down here right now."

Charley frowned. He clutched the kitten to his chest. "Yes, sir. Something wrong?"

Sheila appeared at the door and pushed it open. She swiped at a few strands of raven hair threaded with gray. "Hey, Joe. Wasn't expecting you," she said. "Your package just arrived." She held up a thick envelope. "Something for work, I guess. Not sure why they sent it here …"

Joe's heart lurched. A chain of lightning set fire to every nerve. "Sheila!"

The brief pop of light burned Joe's eyes. Sheila disappeared in a boiling wave of fire that tore a gaping hole through the brick face of the house. The blast wave twisted Joe and flung him face down against the asphalt.

Joe rolled to his side and scrambled to all fours, but stars danced in his eyes, and his ears rang with a high-pitched whistle. "Christ, God Almighty. Help me ..." He tottered and fell again.

Jackson stood at the open door of the Chrysler. The force had cracked full-dark windows and peppered the black clearcoat with brick shrapnel. "What the fuck!"

Joe grunted and pushed to a knee, head swimming. The entire front side of the idyllic little house, wreathed in flame and smoke, crumbled.

Joe squinted and tried to get his brain to engage, to connect the pieces. "Sheila?" he called out, even though he'd seen her vaporize with his own eyes. Then, *Charley.* Joe scrambled to his feet, stumbled, fell against the car, then righted himself again.

"What the fuck!" Jackson shouted again. "We gotta go!"

Joe stumbled toward the car, ignoring the neighbors who gawked and cowered in their homes and yards. He staggered, and his trot became a run as Charley came into view, his body a smoked pile in the street.

"Charley! Charley!" Joe dropped to his knees on the pavement, his heavy hands patting out the embers on the boy's cotton shirt. He scooped the boy up. Charley's lanky body lolled in Joe's big arms. "Hey, buddy, Uncle Joe is here. I'm here."

Charley wheezed. Fluid wept from ruined eyes, his body black, dirty, and distorted. Joe hugged him close.

Jackson had wandered away from the safety of the car onto the sidewalk, a strange, faraway expression on his face.

"Uncle Joe?" Charley rasped.

"I'm here, buddy," Joe said. "Uncle Joe's got you."

Charley sucked in a ragged breath. "I can't see you."

"I'm here. I ain't gonna leave, kid." Joe squeezed the boy, a horrible impotence filling his chest.

"Momma?" Charley whispered. "Momma's okay?"

Joe looked up to the fully involved house and the blackened front stoop where his sister had stood. "She's, ah …" Joe swallowed. "We'll take care of her, buddy. Don't you worry."

The wail of sirens grew in the distance, the sound of a privately operated fire service. A block down, the militiaman in green fatigues sprinted toward them.

Jackson took a step and wrung his hands. "We gotta go, man," he said, but his words lacked conviction.

Charley cried. Joe hunched his body over him and leaned close.

"I'm … scared, Uncle Joe." Charley's voice was faint now. "I don't wanna …"

"I know, kid. I got you. I'm here."

Charley squirmed in the cold grip of death. He gasped, then grew still in his uncle's arms.

The tremors started in Joe's core and spread out to his limbs, a toxic void blooming inside him. Spittle gathered on his lips. "Don't do this." The words hissed from his throat. He shook a quivering fist at the sky. "Don't you do this to me!"

"You there, defiler!" The green militiaman rushed to the car, his rifle raised at Jackson. "Stop!"

Joe shuddered and clutched at Charley's lifeless body.

"It wasn't us!" Jackson lifted his hands. "We were just visiting!"

"Defiler!" the militiaman screamed, his eyes wild white orbs.

"I told you," Jackson started, "we didn't—"

"Why aren't you holding hands?" the militiaman shouted.

Jackson's mouth opened, but nothing came out.

"Why aren't you holding someone's hand?" the militiaman screamed again.

Jackson, bewildered, pointed to the house. "The place blew up and …"

"But you're not holding hands!" the guard said, his rifled trained on Jackson. "You have to hold hands on the sidewalk!"

Jackson half-shrugged. "Fuck, man, I'm fifteen. I don't need to hold anybody's—"

"But you have to!" the militiaman screamed. "You have to hold hands on the sidewalk! It is decreed by the Divine Order!" His finger closed on the trigger. "Defiler!"

Joe squeezed Charley one last time, then lowered the child's broken body to the pavement. He wiped his eyes with his sleeve, got to his feet, produced the snubbie from his waistband, and fired. The round struck the green-clad militiaman in the abdomen.

The militiaman staggered, then howled and swung his rifle at Joe.

Joe limped toward the soldier. His finger clenched the trigger of the snubbie, and it cracked in his hand again and again. The man in green took three more hits, spun, and raked the air with a string of automatic gunfire. He fell on his face in a pool of blood.

Joe released the snubbie's cylinder with his thumb and dumped the empty shell casings on the sidewalk. He dug in his pocket and produced a speed loader. With a flick of his wrist, the cylinder snapped back into the frame.

"I told you to stay in the car," he said to Jackson without looking up from the militiaman.

Jackson just stared at Joe, hands still raised, mouth open. For the first time, the kid didn't have anything smart to say. The sounds of sirens drew closer, nearly drowning out a faint feline whimper.

"Shit, man. We gotta go. Like now," Jackson said, opening the Chrysler's door.

"In a minute," Joe fired back. He stooped beside the body of his nephew and a pall drew over him. He gave the boy's shoulder a squeeze. A disgusting shame to leave him like this. No choice. Joe shook his head and turned to go when the pathetic meow came again.

There on the lawn, Charley's little black and white kitten tottered and fumbled over thick green blades and bits of brick and wood. Something moved in Joe's chest. He stepped onto the grass and crouched to pick up the kitten. The little cat jerked when Joe touched it. He scooped it up, careful not to crush its fragile bones in his heavy hands, and shambled to the Chrysler.

A fire wagon and a squad of security forces rounded the corner.

Joe fell into his seat and dumped the kitten into Jackson's lap. "Hold onto him. Keep him safe," Joe said.

The electric car needed no start and offered no welcome to the future. Joe slammed his foot onto the accelerator. The Chrysler lurched from the curb and tore off down the street.

"Whoa, no, I don't do animals," Jackson said as he tried to handle the squirming kitten.

"You do now," Joe said.

"This is your mess, Genial," Jackson said, the kitten's claws catching in his hoodie. "And slow down, this fur ball is gonna fuck up my shit."

Joe checked the rearview mirror. "If you thought these people were mad about not holding hands, wait until they find out we whacked one of their guys."

"*We* didn't whack one of their guys." Jackson pointed at Joe. "*You* whacked one of their guys."

Joe scowled. "To save your life, you ungrateful little bastard. And do you think they'll care that you didn't pull the trigger yourself?"

"Dude, I have no clue what just happened!" Jackson looked down at the mewing kitten and the little dabs of crusted blood in its ears. "Do I have to hold this?"

"The Don wouldn't …" Joe said. "There's no way he'd go this far … but Svanire would, that evil sonofabitch. But how could the Don allow this?" Joe swallowed, then bared his teeth. He shook it off, looked in the rear mirror, then over his shoulder. "And you violated the Divine fuckin' Order's rules and laws when you got out of the car."

Jackson's eyes flared. "Holding hands on the sidewalk? Really?"

Joe steered the Chrysler, screeching, onto a side street, then looped back onto the main stretch. "I told you. They're wacko. Now, get your head down."

The Chrysler picked up speed, the power core whined, and Joe gripped the wheel with thick, bloodless fingers. At the barricade, the Ali militia scrambled and fumbled with their guns.

Heavy Duty flapped her arms up and down as if she hoped to take flight.

Joe pressed down hard on the pedal and the battery gauge strobed critical. He hunched as low as his large frame would allow and grit his teeth.

The yellow and black wooden barricade exploded as the black Chrysler smashed through it and sent Heavy Duty and her militia members diving out of the way. A bullet thumped against the car's trunk. Three more followed before the back glass popped in a shower of diamond confetti.

"Stay down," Joe hissed, and swerved onto another side street, then back out to the open road.

Jackson laid his seat back and sent air thrumming across his lips.

In the rearview, no one seemed to follow.

Joe followed the signs for the I-90 interchange and accelerated up the on-ramp and onto a freeway dotted with electric cars.

The red battery gauge dinged in rapid succession and locked on.

"Not gonna get far." Jackson swiped the mewling kitten down off his hoodie and it tumbled back into his lap.

"The hell we won't," said Joe. "I ain't gonna stand by and let these fuckers kill another kid." He reached back to the rear floorboard, extracted the sawed-off shotgun, and, with one hand, racked a round into the chamber.

CHAPTER THIRTEEN
Anja

Ralph sat on his hind legs, munching on the carcass of a distant cousin, though Anja couldn't determine which one. She only recognized Ralph due to his distinct black face—now smeared in blood—on an otherwise off-white body. "Ralph, a noted alpha male," Anja said, loud enough for the mic of her tablet to activate, "previously observed to be extremely aggressive and to rape both males and females with no motivation … has progressed to cannibalism."

She had named Ralph, of course, after her late brother. As she had other rats before, each time she ran the experiment. Compelled by a deep-seated need to see if, against the odds, just one Ralph survived.

On her tablet, Anja took note of the pen's temperature—sixty-eight degrees Fahrenheit—and the number of days since day zero—seven hundred and two. She circled the pen, an enclosure larger than her first one-bed studio, replete with multiple watering holes, food troughs, twenty burrow tunnels, and nearly three hundred living compartments. Rat paradise.

Anja had run her ratopia experiment three times, now—her own version of the Universe 25 trial conducted in the 1970s by Dr. John Calhoun at the National Institute of Mental Health. Sure, Calhoun had used mice. But to Anja, a rat's mind just seemed that much closer to a human's. Rats' eyes sparkled with a hint of self-awareness. Nevertheless, Anja's experiment had played out identically to Calhoun's.

She let out a sigh. "Give a society an abundance of what it wants and it will collapse in the most horrific way."

She circled around to the top of the pen to scan the six-hundred-odd mice, which had started as four breeding pairs. They huddled in distinct groups, each easily identifiable by traits so similar to those seen in post-Collapse human tribalism. "The rats, both female and male, who have failed to find a group with whom to breed, have formed their own isolated cells," she said, studying a collection of twenty or so rats clustered in the center of the pen. "As with the previous two universes, one group of incel males is defined by its members' many scars on their bodies, resulting from attacks within their own cohort as well as from other males."

Anja turned her attention to a clutch of rats with bright, shiny coats and clean, sharp eyes who sat high up on one of the perches. "The Pretty Ones, as predicted, have abandoned feeding, interacting, and even mating in favor of preening themselves for inordinate amounts of time." She reached one finger inside the pen, stroked the lush fur of the nearest rat, and shook her head. "All you need is a BingOn account," she whispered.

She wandered to her desk at the end of the stark room and rolled the chair over, then sat down and connected her tablet to the desktop computer. *It's inevitable*, she thought as the colored wheel onscreen spun around and around. *Utopia doesn't last. It can't. Animals—humans—aren't built to accept it.* "We need conflict and suffering to find our way—our place," she said, then rubbed her chin. "But, how to reconcile that with supposed higher human intellect, which abhors pain? We're a walking contradiction."

A furious melee broke out in the pen. High-pitched squeals pierced the air. Anja spun in her chair for a better view. A female rat clasped a pink hairless baby in her mouth and shook it until the squeaking stopped. At her feet lay the corpses of four other pups. A lone, blind baby rat waddled over straw hurdles to escape.

Anja groaned, the weight of the tiny mammal's infanticide heavy on her heart, then turned back to her computer. "As predicted, despite … or perhaps *because* their every need is catered to, mothers continue to abandon or kill their young," Anja said, scanning the raw data in pie charts and line graphs. "Infant mortality approaches ninety percent." A quick double-click opened a document. Using just her index fingers, Anja stamped out her concluding paragraph:

> Ratpocalypse is now in its final stages. The low birthrate, coupled with a lack of social norms for those infants who do survive, drives a total breakdown of rat civilization. I

predict one more generation before total collapse.

"One more generation." She slumped in her seat and her chair rolled back from the desk. "We're out of time."

Anja swiped a strand of pale blond hair from her face, then locked the computer and made for the exit of her windowless basement deep in the bowels of Tarasp Castle. She glanced at her reflection in a glass-walled vivarium, then pushed through the reinforced metal door, pulled it behind her, and tramped up the stone stairs into the bell tower. A quick march through the large wooden inner gate and along the rock corridor and finally Anja made it to the converted northern residence. More than a few of her team had complained about her annexing this space, given it had the largest windows and widest living area in the whole castle.

Tabea hurried up the corridor behind Anja, out of breath, tablet tucked under her arm. "Hey, Ms. Kuhn, I couldn't reach you on the handheld."

"Tabea, how many times do I have to remind you to call me Anja?"

Tabea brushed a lock of bright orange hair away from her face and gasped a little to catch her breath.

Anja checked her belt. "I forgot to grab a radio."

Tabea cleared her throat. "Oh, that's okay, Ms. ... Anja. Just wanted to let you know we still don't have enough coin to pay for Marcel's support over in B.C."

Anja nodded to the two guards either side of the door, who tapped on the stocks of their AR-15s in acknowledgment. "Marcel can take care of himself."

Tabea shrank away behind Anja, who pressed a thumb to the black wall panel.

The door hissed open.

Anja stepped inside, Tabea on her heels. Behind them, the door sealed shut with another wheeze.

A long path cut down the middle of a lush green garden, nourished by bold afternoon sunlight that streamed through a large ornamental window. Anja strolled down the muddy walkway and admired the first broad leaves of the water hemlock plants.

"We still need to get all sites synchronized," Tabea said, tapping away at her screen as she walked. "But it's difficult. The deep web is just way slower, especially in Africa and Siberia."

"Noted," Anja said with a smile. Her fingertips grazed flat-topped clusters of small white snakeroot flowers. "But the countdown is ready?"

Tabea nodded and scratched at her prominent nose. "The electrical signal has to be timed perfectly—globally. Not an easy feat. We've still got a three-millisecond asynchronicity at four sites. And don't get me started on a potential outage in Cape Town."

Anja furrowed her brow at Tabea. "Has our security team fortified the power station?"

"So far." Tabea pulled up a previously recorded video feed on the tablet and waved it under Anja's nose. "The Sixth are doing their job, but again—we're running out of meaningful funds. They don't want altcoins."

Anja stared at the screen where four men in desert camo from the former U.S. Sixth Fleet carried large automatic weapons she didn't recognize. They patrolled the perimeter of the Koeberg Nuclear Power Station. Fossil-fuel stations remained under the control of major oil and gas corporations, but Scarlett Moon had taken ownership of nuclear and green energy plants *before* the Collapse. Scarlett Moon—*Anja*—had had the foresight to buy up as many across the globe as possible. Being such valuable commodities, the plants needed protection by force. Former military types turned mercenaries were an affordable solution. The notion made Anja sick to her stomach.

"There's been no attack on the station, correct?" Anja handed the tablet back to Tabea and strolled away. "The deterrent is working."

"For now." Tabea tottered after her, heels catching in the mud.

"We won't need it much longer," Anja said. She dropped to her haunches in front of a castor bean plant, ran a hand over the big, star-shaped leaves, then plucked off a spiny green capsule.

"You're so calm." Tabea turned away to finger the thin leaves of another plant. "I ... I just wonder."

"Wonder what?" Anja asked.

"If it's right."

"Not this again. You've seen the data." Anja pressed the capsule between her fingers. Mottled beans popped into her hand. "We must save us from ourselves. Humans are built for violence. It's in our nature, our DNA. Even our physiology is designed for war, our hands devised to form fists that deal the most damage while protecting our own bones."

"Those same hands create art and music," Tabea said, and touched what looked like a shiny red ladybug, brighter than her own hair. "The things that make our heart sing."

"You know what else makes our hearts and minds happy?" Anja maneuvered a bean between her finger and thumb. "War." She crushed the bean. "We get the same hit of dopamine eating chocolate as we do by seeking out a violent altercation."

"But … we're more than our biology," Tabea said, her tone more questioning than sure.

"Strip away your idealism, Tabea," Anja wiped the castor bean mush onto her pants. "I once believed human intelligence could overcome our biology, but now I'm convinced we can only paint over it. In the end, we're brutal animals in cocktail dresses." She stood and fixed a pained stare on Tabea. "From the Yanomami people of Venezuela and Brazil, who live in a state of chronic warfare, to the enraged Lebanese father who shoots up the ex-wife that took the children, to the Somalian child paid to drone-murder a property developer in Tokyo—violence is part of who we are, despite any kind of assumed sociological advancement."

Tabea plucked the glossy red and black ladybug from the plant.

"Any time our fragile social etiquette breaks down, we resort to what we know best," Anja said. "Viciousness. Even you and I, here and now, can only communicate because we have agreed to unspoken rules of engagement. But," she pulled a Swiss multi-blade tool from her pocket and clicked it open, "should I simply reveal I'm holding this, your amygdala has already initiated a fight or flight response."

"Damn," Tabea whispered, her fingertips now wet and stained with the ladybug's insides. "Just … as we get closer, and it all becomes real … I have to ask myself, are we giving up on us—on humanity?" She wiped her fingers on a leaf.

Anja sighed. "I wish it didn't have to be this way. But we tried. We clung to hope. Humans have a base, a core. Every-day morality and rules have—over millennia—tried to temper that core, with little success." She put away the blade and placed a hand on Tabea's shoulder. "The internet, the growing anonymity, has emboldened us to engage in ever more hateful interactions. There's no denying all the psychological evidence for this."

Tabea shrugged off Anja's touch, sniffed hard, and wiped away a single tear.

"Tabea," Anja said. "We're no better now than we were in the Middle Ages, killing someone who slighted us. Only, now we can kill that same someone on the other side of the world without getting our hands dirty. But you and I, we can save the world."

"I know you're right," Tabea said, the heel of her palm jammed into her eye socket. "Damn, that burns."

Anja's attention snapped to a plant just starting to produce bunches of red berries speckled with black spots, then to Tabea's stained fingers. "Scheisse."

Tabea doubled over with a grunt and dropped to her knees. A pile of freshly sprouted mushrooms exploded in a puff of debris.

"My eye," Tabea moaned, her words barely audible. Clear fluid streamed down her cheek.

Anja laid Tabea in the grass and sprinted for the entrance. She pressed the release, and the door hissed open. "Radio, now!" she demanded.

Both guards fumbled for their walkie-talkies. Anja snatched the radio from the faster man's hand and keyed it up. "Hans, get up to the garden—now. Bring an ocular flush!"

"What?" Hans asked, followed by a wash of static.

"Just do it!" Anja yelled.

"Copy," Hans said.

Anja bolted back to Tabea and slid into the moist soil. "Hang on, Tabea," Anja said, "help's coming."

Tabea's eye had swollen shut, and little gasps choked in her throat.

Anja's phone vibrated in her pocket. An annoying ringtone blared, but she ignored it and cradled Tabea's head.

Tabea writhed and sucked at the air.

"Shhh, shhh, shhh," Anja soothed, and stroked Tabea's forehead.

The phone rang again.

"*Arschloch!*" Anja said through clenched teeth.

Hans burst into the room wearing his typical sour expression, gut jiggling, a medical kit jammed into his armpit. He dropped to Tabea's side. "In her eye?" he asked.

Anja nodded. "Altered hyperabrin, Hans. She can't breathe."

"Damn," Hans said. "Okay, Tabea, I need to intubate you." He tilted her head back, pulled a laryngoscope from the med kit, and inserted it into her mouth.

Tabea gagged as the dull blade slid to the back of her tongue.

Hans nodded at a bottle of fluid protruding from the open med kit. "Flush her eye." He pushed an endotracheal tube into Tabea's throat, causing her to convulse and gag.

With one hand, Anja pried open Tabea's swollen eyelid and, with the other, grabbed the bottle and squeezed the contents all over Tabea's face and her bright orange hair.

The phone in Anja's pocket blared again.

"In!" said Hans, then attached a hand pump to the tube and began to pump.

Tabea stopped flailing.

Anja's phone buzzed again, and this time didn't cease.

"Vixer," Anja hissed, then jumped to her feet, clicked *Answer*, and held the phone to her ear. "Ja?" she barked.

"Hey, Chura," the husky female voice said, each word spoken with venomous purpose. "When I call, you answer."

Anja's blood chilled.

"I'm busy, Elena," Anja managed.

"We all busy, Chura," Elena said. "Those chafa coins you sent aren't worth shit. You want me to do the job, you better pay up. I don't work de choto, you get me?"

"I get you." Anja paced in irregular circles along the path toward the arched window. "I'll get you the coin, I promise. We've just had a little technical snag. We'll—"

"Twenty-four hours, Chura, then this whole balado go a little ...

armar un desmadre," she hissed. Anja could almost hear the sneer. "Plenty of people pay for that one's head."

The line clicked off.

"*Schiisdräck!*" Anja yelled, and squeezed her phone until she thought the shell might pop.

"Alles okay?" Hans asked.

"Alles guet," Anja said, then tramped back over to Tabea. "Will she live?"

Hans shrugged. "We need to get her to the infirmary. I'll radio for a gurney."

"Do it." Anja turned to face the large glass window.

Warm light washed over her face. No time to worry about Tabea. Just a few more tweaks to the system, a little more coverage in Asia—then she could complete The Solution.

If Elena held up her part of the bargain, Anja could save everyone.

CHAPTER FOURTEEN

Jackson

Jackson stared at the back of Bones' fedora as the old man limped down South Halsted Street. The Chrysler had given out long before they found a Zap station.

Without the protection of his Lenser mask, Jackson scurried from tree to tree, rucksack bobbing up and down on his back. Relief washed over his skin while under the leafy branches, and anxiety stabbed his gut each time he stepped back out into the sunlight.

"So where are we going, kid?" Bones said.

"If you stay behind me, you'll see," Jackson said. "Not sure why your old ass is trying to lead the way."

Bones threw a scowl over his shoulder. "Maybe because you're running around back there like an idiot."

"Can't be too careful, Genial." Jackson scurried to the shade of another buckthorn. "You'll see I'm right when your brains are in the street, stake."

Bones grunted and lumbered on.

The furball in Jackson's hoodie pouch shuffled and squirmed. Sharp claws pricked his skin through the fabric. Jackson moaned about the *stupid cat*, which drew another scathing look from Bones. Jackson reached inside his top and pinned the tiny kitten flat. Under his thin teenage fingers, the animal's fine puff of fur gave way to a skinny, underfed body. "Stop moving, you little shit."

"You give him a name yet?" Bones said, his voice almost lost to the strong breeze.

Jackson hugged a large ash tree. "No."

"Give him a name, kid. *Little Shit* ain't gonna cut it."

Jackson searched the empty street, then darted toward the next tree. Various cat names—Whiskers, Mittens, Socks—rattled around in his skull, mixed with thoughts of his mom, who would have loved a cat if she weren't allergic. The kitten wriggled free and popped its tiny head from Jackson's hoodie. It looked up at him, eyes barely open, raised its paw, and mewed.

"Neko," Jackson blurted out.

Bones stopped in his tracks and turned to face Jackson. "Neko?"

"Yeah," Jackson shrugged. "Like Maneki-neko, you know, those white cats you see in Japanese restaurants holding a koban coin, one paw up."

"Sure." Bones kept walking, his head on a swivel.

"Like you understand," Jackson muttered. "Stupid Genial."

Bones trudged along for another mile, slowed by Jackson's stealth maneuvers between trees. The sound of a drone's quad rotors seized Jackson's limbs, nailing him to the spot. He hugged the nearest tree trunk. Inside the hoodie pocket, Neko mewed.

"The hell are you doin'?" Bones asked, head cocked.

"Staying out of sight, man," Jackson said. "You don't hear that?"

A large drone, a beat-up eboard hanging from its underside, bumbled down the street.

"It ain't a hit, kid. The people gunnin' for us? They're better than that." Bones shook his head. "You get out much? Or you spend all your time whacking off in Momma's basement?"

"Screw you, old man." Jackson peeled himself from the tree, cupped Neko's butt with one hand through the hoodie, and marched ahead.

The drone hummed toward them, Anja Kuhn's face yammering on the eboard screen, bigger than any of Jackson's basement monitors. A large QR code filled one corner of the cracked display. "Things were terrible before the twentieth century," the leader of Scarlett Moon said, her projected voice tinny. "People endured horrific labor. Most women were permanently pregnant from the age of fourteen. Half of all children perished. But then things got better—so good that we forgot what it meant to be human and to suffer for our bread. Without real struggle, our own selfish desires have left us chasing immediate gratification, and we've grown to hate anyone who disagrees with our individual view of the world."

"She ain't wrong," Bones mumbled as the drone passed.

"Help us to help you," digital Anja said, her voice fading as the drone moved farther away. "Give what you can to Scarlett Moon. Help us create a bright new future for all. Help us end omniviolence."

Jackson shook his head. "She's such a whack job."

Bones shrugged. "She's got a point, you ask me. Miss the good ol' days when a man knew what was what. Before all this madness."

Jackson stopped dead. "*Good ol' days*? The hell are you talking about?"

Bones faced the kid, his features all creased up. "When you knew who the good guys and bad guys were, and you picked a side. Back then, there were rules. We all knew them. Everybody had a code. Now—well, look at us." He waved his arm at the rundown street littered with broken drone pieces, overflowing garbage, and kudzu-ridden brickwork. "Shit, kid, even money ain't money anymore. Invisible coins run the world."

Jackson barked a harsh laugh. "Money was *always* invisible, man," Jackson said. "A number on an account. Controlled by crusty old pricks who ran countries and banks. You think a kid like me, folks like my mom, were allowed a piece of that? No—because you had to have money to make money. And some asshole with a clipboard dictated whether my mom's job meant enough to put food on the table, or go on vacation, or have a nice car."

"You could've got an education," Bones said.

"Oh yeah?" Jackson fired back, then barged past. "That work out well for you? Top of your class at assassin school?"

Bones trudged up beside him. "That's not what I meant."

Jackson pulled his hood a little tighter. "You Genials think everything was better before, but it wasn't. Not for most of us. It was all messed up, man. The one percent at the top had all the money and decided how the rest of us got it. Jobs, medicine, food—all decided by some asshole who wouldn't stop to pick up a one-dollar bill, man." He shook his head, the heat in his chest growing. "We took it back. Took back the power. All those bastards tryin' to sell another pair of sneakers. *Do you*, they said. So, we did." Jackson spun to walk backward, made a gun with his fingers, then let the hammer-thumb drop. "Kinda blew up in their faces, stake?"

Bones stared hard into Jackson's eyes but stayed silent.

Jackson stopped and sighed, then pointed across the street to a square brown brick building choked up with kudzu littered with small purple pods. "Trinity Episcopal."

"Your dead drop is in a church?" Bones asked.

Jackson nodded, but made a face. "*Dead drop* is like old-person-speak, man. It's a *throw site*. Say it with me." He dragged the vowels out in slo-mo. "Throw site."

"I don't like your attitude, kid," Joe said.

"And I don't like your old catcher's mitt face," Jackson snapped back.

Jackson stomped to the opposite sidewalk, climbed the broken steps of the old church, jogged up to heavy wooden doors, and pushed his way in. Muted light filtered through colored glass panels and bounced off dust motes. Oak pews with thin red cushions and little racks that cradled dusty bibles framed a small stage with an ornate podium. A large, cracked flat screen floated on the wall behind. Banners with golden crosses hung down from above, and an ancient pipe organ sat in the corner.

Bones shuffled inside, removed his hat, and quickly crossed himself, forehead to sternum and both shoulders.

Jackson rolled his eyes and said, "Oh, man, that was a mistake."

"What?" Joe's brow knit.

Jackson threw his head back and pointed at the TV. "Gesture sensor."

The screen flicked on, revealing a man in a leather hood, his face completely obscured in shadow.

"Don't you keep up?" Jackson said with a sigh. "Scarlett Moon has mega-fans. Science-nerd scythers. Took down most religious organizations—their financial infrastructures, social media, databases. Nuked all of it. Sent churchgoers scrabbling underground. Released a bunch of nasty intel on pedo-priests. Even destroyed some old-as-fuck artifacts. Like, nearly as old as you." He made his way over to the organ. "Hope you like speeches."

"Religion is a global sickness," said the hooded figure onscreen. His voice, digitally warped, rattled the podium. "This illness perpetuates

unchecked authority, intolerance, war, and—perhaps worse—
suppression of those who dare not believe. Religion conditions you, a
power structure fashioned to convince you to give away *your* power for
the benefit of those *in* power."

"It helped a lot of people, too," Bones said, unable to look away
from the TV.

Jackson ignored him and ran his fingers across the organ, feeling for
a concealed switch.

"It's a driving force behind mass insanity," the man onscreen
boomed. "Christian hypocrites spout freedom from sin but live in
shameless depravity. Islamo-dogs imagine that if they blow themselves
up, they will receive seventy-two virgins. Buddhist suckers remain
ignorant enough to believe that they can actually achieve oneness with
the universe.

"Know this," the hooded figure said, "your place of worship has
been scythed. Your coin has been taken back. We are Evil-Ution! End
the slavery that is religion—"

Bones pulled the snubbie from his waistband and blasted the screen.
Glass and electrical sparks flew, the TV fell, and the stage shook.

Neko clawed through the hoodie fabric at Jackson's stomach.

"Hey, geekbag!" Jackson hissed. "You wanna keep it down? We're
trying to keep a low profile, remember?"

Bones shook his substantial head. "Who takes down the world's
religions? Were some of them looney toons? Yeah, but a lot of religious
organizations and their people try to do good in the world. I cook at a
kids' home. They got donations." He looked at the chipped floor. "Or
did. That's how they stayed open through the pandemics. What are those
kids gonna do now?"

Jackson raised an eyebrow. "You cook?"

The muscles of Bones' jaw flexed.

Jackson flopped down on the old swivel chair in front of the pipe
organ, then slid off his rucksack and placed it on the lid of the dust-
covered instrument.

Bones fingered the zip of Jackson's bag.

Jackson's lip curled in a snarl. "You mind?"

"Whatchya carrying around in there?"

"None of your business, Genial." Jackson dragged the rucksack close.

Neko squirmed and tried to emerge from the pouch of the hoodie. Jackson swore and raised a hand to smack the kitten back down.

Bones seized his wrist.

"Hey, get your hands off—" Jackson's words faded under the intensity of Bones' glare.

"Do that again," Bones pointed a meaty finger at Jackson, "and I'll slap you back to the dark ages. Understand?" The old gangster released his grip. "If you're reckless, you'll hurt him."

Jackson scowled. "Stupid-ass Genial grabbin' me over some stupid-ass cat."

"He's ... Neko is just a baby," Joe continued. "A few weeks old, maybe. He don't know any better. You gotta take care of him."

Neko popped his head from the hoodie again and gave a little meow.

Under Bones' watchful eye, Jackson eased Neko onto the ivory and faded-black keys of the old organ, which made no sound under the kitten's scrawny frame. Bones leaned forward and ran a heavy hand gently over Neko's tiny head. A little purr rumbled in the kitten's breast.

Jackson reached under the organ's keyboard, pulled away the flimsy backing, and touched something large taped inside. He dug at the sticky tape and peeled the object away. Cautiously, he pulled his arm back and studied the item in his palm.

"That what you needed?" Bones asked.

"Yeah," Jackson said. A zip-tie-sealed plastic bag held a mobile phone and goggles. "I think."

He ripped open the bag and pressed the power key on the phone for three seconds. It flashed on and scanned Jackson's face. A lock screen melted away to reveal a home area littered with apps. The phone pinged, and an encrypted message app displayed a notification. Jackson hovered his thumb over it, then pressed *Open*.

> Ready for a little VRE exploration, Jackson? Tick tock—HELLCAT.

"And?" Bones said.

"Gimme a minute, man." Jackson scanned the phone and checked the goggles in his lap. "Damn, she's got some kind of Pegasus-based spook app."

"Which means?"

Jackson slid the goggles over his face. "I know you're gonna die, like any minute, from old age, but just chill." The eyewear immediately connected to the mobile phone. "Looks like a ghost-protocol app, too," Jackson said.

"Which means?" Bones asked again.

"It *means* it's masking who I am—my identity in here."

"In where?" Bones pressed.

"The VRE, man, damn." Jackson clicked his tongue. "I mean, this is going to take a lot longer if I have to explain everything to you."

"But I'd appreciate it if you would," Bones said, each word enunciated.

"Fine!" Jackson let out a bloated wheeze. "The VRE, the other reality, where jerkoffs go because they can't hack it in the real world. A while back, peeps made some serious coin flogging NFTs and digital property, but it was a fad, man. Now it's just creepers and weirdos that stalk kids like me." He tapped his mobile phone against the side of the goggles. "I'll use this headset to see it, and my phone to navigate."

"Still don't know where *here* is," Bones mumbled.

Here turned out to be a virtual baseball field with bleachers in the background and a field comprising lush green grass and rusty brown infield dirt. Jackson stood in the batter's box. "Wow. Some serious upgrades on the graphics engines," he said, "even over a dark-web network." He tilted his head down to see a pair of very thin white legs in shorts. They glitched in and out. A disguise. *Figures.*

The field glitched once, then twice, before a young girl, perhaps sixteen or seventeen years old, winked into existence on the pitcher's mound. A flirty smile spread across her fine features.

"Finally," she said, and tugged on the lapels of her cropped leather jacket.

"Hellcat?" Jackson asked, unable to look away from her arresting feline eyes and pinched waist.

"In the digital flesh," she said, and curtsied. "Though that's between me and you." *Sarah146* appeared in sans comic above her head and floated there.

"Always wondered if you were a dude," Jackson said. Perspiration prickled his temple in the real world. "At least, until I heard your voice."

"I always thought you were an old creeper from Asia, Ronin," Hellcat said.

Jackson chortled and studied the digital girl, careful not to pause too long on her deep cleavage. He coughed and attempted to focus his evaluation on the technological aspects of the VRE experience. The rendering of Hellcat's form seemed genuine. Totally fake renders, like the one he wore now, were easy to spot and always looked like a video game, no matter how hard the programmer tried. Little nuances in skin tone, or how they smiled. The tough ones were those built by piecing together real people's faces, hair, and body parts, though Jackson prided himself on being able to see a seam or bug in the pixelation.

"How do I know that's the real you?" Jackson said.

"Your render is glitchy and mine isn't. What does that tell you?"

"It's real?"

"Bingo. Now look, you're ranked seventeen on Dominion right now." Hellcat crossed her arms across her chest, her cat-like eyes squinting with her broad smile. "You want to waste more time, or what?"

"I'm ready," Jackson said. "Where we going?"

"Come on. Can't stay in one area too long," Hellcat said.

A doorway opened in the air over the second-base line and Hellcat slipped through it.

"Shit," Jackson said, then thumbed the screen of the mobile device, which propelled his avatar through the black rectangle.

"Everything okay?" Bones asked.

"Yeah, shut up," Jackson said.

The environment flashed white and Jackson found himself at the edge of a lake with tall, steel-colored mountains in the background. Hellcat stood knee-deep in crystal-clear water, her jeans and jacket exchanged for cut-off denim shorts and a bikini top.

"Why help me?" Jackson struggled to maintain eye contact.

"Maybe I'm helping *me*?" she said, and cocked her head.

"Oh yeah?" He pressed his thumb to the cell phone in the real world and his digital self walked a few steps closer.

"I know the one that's after you," Hellcat said. "A *capo*. High up, too. I don't know what you did to get crossed up with them, but it's bad. And this guy is the worst."

"Yeah," Jackson said. "Sv-han … something …"

"Svanire?" Bones asked. "What about him?"

Jackson waved him off.

"Svanire," Hellcat said, and flicked the water with one hand. "He killed my aunt just for stealing a few Torre Coin. I only found him because he kept her purse as a souvenir, and I connected the pieces using surveillance footage and her air tag. But now he's after you, and the bastard *always* covers his tracks. Though he does seem to be making a pretty big show of taking you out."

"You're hoping he'll screw up and you can peg his location," Jackson said.

"Right," Hellcat replied. "I can get in almost anywhere—get to anyone. But this guy's a ghost. I've never been able to actually pin the slippery sonofabitch down."

"No digital footprint, no calling card?" Jackson asked.

"Who are you talking to?" Bones' voice penetrated the digital façade.

"No one—shut it, Genial," Jackson snapped. "Gimme a sec."

"Kid, I'm gonna box that visor right off your face, here, in a minute," Bones muttered.

"That the hitman?" Hellcat asked, and looked up to the sky as if Bones were some kind of god who boomed from above. "Carboni," she said. "I looked him up. He was supposed to kill you, but turned on his own people instead. That's what I can't figure out. Why?"

Jackson nodded, which made the whole world bob up and down. "Yeah, stake."

"He could help us, you know," Hellcat said. "He knows the whole operation from the inside. I'd keep him close. But careful, cutie, he could change his mind and slay you to get back in The Family's good graces."

Jackson felt his cheeks flush at Hellcat calling him *cutie*. "Got it," he whispered.

"What's happening now?" Bones asked.

"Nothing, Genial," Jackson called into the digital air. "Got anything else on this Svanire guy?" he asked Hellcat.

She shook her head, pixelated tresses swaying. "Only one photo anywhere on any platform." She shrugged, and a window opened in the air beside her. A grainy black and white image of a man in a perfect black suit, so tall and thin, his body seemed stretched. The face was hidden in shadow.

"Guy looks like one of those creepy old-school slenderman characters." A chill prickled along Jackson's spine.

Hellcat nodded. "Stake."

"So, what now?" Jackson asked, hands held up in both the real and digital world.

"You can't stay still for long," she said, "with your name that high on all the slaysites. You're a hot ticket. Easy money. Get to B.C., collect your off-grid coins, and we'll find a way to draw this Svanire out. I've put a few altcoins on this device to help you get going. Oh, and it's got a drone shield emitter. Shouldn't get hit by slaysite noobs with crappy tech."

"Sounds like a plan," Jackson said. "And, uh, thanks."

Hellcat grinned and swished her foot in the digital water. "One question."

"Sure," he said.

"Why keep your off-grid wallet all the way down in El Salvador?"

Jackson shrugged. "Couldn't risk anyone knowing where I stashed it. And B.C. is so messed up, you gotta be a total geekbag to go there. Much better odds that no one would steal it. Just figured I could drone-drop it if I needed it … but now …"

Hellcat pressed her full lips into a thin line. "You got that right. B.C. is whack." She winked. "Okay, later, cutie. Don't get yourself killed." She leaned back, splashed into the lake, and disappeared beneath the surface.

Jackson searched the rippling water for bubbles, but Hellcat didn't come back up.

In the real world, he grabbed the VR goggles and pulled them off his head. "We need to get the hell out of here," he said. "B.C., right now."

"Yeah, you mentioned that," Bones said with a deep frown. "But unless you got wings that sprout from your ass, it's a long walk, and we've got no wheels."

"Ah yeah, you're so funny, Grandpa. I'm dead."

"You will be soon enough, ya little smart ass." Bones pushed away from the organ. "If you don't take it serious, you'll end up like your mom."

Jackson's face burned. "Or blown to bits like your sister and nephew?" He jabbed a finger at Bones.

Bones' eyes flared wide and took on a menace that made Jackson's guts tighten. But as fast as the terrifying look came on, it evaporated.

The tired old gangster turned, head down, and lumbered out of the church.

An unfamiliar and unwelcome sourness filled Jackson's mouth. A low blow—even for him. He shook it off, dumped the goggles, grabbed his rucksack, then scooped up Neko and chased after Bones.

As he fought to slip his arms into the rucksack straps, juggling the kitten from one hand to the other, his nose squashed into Bones' muscular back.

"Hey, what the hell?" Jackson rubbed at his face, then sidestepped Bones, who stood firm in the church's doorway.

There on the street stood a pear-shaped woman, perhaps forty-five years old, with rectangular glasses, a thin floral shirt, a hemp bag over one shoulder—and a revolver so heavy her arms trembled.

"Told you to keep it down, Genial," Jackson blurted out. He slipped Neko into his hoodie pocket.

"You're Jackson," Floral Shirt stammered, and raised the huge weapon.

"Nope," he said, and backed away behind the door frame. "I'm not."

"Don't lie." Floral Shirt's hands shook so badly, the muzzle of the big-bore revolver wobbled from side to side. "There's big money on you."

"That's a 454 Casull," Bones said without turning. "You shoot grizzly bears with those. It'll put a hole the size of a volleyball in you. Ain't that right, Miss …?"

"Doreen," she said, and pushed her glasses back onto the bridge of her nose.

"You don't want to do this, Doreen." Bones held out his hands.

"I've got five children," she said, tears in her eyes. "I owe the enforcers in my neighborhood. You know how much that kid with you is worth?"

"Can't say I do," Bones said. He stepped through the doorway onto the broken steps.

"Five thousand Tribcoin," Doreen said.

Jackson scrunched up his nose. "Tribcoin? That junk? Are you kiddin' me?"

Bones' head turned like an owl's, his eyes hard. "She's got kids and needs the coin," he said, teeth gnashed together.

"Yeah, three kids," she said.

"Wait." Bones whipped back to face Doreen. "I thought you said four kids?"

"Five," Jackson corrected.

"Ah, shit," Doreen said. Her pained expression slipped into a crooked leer. "But I really do want a new purse." The Casull bucked in her hand.

The doorframe of the church exploded, sending plaster and wood flying. Jackson and Bones hit the deck, hands over their heads. A tiny mew escaped Jackson's hoodie as Neko fell out and bumped against the broken steps.

Jackson lay on the stone just inside the heavy church doors and waited for a second blast. He unfurled from the fetal position and lifted his head to scan the road.

Doreen lay sprawled out on the asphalt, her face oozing blood, as Bones pushed back to his feet with a grunt.

Jackson scrambled to scoop up Neko. He stumbled down the

crumbling stairs to Doreen's body. The hemp bag lay open, and a couple of apples and a carton of milk had spilled out. Her busted face wore a large bloody gash from the bridge of her nose through her forehead.

"Damn," Jackson said, head still fuzzy. "You stone-cold slayed her."

Bones shook his head. "I didn't do that." He pointed at the Casull in her hand. "You gotta be strong to handle the recoil on that one." Blood lined the barrel of the gun, a bit of skin stuck to the front sight.

A belly laugh erupted from Jackson. "You mean, she split her own face trying to shoot us!" He gasped for air, adrenaline pushing his laughter to a maniacal level.

"It ain't funny," Bones said. "That bullet would've torn you in half."

"It kinda is funny," Jackson said between guffaws. "She died trying to buy a purse."

"I don't think she's dead ..." Bones eyed Doreen closer. "Eh, maybe she is."

Jackson straightened, hands on his hips, and tried to catch his breath. "Oh, that's good."

Bones looked at Jackson. "She's probably someone's mom."

"Yeah? How many kids did she have, again?" Jackson grabbed up the carton of milk. "She's also a greedy bitch who wanted a new purse so much, she was willing to murder for it."

"You gonna steal her milk?" Bones wagged his finger the way a mother might.

Jackson marched away down the street. "For Neko, jackass." He waved the carton high.

"Where you goin' now?" Bones called after him.

"To snag a ride," Jackson yelled without looking back. "Long way to B.C., and I don't have wings up my ass, remember?"

CHAPTER FIFTEEN
Joe

A bullet-shaped electric car blew past and whipped Joe's long coat about his body. "Sweet Mary." He stepped farther off the road behind the blacked-out Chrysler. "Gonna get run over by one of these stupid AI cars out here."

"What are we even doing?" Jackson asked from the open door of an older, freshly stolen Kia Sorento with sun-faded baby blue paint. "Let's get the hell out of here. Our lat-long is broadcast. It's just a matter of time before some slayer shows up hoping for an easy payday."

"Think I don't know?" Joe popped the trunk of the Chrysler and pulled out the trumpet case.

Jackson shrugged. "I don't know, Genial, because here we are."

"I gotta get some stuff." Joe pulled two more bags out of the Chrysler's trunk, then walked them to the Kia.

"A stupid trumpet?" Jackson looked up and down the interstate. He reached into his hoodie and pressed Neko back into the pocket. Two more electric cars whined past.

"I said, stay in the car and keep an eye on the theft-alert beacon." Joe dumped the bags into the Kia's trunk, then stomped back to the Chrysler.

Jackson slumped and put his head on his forearm. "I told you, that's expensive tech. They don't put it in Sorentos, man, that's ..." He shook his head, still buried in the crease of his elbow. "That's why we took this one."

"Get back in the car."

"It stinks in here," Jackson said, with a sniff of the Kia's passenger seat. "Like spilled box wine and B.O. ... and old people fucking."

"Get in the damn car, kid." Joe grabbed the last bag.

Jackson threw himself into the passenger seat.

Joe tossed two square black bags with handles into the back and slammed the door.

Inside, Jackson sat pouting, the rucksack pulled to his chest.

Neko meowed and wriggled from Jackson's hoodie, only to plop into the gap between the seat and the center console.

Joe sat behind the wheel and pulled the door shut. He jangled the remote in his hand, shoved it deep in a pocket, then pressed the start button by the steering column. "You gotta relax, kid. Not everything is worth getting that worked up about."

"Relax?" Jackson stared at Joe. "Everyone wants us dead, and you want me to *relax?*" He hugged the rucksack tighter. "Sure."

Joe eased the Kia out onto the freeway and gave one last look at the Chrysler as it faded in the rearview. A gust of wind buffeted the car.

They rode in silence for ten minutes.

"So," Jackson started.

"No." Joe looked over his shoulder.

"Oh, so now I'm not even allowed to talk?"

"We got company," Joe said.

Jackson twisted in his seat to see out the rear window.

"See that old Chevy?" Joe said. "The gasoline-powered one?"

Jackson's eyes narrowed.

"It's been tailing us since we dumped the Chrysler," Joe said. In the side mirror, the Chevy surged forward. "Brace yourself, kid."

The Chevy swerved close and tagged their bumper.

The Kia jolted hard.

"Hey!" Jackson cried out and grabbed up Neko.

Joe clenched his jaw and clamped onto the steering wheel. "Where the hell did you come from?"

"Must've been waiting for us. Saw us go back to the car." Jackson hunched lower. "I told you it was stupid, Genial."

"Just shut up for a minute." Joe glanced in the mirror again.

The Chevy guttered, swerved, and tagged their rear fender a second time. The Kia screeched and shook as Joe struggled to keep it on the road. He focused on the blurred rearview reflection. The Chevy's occupants stared out through the windshield.

"Only two guys," Joe said. "Unzip one of those bags. Hand me something."

"Like what?" Jackson asked.

The Chevy slammed into them again. Joe pushed the Kia to its limit, the electrical drive whining beneath them. "Just grab something that kills people. And make it fast."

Jackson stuffed Neko into his hoodie pocket, then reached back and slashed the zipper of the nearest bag open. "Day-um, bro. That's a lot of guns."

"Come on!" Joe shouted.

"Okay, okay." Jackson dug through the bag, metal and plastic parts clacking together. "Here." He heaved an H&K UMP .45 submachine gun from the sack and pointed it with two hands toward Joe's cheek.

Joe snatched it away from him. "Hey, what are you doing? Don't point that at me."

"You asked for one. I gave it to you. Get off my case!" Jackson shouted.

"Could you pick something bigger? Sonofabitch." Joe pinched the ungainly weapon between his knees, collapsed the folding stock, and whipped the charging handle back with a *snap*.

"You said grab *something*. That's something." Jackson threw his hands up.

Neko meowed again, the sound muffled beneath the fabric.

The Chevy groaned and picked up speed. It swerved to the side, accelerated, and smacked into Joe's driver's side. The Kia jolted. Joe twisted to look over his shoulder. Young men, both of them. The driver laughed and clutched the wheel while the passenger gave Joe double middle fingers.

"They're just kids," Joe said, then pulled the submachine gun into his lap. "Probably not even legal to drive."

Jackson screwed up his face. "*Legal to drive?* That's not even a thing anymore, Genial. Shoot them in the face!"

Joe cast a hard look at Jackson. "They're teenagers. The hell is wrong with you?"

"They're trying to *kill* us!" Jackson made a finger gun against his temple and dropped the hammer.

Joe lowered the window and slammed on the brakes. The Chevy rocketed up along their left side. Joe shoved the UMP out the window, one-handed, and opened fire. The submachine gun rattled in the old hitman's meaty grip, stamping out a high-speed staccato. Jackson covered his ears and hunched his shoulders as the stumpy brass .45 cases bounced across the Kia's dash and fell around his sneakers.

The front tire of the Chevy exploded. Rubber and wire extended out in all directions as the heavy rounds shredded the wheel and punched across the hood. Joe floored the Kia and the Chevy swerved out of control behind it, smashing into a series of yellow water barrels that ruptured in a pressurized spray.

"Yeah! Piss off!" Jackson shouted, and waved his middle finger at the back window.

Joe eased off the accelerator, rolled up the window, and grunted with the effort of tossing the heavy UMP into the back seat. "That's how it's done."

Jackson pulled Neko from his pocket and looked him over. "Still think you should've shot them in the face. Neko could've been hurt."

Joe balked. "Oh, *now* you care about the cat?"

"Nope." Jackson laughed. "But I don't want blood on my hoodie."

"It wasn't necessary." Joe pressed his thick lips into a thin line. "Killing ain't something a person should take lightly."

Jackson hocked a laugh. "Never thought I'd meet an assassin who looked for reasons *not* to kill people."

Joe shook his head. "Just because you *can* do a thing, doesn't mean you *should*, kid."

"Sure thing, Genial," Jackson said.

They rode on in silence. Jackson monkeyed with his phone while Joe banked onto I-55 South, away from Chicago and everything they both called home. Joe's brow furrowed. *El Salvador is a hell of a long way away, Joe.*

Minutes ticked past and the miles disappeared beneath the Kia's bald tires. The car was a junker by modern standards, but it wasn't that old, and battery capacity had come a long way in the last twenty years. The dangerous trip to El Salvador was possible if they played their cards right.

The tribal enclaves of Chicago's southwest side, with their spray-painted barriers and cobbled-together sniper towers, gradually gave way to an expanse of genetically modified soybeans, corn, and sorghum. Automated harvesters, like an invading force of H.G. Wells's Martian tripods, bobbed on stalks over the fields, stooping, inspecting, and cutting.

A shiver tickled across Joe's shoulders. He bumped the Kia's climate control up a few degrees. Jackson yawned and held his phone inches from his face, the blue-white glow illuminating his features.

Moisture pattered against the windshield. The gray sky, gray rain, and gray road mixed together in a blur that drove a cramped feeling in Joe's chest. His thoughts turned to Sheila and Charley, to the meals and laughs and games of catch they'd shared. The only good things he'd known in this stupid world. Joe pressed his molars tight until his jaw ached.

He looked over at Jackson, laid back in his seat, phone raised in front of his face. *What the hell are you doing, Joe? Why destroy your whole life to protect this kid?* Joe shook his head. Questions like that didn't have answers. Not yet, anyway.

"Yes!" Jackson pumped his fist and motioned to his phone. "Dink just jumped, like in a big way."

Joe screwed up his face. "What's a dink?"

Jackson pushed a breath over his lips that sent them flapping. "I gotta explain everything to this dinosaur," he said under his breath. He glanced at Joe's still-screwed-up face. "Okay, look. Dinky Coin, it's a penny crypto that you can only get on the shadier exchanges, like Shatterbar. A while back, I opened a side account under a different name and dropped a couple hundo on Dinky just to diversify my crypto holdings a bit. Well," he motioned to his phone, "it just jumped a thousand percent, and I was able to sell out before it dropped."

Joe shrugged. "Okay."

"Okay?" Jackson looked aghast. "Just *okay*? No, it's fucking amazeballs. *That's* the power of crypto." He turned toward Joe. "You have money? 'cause most of mine got scythed just before we met."

"I figure I've been cut off since I went rogue," Joe said. "And keeping stacks of Benjamins in a coffee can under the bed isn't a thing anymore."

"Did you check your account?"

"Don't need to." Joe steered around a clot of wreckage along the interstate. "As sure as I'm breathing, all my assets have been nuked."

"Well, thanks to *this guy*," Jackson thumbed his chest, "and a little good fortune, we now have some cash for the trip."

"Outstanding," Joe said, voice stale. He fixed his eyes on the dreary road ahead.

"It *is* outstanding, actually, you crusty old shit," Jackson said, then went back to his device. "In fact, *I'm* outstanding, and you can say so whenever you're ready."

Joe grunted. "Don't hold your breath."

Hazy and distant, the outskirts of St. Louis loomed on the horizon, clouds clearing to reveal a shroud of smoke from a thousand fires.

"We definitely want to skirt this one." Joe maneuvered the Kia into the left lane. "Take I-255 around the perimeter instead of going straight through town."

Jackson shrugged and held the phone closer to his face. Neko poked his bobblehead from Jackson's pocket and mewed.

As the I-255 access branched off to the left, Joe slowed to a stop on the shoulder. "Shit."

"What?" Jackson looked up, but didn't lower the phone.

"Gimme a second." Joe popped the door and stepped along the edge of the freeway to get a better look.

Across the width of the I-255 offshoot, disabled cars and trucks and minivans, rusted and neglected, formed a barrier. Nose to bumper they sat, stacked three deep and two high. On the front of that massive barrier of steel and glass hung a painted sign that read, *Now entering the Antifascist Republic of St. Louis. All drivers must take I-55 through town and pay all applicable travel taxes.*

Joe took a few steps toward the rusted heap and craned his neck to try to see a way around. At the sight of the collapsed overpass and its demoed support columns, he let out a low whistle and turned back for the Kia.

"What's the deal?" Jackson asked.

"Antifascist types," Joe said. "They're forcing us to go through town."

"We can't take the perimeter?"

Joe shook his head. "Blocked."

"Whatever. I'm starving." Jackson pointed at a flashing electronic billboard that displayed a giant cheeseburger combo meal. "Yippie Burger, next exit. I'm gonna get the triple quarter pounder with cheese, upsized everything." He rubbed his palms together.

"St. Louis is a war zone, kid, has been for years." Joe pulled the Kia back onto I-55 South and accelerated. "And these clowns are on an especially big power trip. We're not stopping unless we get forced to."

Jackson stared at Joe. "The hell we're not! The exit is right there— take the turn, old man. I gotta eat."

"No."

Jackson grabbed for the wheel, but Joe swatted him away. "The hell are you doing?"

"Take the exit!" Jackson grabbed at the wheel again. "Take the exit. Take the exit."

"Fine!" Joe shouted, and wrenched the steering wheel to the right. A smart car blared its horn and swerved to avoid them, but smashed into the side of an older Ford Fusion, causing both to spin out. The smart car and the Fusion screeched to a stop and the drivers, wild with fury, leaped from their cars, produced guns, and opened fire.

"Yes! They're killing each other." Jackson twisted in his seat to watch. "Oohh! Smart-car guy just took a round in the face. But the other guy is gut shot," he said. "That's awesome."

The pop of gunfire blended with the rattle and bump of reflectors beneath the tires as Joe turned onto the off ramp. "Not awesome—they could be shooting at us!"

"Yeah, but they're not." Jackson craned his neck as the two roadragers disappeared behind a concrete bend. "Those people are definitely both dead. Or, gonna be."

"Annoying little prick, grabbing at the wheel like that. Starting shit with people," Joe grumbled.

"Annoying, but effective." Jackson rubbed his hands again and pointed to the Yippee Burger Joint.

"I see it," Joe said, his face flushed.

They pulled through the parking lot past a kid digging through the trash and a half-naked couple making love on the hood of a Tesla.

"Yes. Full penetration." Jackson turned in his seat to watch.

"Show some class," Joe said.

"You want *me* to show some class?" Jackson waved at the public display. "They're the ones out here doing it in front of everybody."

"Still …" Joe pulled the Kia up slowly and rolled to a stop at the speaker box. He felt the pinch of hunger in his belly, the smell of grilled meat activating his salivary glands. Maybe not such a bad idea, after all.

A smiley emoji formed on the speaker box screen. "Can I take your order?"

"Yeah," Joe said. "A triple quarter pounder meal, and—"

"What to drink?" the sterile, non-human voice interrupted.

"Coke," Jackson chimed in. "And upsize everything."

Neko mewed, and his tiny claws plucked against the fabric of Jackson's sweatshirt.

"Coke and—," Joe started.

The speaker box face changed to an emoji with a chubby hand on its chin and a question mark over its head. "Will that complete your order?"

"No," Joe said. "Upsize that meal and—"

"Is that all for you today?" the smiley emoji asked.

A horn blasted from behind Joe. He checked his rearview to see a sunset-orange pickup truck nearly nosed against their bumper. Joe flexed his jaw.

"The total for your order will be twenty-one-point-seven-three Nukes or comparable altcoin." The smiley emoji winked. "Thank you for your—"

"I'm not done," Joe shouted. "Did you get the upsize on that—?"

The emoji shifted to a scolding look. "I'm sorry, but there is no need to shout."

"I wasn't shout—"

"Hey!" The driver of the sunset-orange truck blared the horn again. "Shithead! Order, already!"

"Oh, and double pickles!" Jackson waved his finger in Joe's face. "Don't forget my pickles, Genial."

The emoji face smiled. "Will that complete your order today?"

"Double pickles!" Jackson hissed.

"Genial, move it!" the person in the truck shouted.

With a snarl on his face, Joe twisted his bulk into the back seat and grabbed the blocky UMP, knocking Jackson in the shoulder as he pulled it through the gap in the seats. He shoved his door open, stormed out of the Kia, and leveled the weapon at the driver of the orange pickup. The stringy-haired, wide-eyed occupant dragged an applicator tip wet with hot-pink lip gloss across a stubbled chin.

"Say one more word to me," Joe snarled. "One more word."

The truck's driver released a shrill scream and jerked the wheel away from Joe, the awkward position squeezing the driver's hairy belly and pepperoni-sized nipples tight against the fishnet webbing of an ultra-small halter top. The electric engine of the truck whined and the vehicle swerved from the drive-through lane, bounced over a curb, and crashed through a row of stumpy bushes.

Jackson flopped back in his seat and grabbed his belly in a hysterical fit of laughter.

On the drive-through speaker box, however, the emoji face turned a scolding red, its mouth bent down. "If you are threatening violence, I'll have to cancel your—"

"Cancel this." Joe swung the UMP around and clenched the trigger.

The automatic sub-gun burped fire. Heavy .45 rounds chewed up the base plate, caved in the screen, and shredded the box. Sparks flew and jumped from the speaker. The emoji face winked, fluttered to angry, and back to smiling. "Have a nice day-y-y-y-y …" The top of the box tore free and fell on the curb with a metallic clunk.

"Hey, hey, whoa, man—chill!" Jackson held his arms up. "My food!"

UMP still in hand, Joe left the Kia in the drive-through and marched around the building to the service door. With one hard mule-kick, he smashed the lock and entered.

"Security breach. Security breach," an alarm sounded. "Block security notified."

Joe stormed behind the partition and dodged between an army of automated mechanical arms on rails, all at different stages of meal prep. He grabbed a paper bag and raked in a swathe of cheeseburgers, then turned and marched back to the blue Kia.

"What in the actual fuck, Genial?" Jackson said. "Really?"

Joe threw the bag at Jackson. "Here's your god-forsaken cheeseburgers," he said, and dropped into the driver's seat in time to swat the bag away as it came back at him.

Jackson pouted. "This isn't what I ordered."

"It ain't that burger joint." Joe threw the UMP in the back seat and stomped on the accelerator. "You don't get to have it *your way*."

He reached into the brown paper bag, extracted a half-smashed cheeseburger, pulled the yellow wrapper back with his teeth, and chomped into the soft bun and meat.

"Fuckin' delicious," Joe munched furiously.

He drove the car to the end of the block, crossed three parking lots, and backed up to the rear of a private dentist's office, which had apparently closed for the day.

"The hell are we doing?" Jackson picked through the bag of deflated, single-patty cheeseburgers with mild disgust.

"Wait for it," Joe said around a mouthful of burger. He pointed back to the drive-through. A convoy of cars and trucks that looked as though they might belong to post-apocalyptic wasteland bandits swarmed the restaurant parking lot. The security force, dressed in all black and wearing face coverings, deployed from the vehicles. To Joe's eyes, not a single one of them appeared to be over the age of twenty-five. Each person was heavily armed and wearing black body armor. "The enforcers here are Antifascist types," Joe said. "Very unpredictable."

Jackson picked through the bag, selected a burger, looked it over, and peeled the wrapper back as though it might bite him. He pried the bun off and shoved the topless burger in Joe's face. "Look, man. No pickles. Not one. And I got more meat in my shorts than this stupid little burger."

"Get that outta my face, kid." Joe popped the rest of his burger in his mouth, chewing as a squad of black-clad youth stormed into the Yippee's. A lone soldier, his rifle slung cross-body, toed the drive-through console that lay chewed apart by gunfire.

Jackson inched the open burger closer to Joe's face. "No. Pickles."

Joe turned and licked the patty.

Jackson snatched it back, nose scrunched up and top lip pulled back. "Ewww! Gross! You ruined it!" He dropped it in the footwell.

Joe laughed, still chewing. "That's what you get."

Jackson couldn't help a silly grin spread across his face. "You're nasty, bro. This seriously isn't what I wanted."

"You'll eat it if you're hungry." Joe studied the security contingent as they fanned out into other parking lots. "We'd better get back on the interstate." He crumpled his wrapper and tossed the trash in the back seat.

Jackson pulled another burger from the sack, unwrapped it, and took a tentative bite. He glanced at a curious Neko slinking from his hoodie. "Can he eat cheeseburgers?"

Joe shrugged. "Sure."

Jackson tore off a bit and lowered it to his hoodie pocket. Neko went straight for the meat, gobbling little bites while avoiding the bread. Jackson laughed. "He likes it."

Joe exited the dentist's parking lot and slipped into the thin flow of traffic back in the direction of I-55, though the cars had slowed to a crawl. "Shit," Joe said. Ahead, over another set of concrete barriers, a hand-painted sign read:

No Return Access.

All Visitors Must Proceed to Security Checkpoint Indigo.

The flow turned to stop-and-go traffic as three lanes became one, the barriers blocking off any hope of escape. A surveillance drone chopped overhead as it monitored the row of incoming cars. Along the road, civilian soldiers in all black patrolled, rifles at the ready.

"Damn." The creases in Joe's face deepened. "Stupid to exit here. I told you."

"A man's gotta eat." Jackson chewed, though his eyes remained fixed on the blockade.

"Yeah, but they've got us now."

"These guys are all geekbags." Jackson casually popped the last of the burger into his mouth and fished out another from the bag. "I've run across them online. Always screaming about the benefits of Communism and sharing resources for the common good and all that shit." He waved with his second burger. "I run circles around them."

"Not here, you don't. This is their world." Joe shifted in his seat to track the surveillance drone as it scanned the line of vehicles. "We're in trouble. If we break the line to turn around now, we're done."

"What do they want?" Jackson scarfed down his burger in two bites.

"Power, legitimacy," Joe said, "something to believe in—who knows."

Jackson fed Neko another bite of the burger Joe had licked and craned his neck to get a better view of the blockade, now thick with more civilian soldiers. "They're gonna shake us down."

"Hell yeah, they are," Joe agreed. He eased the car forward to the checkpoint, a fenced-off area built directly on the road. They rolled under a billboard decorated with elaborate graffiti:

Zona Antifash.

One after another, cars passed through the gate. An armed recruit waved them to the right, then they continued down a lane of cones to exit the other side of the checkpoint through a second series of gates flanked by men and women in all black.

"Look," Joe wiped his mouth, "do us both a favor and keep your mouth shut. If you think you wanna say something—don't. And keep that cat hidden."

Jackson let out a sigh and stuffed Neko deep into his hoodie pocket. "I know how to handle myself, Genial. Don't worry about me."

"Oh, it's *absolutely* you I'm worried about." Joe lowered the window. He glanced at the burger wrappers. "Hey, quick, hide that trash."

Joe and Jackson grabbed the wrappers and shoved them into the brown paper bag. Joe crumpled it down and jammed it under the seat just as a young Antifash recruit approached, rifle raised. The man-child, with no more than three hairs on his doughy chin, quivered with anticipation.

"Hands in sight. Show 'em," the doughy man-child said as he jerked the rifle at the Kia.

Joe gripped the steering wheel. Jackson complied by raising his hands, one still holding his smart device.

"Drop the phone," the man-child said.

"It's expensive," Jackson complained.

"Drop the phone!" The rifle shook in the young soldier's hands.

"Just do it," Joe said.

Jackson made a show of pinching the phone between two fingers as he lowered it between his feet. "Happy?"

"Where are you going?" The doughy soldier kept the rifle trained on them.

"South," Joe said.

"Where south?" the man-child demanded.

"To the border," Joe said. When the man-child asked why, Joe sighed. "Because it tickles us. Can we go, please? To the right, correct?" Joe motioned to the cars ahead.

The doughy child soldier leaned forward. He sniffed once. Twice. "You been eating Yippee Burger in here?"

Neko mewed, and Jackson covered the sound with a loud cough.

"Not Yippee's, but we did stop to grab some grub—" Joe started.

The Antifash youth raised his radio to his lips. "Commander Broccoli to Indigo Entrance One!"

"Kill this guy and let's book it," Jackson whispered.

"This ain't some video game, kid," Joe hissed.

The man-child shook his weapon at them. "Stop talking."

"Come on, let's just ..." Jackson's voice faded as an automated M1A3 Abrams tank rolled into view past an opening in the chain-link fence ringed with barbed wire. "Oh, shit."

Joe's expression hardened.

"A few of those got sold on the dark web," Jackson mumbled.

The tank squeaked and ground against the pavement. It stopped, and a turret sporting a 120mm barrel pivoted in their direction. The Abrams' olive-green body sported swathes of luminous slogans and symbols: *ACAB*, *Resist*, the spray-painted image of a raised fist. On the front, just below the cannon, the words *Born to Slay* overlaid a large pink hashtag.

A second young man, lean and wearing a long forest-green wool cloak and matching beret, approached, tablet in hand. The man's face and hands were covered in green makeup, the kind Joe used to get from the old Army Navy store when he was a kid.

"What is it?" the green commander asked.

"This car smells like burgers," said the doughy man-child.

"Oh?" The commander swiped at his tablet.

"Yeah. It does." The doughy youth gave an eager nod at Joe's open window. "Yippee's up the block just got hit. I think they ate it in here."

Joe cleared his throat. "I'm sure a lot of people eat fast food while on the road."

"Shut up, Genial!" the Antifascists said in unison.

Joe pursed his lips. Jackson smirked.

The green-faced commander swiped a few more times, then gave the man-child a curt nod to Joe's left. "Yeah, okay."

"Copy," the doughy soldier said, and waved in the same direction.

"Left?" Joe asked. "But everyone else is—" he said, pointing the other way.

"Left!" The two Antifascists pointed at a lane of cones that disappeared off inside the gate.

"And keep it slow," the green-faced commander added.

Hands on the steering wheel, Joe eased the Kia through the chain-link and barbed-wire gate. "Hey, kid," he whispered, eyes still trained on the soldiers waving them on. "Put Neko somewhere. Hide him."

"What? Why?" Jackson said.

"They'll take him," Joe said, "or hurt him. Just do it."

Jackson opened the glove box. "Here?"

"Quick," Joe said.

Jackson placed the bobble-headed kitten in the glove box and snapped it shut.

Ahead, two large black and red flags whipped in the breeze. The other cars eased to the right, exiting the checkpoint and disappearing from view. Another soldier with her face covered in a bandana waved Joe toward a parking lot. She held out her hand and he stopped.

"Get out," Bandana said, her voice muffled, fingers pinched around a rust-splotched AK-47. "One at a time. You first, fat man." She motioned at Joe.

"Yeah, okay," Joe said. He cut the engine, then popped the Kia's door and stood, towering over the slight female.

Bandana shoved him in the chest, found his bulk immovable, then elbow-checked him. "Move your fat ass. Against the car." She rammed him again, this time with the butt of the gun.

Joe let her move him. "All right, just relax," he said.

"You got guns on you?" Her voice rose in pitch.

"Who doesn't?" Joe looked to Jackson, who jabbed away at his phone.

Bandana gave him another shove. "Don't move." She raked her hands across his waist, snatched the snubbie, and stuffed it into her utility belt. "Anything else?" She grabbed hard at his legs and his groin.

Joe flinched and let out a chuckle. "Easy there, sugar. You gonna take me out to dinner first?"

"My name is Clara," she spat back, "not Sugar, Genial."

"Hey, you, kid!" The man-child chugged up and, a little out of breath, pointed his rifle at Jackson through the windshield. "Put the phone down and get out."

"Chill, bro." Jackson swiped right and tapped twice.

"Now," Man Child barked.

"I got you." Jackson opened the door, dropped the phone onto his seat, and stepped out. "But don't call me kid." Jackson looked the doughy man-child up and down. "What are you, like two years older than me?"

"Shut your face. Hands up," Man Child said.

Shoved against the car and frisked, Jackson complied. Man Child pulled Jackson's arms in front of him and zip-tied his hands together.

"The fat guy has another one on him," Bandana said, pulling the Beretta Tomcat from Joe's pants pocket.

Joe watched as they tugged the cold hard plastic of a single zip tie snug around his wrists. At gunpoint, Joe and Jackson walked away from the Kia Sorento. Behind them, a big-bellied recruit gave a whoop and emptied the duffel bag full of guns out onto the concrete.

Across an open parking lot bookended by large brick warehouses, Joe and Jackson shuffled, rifle muzzles buried in their backs. Overhead, tattered and torn canopies fluttered in the wind. Faded lines of yellow and white strafed the lot in a grid of spaces, punctuated by blue slots marked by stick figures in wheelchairs. In cordoned-off areas, adolescents in safety vests dug through personal bags and separated goods into piles. They'd raked heaps of old leaves and bits of trash into the nooks and crannies and along the edge of a long, graffiti-covered concrete wall where flowing script read *Antifash Checkpoint Indigo. No Nazis. No Law.*

Joe wrinkled his nose. The smell of decay and chemicals and cigarette smoke in the air. His leg still throbbing, he limped past a group of Antifascist laborers spreading dark potting soil over a section of asphalt while a second contingent followed behind, stooping over the dirt.

"The hell are they doing?" Joe murmured.

"Planting crops, idiot," Bandana snapped.

"On concrete? How stupid of me." Joe frowned. "Where you taking us?"

Bandana shoved him between the shoulder blades. "Shut up, fat man."

Joe set his jaw.

They stopped at a tent where the green commander sat behind a fold-out table, swiping through images on a tablet.

"So, you like green?" Joe asked. "And your name is Broccoli? What are the odds?"

Jackson barked a laugh.

Broccoli's lips curled in a snarl. "You won't find this funny for long.

You two are quite the pair, aren't you?"

"Don't know what you're talking about," Joe said.

Broccoli held up the tablet. On the screen, Joe shot the speaker box apart at the Yippee Burger. "You don't know anything about this?" the green commander asked.

Joe shrugged. "They got our order wrong."

"Ah. Well, that's our Yippee's," Broccoli said, "and there are penalties for that sort of thing, here." A smug look settled on his green face.

Jackson raised an eyebrow. He twisted his bound wrists, fingers easing over the large bezel of his smartwatch. "Like what?" He thrust his chin at the graffitied wall behind Broccoli. "*No law*. It says right there. Stupid ass-hats."

The Man Child behind Jackson grabbed his hair and stepped on the back of his leg. Jackson cried out and dropped to his knees. The doughy recruit pushed the barrel of his rifle against Jackson's temple.

"Hey, take it easy," Joe said. "Take it easy. He's just a stupid kid."

Broccoli raised his hand, and the recruit released the teen. Jackson opened his mouth to protest, but stopped short at the withering look from Joe.

"You're right, Mr. Carboni," Broccoli said. "But he's a stupid kid worth a shit ton of crypto." The green commander held up the tablet for them to see the Hunter's Dominion rankings. Joe and Jackson had climbed back to thirteen. "You both are."

"What's that?" Joe stared at the tablet's screen. "That ain't us." He let his mouth hang open and pretended to study the screen. "You got it mixed up."

"Yeah?" Broccoli frowned in mock contemplation. He double-clicked the listing, and their information filled the screen. "A should-be-retired hitman and a fifteen-year-old cryptokiller. Oh, and look. Pictures." He cycled through a dozen drone photos of Jackson and Joe, some before their meeting, others taken via surveillance in just the past twelve hours. "Still think I'm stupid?"

One eyebrow arched, Joe eyed the name tape on Commander Broccoli's breast pocket, then his green make-up covered face.

"Mr. Carboni—may I call you that?" Broccoli said, his tone condescending.

Joe shrugged. "Sure. That's my name, Mr. Broccoli."

Bandana jammed her AK-47 into Joe's ribcage. "That's Commander Broccoli to you!"

Broccoli waved toward the back of the lot. "Mr. Carboni, let me direct your attention over here."

Joe's angry female handler jabbed him again, and he turned to face the graffitied wall. There, a family with young children and an elderly grandfather or uncle shuffled across the back of the lot. Poked and prodded by masked soldiers in black, they were made to stand shoulder to shoulder.

"A decade ago, that old man made a racist comment on social media," Broccoli said. "He never retracted the comment and, as a result, the internet has preserved it forever. Just this morning, we identified him and his family as living on the outskirts of town. Naturally, I sent my people to collect the lot of them so they could all pay for their bloodline's crimes against humanity."

The men in front of the wall hung their heads and the woman clutched her children against her breast and wept. The civilian soldiers had led them to a pit punched through the asphalt. At the bottom, Joe could just make out the crook of an elbow, the bend of a knee, and a shock of blood-matted hair. And that smell of decay.

"This ain't right," Joe said. "You people are crazy."

"Shut up." Bandana shoved Joe with her rifle.

"It was me!" the slump-shouldered old man shouted. "I said those things. Just shoot me! My family didn't do anything!"

"Please don't!" The red-eyed woman by the pit sobbed as the black-clad firing squad formed ranks. "Please ..." she cried. "The children!"

The civilian soldiers took aim. Joe pressed his molars together.

The crack of rifle fire leaped into the air. The family spun, crumpled, and rolled into the ditch.

Joe's hands jerked up and the sharp edge of the plastic zip ties bit into his wrists. Beside him, Jackson looked like he'd swallowed bleach, fingers tapping away at his watch.

The squeal and crunch of the tank's grinding treads started up. The metal beast, turret pivoting back and forth, crawled toward Broccoli's tent.

Broccoli flashed a thin smile, pink gums bright against his green face. "If we'll do this to them for something that happened ten years ago, what do you think we'll do to *you* on a live webcast?" He touched his green-painted chin. "The bounty on you two? That's enough coin to run our operations for quite a long time."

"You're disgusting," Joe said. "Your wall says *No Nazis*, but if you knew your history, you'd know you're doing the same shit they did. You're no better. In fact, your stupidity makes it worse."

"Think that all you want. You'll be dead, and we'll be crypto-rich." Broccoli grinned and motioned to Man Child behind Jackson. "Walk them to the pit."

Bandana shoved Joe hard, right in the spine, with the magazine of her rifle. "Get a move on, fat ass."

Joe turned to glare. "That's enough with the fuckin' shoving."

"Oh yeah?" Bandana snapped. "And you're gonna do *what* about it?" She rammed him again.

The tank ground to a stop and its cannon swiveled toward the body pit.

Broccoli stepped a few paces away to shout at a recruit.

"Get shot to shit, I guess," Joe said.

Jackson took a push from Man Child and stumbled forward.

"All this for a lukewarm, robot-made cheeseburger," Joe grumbled.

"Hey, Bones?" Jackson kicked a dented spray-paint can across the gravel and cocked his head to look at Joe. "Are we gonna die?"

"Looks that way, kid," Joe said.

The smell of chemicals and decay from the pit made Joe's eyes water. A cramp hit his guts as he watched a black-clad soldier shake lime across mangled corpses frozen with rigor.

"I'm sorry," Jackson said.

"Don't be sorry about dying, kid," Joe said. "It happens to everyone."

"Nah." Jackson took a shove from Man Child and stumbled again.

"I'm sorry I've been so difficult. I can be reckless sometimes, ya know?" His eyes twinkled, and his mouth lifted into the slightest of smiles. His index finger hung poised over the watch bezel.

Joe's eyes narrowed. *The hell are you playing at, kid?*

Jackson winked, then touched the watch face.

The M1A3 Abrams tank lurched to life. The power drive whined, gears and treads whirring at max speed as it rocketed across the parking lot. Broccoli turned and let out a cry, his arms flailing high. The tank hit him at full speed and smashed him into a greasy green and red smear against the pavement.

Jackson let out a whoop and twirled his finger on the bezel. The tank turned hard, trenched straight through the asphalt garden, and sent the planters diving out of the way. It turned again, took down a section of chain-link fencing, and smashed a hole in the brick warehouse beyond. Commander Broccoli's blood-splattered cloak flapped along an outer section of the tread.

Joe twisted hard into Bandana and struck her across the neck with his zip-tied wrists.

"No!" Man Child raised his rifle, but Jackson twisted into him and delivered a championship-winning punt to his groin.

Bandana rose with a snarl, which faded to a slack-jawed gape as Joe twisted his arms and snapped the zip-tie restraint with little more than a grunt. He snatched the rifle from her grip and used the weapon to shove her back to the black top.

"If you know what's good for you, you'll stay on the ground, girl," Joe said.

Bandana bared her teeth. "I'm not a—"

Joe leaned closer. "I don't care! Give me back my pistols. Now."

Bandana flinched as the tank crashed through the other side of the warehouse and continued on its path of mayhem. The youth in security vests scattered in all directions. Citizen soldiers in all black dropped their rifles and ran for the tank, desperate to stop its rampage. A crackle of electricity made Joe's neck hair stand on end as the tank's defensive systems came online. The few mad soldiers who'd scaled the metal skin of the marauding beast flashed to nothing more than black, smoldering corpses.

"Give me the Beretta." Joe jerked the rifle at Bandana.

She scowled, dug in her pocket, then slapped the micro pistol into Joe's hand.

Joe shoved it into his own pocket, then grabbed his snubbie from her belt and slipped it into his waistband. "Now, face down and don't move," he said, "and you might just live through this."

Jackson swiped a finger across his watch bezel. The tank's turret pivoted toward the graffiti-covered checkpoint entrance. The ground shook as a blast of fire erupted from the massive barrel. The checkpoint and all those manning it disappeared in a plume of smoke and scattered rubble.

"Yeah!" Jackson hollered. "Here to slay, bitches!" He frowned at Joe's unshackled wrists. "How you do that?"

Joe reached into his sock and pulled out the stiletto that Bandana had missed on her sloppy pat down. "Brute force," he said. With a swipe he cut Jackson's restraints, then slipped the blade back into his sock. "It works."

"Stake," Jackson said, scanning the debris-covered ground. "You're full of surprises, aren't ya?"

"Me?" Joe gave a nod to the tank, which flattened the remains of the entrance and rampaged across the checkpoint.

Jackson hocked a laugh, then dropped to his haunches. "There it is!" He held aloft the dented can of spray paint he'd kicked across the asphalt.

"The hell you doin', kid? Let's go!" Joe grabbed Jackson and dragged him up to run for the Kia.

More Antifash soldiers stormed the tank, forgetting their fallen comrades who'd tried this tactic not two minutes earlier. Their bodies flashed to cinders like flies on a bug zapper. The staccato pop of overcooked internals bursting from crisp flesh echoed across the open lot. The M1A3 churned the pavement, its metal skin now covered in charred smoking corpses—a vision torn right from the pages of the Book of Revelation.

Joe held his arm over his face to block the overpowering stench of scorched flesh and hair. "Mary, Mother of God. Make that stop."

"No way." Jackson laughed as he ran and spun his fingertip on the watch dial again. "It's amazing."

Joe and Jackson careened into the baby-blue Kia, which stood with its doors open, and scrambled over the duffel bags strewn everywhere. "Looks like these morons didn't finish raiding our stuff," Joe said, sucking at the air.

The tank smashed into an apartment building. Smoke and the dust of crushed brick streamed over the metal skin of the metallic titan. Somewhere, a woman screamed.

Joe grabbed the only full gun duffel and slung it back into the car.

Jackson flopped into the passenger seat. "Let's go, man. Before they notice us." He picked up his phone, but dropped it back into his lap. He grabbed at the glove box handle and it popped open. From a jumbled mess of papers, Neko poked his wide-eyed face out and mewed.

"Hey, they didn't find him!" Jackson said.

Joe grunted, turned the steering wheel, and stepped on the accelerator. The Kia swerved hard and angled for the gate at the opposite side of the checkpoint. Joe dodged the car left and right, narrowly missing scattered debris and torn bodies. Jackson grabbed Neko and stuffed the kitten back into his sweatshirt. He touched his watch again and turned in the seat as the tank thrust back out of the ruined apartment complex.

Joe glanced over. "How the hell are you doing that?"

"Told you, Genial. Modified Pegasus app Hellcat gave me. A stealth scythe—I can get into almost anything. Old government spy shit," Jackson said. He ran his finger up the watch bezel and the tank accelerated past them, smashing flat a group of Antifash soldiers as they ran for their lives.

"All right," Joe said, grim-faced. "They're running away. You've won."

"Not yet, I haven't," Jackson said, his face glowing. Flame burst from the tank's cannon and another building crumbled in a swell of smoke and dust.

Joe clenched his jaw and shook his head. He jerked the wheel to avoid an overturned sedan and screeched to a halt. Between them and the closed gate waited Bandana, her soot-covered face furious. Blood was smeared beneath her nose, and she held an AK clutched against her chest.

"Damn ..." Joe murmured.

But Bandana didn't point the rifle at them. Instead, she lowered it and approached the gate control box. With a few taps on the keypad she opened the barrier, the anger in her countenance replaced with a vacant soullessness. "Just go. You've made your point."

Joe pinched his lips and drove the Kia out of the Antifash checkpoint, back toward I-55.

Jackson turned to look out the back glass at the burning checkpoint. His finger traced the watch dial. "And now for the coup de grâce."

Joe fixed his gaze on the rearview mirror.

The tank rumbled back into view amidst the carnage and stopped. Bandana led a group of curious survivors up to the immobile tank.

Jackson tapped his watch and the tank exploded in a rolling blast of fire and smoke. The onlookers flew and tumbled, torn and dismembered, across the lot. Jackson wrestled the paint can from his pocket, yanked off his hoodie, and sprayed #BORNTOSLAY in neon green across the back.

The pungent stink of aerosol assaulted Joe's nose. He slammed on the brakes and the car skidded to a stop on the on-ramp.

Jackson collided with the dash.

"The hell is wrong with you?" Joe shouted, wagging a thick finger in Jackson's face. "And what the hell is this?" He grabbed Jackson's hoodie.

"That's what I do, bitch," Jackson spat. "I'm the reaper."

"But, she just let us go," Joe said, his voice cracking. "You don't gotta keep killing folks!"

"Who gives a shit what happens to these assholes?" Jackson balked.

Joe held up his hands. "I'm not saying they don't deserve it. I'm saying enough is enough. You can't just ... you can't keep ..."

"Man, their lives had, like, zero value. None." Jackson folded his arms.

Neko mewed.

"Whose does, then?" Joe reached down and pulled the stiletto from his sock. With the press of a button, it snapped open. "Does your life matter? Does mine?" Joe offered the handle of the knife to Jackson. "If killing is so easy, then do me."

"What?" Jackson took the knife and held it in a limp grip. "You're crazy."

"Kill me." Joe stretched his chin up, exposing the flesh of his neck. He pointed to it. "Stab deep and rake across. Learn what it really means to take a life. Not with your watch, not with a drone. *You* do it. If life is so meaningless, then cut my throat and dump me here for the crows."

The knife quivered in Jackson's bloodless grip.

"The hell are you waiting for, kid? Put me out of my misery." Joe pointed again at his throat.

Jackson swallowed and put the knife down on the center console.

Joe lowered his chin. For a long moment, the two eyed each other.

Joe blew out a long, measured breath. "If we're in this shit together, the first thing you gotta know about me is this—respect matters," he said. "And just about everybody deserves some measure of it."

Jackson stared straight ahead, eyes wet and large.

"For example," Joe said, "calling me *Genial*. That's done, if you and me are gonna get along."

"Then don't call me *kid*," Jackson said. "I've been doing adult shit since I was eight."

Joe picked up the knife, closed it, and slipped it back into his sock. "I can do that. An' …" Joe swallowed the discomfort of the words and forced himself to say them. "An' I'm sorry if it bothered you."

Jackson shifted in his seat. He looked Joe up and down, then stretched out his hand.

Joe shook it. "It's a deal, then?" he said.

"Sure, Gen—" Jackson pinched his smirking lips shut with his fingers. "Sure thing, Bones."

CHAPTER SIXTEEN
Svanire

Through the window of the blacked-out armored SUV, South Chicago's sea of dilapidated industrial warehouses drifted by. At 1881 West Pershing Road stood his destination, a monolith of worn red-brown brick with scum-covered windows that reflected the steel gray sky. A homeless woman in moth-eaten oversized clothing squeaked a cart along the uneven sidewalk, her head down against a brisk wind.

Svanire's heart beat strong with singular purpose.

He stroked and then squeezed the bare leg of a young tan-skinned boy who'd curled into a ball in the soft leather seat beside him.

Svanire's SUV and the two identical vehicles in convoy—one in front, the other behind—slipped into an alley off West Pershing and glided to a stop. Two thugs stepped down the stairs from a loading dock and rolled their huge shoulders under dark suit jackets.

In unison, the doors popped open on the first and third armored SUVs, and Svanire's security team—all dark suits and sunglasses—emerged. They scanned the alley for signs of danger. A crumpled paper bag touched end over end, then became pinned against the undercarriage of the rearmost SUV. Another gust and the bag unhitched and scraped away, followed by the eyes of the security team.

Svanire shifted in his seat and dug his fingertips into the child's bare thigh.

Satisfied that no danger lurked in the alley, one member of the security detail turned and touched Svanire's door. It released and slid up like a bird folding its wing. Svanire gave his young companion a final loving glance and placed one polished wingtip on the grimy asphalt. He stood from the rear passenger seat, then straightened his ink-black suit and lifted his chin. The chill, dry air carried the dense scent of urban decay. He stood with his security detail, a dozen strong.

A self-drive cab, audio billboards flashing a hypnotic ad, rolled past on West Pershing.

"We have to unite as one people in order to survive." The grating voice of Anja Kuhn echoed off the brickwork. "By nature, humanity is not peaceful. Every time two people meet, a set of assumptions cause each to predict the other's behavior—and violence is sure to follow. The way we treat and react to one another—the outrage machine—has eroded the underpinnings of peace and democracy …"

With a wry smirk, Svanire pulled his suit jacket snug and buttoned it once.

One of the thugs waiting outside the loading dock shuffled from foot to foot. "Mr. Svanire," he squeaked, then cleared his throat. "Mr. Svanire, I tried to stop them, but … well, they're waiting for you inside."

"Of course they are," Svanire said. He gave a curt nod to his security detail leader and the group split. Two remained with the vehicles and ten moved to enter the red-brick industrial complex.

The thugs looked at one another. "Mr. Svanire … uh, Mr. Svanire …" The squeaky one twitched a finger to take in the large group of men in dark suits. "We have orders from Don Rigoletti that your people have to stay outside."

Svanire's alabaster face creased into a rare smile. He stepped over a network of vines and leaves that protruded from the cracks in the alley pavement. Flanked by his team, he took the sullied concrete steps one at a time and knocked politely on the metal door.

It popped open and swung in to reveal a muscular trio sporting dark suits and unwelcoming scowls. One carried a black Scorpion EVO clipped to a single-point sling. Another squat man had the look of a brawler, his fists clenched. The closest of the three stood a foot taller than even Svanire's own ungainly height.

"I do hate it when company comes for a visit—then takes over the place." Svanire released a dramatic sigh.

"Where's Don Giordano?" the Giant asked.

"Sadly, he couldn't make it." Svanire bowed. "I am here in his stead."

"He sent *you*, Squid?" The Giant laughed.

Svanire felt nothing at the jibe, only the swell of his perfect purpose within. "This is Don Giordano's building," he said. "Where are my people?"

"Safe," The Giant said.

"You would act like this with Don Giordano?" Svanire frowned. "You would insult him like this?"

"Desperate times and all that." The Giant glowered down and crossed arms the size of Amazonian constrictors. "No admittance. Not like this," he said. "The council demands adherence to the rule of safety."

Svanire raised a shapely eyebrow. "In Don Giordano's own building."

"Especially here," The Giant said.

"But we invited *you*." Svanire pushed out his bottom lip to pout. "It's *our* party."

The Giant remained immovable. "Not anymore, it isn't. *You* can come in. Your security waits outside."

Svanire's detail leader, a tough plug of a man named Richter, slipped a black briefcase from one hand to the other. "You good, sir?" he said.

Svanire didn't return eye contact. The wind whipped up and scattered a few strands of coiffed hair across his forehead. He gave a measured nod, which made his men uncoil outside the entrance. He waited for The Giant to move aside, then took two steps past the threshold.

The door slammed behind Svanire and a bolt clicked into place, cutting him off from Richter and his security team. Inside, a series of filament bulbs hanging from the ceiling cast weak yellow light into the small room. Paint curled away in brown strips from a single wooden door on the opposite wall. In the corner, a coil of rope lay on a metal chair.

The three thugs closed in around Svanire.

Svanire let out a low chuckle. "Such theatrics."

"Where's your piece?" the Giant asked.

"Firearms disagree with me," Svanire said.

"Bullshit. I know you carry." The Giant reached out to pat him down.

Svanire raised a manicured hand. "I'd prefer you didn't. This suit is handmade by Fabriggio Contessa—the fabric alone is worth more than your life."

The Giant exchanged an amused glance with the Scorpion and the Brawler. "Hey Mike, you hear this fuckin' guy?" His bulk towered over Svanire. "Turn around and put your fuckin' face against the—"

Svanire glissaded past The Giant's outstretched hand, parried away his grab, and delivered a lightning-quick riposte to the man's armpit. The air left The Giant's lungs and he crashed against the peeling wooden door.

Svanire slipped into a pas de basque, his outstretched fingers glancing the neck of the Scorpion. A perfect pirouette, and the snap of Svanire's wrist released a spray of blood from the thug's throat.

Svanire paused in the third position, charcoal over black wingtips pointed outward, one heel touching the back foot's instep. He gave another graceful bow, hand outstretched to reveal a solid black shank of Spanish steel, narrow as a paring knife. It glistened deep red in the yellow light of the room.

Blood spurted from the precision wounds in the flesh of The Giant and The Scorpion.

Svanire's gaze did not waver from The Brawler, who, until this moment, liked his chances.

The Brawler's fingers inched for the heel of a pistol beneath his coat.

"I'll cut you in two before you can break the leather," Svanire said, low and cold.

The Scorpion dropped his weapon and clutched blood-soaked fingers to his neck. He gagged, then stumbled and slid to the floor, leaving a crimson streak against the wall. The Giant groaned and slumped to his knees, then collapsed onto his face on top of The Scorpion. Blood ran like water from an open faucet and pooled around the bodies.

"Brachial artery," Svanire said, with a cruel smile to The Giant. "It's severed easily by way of the armpit. The gun man, a strike to the carotid. Both are quite effective … but messy. Wouldn't you agree?"

The Brawler swallowed hard. "Okay." He raised trembling hands. "Okay, you got me."

"Correct." Svanire launched forward and buried the knife just below The Brawler's breastbone.

The Brawler groaned and grabbed at his assassin's hands against his chest, but Svanire angled the knife up and gave it a good hard twist.

"Heart," Svanire whispered.

The Brawler shook. Red froth bubbled on his lips. He gurgled a moan and his eyes rolled back in his head before he slumped into the metal chair, knocking the unspooling rope to the floor.

Svanire avoided the growing pool of blood and opened the exterior door where his team waited.

Richter took a step in and offered a white handkerchief. "Boss."

Svanire accepted the cloth and wiped the deep red from his blade. He inspected a red dot that marred the otherwise flawless starched white of his shirt front. "The strong-arm methods these gentlemen chose were tiresome and ineffectual." He finished wiping down the black steel of the blade and handed the blood-soiled handkerchief back to the team leader, who accepted it, folded it once, and replaced it in his coat pocket.

"I think it's time I spoke with their employers," Svanire said.

In unison, his detail pulled Glock 19 pistols from beneath their suit jackets. Each man took a conical suppressor, smooth and black, and screwed it flush with the muzzle of his weapon.

"It's a power play now," Svanire said. "Get in and get it done quickly. Find our people—they're detained somewhere in the complex. Link up and wait for my signal." He checked his knife and snapped the blade back into the low-profile Kydex scabbard clipped behind the buckle of his belt. "Don't fail me, Richter."

"No sir," the team leader said, and held out the sleek black briefcase.

Svanire took the case by its handle, stepped over the bodies, and pushed through the peeling wooden door.

Two more gangsters loitered at the end of a long hallway. They stiffened as Svanire and his company entered. The brutes jerked for their weapons and Svanire's men opened fire. The suppressed pistols made no report, only a slight *snap* followed by the *click-click-click* of metal slides feeding subsonic ammunition. The pair of guards fell where they stood.

Through the door where the guards lay, the warm smell of

humming servers filled an open space of high ceilings and exposed beams. Giant racks of computer equipment, manned by just one person, ran the length of the room. Fans whirred and faint blue light seeped from the system housings while bundled networks of cables snaked across the concrete floor.

Svanire motioned with the briefcase to doors off either side of the room, and Richter and his men split and disappeared through them. Svanire then took a slow stroll down the center aisle and stopped at a desk terminal. He checked his platinum cufflinks and black tie and then delivered a courteous nod to a scrawny man with Coke-bottle spectacles who cowered behind the monitor.

"I heard shooting." The scrawny man's Adam's apple bobbed.

"Keep at it, Orlando. All is well," Svanire said.

"Y-yes, Mr. Svanire," Orlando stuttered. "Mining has slowed a little. But ... but we are on top of new chains daily."

"Glad to hear it, Orlando," Svanire said. "Can't let those coffers run dry."

"Of course, Mr. Svanire." The scrawny accountant turned back to his screen and pushed his heavy lenses up the bridge of his nose.

With soundless steps, Svanire glided down the aisle to a heavy metal door at the far end of the cavernous room. He checked his suit one final time, smoothed a few limp strands of hair into place, and pushed through.

The sparsely lit conference room, windowless and smoky, echoed with laughter, but the sound died upon Svanire's entrance. He approached the antique hardwood table that stretched away into the gloom. Around the heavy slab, seven old men scowled from behind curls of smoke and near-empty crystal tumblers. Along the edges of the room, wreathed in shadow, the dons' henchmen waited, as still as gargoyles on a moonless night.

"Gentlemen." Svanire placed his thin hands on the back of the only empty seat. "My deepest apologies for keeping you all waiting."

"Where're my fuckin' guys, Squid? The ones that were supposed to escort you?" said an olive-skinned man with heavy jowls at the far end of the table.

"Those were yours?" Svanire said.

The jowled man's fleshy face quivered. "Where's Don Giordano?"

"Sadly, he cannot join us today, Don Rigoletti." Svanire gave a deep bow. He raised the computer case for the men to see. "As a sign of his commitment to The Family, and as a token of his remorse at not being able to attend, he has authorized a one-time payment to each of your houses in the amount of ten million Torre Coin."

"As well he should," said Boston's withered Don Russo in a three-piece pinstripe suit.

A series of murmurs and nods of agreement passed around the table.

"We don't need Giordano's charity." Rigoletti's jowls jiggled as he fiddled with the smart Rolex strap, too tight around his obese wrist.

"Are you declining this generous gift?" Svanire asked.

Rigoletti licked his lips and motioned for the computer. "I didn't say that."

"Very good." Svanire opened the case, extracted a small laptop, and passed it to Don Russo. "To receive your payment, you will need to verify your identity via fingerprint recognition and facial scan."

Don Russo took the laptop and placed his delicate palm on the black glass of the sensor. The screen registered a picture of his face, and a window opened to show his information. He cleared the screen and passed the laptop to sweaty Don Colombo.

"Where *exactly* is Don Giordano?" Rigoletti asked, eyes narrowed.

"Indisposed, I'm afraid," Svanire said, "but he sends his best regards."

"Indisposed," Colombo repeated, his lips smacking as if tasting the words. "Nah, that ain't the right word, see? The right word is *scared*."

"Oh?" Svanire inspected his manicured fingernails for blood.

Rigoletti tugged at the strap of his smart Rolex again.

"I always knew Giordano was a chickenshit," said Don Ricci, a toady man with bulbous features. The computer continued its trip around the table. "Now he wants to throw money at us—'cuz somehow that makes it better?"

"He started this mess," Rigoletti said, then lit a thick cigar with a match. "Killing his own guys, that shit spreads to us." He shook the dying flame from the match and sucked on the cigar. "Dysfunction in one family means dysfunction in all the families. And now he thinks he can make it better by bribing us while he hides away—like a *rat*."

Svanire removed his hands from the back of the chair, clasped his wrist, and scanned the faces of the kingpins around the table. "I would ask if you all felt that way, but it seems Don Rigoletti and Don Ricci's vulgar tone has your attention."

Rigoletti frowned. "We don't give a shit what you think, Squid. These bloodlines make up La Nueva Cosa Nostra." He rolled the thick cigar between even thicker fingers. "*We* rose from the ashes of the Collapse."

"*We* founded this coalition," Don Ricci said. "*We* saw the future in crypto. And *we* created Torre Coin.

A sneer crawled across Don Rigoletti's jowled face. "You're not blood, Squid—*you* didn't contribute, you're just Giordano's pet."

A chorus of murmurs arose from the table.

Rigoletti sucked at his cigar again and huffed out a thick cloud of smoke. "We've run this coalition for decades, and you, orphan boy—you think you can come in and address us as equals? Get the fuck outta here."

The computer finished its rounds. Don Bianchi slid it across the table to Svanire, who closed it with two manicured fingers, and raised his wrist to inspect the face of his platinum Audemars Piguet Royal Oak timepiece.

Rigoletti's face reddened. "If Don Giordano can't show us the respect we deserve by coming here himself, then it's time someone else took lead chair." He stood and placed his fat hands on the table.

"And I assume you think that person should be you, Don Rigoletti?" a balding Don Bianchi shouted in his thick Philadelphia accent.

"Why the hell not?" Rigoletti spat. "I've run *The Island* for years. Nobody else in this room has the balls to organize this group."

"Is that so?" Don Ricci jabbed a fleshy digit in Rigoletti's direction. "My boys in Miami can run it better than you clowns in Manhattan."

"Now, wait just a second!" Don Colombo jumped to his feet. Two more dons stood, and the room filled with shouted threats as the men at the table gesticulated and spat.

Svanire eyed the dons' bodyguards around the fringe, who seemed to inch closer from the shadows. He raised a hand. "Gentlemen, may I have your attention, please." The shouts continued, Svanire's plea unnoticed. He put his fingers to his lips and whistled high and sharp.

Silence. Amid the smoke and gloom, all eyes shifted to him. Svanire allowed the stillness to deepen.

Don Rigoletti's jowls shook. "I think you forgot that adults are speaking here, boy."

Svanire touched his chin in contemplation.

"You got some brass balls on you, I'll give you that." Rigoletti curled his lip. "Whistling at us like we're a bunch of dogs."

"It's what you are." Svanire smirked. "Little more than a pack of toothless old dogs fighting for scraps."

The smoky air swelled thick with hate.

"Hey, Tommy—this gangly prick thinks he can talk to me." Rigoletti pointed at Svanire. "Cut his throat."

The dons shifted to look for Rigoletti's bodyguard.

"Tommy!" Rigoletti twisted in his chair, his face furious. "You fuckin' deaf?"

A slight wheeze escaped Tommy Orsatti's throat. He slumped to the polished floor and rolled to his side, a knife buried in his spine.

Out of the gloom stepped Richter.

Then another of Svanire's detail.

And a third, until Svanire's own operatives ringed the opulent table.

A chorus of bodies slapped and thumped against the concrete floor as each operative discarded a don's bodyguard at his feet.

"Th' fuck …?" Rigoletti opened his mouth again, but no more sound came.

"This won't stand, you mothafucka," Don Russo squeaked.

Rigoletti jumped up and threw his cigar across the table. "We … we got here first—we brought ten men a piece!"

Svanire touched his lips. "Tactics, Leo. Can I call you Leo? While you squabble like children, Leo, I take action. You said it yourself—it's time someone else took charge."

"What is this?" Don Russo stood slow and ran his hands down his suit. "Some kind of coup?"

Svanire inclined his head. "Please, everyone, sit down."

Rigoletti, Russo, and the others eyed one another, then reluctantly took their seats.

Svanire leaned forward and opened the small laptop. He unlocked the screen, pressed play, and swiveled the screen for the dons to see. The display filled with seven small boxes—recorded video calls of each of the dons speaking with Giordano. Svanire paused the playback, tapped a few keys, and the image of Giordano dissolved until he was revealed as Svanire in a milk-white silicone mask.

Gasps rippled through the room. Don Bianchi clutched at his tie and loosened it.

"You're a fraud! A snake!" Don Rigoletti spat. "Have you no respect for the old ways?"

"The old ways are dead." Svanire shut the laptop. "You are all relieved of your positions and influence. In your places, leaders of my choosing, loyal to me, will keep order and synchronicity within the organization—"

"Then Giordano is dead." Rigoletti tapped at the face of his smartwatch to wake it. "You fuckin' snake."

"Leo, please. Your tech won't save you—"

"Think again!" Rigoletti stood, furious. "I got a high-altitude combat drone that'll hit this place with a bunker buster in seconds. We can burn in Hell together!"

"Leo—"

Rigoletti's finger hovered over his watch. "One tap. You ready, you skinny sonofabitch?" Rigoletti tapped his watch. Stared at it. "The fuck?" Tapped it twice more. Then he shook his wrist.

Richter lurched over a pair of dead bodyguards, seized Don Rigoletti by his thinning hair, slammed his face against the hardwood table twice, then stepped back. Rigoletti moaned as blood dribbled from his nose onto the varnished tabletop.

"Enough talking, Leo," Svanire said. "No more interruptions, please." He plucked a white square from Don Bianchi's pocket and slid it across the table to Don Rigoletti. The moaning Don, pinching his nose, scowled at the cotton, then picked it up and held it to his face.

"Each of you has grown fat and rich off the backs of others," Svanire said, "too accustomed to having your way. Ignorant of technology. Bloated with power. That ends today. Today, La Nuevo Cosa Nostra moves forward into the next generation—an era that does not include you." Svanire tented his fingers on the tabletop. "You have given me the biometrics necessary to seize your station and your accounts. Everything you have now belongs to me. You've had a good run, gentlemen. I hope you enjoyed it."

"You're what? Gonna kill us, now?" Don Rigoletti whined through the cloth pinched to his nose. He flinched as Svanire's men stepped closer.

Svanire raised a hand and his team stopped. From inside the computer case, Svanire produced a black velvet box. He eased the black lid open, placed it on the table, and swiveled it so the old men could see inside.

A hush fell upon the table as Don Bianchi and Don Russo leaned forward to inspect the box, squinting to see through the smoky air. Inside the box sat a black ring surrounded by eight golden jewels, oblong in shape and no wider than an adult's little finger. The ring and each jewel sat in an individual pocket in the velvet tray. Symmetrically identical, the jewels glittered with specks of yellow and orange and black.

Bianchi, the bald don in the three-piece suit, drew very close. "What the hell are they?"

"The future." Svanire motioned to the velvet box. "The independent development team over at what was MIT have been busy little bees." He chuckled and held his index finger to his lips. "Don't tell anyone they shared their research on alternate pollination."

Svanire took the matte black ring from the box and slipped it over his middle finger. Each of Svanire's detail in turn produced and slipped on a carbon-gray mask adorned with the image of a skull. Richter handed Svanire his own mask, different from the others. Svanire pulled it over his head, careful not to disrupt his coiffure, until the mask's angles hugged the contours of his forehead, cheeks, and jaw. Dark lenses covered his eyes like hollowed sockets and the mask wrapped around to cover his ears.

The other dons sat staring, their faces a mix of confusion and dread. Svanire passed his ringed finger over the open box and the jewels shivered.

Bianchi abruptly sat back, knocking over the computer case Svanire had set on the floor, and pointed. "Look—"

Independent of one another, the jewels shifted and rocked, unseating themselves from their snug pockets. The little charms crawled on tiny stalk legs across the box and formed a neat row along the rim.

Rigoletti shook his head, a sheen of perspiration on his brow. "You come here, trying to shake us up with your ghost masks and your parlor tricks …" he muttered.

Svanire reached his hand down and one of the little stalk-legged jewels climbed onto the tip of his finger. "Oh, it's no trick, Leo, I assure you," Svanire said. "In an age of such technology, your biometric signature can be used for so many things." He held his hand out and translucent wings popped free from the little golden jewel and began to flutter. "Such as a tracking beacon for this microdrone."

"The hell—" The words weren't out of Don Rigoletti's mouth when the bumblebee drone zipped the length of the table, dodged a swipe of his fat hand, and landed just beneath his nose. In an instant, it disappeared into his nasal cavity.

Rigoletti gasped and screamed—he clawed at his face and eyes as blood streamed from his nostrils. He gagged, grabbed at his throat, and toppled from his chair across two of the dead bodyguards. The chair's wood backing clattered on the polished concrete.

Don Russo shoved out his chair, tripped over a lifeless bodyguard, and was pinned to the floor by one of Svanire's men.

A cacophony of screams and curses raked the air. Svanire's skull-faced men forced the remaining dons, writhing, back into their seats. At the end of the table, Rigoletti writhed and shrieked on the concrete. His fingernails clawed bloody furrows into the flesh of his face.

"You see," Svanire said, "it's the constant digging, digging through the bony structures on the way to the brain, that drives one mad."

"You're sick! You're … you're twisted!" Bianchi screamed. His eyes bulged from their sockets as he struggled against the hands that held him fast.

"Correct." Svanire's skull-faced mask grinned with toothy malevolence.

He reached into his jacket and swiped open his phone. At the top of a playlist was Rimsky-Korsakov's "Flight of the Bumblebee." A chuckle resonated in Svanire's throat. He passed his ringed hand over the drone box and touched *Play* on the phone.

The room filled with the dizzying ups and downs of Korsakov's orchestral interlude and the hum of tiny wings. The dons bucked and twisted under the grip of Svanire's skull-faced detail and slung threats, to no avail. The bumblebee drones took flight, zipping and diving in a beautiful dance of death timed to the music. Each found its mark—up noses, down yawning throats, and into exposed ear canals. The old men, released by their captors, flailed on the polished concrete and twisted on top of their dead bodyguards like wounded snakes. In minutes, all lay prostrate, more than a dozen bodies spread about on the concrete around the chairs like debris after a storm.

Svanire tapped the screen of his phone and the song abruptly stopped.

"Come home, my lovelies," he said. He took the black ring off his middle finger and replaced it in the velvet tray in the box. Then he leaned forward on his toes and clasped his hands behind his back, eyes roving with expectation over the bodies of the dead men.

Don Rigoletti's head twitched, then trembled. After a moment his left eye bulged out ever so slightly. Along the side of the white of his eye, the bumblebee drone emerged. Gold and crimson and flecked with bits of white bone, it crawled along the bridge of the dead man's nose, down to the tip, and spread little blood-matted wings.

The other drones emerged, crawling from their dead hosts to spread their wings. A hum filled the room once again as the microdrones took flight, circling in little loops back to the box. One by one they landed along the rim of the box. Their miniature wings fluttered and folded.

Little beautiful murderers, every one. Svanire slid the black velvet box toward the edge of the table where one of his detail waited with a can of electronics cleaner. Blood and bone were sprayed from each little drone. Then, one by one, the operative placed them back in their pockets and snapped the box closed.

"I do love a good performance," Svanire said. "Speaking of which, what is the status of my favorite odd couple?"

Richter opened the laptop and with a few keystrokes turned it to face Svanire. "Looks like they're approaching the border with Mexico, Boss. El Paso-Juarez."

Onscreen, a high-altitude predator drone zoomed in for maximum detail. It followed the beaten blue Kia Sorento south toward a welcome/bienvenido sign stretched above a ten-lane highway swarming with Texas Law Enforcement. Along its length, open toll booths topped with gun turrets pointed their striped barrier arms permanently toward the sky.

Svanire's countenance darkened.

"Boss." Richter looked from the screen to Svanire. "We have their active GPS location and the munitions to hammer them from twenty-five-thousand feet. Why not hit them now?"

Svanire clicked his tongue against his teeth. "A vulgar man smashes a cockroach beneath his boot heel. Out of fear. And the roach can still flee, if it's lucky. But to force it in a direction where it cannot escape," Svanire's spidery fingers danced in the air, "to let it run in circles until it's exhausted, then pull off its legs and its wings one by one, until it has no other recourse but to lie on its belly and wait for a slender pin to slip between the gaps in its armor ..." Svanire sighed. "Ahh, now *that* is artistry."

Richter gave a faint, confused nod. "You know this is gonna bring a shit storm from the other coalitions. They'll come lookin' for you."

"Indeed." Svanire composed himself with a tug of his shirt sleeves. "Finish up, here." He turned for the door, reached inside his coat, and slipped on a pair of black leather driving gloves. "I have a few things before we disembark."

"Disembark? For where?" Richter looked up, but Svanire had vanished into the gloom. At the end of the darkened space, the door eased shut with a *click*.

CHAPTER SEVENTEEN
Jackson

Jackson groaned, his eyelids glued together and throat parched. He rubbed away the stickiness around his lashes and looked down to Neko who, curled up on the rucksack in his lap, breathed slow and steady.

Bones' heavy hands gripped the steering wheel. Jackson followed the old gangster's gaze to the dusty stretch of road ahead. Rows of butter and carrot-colored buildings, once homes with ornate window treatments, now wore unlit neon signs that touted cheap booze and naked women.

"Where the hell are we?" Jackson worked his tongue around in his mouth, brain itching for a vape of Strawberry Fields or Banana Sunshine. Hell, at this point, he'd even go for a hit of Winter Cherry, which everyone agreed tasted the way glass cleaner smelled.

"El Paso-Juarez," Bones said, without looking over.

"Mex?" Jackson blinked slowly. "Or Tex?"

"We left the Free State of Texas a while back," Bones said. "You were sleepin'. Huge checkpoint. Dogs sniffed around the car and everything."

"Too uptight for me," Jackson said, shaking his head.

Bones shrugged. "Texans are serious about their sovereignty."

"Place still uses paper money, has a state government and militarized police and shit." Jackson rubbed at his eye-booger-crusted sockets. "Same right-wing geekbags that attacked D.C. to *take the country back*, but then fucked everything up when part of their own mob took out Washington D.C. with a MOAB." Jackson swiped a knife-hand through the air and laughed. "Slayed everyone and everything."

"Sure," Bones said. "Still, FST reminds me of the good ol' days."

"When you ate brontosaurus steaks?" Jackson side-eyed Bones. "And you pedaled your stone car with your feet?"

"You know *The Flintstones?*"

"It's on the net, man." Jackson rolled his eyes. "Everything is. You'd know that if you came out of the dark ages."

Bones showed the hairy back of his hand. "My old man would've clapped me a good one for talkin' the way you do."

"I ain't got an old man," Jackson said.

"Hell, yeah, you do," Bones said. "That little shrine in your mom's house. The one you took the gun from."

Jackson swallowed and clutched the rucksack a little closer. Neko wriggled on top, but didn't wake.

Dad's desk. His mom hadn't let anyone touch it—not that anyone came to the house. But she insisted that *James wasn't coming back.* Jackson had given up trying to understand. The memories of an eight-year-old were muddled. The silhouette of the man's face. His smile.

That mole.

Had Dad run off to join Anja Kuhn's cult? The thought left an odd hole in the pit of Jackson's stomach, which turned into a grumble.

"Hey, I didn't mean to …" Bones started.

"I'm hungry," Jackson announced. "And thirsty."

Bones studied Jackson, then Neko. The kitten stretched the length of Jackson's thighs.

"I'm sure there's a bit of old burger lying around under the seat," Bones said with a thin smile.

Jackson smirked.

Bones eased down a street past a skeletonized church, its bell lying on a kudzu-choked lawn. Save the dry wind howling between candy-colored brickwork, the roads were quiet and devoid of life or traffic. Not even a stray dog roamed the trash-strewn, overgrown sidewalks.

"Where's all the water at?" Jackson asked.

"It's a desert," Bones said. "You've read about those on your internets, right?"

Jackson pulled at his face and groaned.

"I'll find a place, just gimme a minute," Bones said. "You missing your frozen yogurt treat or something?"

Jackson flipped Bones the bird, then opened the phone Hellcat had given him.

One new message sat in the encrypted app. He pressed *Open*, and an image appeared onscreen. A tall white man with bony hands wore a crisp white shirt and sharp black tie. The distorted picture imbued the man with a terrible, ghoulish appearance.

Hellcat's voice boomed from the tiny speaker, and Jackson almost dropped the phone. Neko dug his claws into Jackson's lap, then fell into the footwell and lay there, heaving tiny, exhausted breaths. Bones barked to turn the volume down. Jackson smothered the speaker with his palm and thumbed the volume key until the decibels had reached tolerable levels.

He dragged the audio note back to the beginning and let it play.

"So, first of all, bravo on the checkpoint in St. Louis," Hellcat began. "You just jumped up a couple places on the slaysites. Way to stay off the grid." The sound of her slow clapping rattled the speaker.

Jackson coughed into his hand.

"Anyway, love, check this out—that Svanire guy," Hellcat said, her voice an octave higher than usual. "His name literally means vanish, so this is the best image I've gotten. He went into your house and picked around looking for … well, who knows what."

"No way," Jackson said. He paused the audio and held the phone out to Bones. "This him? This your guy?"

Bones squinted, then nodded. "That's the Squid."

"Squid?" Jackson asked.

Bones let go of the steering wheel to waggle his arms like a giant cephalopod. "Thinks he's some kind of dancer."

Jackson curled up a derisive nostril.

"You actually got a picture?" Bones glanced over again. "I've never seen a photo of him, ever."

"Hellcat did," Jackson said.

Bones bobbed his head. "She's a resourceful one."

"But dude was in my house, man," Jackson said. "Messing around after we left. I don't like it." He shook his head and pressed *play*.

"Latest intel indicates this Svanire guy might also be making a power play against the other factions of La Nueva Cosa Nostra," Hellcat said.

"If he's able to do that, then he could take on the Triads or the Yakuza or the Sureños, next. Topple them one by one. He's hard-jacked into every CCTV and all the surveillance drones, so we can't use them. I've scythed every device I can find just to see if he shows up—still nothing. Guy is a damn ghost."

"She's right," Bones said, then curved the car down another deserted street.

"He's got all kinds of tech—not a Lenser mask, but all kinds," Hellcat said. "I mean, I've scythed every cell device in the damn city using the Pegasus upgrade I gave you."

Jackson slapped his palm to his forehead. "That's how she did it. Not onsite," he said. "She scythed people's tech. For her news stories."

Bones grumbled something, but Jackson hushed him with an upheld finger.

"Svanire's camo-tech doesn't just mess with his face, but his gait, everything," Hellcat continued. "Can't even track his movements. I'd need a serious global network and some next-level computing power to rebuild this guy. I'll try to figure out his next move. Be in touch soon, stake."

The audio message stopped.

"We'd need access to, like, every piece of surveillance on the planet," Jackson muttered to himself. "To see everywhere, so this bastard can't hide …"

"Too much for the master hacker? Can't crack a blockchain?" Bones said.

"First off, I'm a cryptokiller, not a hacker, man," Jackson fired back. "What is this, the 1990s? It's called *scything*. Second of all, *blockchain*? Did you just read that word on the back of a cereal box?" He shook his head. "Blockchain is old school. Only dumbasses use it. Every bit of data on every computer has to be stored on a particular network. It's called global consensus—totally flawed and inefficient."

"Even the cat's bored," Bones said, and pointed at Neko yawning in the footwell.

"New network chains function different." Jackson stuffed the phone into his hoodie pocket and grabbed the kitten. "Data goes from person to person. A geekbag on the other side of the world doesn't need to store all of your transactions and data. It's an agent-centric approach. Totally more efficient, with even less centralized control."

"They look like trouble," Bones said, eyes now fixed on three teens huddled around a streetlamp, who hooted their approval as one kid danced and waved chromed-out .45s above his head.

"Hey, old man." Jackson raised his voice. "I'm dropping knowledge, here."

Bones flicked his attention back to Jackson. "You were talking?"

"Do I need to break out the crayons and draw you a picture?"

Bones sniffed hard. "Nobody's gonna be making jokes if Svanire catches up with us."

"Don't know why I bother," Jackson said.

Bones checked the busted side mirror. "You ever figure out why ol' Squiddy is after you in the first place?"

"I dunno, man," Jackson said with a shrug. "Not enough data. Yet."

"Think." Bones tapped on his temple with a sausage finger. "What was your last job?"

"I got chucked off my last job." Jackson threw his hands in the air. "Some amateur took out half of New York just to slay one programmer."

"Okay, so the last job you *actually* did," Bones said. "You know—whose eyes did you close?"

"Oh," Jackson said with a frown. "Hmmm …"

Bones' craggy face twisted up more than usual. "You don't *know?*"

"They're just usernames most of the time, man." Jackson stroked the kitten's bony frame. "They have an IP address and I get a drone, or someone close by, to hit them. I might route the job to a proxy in Rwanda, say, who does it for a fraction of a coin, and I don't have to get my hands dirty. I do that mainly if the hit is in Chicago or Illinois—close to home. Depends, though, you know?"

Bones flexed his fingers around the steering wheel. "Yeah, I guess I do."

"Look, man," Jackson groaned, "I think my last job was some dickhead called CasperRasper. A pedo out of Philly who ran a child trafficking ring."

Or so he'd been told. Truth was, Casper could have lived as a monk in celibacy. Jackson didn't do too much digging. Never a good idea. Just enough info to slay the mark, collect the coin, and move on. Casper had lived far enough away, with so little human contact, that Jackson could slay the guy himself. A claymore in a box of Casper's favorite donuts. Sprinkles, frosting, and bits of CasperRasper had splattered his porch on a warm Saturday morning in Washington Square West.

The Kia screeched to a stop at the curb, jolting Jackson from his thoughts. He grabbed Neko, who mewed and nearly fell back between Jackson's feet.

"What the hell, man?" Jackson stroked the kitten's back to calm it.

Bones pointed out the windshield. "Water."

Jackson frowned at a neon green sign that strobed an ad for *Girls, Girls, Girls*. "We're going to get water in *there*?"

"If you count the ice in my bourbon, maybe." Bones yanked on the car door handle and stepped out. He wedged the fedora onto his head, slammed the door shut with a metallic clang, and stomped around the Kia toward the club.

A powerful gust of wind clattered sand across the Kia's windows. Jackson chewed at a fleshy hangnail. "Screw it," he whispered. "You stay here, Neko." He placed the kitten and the rucksack in the footwell, pushed the door open, and climbed out. He clicked the door shut, careful to make sure Neko wasn't in the way.

The bar ahead—just like Jackson's favorite shrimp joint—stood obscured behind thick vines, leaves, and purple pods. Only, instead of the delicious scent of deep-fried crustaceans, the stink of piss and cheap alcohol clogged the air.

Bones stooped down and disappeared behind a row of rusted choppers. Jackson shuffled around the broken-down motorcycles. In the gutter, an emaciated corpse—its jaw open, twisted and buzzing with flies—stared up at the morning sky. A catheter protruded from a blackened vein in the papery crease of its elbow.

"Damn junkie," Bones murmured. "Look at him."

Jackson shook his head. "Nah, man, he's a juicer."

"Steroids?" Bones studied the corpse's weedy frame. "I don't think so."

Jackson hocked a laugh. "No, an *actual* juicer." He dug at the red dirt with his fingers and followed the catheter until he reached a dried-up husk of a grapefruit. "It's a thing, man. All over the web. Can't get medicine, dose yourself with Vitamin C."

"Like this?" Bones asked, then stood with an old man's groan and covered his nose.

"Not everyone can afford the fancy bags of C from a drug corp." Jackson threw the shriveled fruit, which bounced off one of the choppers and skipped across the dirt. "Some kid posted this on BingOn and, course, now these idiots are dying from infections."

Bones shook his square head. "This is what I'm talkin' about. There used to be an FDA to stop this sort of bull squeeze."

"Your old ass is forgetting," Jackson said. "Folks were self-medicating back when old guys like you controlled everything because no one trusted them." He rolled his eyes. "When are you gonna get it, man? Control stopped ingenuity."

"It stopped people from dying, too," Bones said, "from taking stuff that wasn't tested by a professional who studied medicine his whole damn life."

"Blah blah blah." Jackson puppeted the words with his hands. "Only medicine that turned a profit got made. Not enough patients to make money from selling it? Don't make the drug. Can't sell the drug for much money? Don't make the drug. Now a good idea *alone* can go viral. Get support from all over the world, crowdfunded by coin. No red tape, no barriers."

Bones waved at the corpse. "An' shit like this happens."

Jackson shrugged. "But freedom from big corps who just sell my data to pseudo-fascist regimes hiding behind rigged democracy means I get cell service from a guy who built his own satellites, earned the coin to launch them, and set up a secure network free from Bill Musk's eyes wanting to see when I take a shit."

Jackson and Bones pushed through the bar door into a murky room full of dense cigar smoke and the source of the piss stink he'd registered outside. Unkempt men sat like gargoyles on tall stools at a bar with no bartender, all focused on a stage off to the left. A bedraggled woman with meth sores gyrated on a pole, a bright red thong tucked under her paunch. She tossed around bad hair extensions and shook breasts that looked like a couple of socks, each stuffed with a billiard ball.

"Eugh," Jackson said, unable to look away.

"You don't like girls?" Bones asked.

"That ain't a girl, bro." Jackson squinted one eye. "She got an ass like an old orange."

"You mean, she's a real person?" Bones studied the twirling woman.

Jackson blinked away the grotesque image. "Strippers don't look like that."

Joe laughed. "Hell, yeah, they do. All but the high-dollar ones. None of your fancy filters and AI in real life." He nodded to the bar. "C'mon. Water, remember?"

Jackson pulled his gaze from the stripper's jiggling meat curtain, swallowed back the bile in his throat, and followed Joe to the old wooden bar.

A few bulbs hung from the ceiling to barely illuminate the regulars. Bones stood between an obese gargoyle with tattoos where his hair should be and a cowboy in a red flannel shirt. Another gargoyle in a paper wolf mask sat hunched two seats down. All three men kept their attention on the world's ugliest pole dancer.

A man with long straight black hair tied back and hairy forearms popped up from behind the counter. He eyed Bones before settling on Jackson. "No kids," he said, words heavy on the vowels, the waxed ends of his thick mustache twitching.

"He's with me," Bones said. "Just need a drink. Bottled water for the k—uh, my friend here—and a glass of bourbon on the rocks for me."

"He got any BrainStorm?" Jackson whispered.

"Look at this place." The bartender grunted. "Does it look like I sell bourbon, rich man?"

Bones' eyes narrowed.

After a dead cold stare, the barman trudged away then came back and slammed down a pathetic jug of water. He pulled a dusty bottle of brown liquor from under the counter and poured a swallow into a tumbler, then tipped the water jug and splashed a few mouthfuls into a dingy glass.

Joe balked. "Tap water? You want him to get sick or somethin'?"

"Drink it or don't," the bartender said, palms resting on the bar. His thick mustache twitched. "Tap water and rotgut is what we got. Five hundred Zip Coin."

Bones raised an eyebrow.

Jackson pulled out his phone and opened a trading platform. "I'm thirsty," he said. "I'll take my chances, but I don't got any Zip." He rattled through a conversion estimate. "Five hundred?"

"That a lot?" Bones asked.

Jackson waved his device in the gangster's face. "Like, I could buy a top-of-the-line e-bike from Streetblädz for that. And those guys are the shit. Darren, the CEO, man, he's a legend. He's like twelve, but he set up out of his gara—"

Joe's face darkened. "You trying to screw me?" he asked the barman.

The gargoyles shuffled in their seats and pulled their attention from the pole dancer.

"El Paso-Juarez city tax," the barman said.

"I think," Bones sucked at his teeth, "you see a couple of out-of-towners and think you're gonna make a few coins off us. That's what I think."

"Oh yeah?" the bartender growled. "Well, *I think* you and your little twink boyfriend here can—"

Joe held up his hand, his eyes hard. "Now, don't go saying something you're gonna regret, pal."

Jackson's eyes grew wide and the gargoyles climbed off their stools. Even the stripper stopped rubbing her flaccid bits on the greasy pole.

"You know what?" Bones shooed Jackson away from the counter. "We'll find a drink somewhere else."

"You ain't leaving 'til you paid up," the barman said, and pointed at the two glasses beside the dusty brown bottle.

Bones stared at the barman for a moment, removed his fedora and suit jacket, and placed them on the bar. "Fair point." He rolled up his shirtsleeves and knocked back the glass of rotgut in one gulp. Without looking, he used a heavy hand to shove Jackson in the chest.

Jackson stumbled back and crashed into a chair, then rolled on the sticky bar floor and under a table.

The old gangster threw the empty tumbler with pinpoint accuracy and hit the barman square in the nose. Blood poured over his waxy mustache, and he stumbled back. His outstretched arms raked a row of shot glasses onto the floor.

The gargoyles descended on Bones from both sides. He stomped Wolf Mask in the groin.

Wolf Mask howled and dropped to his knees.

Red Flannel grabbed the chair Jackson had toppled and swung it hard.

Bones ducked low and threw a hammer-like fist into Red Flannel's solar plexus, which sent him tumbling into Jackson's hiding place. The table splintered and Jackson scrambled on hands and knees to avoid being crushed. Red Flannel lay unconscious in a pile of wood splinters.

Bones stood, shoulders heaving. "Who else?" He held up two meaty fists.

The barman fumbled against the counter and disappeared through a partition into the back, leaving his customers to take on Chicago's scariest old-school hitman.

The bald tattooed guy stormed up behind Bones. Brass knuckles gleamed on a closed fist.

"Bones, look out!" Jackson yelled, too late.

Tattoo punched Bones behind the ear, hard. The old hitman fell against the bar. Blood streamed from his hairline, the collar of his dusty white shirt now red.

Bones' hand closed on the neck of the bottle of rotgut. He swung it in a huge arc and straight into Tattoo's fat face. The sweaty biker rocked, then his knees buckled. Bones whipped the bottle under Tattoo's chin, and the solid impact opened a deep gash in his fleshy neck. Bones grasped Tattoo by the shirt collar and struck him in the face again and again until the bottle cracked and his face pulped into a soggy red mess.

"Yeah!" Jackson yelled from the floor, his shout cut short as hands closed around his ankles and dragged him toward the stage.

Jackson flipped onto his back. The pruned face of the stripper screamed at him. Dark blue eye shadow framed bloodshot eyes. Jackson screamed back, high pitched and hysterical, as the dancer—her sock-breasts swinging—dug into him with acrylic nails. Jackson grabbed one tit, yanked hard, and she shrieked. His free hand seized a tangle of hair extensions which he jerked so violently the stripper rolled across the tacky floor. Jackson leaped up and kicked her in the ribs. The stripper's eyes bulged from their sockets, and she curled into the fetal position.

Jackson stepped over the scraggly dancer and shuffled around the still-out-cold Red Flannel gargoyle. "Bones! Bones!" he called. "What now?"

A concussive blast shook the room—tiles and debris shattered across the floor.

Joe sucked at the air; fists still raised. Wolf Mask clutched at his groin. Tattoo lay dead in a spreading pool of blood, and the stripper groaned.

Jackson followed the echo of the blast to the partition, and a three-foot-long, neon-pink penis clutched in the barman's hands. Smoke snaked from the oversized hole in the glans. The barman worked the gun's pump action.

"What the hell is *that*?" Bones said, lowering his fists.

"It's a gun!" said Jackson, frown deep and hands up.

"Nobody move, assholes," the barman shouted, blood caked thick in his mustache.

"No way," Bones said between stuttered breaths.

"A shotgun," Jackson said, backing away. "Free plans all over the net. Just 3D-print it."

"And make it look like ... like ... *that*?" Bones motioned to the luminous phallic blunderbuss with its pair of jiggling testicles.

"I said don't move!" the barman yelled, and pivoted the weapon, its testicles swinging.

"Just put it down." Bones took one step toward the barman, then another.

The bartender bared blood-covered teeth. "I said—"

"Yeah, I heard you." Bones slapped the giant penis head to the side and the gun discharged into the wall, sending wood and brickwork flying.

Bones clasped the pink member in both hands, wrenched it away from the barkeep, and stroked another round into the chamber. He leveled the blunderbuss at the barman's face, pushed the end in the guy's mouth, and pulled the trigger. The shotgun penis flashed and the barman's skull exploded against the back of the bar.

Bones shook the penis gun at the beaten gargoyles. "Had enough? 'Cause I'm feelin' frisky."

Jackson blurted out a laugh, then covered his mouth.

"No? Good." Bones grabbed the glass of water and a bar rag and marched over to Jackson.

"Dad joke, but funny." Jackson took the glass and slugged back a gulp of the water.

Bones pressed the rag to the cut the brass knuckles had left at the base of his skull. "You good?"

Jackson nodded and took another gulp.

"Save some for the cat," Bones said, then threw the phallic-shaped weapon onto a cluttered table and limped for the door.

CHAPTER EIGHTEEN
Anja

Flanked by two armed guards, Anja hovered in the doorway to Tarasp Castle's makeshift medical center. Inside, six beds made with pristine white sheets contrasted against water-stained stone blocks. A narrow window in the castle wall guided in a blade of light that cut across the first bed with its peeping heart monitor—and Tabea's limp form.

Anja waved for the guards to leave and closed the door behind them. "Hey," she called into the room, her voice barely audible.

Tabea looked up. Her trembling fingers gathered the cotton bedding tucked snugly around her legs.

Silence, save the rhythmic *peep* of the heart monitor.

Anja bit her lip. "How are you, Tabea?"

"You know ..." Tabea said, finally, as she studied her ruffled bedclothes. "My mom used to show me old movies ... like, from those old Hollywood studios. Before ... before it was cheaper to crowdfund some influencer to make something no one cares about." She tried to shuffle into a more comfortable position, but winced and gave up.

"Is that so?" Anja considered sitting in the nineteenth-century wheelchair parked in the corner, its eggshell-colored canvas stretched over a slim metal frame, but she changed her mind. "I must say, in Switzerland we're never very good at knowing what's popular on the international stage."

"In Germany, we are." Tabea sniffed and drew her forearm across her wet nose. "You ever watch one?"

Anja sat at the foot of Tabea's gurney, the foam mattress so thin she could feel the metal springs groan underneath. "Can't say I have."

"I loved the sad ones, you know?" Tabea looked away to the slender opening to the outside, a blue sky peeking through. "If it made me cry, even better."

"Sometimes a good cry helps the soul," Anja replied, slipping her hand across the sheets into the warm ray of sunshine. "At least, that's what my mother said."

A bird flapped past the window.

"They're always so peaceful," Tabea said, her stare fixed on the cloudless horizon.

"Peaceful?"

"When they die," Tabea whispered. "In the movies. When they know they're going to die ... they become peaceful. They say goodbye to those they love and tell them not to grieve. They're so brave and ... magnanimous."

Anja pursed her lips. "Well, I suppo—"

"They lied." Tears welled in Tabea's eyes, building until they tumbled down her red cheeks. "The movies don't show how it really feels." She hacked a raspy cough.

Words formed in Anja's throat, but never made it past her lips.

Tabea bared her teeth. "I'm not ready to die, Anja. I haven't lived, haven't loved. I've never had a man touch me." Anja flinched. "Never swam in the ocean or tasted champagne. It's not fair!" Tabea grabbed the bed sheets and ripped them away. "And it's your fault!" she screamed, sputum hanging from her lip. "*You* did this to me."

"Tabea," Anja said, shrinking away. "I'm sorry, but I warn everyone not to touch the plants, especially—"

"You're *sorry?*" Tabea bawled. "You created this poison. You owe *me!*" Tabea jabbed at her own chest with two fingers.

"*Owe* you?" Anja pushed herself off the bed and backed away. "What do I owe you? Coin?"

"Who needs coin when they're dead?" Tabea asked. "No, I want ... I want ... The Solution."

Anja's brow knitted.

"Anja ..." Tabea's voice cracked, and more tears fell. "It burns me inside ... it's not my time.

"I don't want to die like this!" she cried. "You can stop it."

A tightness grew in Anja's chest, and her heart fluttered. Tabea held her gaze, eyes full of expectation. "I can't do that," Anja said.

"Yes, you can." Tabea's bottom lip quivered. "We're all going to get it, anyway. Don't make me beg."

Indecision swarmed Anja's mind, if only for a moment. She stood and crossed the room to the wheelchair. She pushed it over to Tabea's cot, then rounded the bed frame and switched off the heart monitor. "Quickly," Anja hissed, stripping Tabea of the wires.

Tabea shuffled, grimacing and moaning, to the end of the gurney.

Anja rounded the bed, grabbed Tabea as tightly as possible, and lowered her into the wheelchair. Without another word, she opened the door and pushed Tabea out into the corridor. The hard tires of the wheelchair rattled on the rough stone floor. Anja made for the bell tower.

Hans marched down the passageway. "Ms. Kuhn," he said, his usual sour expression fermented into a full scowl. "We've not heard from Marcel. You're going to need him to—"

"Not now," Anja said without slowing. "I'll deal with that shortly."

Hans held up his palms as they passed each other. "But—"

Anja pushed on, then used Tabea's knees to open a door into the bell tower stairwell. "Come on," Anja said, and tried to pull Tabea up by the arm. "I'll help you down."

Anja ducked her head under Tabea's arm to help the young woman from the wheelchair. They fell into the banister, Anja's hip taking the brunt of the impact. Still supporting Tabea's lame body and using the banister as support, she struggled down the cold spiral steps one at a time.

Lungs heavy, skin damp, Anja reached the bottom and dragged Tabea along the passageway to the large door to her lab. After another struggle with an iron key, they pushed inside the room and hobbled toward a transparent vivarium the same size as the garden greenhouse Anja had once owned.

"In here," she said, then pressed her thumb to a keypad embedded in the glass wall. A door popped open under pressure, releasing a fine mist. She eased Tabea to the tender, grassy soil. "Just stay there, it'll be over soon," Anja said between deep breaths. She clicked the clear door shut, and a hiss ensured a positive seal.

Anja closed her eyes and pressed her forehead to the warm glass vivarium wall that dulled Tabea's sobs. She wished the darkness behind her eyelids were another world, free from pain and duty.

Tabea's wailing inside the vivarium grew louder and forced Anja back to reality. Tabea had curled into a ball on the sodden grass, fingers entwined in a mat of vines with broad, heart-shaped leaves and purple pods. Anja pulled back her gaze to the dried, bloody smears on the inside of the transparent vivarium wall.

Finally, her own reflection came into focus. Tired eyes looked back out of dark circles; her likeness judgmental. "Nearly done," she whispered to herself.

Tabea convulsed, her howling uncontrollable. "I don't want to die!" she screamed into the climate-controlled air.

Anja turned away, sniffed back tears, and headed to the control console between her rat experiment and the vivarium.

A bloodbath of intestines and half-eaten corpses littered the sawdust-covered floor of the rat enclosure. Ralph swayed from side to side in the shadows, black eyes in a white face fixed on some imaginary foe. Anja swallowed. He'd survived this Ratpocalypse, but at what cost? She twisted back to the control console, keyed up the test protocol, and studied the system-ready checks. Onscreen, the closed-circuit diagram comprising a power source, the conductive pathway, and the vivarium lit up green.

A message popped up: *Do you wish to stimulate the root network?*

Anja's finger hovered over the *Yes* button.

She followed the path of the power cable from the console along the floor and under the vivarium wall into the earth on which Tabea lay. *Do it, Anja.* She pressed the key.

A timer appeared: thirty seconds. Twenty-nine, twenty-eight, twenty-seven ...

Anja stepped over to the vivarium and placed both hands on the glass wall. "It's done, Tabea," she said. "It'll soon be over."

Tabea unfurled from her fetal position and looked up.

"You remember how this goes, right?" Anja said.

Tabea sniveled and nodded.

"The electrical impulse will stimulate the root network that connects the plants." The mechanical task of explaining how The

Solution worked somehow gave Anja a renewed strength of purpose.

"I'm scared." Tabea sobbed, then spasmed, kicking clods of dirt to splatter the vivarium wall. "Wait, Ms. Kuhn ... Anja ... Anja, let me out."

Anja shook her head and took a step back from the glass.

"Let me out, I changed my mind." Tabea screamed and clawed at the soil.

"Almost there, Tabea," Anja said, her mind now locked into the sequence of events.

"No, no, no ..." Tabea moaned, and rolled onto her back, filthy hands over her face.

"The impulse will ... will activate the dormant DNA ... just in the way I designed," Anja stuttered. The computer began the final countdown aloud. "Immediately, the pods will release the altered pollen," Anja said. "They rupture. Do you remember, Tabea? They rupture a bit like *Ecballium*."

"Anja!" Tabea, now on all fours, screamed long and loud.

"Three ... two ... one," the computer said.

A low hum sounded, then, inside the vivarium, the purple pods detonated like firecrackers, one by one releasing a black smog that filled the enclosure.

Tabea coughed and grasped at her own throat as the particles filled her mouth and nostrils. She screamed; her bloodshot eyes wild. She beat on the glass and scraped at it with her fingernails until they broke and ripped from her flesh.

"It'll be over soon," Anja said, tears in her eyes. "Just a little longer."

Tabea threw herself at the barrier, splitting the skin of her forehead. Anja reeled.

One last primal shriek, then Tabea slumped into the mud.

The smog dissipated and a series of extraction fans in the ceiling of the tank clicked on, purifying the air.

Silence settled over the lab. Anja waited, fingers fiddling with her scarf.

"Tabea?" Anja whispered, crouching down to see better. "Tabea?"

Eyes fluttering, Tabea turned her head toward the glass wall. "I'm fine," she said. She sat up, and a drip of blood ran from the gash in her forehead down her nose and across her slight smile.

The console behind Anja beeped in repetition.

She stood and sauntered over to the screen.

Activate trial motivation? the message read.

With another heavy exhalation, Anja pressed *Yes.*

Speakers within the vivarium blared—voices screamed insults in rapid succession.

"You're a useless whore," one screamed.

"Fuck your pathetic life, ugly-ass pig," another bawled.

"Your whole family is racist—you'd be better off dead!"

The onslaught continued—not a moment's reprieve in between. Each and every affront more horrific than the last, designed to hack through even the toughest of skins.

Tabea didn't respond, instead sat on the grass with her little smirk and blood dripping off her chin.

Two circles slid open in the vivarium's ceiling to allow thin robotic arms to reach down, and fire blue arcs of electricity zapped across her skin.

"Hey," Tabea said, vaguely amused. "Come on, cut that out."

The arms withdrew and the circles above closed.

Anja checked the console to confirm decontamination, then stepped over to the vivarium and unsealed the door open with a press of her thumb. She dropped into the mud, littered with burst pods, and stared at Tabea, who stared back. Anja reached out to stroke Tabea's face—then slapped her as hard as she could.

Tabea's head jerked and blood spattered the green blades of grass.

"You're going to die, Tabea, and it's my fault!" Anja tried to shout but choked on the words. "It's my fault, do you hear me?" She swallowed away the dryness in her throat. "You'll never experience life. I took that from you!"

"It's okay," Tabea said, and broke into a goofy smile. "I can't change any of that."

Anja released a long sigh, then shuffled behind Tabea, slid her arms around the woman's thin waist, and pulled her close. "No, you can't, but you get to die without rage in your heart," Anja whispered. "It's been purged from you. Just like it'll be purged from us all."

Tabea tilted her head back to peer into Anja's eyes, a crooked smile on the dying woman's face as blood snaked from the wound in her forehead and dripped from the end of her nose.

CHAPTER NINETEEN
Joe

Joe sat on the curb of the deserted Zap station, waiting for the beat-up blue Kia to finish charging. Overhead, a waxing crescent moon hung low and yellow, and distant stars glimmered across the purple-black expanse. A pleasant breeze stirred the twisted branches of the flowering jacaranda trees. Beneath the mismatched tangerine and sterile white lights of the ramshackle shops and cantinas, slump-shouldered farmers and tired street vendors rattled their wares in carts over uneven cobblestones.

The light on top of the Zap terminal switched from red to green. With a grunt, Joe dragged himself to his feet, the pain in his leg now familiar. He lumbered to the charging cable, pulled it from the Kia's connection port, and hung it back up. A message popped up on the display, showing a fee of over four thousand coin for the Zap charge.

"You got this?" Joe said.

Jackson lay reclined on a bench, staring at his phone. "What coin do they want?"

Joe squinted at the display. "Maya Coin?"

Jackson made a retching sound. "Let me convert something with actual value."

"Convert extra, if that's how they wanna get paid around here," Joe said.

Jackson tapped on his phone, rolled off the bench, and sauntered over. Neko's fuzzy head poked from the hoodie pocket and bobbed with Jackson's gait. He held up his digital wallet and the Zap terminal blipped.

"Where's here, anyway?" Jackson stuffed his phone back into his pocket.

"Antigua, Guatemala."

"Another shithole, backwoods town. How much farther?" Jackson asked. "To Bitcoin City?"

"Seven hours, but I won't make it tonight." Joe watched a stray dog with bony ribs and hungry eyes trot across the far corner of the lot and disappear into the undergrowth.

"I can drive," Jackson said.

"No, you can't."

Jackson scowled. "There's no law about it. So why not?"

"Because I value my life." Joe chuckled. "Come on. There's a hotel just down the way."

Jackson pointed to the car. "We just gonna leave it here?"

Joe popped the trunk and gestured inside. "The important stuff goes with us. We need this ugly bastard, but it's a bullseye. If someone comes looking—"

"I got you." Jackson held up his hands.

Joe pulled a duffel bag from the trunk and left his heavy coat and fedora in place. He slung the duffel over his shoulder, then grabbed the Diora Brass trumpet case and elbowed the trunk shut.

"Ooh," Jackson said. "Get ready to wet your panties, ladies. The old man is breaking out the brass."

"Stow it, Jackson." Joe limped ahead.

With a snicker, Jackson slipped on his rucksack and followed along. He reached into the hoodie's pocket and extracted Neko. Jackson placed him on his shoulder where the little cat perched, bobbing and swaying like a parrot. "Ow, hey, chill with the claws, bro," Jackson said. He reached up and stroked the back of his hand along the kitten's tiny, ribbed flank. Neko mewed.

From the edge of town, they wound their way into a warren of quaint cobblestone streets and Spanish colonial structures toward the city center. Simple shops and cafés lined the street in an unending row, differentiated only by changes in color, from lemon to seafoam to cherry to peach. Joe gave a little tip of his hat as they passed the Iglesia de la Merced and the exquisite baroque statues set into her canary façade.

"That old church still looks alive and well," Joe mused.

"Must be off grid or something," Jackson said.

Joe trudged on and cut the corner onto Avenida Norte. The lane passed straight as an arrow through the heart of town and beneath the

Santa Catalina Arch, where a few stubborn street vendors had yet to pack up their wares. In the distance, lit by the pale-yellow moon, the smoke-shrouded and majestic Volcan de Fuego brooded.

"Hello," said a señorita with jet black hair. She floated from her mat beneath the Arch and walked as if on a cushion of air, her sandaled feet hardly touching the stones. She'd tied a beautiful sash around her waist. A kaleidoscope of colorful thread, the sash rocked with the sway of her hips. She passed Joe and approached Jackson with a genuine smile, another multicolored sash tangled in her fingers.

Joe slowed and eyed the girl. Jackson seemed anchored to the spot.

"You are staying here? At the convento?" she asked.

"Uh …" Jackson looked warily at Joe.

"Sure," Joe said.

The señorita seemed to glow, her sun-bronzed skin radiant. She looped the sash around Jackson's neck and kissed him on the cheek with pillowy lips, then extended a finger and tickled Neko under his chin.

Jackson swallowed. He touched his cheek.

Neko snuggled into the sash.

"For luck," the señorita said, and winked.

"Oh … okay … ah … thanks? Gracias …" Jackson stammered.

Joe shuffled over to get a closer look at her, the corners of his mouth teasing upward. "You're good. How much for the threads?"

The señorita played with her raven hair. "For him?" She touched Jackson's chest. "Five thousand Maya Coin."

"One thousand," Joe said.

"Thirty-five hundred," she said.

"Two," Joe said.

"Twenty-five hundred," she said with another genuine smile, "and I give him an actual kiss."

"Sold," Jackson blurted out, a goofy grin fixed on his face.

The señorita produced a digital wallet from beneath the sash at her waist and held it out. Jackson keyed the fee into his device and touched it to hers. A twin chime sounded on the phones. The señorita took a step closer to Jackson, placed her hands on his chest, and kissed him slow on the lips. Jackson touched her hips and gently pulled her against him.

"Okay, lover boy." Joe slapped a hand on Jackson's shoulder. "I think that's enough."

"Bones ..." Jackson said, eyes glassy and full of fire, "you're *ruining* the moment."

The girl pulled free and pressed her wrist to her lips. Her face flushed and the corners of her eyes crinkled in another winter-thawing smile. "Maybe I see you later?"

"Yeah," Jackson said.

"No," Joe said as he pulled Jackson away.

"Yes," Jackson said over Joe's shoulder as he strained against the old man's bulk. "Definitely."

Joe ushered Jackson to a rounded doorway.

A brass plaque read *Hotel Convento Sta. Catalina. Since 1613.* As Joe led him through the entrance, Jackson strained to see his newfound love.

"Whooo!" Jackson called. "Bro ..."

"I know," Joe said. "Come on, before you draw too much attention."

The two stopped at the front desk, checked in under a false name, and followed a plump matron to their room via an open-air walkway of red and yellow tiles. She opened a heavy wooden door and motioned for them to enter. Joe stepped in first and did a quick safety check of the room.

"Bars on the windows. That's good," Joe mumbled.

"Everything is okay, señor?" the woman asked with a tilt of her head.

"Stake." Jackson flopped down on one of the beds, squashing the rucksack beneath him. Neko popped from the sash around Jackson's neck and bobbled onto the end table, where he arched his back and slumped into a lazy sprawl.

"Muchos gracias," Joe fumbled in broken Spanish.

The matronly woman bowed and closed the heavy wood door as she left.

Joe dropped his bag on the red tiles and wilted into a chair with a sigh. "Get some rest. I'll take first watch."

"Rest?" Jackson pulled the sash from his neck and smelled it. "Nah,

I got plans."

"The hell you do." Joe leaned back in the thin-cushioned chair. "We got a major hit on us, remember?"

"But, Bones—I mean, you saw her, right?" Jackson whistled.

"I saw her," Joe said. "She's beautiful. And she'll destroy you."

Jackson pulled his face out of the colorful sash. "No way. Not a chance."

"That's what women do." Joe felt a pinch in his chest as Jackson's usual sour attitude faded behind flushed cheeks and the glow of a life yet lived.

Been a long time since you felt like that, Joe. That's love. The sound of his trumpet filled Joe's mind, five-year-old Charley giggling and clapping along under a tent for Sheila's thirtieth birthday, and the memory stole his breath away.

Joe worked his teeth together.

Jackson looked at him hard. "You okay?"

The horrors of the world will smother the light out of him too, Joe.

"Dammit," Joe said, and slapped the arm of the chair. "Yeah. Come on."

"We going back to see her?" Jackson popped up off the bed as if loaded with springs.

"Just come on." Joe pulled the door open.

"Neko's okay?" Jackson asked and looked around. The kitten rolled on his back, pawing at the bed sheets.

"The shutters are closed," Joe said. "He's not going anywhere."

With the door shut behind them, they walked out to a small open-air café strung with little lights in the center of the hotel. Joe motioned to a table. "Wait here a minute, okay?"

"Sure, Bones." Jackson took a seat and dumped his rucksack on the table.

"You hungry?" Joe asked.

Jackson rubbed his belly.

Joe hobbled across the courtyard past a bubbling stone fountain and wandered into the kitchen uninvited. A moment later he emerged with a couple of bottled beers and a plate of small bean and cheese soft tacos.

Behind him, the plump matron filled the doorway to the kitchen, wiping her hands on a towel.

"There you go." Joe set the plate of tacos down and took a seat.

Jackson shoved one of the little tacos whole into his mouth and made a *Mmmm* sound as he chewed.

Joe pushed a beer in front of Jackson.

"Yeah?" Jackson asked around a mouth full of the second taco.

"You ever had one?"

Jackson shook his head. "Mom … she didn't let me drink."

Joe popped the top off his own beer, a brown bottle marked *Gallo* which displayed the head of a rooster. "She was a good person, and she loved you." He leveled his gaze at Jackson. "But you told me yourself—you ain't a kid no more."

Jackson worked the cap off his bottle.

"Here's to your mom." Joe held his beer out.

Jackson swallowed the beans and cheese and seemed to think a moment before raising his bottle. "And your sister and nephew."

Joe cleared his throat. "Good folks. All of 'em. Worth remembering."

They clinked the bottle necks together and each took a long slug. Jackson held the mouthful a little too long, his eyes scrunched up, but swallowed.

Joe chuckled and took another drink.

Jackson appraised the bottle and took a smaller sip. He touched the kaleidoscope of threads bunched around his neck.

Joe drummed his fingers on the table while Jackson seemed to search the restaurant for anything to look at other than Joe's eyes.

"You gonna tell me what's in there?" Joe motioned to Jackson's rucksack.

Jackson took another sip of his beer, then set it down. He looked at the rucksack, then Joe, and back again.

"You take it everywhere," Joe added.

Jackson pulled the bag close, unzipped it, and rummaged inside until finally he inched out an old photo. He slid it across the table to Joe and hid behind his beer.

Joe eyed the handsome features of the man who looked so much like Jackson.

"Don't know why I keep it," Jackson mumbled.

"Because he's your dad." Joe passed the picture back. "Simple as that."

Jackson slipped the photo back into his rucksack.

Joe took another swig. A rumble sounded in the distance, followed by a *pop*. "Hey, how 'bout that?" Joe pointed.

Bright orange magma burst from the crest of a distant volcano and sailed into the midnight sky. A river of fire crept in slow motion down the mountainside, the slope lit by the smoke-tinged moon.

"Wow," Jackson said. "Epic. Perhaps not a shit-hole town after all …"

Joe kept his eyes on the distant eruption. "Fuego is one of the most active volcanoes in the world." He shrugged. "At least, that's what I heard. What do I know?"

"More than most Gen—," Jackson said and grinned. "More than me."

"I dunno about that, buddy. You're pretty sharp." Joe stuffed a taco into his mouth.

Jackson smirked, but the look faded to seriousness. He rotated the beer bottle between his fingers. "Tell me something straight up, Bones."

Joe set his empty bottle down, chewing.

"Why didn't you do it?" Jackson said. "For real?"

"Do what?" Joe asked as the smoking lava flowed down the mountain.

Jackson nursed his mostly full beer. "You could've slayed me when you came to my house. Easy. Your life wouldn't have missed a beat."

"And your life would've ended."

"Yeah," Jackson scowled, "but you didn't know me. Why not kill me?"

Joe swallowed a bolus of taco. He chased it with a swig of beer. "Killin' should have rules. And there ain't rules no more. And … then one day you get asked to do somethin' you know ain't right."

Jackson studied Joe with genuine interest.

"Right before you," Joe said. "The Family ordered me to take out one of our own …" he said, "… and his little girl."

"Damn." Jackson leaned back in his chair.

"The boss ordered the hit anyway," Joe said, a meaty finger picking at the label of his beer. "But that never made sense, because the boss is a good man. He wouldn't …" Joe shook his head. "Anyway, they were pissed I didn't do it their way. You were my redemption job." He rolled his eyes. "My way back into the Don's good graces."

Jackson rubbed at the back of his head.

"I figured it's time for a change. Too much blood." Joe held up his hands. The beer made his head a little lighter and pushed his emotions a little closer to the surface. "Maybe something else is going on. The whole setup don't feel right—killing a kid ain't the Don's style. But," he said, "it *is* Svanire's." Joe pinched his lips tight.

Jackson lowered his head. "Some folks would probably say I deserved it for the things I've done."

"I don't care what you did. You're just a k—" Joe squinted, and a flash of color made him smile. He touched a meaty finger to his temple. "A kid! You *are* a kid. You shouldn't have to live like a killer—your whole life is ahead of you, and you deserve a chance to experience it."

"Yeah, stake." Jackson took another gulp of beer.

"Let me ask *you* somethin'," Joe said. "When she kissed you, how'd it make you feel?"

"Oh, man." Jackson's face lit up. "I mean, I've been with girls before, ya know? But online, like in VR and stuff. This was different, man. She was … electric." He tried to rein the smile in and couldn't. "And I can still smell her, like vanilla and spice." Jackson put his face in the bright-colored sash around his neck.

Joe smiled. "Because she's real, Jack. Nothing beats a real human connection."

"Stake." Jackson grinned, but his face darkened. "And I'll never see her again." He swirled the beer in his bottle.

"Don't be so sure." Joe winked. He thrust his chin toward the front of the hotel.

Jackson spun in his seat.

In the entranceway, his señorita leaned against the arch, that same brilliant smile on her face.

"Look at you." Joe pointed at the goose flesh on Jackson's arms. "Someone who does that to you don't come around every day." He nodded. "You should do somethin' about it."

Jackson glowed. "Are you serious with me right now?"

Joe shooed him off and leaned his heavy bulk on the table. "Don't spend your whole evening with an old man. Go." He reached out and touched Jackson's elbow. "But, hey, listen to me."

Jackson stopped.

"Treat the lady with respect," Joe said, "and don't forget there's an enormous price on your head. Have a plan if things go south."

"I got you." Jackson stepped away from the table and waved to the girl, who waved back. He turned to Joe. "I'll be safe, Bones. I swear."

"Be here first thing in the morning so we can shove off," Joe said.

"Stake." Jackson grinned.

Joe watched as Jackson strutted across the space and he and his señorita drew close. She looked at Joe, then kissed Jackson again. His face mashed against hers and Jackson gave Joe the thumbs up. Joe chuckled. As the couple disappeared around the corner, snuggled close, Joe felt the dimmest of lights brighten within his chest.

The sun rose fierce and hot in the cloud-scattered morning sky, burned through the slats and bars of the old convent, and splashed across the red tile floor. In the middle of one shimmering golden band of light, Neko lay curled in a tight little ball, bits of half-eaten taco in his whiskers.

Joe roused himself from the chair he'd napped in overnight and rubbed at his white-stubbled jaw. His gut soured and he sat up straight.

"Jack?" he called out.

Relax, Joe. You told the kid to have a good time. He did.

He pushed from the thin-cushioned chair and shuffled to the spacious tiled bathroom, where he took a quick shower. The blistering hot water washed away the madness and the grime of the past few days. It felt counterproductive to put on the same suit he'd worn since this little road trip started, especially now that blood stained the collar of his shirt, but to his eye, the rest of the wrinkle-free suit looked serviceable.

As Joe combed back his thinning hair, the door to the room clicked.

He peeked around the corner just as Jackson groaned and flopped onto one of the beds, both of which were still made.

"Hey, it's lover boy." Joe tried to sound as relaxed as he had the previous evening.

Neko clawed at the bed sheets until Jackson scooped him up and placed the kitten on his chest.

Joe wiped the foam from his chin with a red towel and stepped from the bathroom, rolling his sleeves back up. "You wanna grab a shower? It's hot."

Jackson didn't reply but raised his hand to stroke Neko's fur. The cat purred and twisted against Jackson's fingers.

Joe hung up his towel. "So, no shower?"

Jackson stroked Neko.

"Okay, then. We need to get moving if we're gonna get to your stash in B.C." Joe grabbed his duffel and the Diora Brass case and double-checked to ensure he had everything. "Let's go, Jack. By my guess, it's a good seven-hour trip." He slung the duffel over his shoulder and tugged the heavy wooden door open.

Jackson rose with a loaded sigh, slipped on his rucksack, plucked Neko off the bed, and wandered out after Joe, out of the hotel and onto the cobblestone street. Joe bid farewell to the matronly woman at the front desk, then he and Jackson headed toward the Zap station.

Sunlight and shadow dappled the narrow lanes of the town and added to the eerie sense of serenity. "Kinda weird we ain't been shot at, kidnapped, or set upon, here," Joe said as he peered around another corner. *Must be something in the water.*

Jackson didn't reply, and they made the trek across town in silence, back to where they'd parked the beat-up Kia.

When they found the vehicle, they both stood for a full minute staring at its stripped-down frame. The Kia teetered on blocks with no wheels, the hood and trunk open. The vandals had picked it over and plucked the battery compartment bare.

"Violent crime might be down, but they have thieves." Joe hitched his gun duffel higher over his shoulder. "Bastards took my coat and hat."

"Guess that means we have to stay." A little smirk pulled at Jackson's mouth before disappearing again into a morose mask.

Joe shook his jug-head. "Much as I'd like to—we can't. Not until this business is over." He scoured the empty service-station lot. "We need a ride."

A four-cylinder, primer-gray Nissan truck rattled down the row of rundown businesses and stopped. An old man in a straw hat left it running, got out, and tottered around the back of a dusty cantina.

Joe looked at Jackson.

Jackson crossed his arms. "Thieves everywhere."

"Come on." Joe hobbled up, dropped his bags in the bed of the old gas truck, and opened the driver's side door, but stopped.

"What?" Jackson said, already halfway in the passenger door.

Joe clasped his hands. He picked up the Diora Brass case and opened it. Gently, he removed the gleaming brass trumpet and set it gently on the curb, cloaked by the knocking of the four-cylinder engine.

"What are you doing? Let's go." Jackson scowled. "That dirt farmer doesn't want a stupid trumpet."

Joe snapped the hardcase closed, placed it back in the truck bed, took one last look at the family heirloom on the curb, and got into the truck.

Joe shifted into first gear, released the brake, and pressed the accelerator. The truck rattled away from the curb. In their rearview, the old farmer tottered back out of the cantina, shouting and waving his arms. In apparent confusion, he bent and picked up the pristine brass instrument.

Joe pressed his lips into a line. "He may not know it yet, but that's more than a fair trade."

"A trumpet?" Jackson scoffed. He pulled out his phone.

"That trumpet will feed his family for a month *and* buy him a new truck," Joe said, "if he sells it to the right person."

Jackson looked up from his phone. "It meant something to you?"

"Was my father's." Joe sucked his teeth. "They don't make 'em like that anymore."

Jackson eyed Joe for another moment before turning back to his phone. "You should've just stolen the truck."

Neko mewed and poked his little head from Jackson's sash.

Joe shook his head. "That old man didn't do nothin' to nobody. He deserves a little—"

"Respect. I know." Jackson let out a huff. "But everyone's done something to somebody."

Joe dipped his chin in acquiescence. He looked the grumpy teen over. "You at least gonna tell me her name?"

Jackson touched the sash and worked his jaw. "No. That's just for me."

"Okay, pal," Joe said, and focused back on the road. "I get it."

Joe drove, Jackson fiddled with his phone, and the miles and hours passed without incident. Neko curled into a ball on the dash and slept. The cramped alleys and sunlit lanes of Antigua gave way to twisting, arid landscapes and dense, humid jungles as Joe and Jackson wound farther into the heart of Central America. The four-cylinder Nissan rattled and squeaked over potholes, uneven asphalt, and dirt roads. More than once, the two killers had to stop to barter, argue, and cajole for gas.

The truck jostled across a partially washed-out section of road, the jungle close and dense, a smothering wall of endless green. In the truck bed, the duffel rolled from one side to the other with a *clump-clump* sound. Jackson's nose wrinkled and he pulled away from the phone.

"What?" Joe asked.

"Hellcat just asked if I had fun last night," he said.

Joe leaned over to glimpse the screen, and a new Hellcat message that said: *Don't make me watch you with someone else!!!* followed by several crying emojis.

Joe's eyes narrowed. "Creepy. If she's got an eye on us, others might, too."

Jackson waved him off. "Hellcat can always get into places no one else could," he said. "She's looking out for us."

"Or watching you take showers and stuff, like some weirdo voyeur," Joe said.

Jackson stuffed his phone into his pocket and groaned. "Fucking twisty jungle highway. I feel like I'm going to toss my cookies." He tucked himself down into the seat and closed his eyes.

Joe piloted the primer-gray truck away from the jungle road and up an on-ramp of fresh hot top that arced through a winding pass between two great mountains. Between the hunched and sleeping giants, the choked jungle opened up and a blinding flash of light seared through Joe's retinas. He grunted and pulled down the visor.

Jackson covered his eyes. "What is it?"

"I'll be damned." Joe held up his hand against the glare. "I think we made it."

As Joe's eyes adapted to a brilliance that seemed greater than the sun, a tingle formed at the base of his neck. On all sides lanes from far-away places trickled together to form a massive highway, which then spread into wide concentric streets of steel and glass. Skyscrapers by the dozens stretched to the clouds as if trying to reach God Himself, their sleek mirror surfaces reflecting the powerful afternoon sun.

Beyond the shimmering cityscape, the smoking Conchagua volcano slumbered. Cut into the volcano's ancient mountainside, broad stone stairs led up and up and up to an enormous flat ring that jutted out horizontally into the air. On its surface, tourists wandered back and forth like little photo-snapping ants.

"Epic," Jackson said.

"I don't like it already." Joe leaned forward to get a better look. "We could take a hit from anywhere. Never see it coming."

"Chill, dude." Jackson pumped his hands down. "We'll pop in, get my stash, and bug out. Then we can go wherever we want to and jam this Svanire guy up."

"Still don't like it," Joe said. The massive skyscrapers loomed closer, surrounded by a warren of streets packed with pedestrians, electric cars, and triple-decker busses that blared their horns and swerved through traffic.

"Just think of it like any other big city, like Chicago or Manhattan," Jackson said.

"That's what I'm worried about." Joe tightened his grip on the steering wheel, ready to swerve at the first sign of danger. An electric car honked, zipped past, and the driver flipped them the bird. "Where'd the money for all this come from?" Joe asked.

"Bit. Coin." Jackson opened his eyes extra wide and pointed to his brain. "Bitcoin City? Hello?"

Joe scowled. "Obviously, genius. But Bitcoin got mined out a long time ago. So, where's fresh money come from?"

Jackson plucked Neko off the dash and placed the kitten on his chest. He leaned back in his seat. "After Bitcoin went down, all the miners needed work, right? Giltcoin was the next big thing, so B.C. got on board and sold the transition to everyone else."

"Sold the transition?" Joe repeated.

"They didn't gamble on it, man. They *ensured* it was the next big thing. And, boom," he raised a fist and spread the fingers out wide, "when Giltcoin took off, it took B.C. with it."

"On or off?" Joe grumbled.

"Off." Jackson pointed and rolled down his window. "Ooh, I smell the ocean."

Brow knit, Joe exited the sea of traffic and merged down the ramp onto a broad street framed by palms that reminded him more than a little of Sunset Boulevard. Beyond the strip, to the west, the sun dazzled its way across the whitecaps of the Pacific and white sand beaches that extended for miles.

"Still don't like it," Joe grumbled.

Jackson gawked at the spikes of glass and steel that towered overhead, and the sun-bronzed ladies along the boardwalk. "I mean, look at this place."

"No."

"Okay, grumpy ass." Jackson spotted Neko with open hands as the tiny cat picked with needled paws up the front of Jackson's hoodie. "You're just over sensitive to—"

Joe slammed on the brakes as they crested a rise. Their four-cylinder rattletrap slid to a stop, a trail of black rubber skids in its wake. Across the road, old military Hummers, armored personnel carriers, and pickup trucks with faded police lettering blocked the intersection. On the side of each vehicle, *La22* had been hastily stenciled in yellow over the deep crimson of a scarlet moon.

Joe ground the gears of the old pickup into reverse, but before he could mash the pedal, more trucks with belt-fed heavy machine guns screeched up behind, blocking them in under a rocky outcroping. Drivers along the boulevard slowed to gawk and pedestrians ran for cover.

"Danger?" Joe turned to Jackson. "Were you gonna say *danger?*"

Jackson swallowed and shoved Neko deep into the hoodie pocket.

Electric cars by the dozens piled up behind the blockade. Their horns blared and their occupants leaned out to scream obscenities. Along the edge of the road, a large red tour bus came to a full stop, its stunned patrons ready to capture the excitement on their smart devices.

Static scratched over a megaphone. "Atención! Apague el vehículo y saque las manos por la ventanilla. ¡Hazlo ahora!"

Joe pressed his lips together in a grimace. "We're about to make the news. You speak Spanish?"

Jackson frowned. "I think he said hands out the window …"

Joe raised his open palms slow and stuck them through his open window. Jackson did the same.

Soldiers in jungle fatigues rushed the old Nissan, their rifles raised. They snatched the doors open and jerked Joe and Jackson out onto the ground.

"Okay, all right," Joe said, face down on the tarmac. "Everything's good. No problema."

A burn-scarred man pushed the barrel of his battered FAL against Joe's cheek. "No problema?" he repeated.

"No problema," Joe said as another soldier pulled his hands behind his back and cinched them together with two interlocked zip ties.

Four uniformed thugs, strong but not large, gathered around and pulled Joe to his feet. They walked him to the front of the old truck and shoved him back against the hood. Joe scanned the group. *Twenty-five foot soldiers. Maybe thirty. No way out, Joe.*

Jackson, hands bound behind him, got shoved against the hood next to Joe.

Joe looked at the kid. They'd busted his nose. "You good?"

"Peachy." Jackson sniffed at a dribble of blood on his lips. "Perras estúpidas!" Jackson spat blood at the closest soldier. The man cocked his FAL rifle over his shoulder like a club.

"Hey, hey," Joe leaned over between the two. "Don't do that. If you gotta hit someone, hit me."

Jackson side-eyed Joe, who held firm, shielding the teen with his barrel chest.

"Shoot them, already!" one of the tourists shouted out the tour bus's window.

A soldier with buck teeth bent Joe back over the Nissan's hood and shoved a rusted steel machete in his face.

Another uniformed thug with cropped, dyed hair the color of carrot juice jammed the barrel of his rifle hard into Jackson's stomach, making him wretch and drop to his knees.

Neko hissed from within the hoodie.

The La22 soldiers looked at each other, confused. Carrot Juice lunged forward, groping at Jackson's front.

"No!" Jackson tried to twist away. "Stop!"

Carrot Juice leered as he pulled Neko from Jackson's pocket by the scruff of his neck.

"Stop! Give him back!" Jackson shouted.

Joe lay pinned against the hood, the tip of the machete inches from his face.

Carrot Juice held the kitten high for the men to see. "Es solo un gatito!"

The gang members laughed. The entire city seemed to freeze and gawk.

Then applause, slow and deliberate, echoed off the sodden concrete.

A woman emerged from the midst of the army of male soldiers. Dressed the same as the others, she wore a yellow cap and flashed teeth crusted in diamonds. Perhaps in her late forties, deep brown eyes sat in a handsome face. A hard musculature pushed against the fatigues when she moved. A woman with a purpose. She stopped before Joe and Jackson and clapped a few more times.

"Oh, shit," Joe said.

"Joe Carboni." The Hispanic woman flashed an ice-caked smile. "How long has it been, chero?"

Joe grunted. "Not nearly long enough, Elena."

"*Puya!*" She batted her smoky eyes and stepped closer to him. "How could you say that to me? After all we went through?" The two uniformed thugs held Joe fast against the hood, but Elena gently redirected the machete to the side and stroked her fingers along Joe's cheek. She ran her hand down his chest. "You remember, Joe?"

"That was twenty years ago," he said. "Maybe twenty-five."

Jackson looked from Joe to the woman and back again. "No way."

Buck Teeth pushed Jackson farther back. "Cállate."

Jackson grunted. "Gimme back my cat."

The diamond-mouthed vagenda turned to Jackson and extended her hand. "Elena De León."

Restrained, Jackson just stared at the offered hand. "Getting down with the old man, huh?"

Elena retracted her hand and checked her painted nails. "It was years ago. Joe and I met at an arms deal in Dallas back when I was brokering for the Sinaloa Cartel. He was so powerful. Dangerous. The most feared man on the North American continent." She winked at Joe. "How could I not be taken with this man?"

Joe frowned.

"But when the business was done, he used me and threw me away. Like some dirty chucho." Elena mimicked the wiping of a tattooed tear.

"Now, look." Joe flexed his fingers open, the only part of him he could move. "That was a mutual encounter. I did *not* take advantage of you."

"I was just a girl, Joe." She batted long eyelashes. "When I looked at you, I had stars in my eyes. How could you do what you did to me?"

Joe shook his head and licked his lips. "Look, I'm—"

Elena held up her palm. "I have waited very long, handsome man," she said, every *H* heavy as lead. "I want to savor this moment."

"I have nothing to do with this," Jackson said. "Can I have my cat back? I'll just walk away like I didn't see nothing."

Joe's head twisted in Jackson's direction. "Go ahead, throw out your own life raft."

"Her problem is with you. I have nothing to do with your irresponsible conquests." Jackson rolled his eyes. "Giving me a lecture about treating girls with respect back in Antigua. Now look at us."

"Irresponsible con—" Joe started.

Elena held up a finger to Jackson. "Don't be so quick to jump to conclusions, my young friend." She produced a smart device. On its screen, the rank listings for Hunter's Dominion showed Joe and Jackson back at the top. "You both are worth quite a chunk of pisto, no? How fortuitous for me."

"Come on!" another passenger shouted from the tour bus. "Cut them apart!" More horns honked from the gathering traffic.

Elena sucked her diamond-studded teeth. "The bounty is up to one million Giltcoin now. Impressive."

"Elena, I never meant to …" Joe said, trying to wriggle off the primer-gray hood. "Look, it's true we've got a lot of heat right now. But if you help us out, I'll cut you in when we get the score we came here for."

"What score?" Elena asked.

"Cut her in?" Jackson balked; his back arched against the truck's hood. "No way."

"Oh, that!" Elena smirked. "You think I don't know what sits in the banks of my city? Perhaps you have an encryption key in here?" She motioned to one of her men, who stepped forward and handed her Jackson's rucksack. She zipped it open and dumped out the crushed can of BrainStorm, an empty Strawberry Fields vape, and the photo of his dad onto the tarmac. "What do we have in here, baboso cipote?" she said with a sneer.

Jackson's eyes grew wide. "Give it to me."

Elena picked up the photo and studied it. "This your favorite uncle? The one who touched you in your special place?"

"Fuck you!" Jackson fired back.

Elena cackled and threw the picture over her shoulder. A breeze stole the photo and dragged it down the highway.

Elena cut her smoky eyes at Jackson. "Tell me how to access your cold storage and I'll kill you fast. Refuse, and I'll make sure you live long enough to regret it, vea."

An eager tourist in a gaudy Hawaiian shirt pushed his torso halfway out an open tour-bus window. "Do something! We're waiting!"

Elena snapped her fingers and two of her men pivoted and ripped off a string of gunfire that smacked the body and windows of the tour bus. Jackson flinched and Joe pulled at his bonds.

Perforated with half a dozen new holes, Hawaiian Shirt toppled from the window into the street and lay there in a bloody heap. A moment later, the traumatized faces of the silent tourists rose again to peer out of the shattered ports.

"I'm not giving you shit," Jackson said. "Now, give me back my cat!"

Carrot Juice sneered as he dangled a mewing Neko by the scruff of his neck.

Elena crossed her arms and rocked her weight onto one hip. "A shame. I will have to make a spectacle of your deaths." She snapped her fingers again and pointed to Carrot Juice. "Un gatito."

A savage grin spread across Carrot Juice's face. He bent and placed a mewling Neko on the asphalt and covered the kitten's squirming body with his boot.

"Stop!" Jackson wrenched against Buck Tooth's grip. "Don't!"

Elena stepped closer to Joe, and he stiffened. She ran her hands down his chest, over his belly, to his belt. It jingled as she unclasped it.

His pants fell to his ankles. Another tug and his briefs dropped to his knees.

A warm breeze tickled Joe's bare skin. He tugged fruitlessly at his plastic shackles.

"You've gotten old, Joe. But I guess age comes for us all." Elena smiled, touched her own crow's feet, then held out her hand. One of her men filled it with a boot knife. Her gaze dropped to Joe's genitals, then to the purple-black bruise covering the back of his calf. "Ooh, I bet that hurts, no?" She brought the knife point up beneath his testicles and leaned to whisper in Joe's ear. "But not as much as this will."

Carrot Juice shifted his weight slowly over the squirming cat.

"Please don't!" Jackson spasmed, his voice breaking.

"Hey, hey, Elena, stop," Joe stammered. "I swear to you, I'm sorry. I am. I never meant—"

"Shhh." Elena pressed a finger to Joe's lips. "You never loved me, Joe. You took what you wanted from me and left," she said, then pouted. "And now I'm going to take something from you—"

Carrot Juice coughed, stumbled to the side, and grabbed his face. Blood gushed through his fingers as he fell. A spray of fabric and blood exploded from Elena's shoulder. She toppled back and rolled across her shoulder, but rounded onto her feet, fingers clutching her arm. The double report of precision rifle fire echoed across the intersection.

"*Ellos estan atacando!*" Elena shouted and took off at a dead sprint for the La22 convoy.

A barrage of gunfire opened up from a rocky outcropping along the edge of the boulevard.

Buck Tooth released his white-knuckled grip on Jackson's hoodie and fled for cover even as a storm of bullets shredded the stunned La22s. The buck-toothed thug tripped, took a round in the spine, and dropped like a pile of empty clothes.

Neko scrambled between Jackson's feet.

"Get down!" Joe twisted and threw himself beside the truck, shorts and pants still around his ankles. From the other side of the vehicle, Jackson flopped onto his belly and wormed underneath.

Past the undercarriage of the old Nissan, across the boulevard, commandos in stone-gray fatigues advanced on La22, clean Scarlett Moon logos on the battle armor of the new arrivals. A rocket ripped through the air and slammed into an armored La22 personnel carrier. It erupted in a blast of flame. Men howled and stumbled down the ramp, their bodies engulfed in fire. Smoke canisters popped and gushed their contents, hissing through the air. A haze of white and black smoke obscured the battlefield.

Joe crunched his body against the truck's running board. Between his legs, he felt the wet tickle as blood stuck his bare thighs together. He pinched his eyes shut and prayed that a cut from Elena's knife or a random ricochet hadn't made an already bad day worse.

From somewhere beyond the smoke, Elena shouted something unintelligible, then repeated the word *Retiro*. The La22 convoy rumbled and tires screeched on the asphalt as the gang retreated into the smoky haze of the boulevard. The pop and whiz of gunfire slowed, then stopped. Joe listened to the Pacific breeze as it carried the cries of the wounded.

He sat up, blinked, then, with one eye closed, checked his crotch. His eyes rolled back and he let out a sigh of relief. "Oh, God. Oh, thank God," he whispered, though Elena's boot knife had left a nick high in his groin.

A tall commando with dark skin, graying temples, and shark-black eyes strutted toward them. His armor carried that same Scarlett Moon logo, but without the yellow *La22*. The surefooted commando navigated around the shot-up tour bus, his blocky G36 rifle raised at the high ready. An unorganized group of La22s, cut off from the retreat, charged the Scarlett Moon commando. He fired three rounds and dropped three men with perfect headshots. His weapon ran dry. He performed a quick chamber check, slung the G36 to his back, and drew a sidearm and combat knife from his rig.

Two remaining La22 goons in fatigues and yellow bandanas rushed the Black commando, machetes in hand. He sidestepped a swing, twisted, and fired the pistol into one goon's face at point-blank range. The second thug thrust at the commando's gut with his machete, only to see it parried away by the smaller blade. With a scream, the gang member swung again, but the commando was on him with a triple tap to the pelvis, chest, and head. The La22 goon crumpled.

The Scarlett Moon commando stepped over the bodies of the downed men and stalked toward Joe, pistol leveled at his chest. A wounded La22 gang member writhed between them on his back, waving an old revolver into the air. The commando thumped two slugs into the gangster's chest without breaking his stride.

"You Joe Carboni?" the commando asked, his pistol pointed at Joe's face.

"Who's askin'?" Joe said.

"The guy aiming a gun at your head," said the commando, "that's who."

Jackson ran up beside the commando, arms still tied behind his back. "Dad? Dad, is … is that you?" Jackson's face seemed to glow.

Two Scarlett Moon mercenaries flanked the tall commando. "Step back," one said to the teenager.

"He's fine." The commando holstered his weapon.

"Jackson, you okay?" Joe asked, but the kid ignored him.

"Jackson," the commando said. "Well, no shit."

"Dad … what …" the boy stammered. "How?"

"Dad?" Joe looked from the commando to Jackson. They bore a powerful resemblance to one another. He thought of the photo Elena had tossed in the wind.

"Sorry, Jackson," the commando said with a shake of his head. "I'm not your dad. I'm your uncle. Name's Marcel."

Jackson cocked his head. The glow on his face faded and he studied the man.

The silence ballooned, save the grunting and growling of tour buses navigating the wreckage of burning cars and dead La22 soldiers. Marcel's other soldiers, in crimson-marked gray armor, stopped here and there to put some poor soul out of their misery.

Joe clambered onto his knees, gritted his teeth, then got his feet under him. He stood slow. "Someone wanna untie me?"

Marcel's shark-black eyes crinkled at the corners.

Joe sighed. "Long story. You wanna let me pull my pants up or what?"

Marcel held up the knife.

Joe turned and let Marcel cut the zip tie. "What are you doin' here?" Joe rubbed at his wrists. "And you're Jackson's uncle? What gives?"

Marcel motioned to Jackson's restraints. "I head up Scarlett Moon's Critical Strike Team. Here to reestablish a working government and take back the city from La22," Marcel said. Jackson's restraints popped free with an upward pull of the blade. "That crazy bitch Elena has been a thorn in my side for far too long."

Joe touched the trickle of blood on his inner thigh before pulling up his pants and fixing his belt. "You got no idea."

Jackson bent and grabbed Neko from where the kitten had scurried behind the truck's wheel. He stroked the quaking kitten a few times and placed him back in his hoodie.

Marcel sheathed his knife. "Someone named Hellcat reached out and told me you were in a bit of trouble. Weird tip, but I had to check it out." He stepped toward Jackson and touched the teen's shoulder. "I thought you were still in the States. Haven't seen you since you were a baby. And look at you, grown into a young man."

Jackson's expression softened. "I didn't even know I *had* an uncle," he said. "You look *exactly* like Dad. Where have you been?"

"Around the world, trying to restore some sense of safety and order for the common man," Marcel said, puffing his chest out with pride, his silhouette sharp against the blinding cityscape. "A safe and equitable world for all."

"Stake," Jackson said with an enthusiastic bob of his head.

Joe scowled. "I've been saying that this whole time and you've all but told me to piss off ..."

"Do you know ..." Jackson's voice trailed off. "Like, what happened to my dad?"

Marcel gripped Jackson's shoulders and leaned close. "Your dad and I ..." He seemed to search for the right words. "Our relationship was strained. Our paths were very different. I wanted to fight for something better, and Jay—James—was more ... chill. A tech guy.

"Funny," he said, and looked down. "We both found our way to Scarlett Moon."

"Dad worked for them?" Jackson's voice squeaked.

Joe watched the blood pool around a La22 corpse. "Hey, are we safe out here?"

"Few people knew your dad worked for us, Jackson," Marcel said.

"So, where did he go?" Jackson frowned. "Why would he leave?"

Marcel stepped back. "He didn't leave, Jackson. Someone killed him."

"What?" The word hissed over Jackson's lips.

"He was deep into crypto," Marcel said, "and got himself in trouble with some mob types in Chicago. I'm sorry, kid."

Jackson, his eyes wet, looked at Bones. "Mob types?"

Joe shook his head. "Not me, Jack. I don't know nothin' like that. I would've heard."

"I told your mom," Marcel cocked his head. "She didn't tell you?"

Jackson just stared up at his uncle.

"I'm sorry, kid." Marcel put his arm around Jackson. "But I'm here now. I'll look after you."

"He don't like being called kid," Joe said, but his words went unnoticed.

Jackson hovered on the spot, swaying just a little, then leaped forward and threw his arms around Marcel. The two hugged tight.

Joe let the moment hang for as long as he could. "I hate to interrupt," he said, "but I'm out here in B.C., uh, on the lam."

Marcel released Jackson. "What about you?"

Jackson wiped his face.

Joe studied the teen and his uncle. Similar nose and eyes. The way the corners of their mouths moved when they smiled. Not exactly the same, but close enough. Enough to know they were family.

Just like Charley and you, Joe.

Joe lowered his eyes. "I just did my best to keep the boy safe. That's all."

Marcel extended his hand and Joe shook it. "And for that," Marcel said, "I'm grateful." He gave Joe's hand a good squeeze, then turned back to his men. "Rally up!" Marcel waved an index finger in a loop over his head.

The remaining Scarlett Moon commandos, a squad of twelve or so, navigated the wreckage of the boulevard battle and gathered on his position.

"Where are we going?" Jackson asked.

"You ever been to Switzerland?" Marcel waved Jackson on.

Jackson's smile broadened. He wrapped the Antiguan sash around his neck a little tighter and fell in behind his uncle.

Joe took a step to follow, then stopped, an emptiness pooling in his guts.

What the hell are you doing, Joe? Switzerland? You can't go to Switzerland. You did what you said, and you got him here.

He rubbed at the zip tie indentations in his wrists, eyes downcast, as Marcel and Jackson and the rest of the Scarlett Moon commandos crossed the highway to a convoy of electric four-by-four pickups.

You're not his father, Joe. Let the kid go.

Joe retrieved his things from the old Nissan and waited another moment, but the teen never looked back. Joe dropped his head, coughed at the windblown smoke, and limped off across the corpse-strewn wreckage of the boulevard.

CHAPTER TWENTY

Jackson

The four-by-four electric truck gunned down a stretch of black highway that ran the length of the coast along the edge of Bitcoin City. Looking out one window, Jackson took in the pure white sand and endless expanse of the Pacific, sparkling in golden sunlight. On the other side, knife-shaped skyscrapers draped in climbing greenery sliced through a cloud-scattered sky. Marcel's militia traveled on all sides of them as though Jackson were some VIP.

He made himself comfortable in the rear passenger seat, Neko curled in his lap, while a gruff driver and his uncle Marcel sat up front. The vibrations of the road rumbled through the cab and into his chest.

Though he'd almost gotten butchered by some diamond-toothed vagenda who had a grudge against Bones for boning her a million years ago and never calling back, Jackson's mind remained fixed on one thing. The mob had killed his dad. Probably La Nueva Cosa Nostra. And, perhaps now Bones had been sent to finish off the Cross family. He swallowed and chewed at his fingertip.

Your dad's not coming home—that's what his mom had said. Plain and matter-of-fact. She hadn't cried, and neither had Jackson. But traveling in a militia convoy in El Salvador, the target of some ghoulish mob capo and every other coin-hungry geekbag this side of the Atlantic Ocean, Jackson's heart hurt. Deep inside, a lonely eight-year-old boy still believed his dad would walk through the front door. For seven years, Jackson had masked hope with indifference. Until thirty minutes ago, indifference was an option because his dad still existed out there in the world. Until now, there had been a chance.

"Why do you think Mom never told me?" Jackson said, prodding at his busted nose and wincing.

"About your dad?" Marcel called back over the road noise and scratched at the mole on his chin. "Who knows, kid? She didn't like that

Jay worked for Scarlett Moon. Damn sure she didn't want you following him down that path."

Jackson averted his gaze out the window.

"Which begs the question: what are you doing down here?" Marcel's shark-black eyes darkened. "Your mom's gotta be freaking out."

The empty feeling in Jackson's gut deepened. "Mom's dead."

Marcel slung an arm around the headrest of his seat to face Jackson properly. "What?"

"There's a hit out on me." The colorful Antiguan sash muffled Jackson's words. "They got her, trying to get to me."

Marcel's heavy brow lowered. "You're fifteen years old," he said. "You post something someone didn't like?" He smacked the headrest.

Jackson stuttered, debating whether to tell his uncle what he did for a living; wondering if the man was too idealistic to understand. "I had a stash of crypto in an offline wallet down here. From back when B.C. just got started. I wanted to grab it and get Mom out. You know, to an island somewhere."

"You're a smart kid, Jackson." Marcel faced the road ahead. "I'm sorry about your mom. I got you now. We'll get you to Switzerland. Scarlett Moon HQ is as secure as it gets. No one will touch you there." He grabbed a satellite phone from the center console and keyed it up.

Jackson pulled his knees in, shrunk into a ball, and fished out his own phone.

A tiny red slice showed the low battery life. He searched the four-by-four's interior. Plenty of charging ports, but no cable. A message from Hellcat sat in his box, so he thumbed it.

Hellcat_59: Hey, love, what's up? I saw you got
into trouble with the locals down there in BC.

"Hey, yeah, Christian?" Marcel said into the satellite phone. "I'm coming in hot, St. Gallen Airport. Have the security team ready to receive us." He peered over his shoulder at Jackson. "We take off from B.C. in one hour. Got a passenger with me. Name's Jackson. Make sure the ground team knows I've cleared him, okay?"

Jackson's thumbs tapped on the phone screen.

OMNIVIOLENCE

CyberRonin81: I'm okay. Turns out I have an uncle. His name's Marcel. Works for Scarlett Moon.

Hellcat_59: I saw that, so I sent him your way ;)

CyberRonin81: Huh? How?

Hellcat_59: I'm always watching. <3

Jackson pursed his lips. His fingers hovered over the screen.

CyberRonin81: Like in Antigua?

Hellcat_59: :(wasn't trying to stalk. I think I felt a little ... jealous. Sorry ...

CyberRonin81: Thanks. I'm sorry too. Anyway. Now off to Switzerland with SM.

"What?" Marcel shouted into his phone. "Why would Tabea do that?"

Jackson glanced at the back of his uncle's head.

Hellcat_59: What are we going to do about Svanire?

CyberRonin81: You think he can get me there too?

Hellcat_59: Maybe. But, love, we agreed to take this bastard out. Together. For your mom. For my aunt. You still in?

"Watch that. Watch that." Marcel pointed at the lead convoy vehicle as it swerved to avoid a cardboard box.

The driver veered into the next lane over. The dense green jungle passed in a blur outside the windows.

"Everything okay?" Jackson asked.

"La22 loves their IEDs," Marcel shook his head. "Can't be too careful." He winked at Jackson.

Jackson's thumbs lingered over his phone's keyboard display. He reread Hellcat's last question. Jackson reached for Neko and scratched under the scrawny cat's chin, his eyes never leaving the screen.

Hellcat_59: SM is plugged into EVERYTHING.
Global surveillance. FULL COVERAGE. Use it to
find Svanire, then I can slay the slippery bastard.

CyberRonin81: Stake.

Jackson's phone chimed and the battery icon blinked red.

Hellcat_59: Okay, I got a modification to the
Pegasus program on your device. It'll help you
get past their firewall. You'll need to hardwire
into their system. Imma send you the update, k?

CyberRonin81: K. Let's do this!

Hellcat_59: Stake.

Hellcat_59: I'll come find you in Swiss land. I got
some coin.

Hellcat_59: Oh, btw, the Genial still with you?

The phone screen went black.

"Shit," Jackson mumbled. He touched the power button, then shoved the black mirror back into his pocket.

"Just hold Anja off 'til I get back," Marcel said, then ended the call on his satellite phone.

"Hey, uh, where's Bones?" Jackson asked. "Did he get into the car behind us?"

"The old guy?" Marcel replied.

"Yeah." Jackson held on to Neko with one hand and grabbed Marcel's seat with the other.

"Don't know," Marcel said with a shrug.

"Can you check?" Jackson looked out the back window in hopes of seeing the gangster in the passenger seat of the car behind. Nothing.

Marcel keyed up a built-in dash radio. "Anybody carrying extra weight? Who took the old man?"

Voices talked over each other, penetrating a wash of static. None of the other trucks in the convoy had Bones.

"Wait, you left him behind?" Jackson sputtered. "Svanire will kill him!"

"Who?" Marcel asked, twisting around again.

"Are you even—?"

The lead truck exploded, cutting Jackson off. Its black frame tumbled end over end down the highway. Jackson shot forward and clutched Neko against his belly as the truck's brakes locked. His busted nose smashed into Marcel's headrest and he yelped, then fell into a ball on the truck floor, wedged between the front and rear seats.

The door flung open and Marcel dragged Jackson out by his hoodie. Jackson managed to clasp his fingers around Neko's skinny torso and pull the infant kitten along. He stuffed the cat into his hoodie, then stumbled to the road shoulder, where Marcel hid under a guava tree.

"… the hell?" Jackson wheezed.

The lead convoy truck lay burning, its chassis riddled with bullet holes. A rusted-out pickup screamed past, its flatbed packed with hooligans who fired their AK machine guns, spraying the highway with abandon.

One hooligan lobbed a grenade at no apparent target. A palm tree's trunk took the brunt and shattered, sending splinters floating on the breeze. Dried-up fronds caught fire and smoldered in a chain reaction down the length of the highway.

"Fuck." Marcel scanned the blacktop battlefield.

The remaining Scarlett Moon militia had deserted the last three electric trucks in their convoy, which now only served as target practice for the pack of whooping La22 thugs who revved flatbeds and dirt bikes in rubber-burning circles on the tarmac. Civilians who happened to be coming through abandoned their family station wagons and SUVs and scattered like ants from a kicked anthill. Only half escaped the melee.

"Move!" Marcel yelled over the pandemonium. "Go!" He sprinted away from the safety of the guava tree.

"Where?" Jackson shouted back, and stumbled after his uncle.

Marcel yanked him down behind the wheel arch of a shredded transport. Jagged metal poked at Jackson's skin through the thick cloth hoodie. He slipped a hand in his pocket and cupped Neko's limp, shaking body.

"Fucking 22s," Marcel said, breathing hard.

Jackson's broken nose throbbed. "What do we do?"

"We can still make it to the airport," Marcel said.

"How far?"

"Too far to walk." Marcel grabbed Jackson's hoodie again. "Come on, move."

Crouched low, Jackson followed his human shield. Marcel slunk between wrecked Scarlett Moon trucks and civilian sedans now abandoned along the highway. A palm tree crackled in flames overhead. Keeping the beach on his left, Marcel ran—almost too fast for Jackson's tired legs.

A scraggly, yellow-clad hooligan vaulted the hood of a busted Toyota. His tattooed face red with fury, he squeezed the trigger of a janky Glock, and 9mm rounds smacked and thudded across the fractured tarmac.

Marcel jerked his Sig P220 from its holster and fired twice. One hole in the chest and a second in the middle of the forehead. The hooligan's momentum carried him forward and he crashed face-first into the road. The Glock slid to a stop a few inches from Marcel's feet.

"Here," Marcel said, handing the hooligan's Glock to Jackson. "You know how to handle this?"

Jackson took the blocky weapon, heavy in his hands. He thumbed the magazine release and checked if it still had rounds. He pushed the magazine back into place with a *click*. "I've seen a lot on the internet."

Jackson knew, in theory, how a handgun worked. He'd never pulled a trigger before, but the weight of the gun in his hands came with an innate sense of power. The old Genial would see this as a moment to teach, Jackson thought. *Bones, where are you?*

Jackson scanned the highway as the battle haze of smoke and debris engulfed everything. "What about your guys?"

"They can take care of themselves." Marcel nodded as a La22 hyena took a blast in the chest and tumbled from his dirt bike. A noise from the shadow of a folded-over palm drew Jackson's attention to a Scarlet Moon soldier racking the action of his Mossberg 500, then sprinting off into the smoke.

"Stay close," Marcel said.

An armored tour bus idled in the breakdown lane. Bullet strikes pockmarked the steel plates welded beneath fractured windows on either side. The driver lay slumped against the wheel. A few civilians hung from broken windows or lay collapsed in their seats, bodies shot through and through.

Marcel pointed to the bus. "It's slow, but it'll be hard to stop."

Up the road, six soldiers in yellow caps and bandanas with M-16 A1 rifles moved in formation through the smoking chaos. At their fore marched Elena, blood streaming from a bullet graze on her shoulder. A maniacal grin flashed the diamonds in her mouth.

Her squad prowled the edge of the road, rifles held at the ready. Anyone still writhing on the debris-scattered road took an extra round for good measure. A middle-aged man with a briefcase clawed at a sucking chest wound, and a young woman in a flower-print summer dress crawled on her belly—both were executed with rifle fire.

Marcel pulled Jackson close, and together they shuffled to the open door of the tour bus. Crouched low, they navigated around the corpse of an older woman collapsed on the stairs. Marcel gently teased her free and rolled her onto the highway, then made for the driver's seat.

Beneath Jackson's feet, the bus rumbled, diesel fumes sharp in his nose. He crunched down into a cloth seat, Glock in hand, and peeked out the windshield at Elena and her squad of La22s.

Between Elena and the bus, a toddler, perhaps three years old, clutched a ragged, one-eyed teddy bear and bawled for her mommy.

"We gotta help that kid," Jackson said, the words a surprise even to him. The image of Bones' nephew Charley, charred by the blast, surfaced from the depths of Jackson's mind.

Marcel worked the heavy bulk of the dead bus driver from the driver's seat and laid him on the floor. "Nothing we can do," he whispered.

"Nothing?" The word scratched across the back of Jackson's throat.

In front of the bus, one of Elena's soldiers approached the toddler. The girl looked up at him, eyes large and misty, tears cutting a path through the grime on her cheeks. The soldier cocked his head for a moment, grinned, then lifted his M-16.

Jackson pinched his eyes shut. The sharp report of the rifle cracked in his ears.

"Those motherfuckers," Marcel hissed through a set jaw. He slunk into the bus driver's seat.

A voice crackled over the radio on Marcel's belt. "Kilo to Alpha, we're pinned—"

Marcel clutched at his belt to silence the voice.

Elena's head snapped up and she gestured to her soldiers. Weapons swinging left and right, they circled the bus, searching for the source of the radio traffic.

Jackson's shoulders burned from the weight of the outstretched pistol. The idea of poking his head up to take a shot sapped his gun-given bravery. "Shit," he whispered, "what do we do?"

"Hold on to something," Marcel said, voice low. Lying back in the driver's seat, he slammed it into gear and jammed his foot down on the accelerator.

The bus lurched and a plume of black smoke guttered from its tailpipes. Elena and her men stumbled back, fumbling with their weapons. The gang leader shoved one soldier to the side and fell with him. Another hooligan, terror-stricken, bungled with his rifle, raised it, and fired. A single bullet smacked the windshield into a spiderweb just as the diesel-powered hulk slammed into him at speed. The hooligan screamed as the bus tires ground his body into the road. The bus smashed into a sedan and spun it off the roadway in a shower of glass.

Elena screamed, the M-16 rattling in her hands. Bullets pinged off the armored sidewalls of the bus.

"Alpha lead to all units!" Marcel shot up in the seat, the radio pressed to his lips. "Fall back to rally point echo. Get there however you can. Over!"

Jackson raised his head to peer out of the window and watched as the smoke and chaos of the battle receded behind them. "Rally point echo?" he shouted.

"The airport." Marcel squeezed the wheel. "We might make it if they don't give chase."

Neko squirmed in Jackson's hoodie.

"You good?" Marcel called over his shoulder.

On the floor of the bus two rows back, the enormous body of an obese man, riddled with holes, jiggled and jostled over the bumpy road.

Jackson refocused his attention out the back window and on the road behind them. A beat-up red sports car and two flatbeds loaded with hooligans in yellow screamed from the smoke behind the tour bus. Jackson licked his dry lips and adjusted his sweaty grip on the Glock. "Ah, Marcel?"

"What?" Marcel's black eyes hit the rearview mirror. "Shit. Can you keep them off us?"

The Glock trembled in Jackson's hand.

"How about driving?" Marcel barked. "Can you do that?"

"Stake." Jackson threw the Glock down on the bench seat.

Marcel waved him up. "Come on, move!"

The bus's ruined chassis squealed as they barreled down the coastal highway. Jackson pressed Neko to his belly and staggered up the bus, grabbing at the seat backs. In the distance, an expanse of concrete runways crisscrossed one another.

"Right there. Just take us in." Marcel pointed ahead, then slipped from the seat as Jackson squeezed in behind.

"I got this." Jackson seized the wheel in a death grip, the weight of the Glock now dwarfed by the feeling of piloting thousands of pounds of steel.

In the rearview, Jackson watched Marcel hunker low, using Fatty Arbuckle's bloated corpse as a shield. Two more sedans raced up behind the bus, the yellow accents of their occupants visible through fractured glass.

Marcel pulled the Sig from its holster. "Too many …"

"We good?" Jackson called back. He swallowed again, unable to wet his throat.

"No! We're definitely not good!" Marcel said as he checked the magazine of his Sig. "Don't stop. No matter what."

Jackson couldn't answer. A high-pitched whistle pierced his eardrums. "You hear that?"

Marcel hissed a curse.

The whistling grew louder.

Something shaped like a rocket, sporting six two-foot-long blades, screamed past. The crack and squeal of torn metal scratched Jackson's eardrums. In the bus's large side mirror, the beat-up red sports car, now torn in two and drenched in human gristle, slid to a stop in the middle of the highway. The other flatbeds swerved around the wreckage and backed off.

"Holy shit," Jackson yelled over his shoulder. "The hell was that?"

"Ninja missile," Marcel said, climbing to his feet. Through the side window, he tried to scan the heavy sea of dark clouds above. "Someone has a Predator in the air. Eyes on the road."

"The fuck is a ninja missile?" Jackson said, trying to concentrate on the highway in front. "Scarlett Moon tech?"

"No," Marcel said, breathless. "Just drive."

The rumble of petrol-powered heavy vehicles thrummed in Jackson's ears. Up ahead, a convoy of open-top Jeep Gladiators and Toyota Hilux raced straight at him, going the wrong way down the highway.

Jackson slammed on the brakes. The tour bus shuddered to a halt and the engine stalled.

Marcel fell into Fatty's gelatinous gut. "The hell, kid?"

One of the Hiluxes slid to a stop, its brakes smoking. In its rear, Jackson saw half a dozen dark-skinned boys and men in jeans and T-shirts overlaid with camo-colored body armor. The newcomer's cavalcade slid to a halt, forming a makeshift barrier.

The airport, a gray blur encased in a chain-link fence, lay beyond the blockade.

Marcel clambered past the seats to the front of the bus.

"Hosh, jy raak wys!" a child no more than ten years old screamed, his words barely audible over the rumble of janky engines. He thrust his AK-47 into the air, revealing a chest plate with *HL* spray-painted on it.

"The Hard Livings?" Marcel pulled the radio from his belt and keyed it up, his head whipping back and forth to see out each of the windows. "Critical Strike Team, we have a new player on the field."

Behind the tour bus, the La22 hooligans in their SUVs pounded up the highway.

Marcel's dark eyes hardened. "What the hell are you into, kid?"

Jackson's tongue stuck to the roof of his arid mouth.

"Move," Marcel growled. He grabbed a fistful of Jackson's hoodie and yanked him from the driver's seat.

Jackson tripped over the dead driver's body and fell into the stairwell. With his forearm, he shielded Neko's tiny skeleton from being squished against the railing.

Marcel crammed his bulk into the driver's seat once again and stomped on the pedal. The diesel engine revved high. He jostled the shifter into gear, then clamped bear-like hands on the wheel. The tour bus jolted forward, gaining speed as it careened out of control toward the Hard Living's barricade.

CHAPTER TWENTY-ONE

Joe

One hand thrust deep into his pants pocket, the other clutched around the handle of the Diora Brass case, Joe sized up the façade of the Cathedral de la Santa Madre. White and cream with round open windows and medieval, tower-like architecture, something about the old church called to him. He set the case down and rolled up shirt sleeves damp with sweat, then unbuttoned his shirt once and picked up the case again. Slump-shouldered, he limped out of the public park toward the cathedral. An army of pigeons parted before him like Moses at the Red Sea.

At the edge of the busy street, an odd assortment of electric and gas vehicles whined and sputtered past. Pedestrians, many of them dressed in the latest crypto-riche garb designed by an eight-year-old with a crayon, walked with purpose down the crowded sidewalks. They came and went from the many skyscrapers that jutted like thorns of glass and steel into the clouds. Courier drones zipped between the towering structures, missing each other by the narrowest of margins.

"Bitcoin City," Joe mumbled.

What the hell are you doing here, Joe?

A block down, someone screamed. Two men, machetes raised, converged on an unarmed third. The hapless man held up his hands and waited for the blow. The criminals hacked at him until he fell, then fled into a side street. The victim lay in a bloody heap on the sidewalk, ruined hands outstretched in an unanswered plea for help. The other pedestrians hurried past, smart devices capturing everything in high definition, looks of pity and disgust on their faces.

A stiff ocean breeze tossed the tops of the palms lining the street and sent pigeons flapping away. Joe instinctively reached for his fedora and instead touched wispy, graying strands of hair across his crown. "Who takes an old man's hat and jacket?" he muttered.

Joe hesitated on the curb. He refocused from the church to the rat-hole bar one lot over, complete with a gaudy flashing sign mimicking liquor poured into a martini glass. Joe licked his lips, then bared his teeth and shook away the thought. "Need answers, not a hangover," he said.

He crossed the busy street and entered the church grounds through a pair of iron gates that led to an off-white brick pathway. In his hand, the Diora Brass hardcase swayed on its handle and bumped against his thigh—though it felt a lot lighter without his father's trumpet inside.

You gave away Dad's prized possession, Joe. A bitter tang formed in his mouth.

"And for what?" he grumbled. "To who? Some dirt farmer who won't recognize what it's worth."

Joe stomped up the stone steps of the cathedral and entered. The acid burn of reflux tingled his upper chest as he stopped and crossed himself, forehead to sternum and both shoulders.

Ornate eggshell-white and yellow columns reached from floor to ceiling, framed by arched windows of beautiful stained glass. Down the center of the marbled floor, hardwood pews lay empty save the hunched form of an old woman near the altar. The light through the stained glass glowed with soft pastel colors, and Joe detected the faint scent of spice in the air.

At a long dark table by the door, he lit one of the votive candles inset in small rose-colored jars. His chest empty and his soul no closer to feeling absolved, Joe lumbered to the closest pew and sat alone in warm flickering candlelight.

Sheila and Charley might still be alive if you hadn't taken on this stupid crusade to save the kid. All you do is kill and get people killed, Joe.

He pointed at the altar and the cross that hung above it and wondered if God even cared. "What the hell are you doing?" Joe bellowed into the air. "My life is falling apart, and you're silent!

"I know I'm not a good man, but I need to hear from you right now," he said. "Are you even there?"

The silence of the cathedral felt louder than a crowded concert hall. Joe's ears ached with it.

"Answer me!" he shouted.

The old woman up front stood and hurried out, her wrinkled face scolding him as she shuffled past.

Joe gritted his teeth and grunted to his feet. "I'm trying to believe in you, here. To hold onto something decent." Joe's words echoed and died in the space.

"Why are you always silent?" he cried.

A hand touched his shoulder. Joe twisted, ready to fight.

By his side stood a short, balding man in a decorative robe.

"Señor," the priest said with a bow of his head.

"Oh," Joe stammered. "I didn't see you there, Padre."

"Es hora de confesarse." He motioned to the confessional.

"Confession," Joe said.

"Sí, Señor." The priest held out a small square crypto wallet. "Only ten thousand Maya Coin."

Joe's mouth hinged open. He stared at the device, then at the priest's grin. He lurched forward and grabbed the holy man by his robe.

The priest screamed. The square wafer flipped from his hands and clattered on the marble. He pried at Joe's heavy hands.

"Señor, it is the only way to be absolved of your sins!" the priest whined.

"The world is on fire, and you're gonna extort me for a confession?" Joe spat through clenched teeth.

The priest's eyes swelled, large and white. "I have to eat."

Joe shoved the priest into a seated position on the pew, then jerked the Beretta Tomcat micro pistol from his pocket and shoved it against the bridge of the priest's nose. "You hungry?" he asked. "How about I do the world a favor and feed you a bullet?"

"No, Señor, no! Por favor!" The priest's hands shook with violent tremors.

"Repeat after me." Joe's voice grew low and his finger moved to the trigger. "Forgive me, Father, for I have sinned …"

"Please!" the priest cried. A dark yellow stain spread across his robe and ran down his legs. Urine soaked the pew and spattered on the marble floor.

Joe wrenched the gun to the side and fired off a round by the priest's ear. The little man screamed, clutched his head, and shrunk down into the pew. He stared up at Joe, eyes terror-stricken.

Joe angled the pistol up. A thin trail of smoke wafted from the barrel. He eyed the quivering, piss-soaked priest and, without another word, grabbed the trumpet case and made for the door. Joe pinballed off two people as they entered, a man and his wife, the impact eliciting a stream of Spanish curses. Joe stomped down the front steps a little too fast and set his jaw at the throbbing pain that radiated from his injured calf. He hit the sidewalk, curved left, and marched one lot down from the church to enter the rat-hole bar. Above the door, the flashing martini glass received a green olive on a toothpick.

Warm body odor hit Joe like a punch. The place was crowded with people packed elbow to elbow. Joe stopped at the threshold to get a feel for the place and a hush fell over the bar. He felt a tickle at the base of his neck.

Anyone in this place could know the price on your head, Joe thought. *Screw it. Everything you ever cared about is dead and gone. Your life might be worth taking, but it ain't worth living.*

He pushed through the crowd and the chatter swelled again. He made for the worst seat in the house, the seat he never wanted—one at the bar. With the entire place to his back, Joe slumped onto a barstool, tucked the trumpet case in front of his feet, and waited for the pain of a kitchen knife to slip into his liver. He leaned on the bar, the flesh and hair on his forearms sticking to the surface.

A barkeep with deep black circles framing hollow eyes rubbed her hands on a soiled rag. Purplish-yellow bruises splotched her arms. Her posture screamed defeat.

"You gonna wipe this shit-show down or what?" Joe said as he examined his hairy, sticky forearms.

The hollow-looking barmaid stared at him from the black pits in her face.

Joe let out a loaded sigh. "Cerveza?"

The hollow woman stepped away and, a moment later, clunked a mug down in front of him. Joe grabbed the handle and took a slug of the room-temperature lager. He wiped his chin with a tacky forearm, then drained the glass.

"Another one," Joe said.

The barkeep's sad eyes bored holes into him, and Joe wondered what sort of hell she'd lived through to look like that.

Joe opened his hands in a silent show of desperation. "Please?"

She bent to retrieve a fresh glass from a low shelf and a tiny crucifix on a gold chain tumbled from her shirt. She glanced up at Joe and, empty glass in hand, tucked the tiny keepsake back into her shirt.

The barmaid stepped away, filled the fresh glass at a tap, and set it down in front of him. Joe raised it, but as the glass touched his lips, a loud patron entertaining two bleary-eyed androgynous hookers swung his arms wide and knocked Joe's glass.

Beer splashed on the countertop and ran down to Joe's arm.

"Hey, hey," Joe snapped, "stupid asshole."

"Vete a la mierda, gringo," the john spat, then laughed and slapped one of the hookers on the ass.

Joe's eagerness to fight over spilled beer ebbed. He slumped forward on his elbows and took another swig. A bout of laughter broke out and the din of the place swelled to deafening levels. Joe pinched his lips and sank into a sea of alcohol-inspired self-loathing.

The door to the bar jerked open, then clacked shut. A woman, malnourished and no older than nineteen, shuffled through the crowd. Dark tangled hair clung to her grimy cheeks. The ripped toes of her shoes scuffed at the gummy floor. She stopped by the old hitman's shoulder.

"Joe Carboni?" she asked in a heavy accent.

Joe twisted on his stool and stared hard at the disheveled young woman.

The disheveled woman held out a smartphone.

Joe ran the back of his hand beneath his chin. "What is it?"

She shook the phone, hand outstretched. "Please, take it."

Joe gave the phone a once over and held out his hand.

The girl dropped it into his palm and turned to leave.

Joe grabbed her frail arm. "What's this?"

"Por favor, Señor Carboni," she said, her whole body trembling in his grip. "She tell me to deliver this to you, and she pay me."

"Who's she?"

"Please, Señor," she sobbed. "I don't want nothing to do with this." She wrenched away and fled the cramped bar, knocking into drunken patrons as she went. She hit the exit at full stride, bowled the door open into a wash of gray afternoon light, and was gone.

Joe frowned and rotated the black-faced device in his hands. The phone powered on with a single touch, and he waited for it to boot up. A generic background of swirled colors filled the screen. One app blinked in, entitled *Open Me*.

Joe touched the icon and a message leaped onto the screen. A timer at the top ticked down from one minute.

> A friend: BC Airport. Go now. The GPS will guide you.

Joe tried to make sense of the words as the timer shot down below forty-five seconds. Then a second message dropped in below the first.

> A friend: J' s life is in your hands. Always has been.

Joe frowned. The counter reached thirty.
Joe's thick fingers moved across the touch screen keyboard. *Hellcat?* he typed. A response popped right up.

> A friend: The one and only.

> Joe: How do you know this?

Joe searched the room, but no one paid him any attention as the timer fell under ten. A new message appeared.

> A friend: Stop wasting time. Go now and bring your toys, or he dies.

The timer hit zero, the screen blipped, and a GPS navigation app filled the screen.

He could barely hear the electronic voice through the noise of the bar. "Turn left on 8 Avenida Norte," the GPS said.

Joe backed off his stool and felt his pockets for his wallet. "Well, shit." Jackson always paid. *You ain't got any coin, Joe.* The empty eyes of the barmaid fixed on him from behind the counter. "Hey, uh," he stammered, "look ..."

"Go," she said. The dark eyes blinked slowly. "It's on me."

Joe's face screwed up in a wrinkled grimace. "You shouldn't pay for it."

She reached across the bar and touched his hairy knuckles. A ghost of a smile crested her mouth. "Sometimes people just need you to care about them," she said. "They need kindness without expectation of return. They need hope."

Joe pressed his lips into a line and lowered his eyes.

"Go," she squeezed his hand, "and pay it forward to someone who needs it." The corners of the sad woman's sunken eyes crinkled with hard-earned wisdom.

Head down, Joe's eyebrows gathered as he touched the woman's hand with the outside edge of his pinky. With barely another look, he grabbed the trumpet case from the floor and hurried for the street.

CHAPTER TWENTY-TWO
Jackson

Another round *thunked* against the armor of the tour bus. Jackson hunched down behind a blown-out tire that could only provide minimal cover. With the Glock—which Marcel had thrust into his hand—pinched between his fingers, Jackson poked his head up just enough to see over the hood and across the tarmac. Two hundred yards away lay their destination: a private hangar housing a Scarlett Moon jet, fueled up and ready to roll.

But between Jackson and freedom, a sea of destruction.

Jeep Gladiators and Toyota Hilux troop carriers careened across the runway, skidding and power sliding past the bus as if the drivers believed themselves part of a VRE game. In the flatbed trucks spray-painted with *HL*, kids younger than Jackson rattled off entire magazines of ammo from rusty, cobbled-together AK-47 rifles. La22 hooligans on foot swarmed the airport by the hundreds with screams on their lips. Row after row of the El Salvadoran hyenas fell beneath a hail of HL gunfire, only to be replaced by more from the rear. The wildness in their eyes spoke of drug-induced bravery—or stupidity.

A Scarlett Moon soldier slapped his comrade's shoulder and called, "Last man," then darted for the next point of cover.

Jackson detected no particular strategy or common enemy in the airfield melee. It just rolled over the black tarmac in a fury of fire.

Thunder rumbled overhead and raindrops smacked the roof of the bus in a drum-like staccato.

"Alpha to Kilo, do you copy?" Marcel yelled into his radio as the rain pattered his face.

Static wash.

"Repeat, Alpha to Bravo," Marcel barked. "Delta! Anyone copy?"

The words came clipped by interference. "—Damn massacre."

"Kilo!" Marcel slid to the ground with his back pressed to the bus.

"Who are the HLs targeting?"

"Everyone." Ragged breath rattled the speaker. "Us, the 22s. They're animals."

"Fuck sake," Marcel muttered, and turned to Jackson. "You've got to know something."

Jackson shook his head. "I told you—the mafia wants me dead. Some guy named Svanire."

Marcel grimaced, then keyed up his radio again. "We have to get to the hangar. Can you provide cover?"

More static hissed from the radio.

"Kilo—you copy?" Marcel yelled, the microphone pressed to his lips. "I need to get this stupid kid out alive."

A fork of lightning pierced the swollen clouds, followed by a deafening clap of thunder. Fat raindrops gushed from above and quenched the burning battlefield with a rush of white noise.

The back of Jackson's neck prickled. "Stupid kid?"

"We're getting slaughtered, and it's your fault," Marcel said, his cold expression slick with rain. He keyed the radio. "All units—we're two hundred yards south of the hangar, behind the tour bus," he spat into the radio. "We're gonna make a run for it. On my mark."

"Delta, copy." The radio crackled. "We'll do our best, but you gotta haul ass."

"Copy," Marcel said, then snatched at the soaking Antiguan sash around Jackson's neck and yanked him close. "Kid, if we make it out alive, you got a ton of explaining to do, you hear me?"

Rain poured across Jackson's face and masked the tears rolling down his cheeks. His uncle, a man who resembled his father in every way, bore a hateful stare into him with those shark-black eyes. Neko cried inside Jackson's hoodie, an echo of his own childish whimper. Jackson's chest tightened and he forced his lips into a defiant line.

"Fuck you, man!" He wrenched the scarf away. "This is *your* mess. You Scarlett assholes with your anti-omniviolence bullshit!"

"Don't open your mouth at me, boy," Marcel fired back. "My brother's kid or not, I'll slay you *myself*. You hear me, you little bastard?"

Little bastard. That's what my uncle thinks of me. Jackson's face burned hot. He scrambled to his feet and swung the Glock down hard. The barrel whipped against the top of Marcel's head. His uncle cried out and clutched at his split scalp. Blood and rainwater mixed and washed down the front of his plate carrier onto his thighs.

Heart thrumming, Jackson sprinted for the open hangar. Away from his uncle, away from the fight, away from all the death and destruction. Bullets zinged off the tarmac at his feet. He staggered and fell. Arms out to break the fall and protect Neko, he landed hard on his elbows. Neko cried out, the Glock clattered away, and Jackson rose again. Elbows throbbing, he ran, thin legs pumping like pistons at full throttle.

Deep in his memory, his mother's voice begged him to come home—and a raw emptiness filled Jackson's chest. Bitter tears of sorrow mixed with the rain to blur his vision. He slipped and crashed to his side in a puddle not twenty feet from the hangar. The concrete tore the denim of his jeans and raked at his bony knees.

Neko cried and clawed at Jackson's stomach through the hoodie.

Jackson lay panting. "I'll show you," he blubbered into the water. "I'll show you all." His fingers trembled and fumbled over the face of his smartwatch, but rain slid over the glass and obscured his commands. "Come on, come on." Tears choked his words.

A hand grabbed him by the hoodie and dragged him to his feet.

"Damn you, stupid-ass kid," Marcel said, face drenched in blood, his head on a swivel. "We gotta move."

Marcel hauled Jackson toward the yawning hangar door.

Another *crack* echoed across the runway, but no flash of lightning followed.

Marcel faltered, heavy rain rinsing claret from a hole in his side an inch below his plate carrier. He stared at Jackson, then collapsed to the tarmac.

"Get up!" Jackson tried to pull his uncle to his feet. "Marcel!"

Marcel gulped at the air.

"He can't talk, bicho," Elena said as she stalked out of the hangar, accompanied by two of her thugs, into the tropical storm. "That's what happens when you're shot in the diaphragm." She flashed diamond-studded teeth. "And because the money is so good, you will die, too, chucho." She raised a Browning Hi-Power pistol.

Fury boiled in Jackson's heart and bolstered his courage. He stuck his chest out and beat it with his fist. "Do it, bitch."

Elena grinned, her grill glinted. Her finger moved to the trigger.

A projectile zipped past and whined as it ricocheted off the tarmac. Elena collapsed to a knee and clutched her side. "Mierda!" The Browning tumbled from her open hand and clacked where it fell.

Elena's guards spun with their FAL rifles and fired, absent a target.

A second high-pitched *zing*. One of the La22 soldier's heads popped like a watermelon wrapped in too many elastic bands, and he collapsed into a heap.

Another *zing*. The remaining thug's chest thumped with the impact, and a puff of red mist disappeared in the wind-blown rain. The man gargled and flopped face-first into the body of his dead comrade.

"Run, Jack! Get inside," a gruff voice called out.

Jackson sat bolt upright and squinted. "Bones!"

On the roof of the hangar, the old hitman lay prostrate, a bullpup rifle welded into his cheek, the scope level with his eye.

"Run!" Bones called out again.

Jackson glanced down at his uncle, who laid still, the rain pattering his unblinking, shark-black eyes.

"You little bastard!" Elena shrieked, and grabbed at Jackson's ankle.

Another bullet whined past Elena's head and zipped off the tarmac. She flung herself prone, face buried in her arms.

Jackson sprinted for the hangar.

A Jeep marked with the letters *HL* careened up beside Jackson, then swerved in front to cut off his path. Jackson held up his hands. The driver, no more than twelve, shouted to his passenger—another kid armed with an AK. Amid shouts Jackson couldn't understand, they studied an e-tablet fixed to the dash. Again the driver pointed at Jackson, then back to the tablet.

Jackson raised his hands up higher. "Whatever I'm worth," he said. "I'll pay you."

The driver made a circle in the air with his index finger and the truck swerved away.

The HL boys tore off down the runway with a "Whoop!" and plowed right through a pack of La22s, leaving a greasy red smear on the road.

Jackson threw his hands in the air. "What the hell is going on?"

"Let's go!" Bones called out from the roof.

Jackson flew into the dark hangar and slammed onto the stairs of the waiting jet.

A tall man in alpine-camo fatigues scrambled from the open jet door. "Hey, you okay?"

Jackson gasped for air under the deafening rattle of rain on the hangar roof.

"Back up, pal." Bones stepped down off a ladder leading to a hatch in the roof. He edged around a tall crate, the muzzle of his bullpup rifle raised.

Jackson launched into Bones' barrel chest and hugged him tight. Under a soaked dress shirt, the old hitman's heavy frame wasn't the same as an embrace from his mom—but it was enough.

The gangster patted Jackson on the back. "Okay, easy there, pal. We gotta move."

"You're Jackson?" the camo guy asked from the foot of the jet's staircase.

Jackson pulled away from Bones, wiped his eyes, and sniffed hard. "Who's asking?" he said, chest puffed up with Bones at his back.

"Can we move this along?" Bones gestured to the jet stairs.

"I'm the pilot," the camo guy said, then glanced out through the hangar door at the melee now rolling away with the storm. Elena still lay on her back, wailing in half-Spanish.

"Where's Marcel?" the pilot asked.

"Dead." Jackson took a few steps closer, his courage growing with each breath. "But he said to take me to Scarlett Moon in Switzerland, right?"

The pilot looked to Bones, who still had the bullpup rifle held at the ready. "And this man?"

"That's Bones," Jackson said. "He comes, too."

"Fine, fine, no problem," the pilot said. "Come on." He disappeared up the stairs into the cabin.

Bones placed his weapon on a crate. "Gimme a second, would ya?"

Jackson trailed behind the old gangster as he limped back to the hangar door.

Bones stepped out into the rain and offered Elena a hand. She grasped the gangster's meaty paw, and he hauled her up into his arms. He limped back inside, straining under her weight, then eased her down to rest against a tall wooden crate.

"You shot me, Joe." Elena wheezed, blood seeping through her fingers. "How could you?"

Joe sighed. "Sorry, darlin', but I can't have you killing my guy here." He nodded to Jackson at his side.

Jackson stood tall, shoulders back, chest out—though his elbows, knees, and nose all burned.

Elena pressed her palm to the wound in her side and winced. "But you shot me …"

"I missed your liver, doll. You'll live." Joe wagged his finger at her. "But you almost castrating me made it a lot easier to pull that trigger."

Elena laughed, which morphed into a rasp. "What happened to us, Joe?"

"I suck at relationships, and you're crazy." Joe shrugged. "It was doomed from the start."

"You're right, of course." Elena looked up at him with smoky eyes. "But we are older, wiser now. And look at you, coming to this boy's rescue. So dashing, so … dangerous." Her lips curled back into a diamond- and blood-coated leer.

"No way," Joe said, and took a step away. "Not happening."

"Come on, Joe. One last fling," Elena said, and licked her jeweled teeth.

"I gotta go." Joe hobbled toward the plane. "Take care of yourself."

"Think of me, Joe. We'll see each other again one day," Elena called out.

"God, I hope not." Joe put his arm around Jackson's shoulder and ushered him to the plane.

The engines turned and a whine rose from them, all systems coming online as the pilot prepped for takeoff.

At the base of the stairs, Jackson stopped. "Where you been, you crusty old prick?" He punched Bones in the arm. "You look like shit."

"And you *are* a shit." Bones smirked, but his eyes narrowed. "You got my cat?"

Jackson pulled the kitten, sodden and mewing, from his hoodie. "*My* cat."

"Let's get the hell out of here." Bones cupped Jackson's shoulder and helped him to the jet stairs.

"Stake. Fuck this place." Jackson took the stairs two at a time. He paused at the top, waiting for his guardian angel. Bones took one last look out at the tarmac, where the melee had moved on, then gave a firm nod and hobbled after the teen, taking the steps one at a time.

CHAPTER TWENTY-THREE
Svanire

The most opulent room in the underground complex was, without question, the dining room. While many of the bunker's spaces were originally designed for military efficiency, stacked over one another in economical precision, Svanire had insisted the dining room deserved special attention during the remodel.

He sat at the head of a long, rich sandalwood table which occupied the center of the space atop a seventeenth-century Rothschild Tabriz medallion carpet. Along the length of the table sat ornate candelabras of pure silver and the finest bone-china crockery. Warm modern lighting lay inset into the dark wood-paneled walls and, over the room's hidden sound system, the percussive piano of Liszt's *Totentanz* trembled the air.

Svanire poised the tines of his antique silver fork against the last portion of seared foie gras. He pressed his fork against the rare flesh, tender and willing. With slow, deliberate pressure, the tines indented, then punctured the surface. Svanire allowed himself a gasp of pleasure, then moaned as juice dribbled out from the wound onto the plate.

An icy smile played across his thin lips.

He closed his eyes, then popped the foie gras through the gap in his perfect white teeth. The morsel melted in his mouth and he raised the fork like a conductor's wand to punctuate a moment in the score.

A bald, portly man in a white apron emerged from a side door. He approached with hurried steps, but stopped shy of the carpet.

Eyes closed, Svanire swallowed the bite and placed the fork gently on the plate. He dabbed the corners of his mouth with an embroidered white napkin. "What is it?"

The chef thumbed his ear, averted his eyes, then leaned forward with an open hand. "May I step on the carpet, monsieur? To take your plate?"

Svanire opened his eyes, then folded the napkin, but did not turn in the chef's direction. "It was dry."

The portly chef pursed his lips and gave a hesitant nod. "Dry?"

"Are you a parrot?" Svanire turned his cold eyes on the chef.

"No, monsieur," the chef said, sweat studding his brow.

With manicured fingers, Svanire plucked an engraved silver dinner knife from beside his plate and inspected the flawless craftsmanship. "Foie gras must be cultivated with extreme attention and care so as not to cause it to burn or melt. This piece," Svanire jabbed at the plate with the knife, "was cut too thin, and thus you overcooked it."

The chef wiped his brow and bowed. "I'm sorry, monsieur—"

"You're sorry?" Svanire interrupted. "Sorry is what one says when he absently forgets to return a call or complete some trite errand for an acquaintance. Sorry is not what one says having just destroyed an important meal for his employer."

The chef bowed low and held the posture of submission. "I deeply apologize for my miscalculation, Monsieur Svanire. It will not happen next time."

"Correct." Svanire stood with the knife in hand, and his tall, slender form towered over the bowed chef. "Because you'll be dead, and I'll have a new chef—one who knows how to prepare foie gras."

The chef straightened slowly, face drained of all color, and pulled down on the hem of his apron. For the first time, he raised his terror-stricken face. His throat moved once, twice.

Svanire's narrow eyes closed to slits and his lips parted, showing the stark white of his teeth. "I'm joking, of course." He dropped the knife on the plate.

"Monsieur ..." the chef said, the words tangled in his throat. "Yes, monsieur. Of course."

Svanire slipped his hand beneath the plate and extended it to the chef.

The portly man reached out, hands trembling, and took the empty plate. He held it out before him as though it were a shield.

"You're dismissed." Svanire turned away from the table and made for the central corridor, his light pas brisé steps contrasted against a wintry expression.

Within the bowels of the converted Cold War missile silo, he passed the long-term food vault, filled with case upon case of metal tins and nitrogen-packaged food, the water reclamation unit backed up by a deep-water well, and the generator housing group, supported by underground hydropower.

His personal library, replete with a wine vault—all his own additions—lured him inside to well-worn oxblood Chesterfield couches, a place even more important than the dining room. His loins ached and he stepped to the only other door in the room—a heavy, dark metallic portal—and traced his pale fingertips across its surface. He leaned close and listened to the rustle of chains on the other side. His tongue tingled with the thought of licking Château Lafite 1787 from the navel of one of his pets.

"I'll be home soon, my loves," he whispered, then placed a tender kiss on the smooth steel of the door. Svanire took a step away, but his fingertips lingered with a lover's touch.

With a crisp ballerina's turnout, Svanire strode out of the library, then rode the elevator up to his private quarters. The doors pinged open to reveal dark hardwood. Twenty-foot-long oil paintings hung in gilded frames. He tapped his smartwatch and for a moment recoiled at its square, uncultured aesthetic. "Would much prefer a Patek," he moaned, "but needs being what they are …"

A series of monitors fixed to the back wall of the parlor flicked on to display independent blogger news feeds from around the world. One headline read: *Scarlett Moon Forces Clash with La22 in the Bloodiest Battle for BC Yet.*

A smirk teased at the corners of his mouth.

Svanire touched the wood paneling. It slid back to reveal a massive wardrobe full of onyx-black suits. He ran his fingers down the row of jacket sleeves and stopped at a series of hangers loaded with dark tactical clothing. He stepped out of his charcoal-over-black wingtips and slid out of his jacket and pants, then placed them all neatly inside the cupboard. Near-translucent fingers worked at the buttons of his shirt until he could open it and pull it off. He hung that too, though on a second rod for clothes to be collected and cleaned.

At the far end of the luxurious space from whence he'd come, the elevator doors slid back. Inside, Richter stepped forward to the open elevator door. Dressed in midnight fatigues with a suppressed pistol secured on his hip, Richter possessed an explosive, restless energy that simmered within his compact but muscular frame. "You asked for me, Boss?"

"Please, come in," Svanire said.

The security team leader crossed the space, but stopped short of the bedroom.

"I assume everything is in place?" Svanire extracted a pair of midnight-black tactical pants and pulled them up over his lithe legs.

"The team is ready on the surface," Richter said. "They're the best I could find."

"Good. I shall only be a moment." Svanire selected a matching tactical blouse from the hanger. He tucked his head through and pulled it down over the thick scars that traced his back in a patchwork, then stepped into a pair of black tactical boots and tucked a series of razor-sharp knives into sheaths concealed behind his belt. "Will you accompany me?"

"Of course." Richter turned back for the elevator, tabbed the button, and held the doors.

Svanire entered and pressed the button for the fourth floor.

As the elevator groaned upward, Svanire clasped his hands at his waist.

"Have the chef disemboweled." Svanire checked his manicured fingers, then straightened the tiny wrinkles from his blouse. "I don't like his foie gras."

Richter pursed his lips. "You have a replacement?"

Svanire shooed the thought away with his fingertips. "The other candidate from L'atelier Des Sens should suffice. Just make it happen."

"Yes, sir." Richter produced a small tablet from a cargo pocket and tapped at the screen.

The elevator came to a full stop, but the doors did not open. Svanire touched his full palm to a black glass panel above the floor call buttons. A blip sounded. He raised his face to be scanned by the camera overhead.

"Hello, Mr. Svanire," an artificial female voice said. "Welcome."
A chime rang and the doors opened.

Svanire danced out into the ivory-colored open floor plan with its ten-foot-high ceilings and row upon row of tables. "What do you think?" he asked Richter.

Upon each row of tables waited dozens of computer terminals, their screens dark.

Richter stepped from the elevator, but not an inch further, and allowed the doors to shut behind him. "My clearance doesn't allow me on levels three through nine."

Svanire waved at the room. "Entertain me. What is this?"

Richter eyed Svanire, then walked to the nearest terminal and bent to inspect the dark screen. "I don't know," the security leader said. "A ton of computers and no human operators."

"With six more floors just like this one," Svanire added. "Go on."

Richter shrugged. "Not my specialty, Boss, but with this much computing power … crypto?"

Svanire chuckled. "Nothing so crude." He strutted to where Richter stared at the terminal and woke the screen. A single box appeared: *Password*. Svanire's fingers hovered over the keyboard. He looked at Richter.

Richter turned away.

Svanire typed his password into the block: *#9ower9leasure9ain*. It immediately masked itself with a string of asterisks.

"Ready?" Svanire held a slender finger over the *Enter* key.

Richter waited, hands behind his back.

Svanire tapped the key and a small camera above the screen imaged his face to confirm identity. Hundreds of terminals sprang to life around the room, each monitor filled with a different task. Engaged in an effortless digital ballet, the AI on each screen jumped from tab to tab.

"So, what is it all doing?" Richter asked.

"My HKT Artificial Intelligence is the most sophisticated in its class," Svanire said. "It can execute almost any cyber-attack you can imagine and get into nearly any system." He motioned to the next terminal.

"Nearly?"

"Nearly," Svanire repeated, eyebrows raised.

Richter frowned, but held his tongue.

"This one hacks the defenses of the South Korean people," Svanire continued. "I'm sure you'll hear about a little wholly unprepared run-in with their northern neighbors soon enough. How awful." He feigned a despairing pout, then directed Richter to the next screen. "This one spreads viral disinformation, pedaled as fact-checked *truth*, to the left-controlled New Zealand Justice Coalition. Quite amusing, as they currently burn all their livestock because of a non-existent prison outbreak." He pointed to the next screen. "And that one redeploys the Chinese supply lines as they deliver aid to the annexed U.S. West Coast."

"Didn't Rigoletti experiment in Chinese aid?" Richter said. "That was his side hustle."

Svanire sneered and tapped the side of his head with a spidery finger. "Crafty bastard. Some tough cybersecurity for that op, too. But my HKT had little difficulty penetrating. Once it did, I took Rigoletti's toy away. All those greedy dons dabbling on the side, and now every bit of it belongs to me." His chest swelled. "Pieces in a jigsaw puzzle."

Richter watched a screen populated with colored chat boxes. He leaned in closer to inspect it. "And this one?"

"Oh, this one is a favorite." Svanire's face glowed. "Watch." He clicked on a tab that read *Suicide and Crisis Hotline*. One of the live chat windows expanded. Text flashed up in quick spurts of characters.

> Maurice: Hi, nice to see you again.
> Chloe: Hi, Maurice. I got one, just like you told me.

"Maurice is your HKT AI? A bot?" Richter rubbed the back of his head.

Svanire smiled. "Not always." He flexed his fingers, then tapped a few keys, taking control of Maurice.

> Maurice: Good, that's good. Are you ready like we talked about?
> Chloe: I think so ... I'm scared.

Svanire grinned at Richter before responding.

Richter leaned in to better see the conversation.

Maurice: Don't be, this is the right thing to do. The world is messed up. Your dad killed himself because he couldn't stop the thoughts. You can't either. Living just isn't an option anymore.
Chloe: Ur right.
Maurice: Okay, Chloe. Camera on.

A window pinged open to reveal the wet, gaunt face of a thirteen-year-old child with empty eyes, standing before a dirty bed populated with only a few old stuffed toys.

Maurice: Remember, it has to be a sturdy branch.

"I know a good one," Chloe said, her voice barely audible. The image from her smartphone jostled, then turned sideways. The child's legs shuffled, dingy pink slippers scuffing across a peeled linoleum floor. The camera view bobbed with her shambling steps as she made for a screen door. She plodded down the stairs and out the front door into an open area crossed with laundry wires. Patches of brown grass and dirt crunched beneath the girl's feet. The camera angled up to show the thick limbs of a laurel oak and the crumbling red brick of project housing, broken and cruel.

Chloe: How about this?

Svanire licked his lips and tapped three letters.

Maurice: Yes.

The girl sat the camera down, propped against some unknown object. She shuffled off the screen, then returned with a plastic chair and an orange coil of an extension cord. She bent back down before the camera lens, her youthful face streaked with tears.

Svanire eyed Richter, whose marble expression had cracked just a little, then typed again.

Maurice: Go live to your socials. They need to see what they made you do.

Chloe bit her bottom lip and tapped and swiped at the screen a few times before clearing her throat. "I'm recording this so you all can see … what you …" She choked out a sob. "What you made me do." She climbed onto the chair, slipped the power cord around her neck, and drew it tight. "Bye, Momma."

Svanire stood, unable to contain a Cheshire grin. He turned to savor Richter's expression of disgust.

The plastic chair squealed in protest, and a leg snapped as it toppled over. Chloe grunted and gasped, and the extension cord strained with the kicking of her legs. A little shower of leaves rained over her.

"Damn," Richter said, his upper lip curling. "That's cold …" He shook his head.

Svanire allowed the AI to resume. "And I'm just one man," he told Richter. "HKT is doing this around the world, in every language, across social media, to hundreds of people a second. And the entire operation is foolproof."

Richter squared his shoulders. "Why are you showing me this, Boss?"

"Because, dear Richter, we now arrive at the pièce de résistance." Svanire leaned over another terminal and punched a few keys until a new image filled the screen.

Down the length of an airport runway littered with corpses and a wrecked tour bus, fires burned despite the heavy rain. Gunfire rattled over the monitor's speaker and men screamed in the distance. A pickup crashed headlong into a group of riflemen in yellow bandanas.

Svanire tapped the keyboard, and the drone footage froze. Another tap, and the video zoomed in on the entrance to an open hangar. Svanire inched the footage forward frame by frame. A barrel-chested man lifted a woman in fatigues off the tarmac and carried her to the hangar as a young black male watched.

"Carboni," Richter said.

Svanire nodded. "And young Mr. Cross. Just a few hours ago, before they boarded a plane bound for Switzerland."

"Mmm," Richter said.

"They've survived thus far." Svanire rubbed slender hands together. "But it's time to put ol' Jojo out of his misery."

Richter clenched his jaw a little tighter.

"Come, let's not keep our boys waiting," Svanire said.

With Richter in tow, Svanire returned to the elevator and together they rode the rest of the way to the surface in silence. They exited the elevator between two massive doors of armored steel filled with poured concrete. Svanire tapped his smartwatch and the doors groaned shut behind them.

Outside, the pristine mountain air whipped and bit at Svanire's alabaster cheeks. He turned to admire his fortress embedded in the snowcapped České Středohoří mountains, silhouetted against the forgotten Czech capital of Prague. He hadn't felt this much excitement since getting that initial buttery whiff of his first love, Christopher, a boy with cobalt eyes and strawberry hair that Svanire had specially imported from England more than a decade ago.

Svanire pressed away his growing arousal and trained his thoughts on the mission ahead.

He stepped from shade into sunlight and completed a curt pirouette to face a group of twenty stoic mercenaries in tactical gear that Richter had gathered for him. The best of the best, he'd been assured. Behind them, on a small grassy rise, four MH-7M Little Bird rapid-assault helicopters waited.

"I'm coming, Jojo," Svanire whispered. "The game is almost over."

CHAPTER TWENTY-FOUR
Jackson

Jackson awoke to the stench of cat urine clawing its way up his nostrils. He groaned and pulled himself upright in the soft leather seat. "What the hell, Neko?" He pinched his nose.

Bones looked over from his chair across the aisle. He stroked Neko's back with a hairy hand as the kitten purred. "My man had to go some time."

Jackson covered his face with his sash. "Damn," he mumbled through the fabric. "That's nasty. Though, with the bathroom out of order, I could stand to lose a couple of pounds myself."

Bones chuckled. "First thing we can agree on."

In the light of day, the full audacity of the plane's plush cream linings, wooden furnishings, and star-speckled ceiling came to life. Jackson had only ever seen this kind of private jet in old music videos. The sort of crypto millionaires for whom he normally worked probably had one, perhaps even five. Now he—Jackson Cross, a teenager from Englewood, Chicago—rode one on his way to Switzerland.

A smile spread across his lips. *If only Mom could see me now.*

"Buckle up, gentleman," the pilot said over the intercom. "Touchdown in ten."

Below, huge veins of snowcapped mountains pushed through swathes of green countryside. Unlike the crowded streets of Chicago, full of concrete and glass, Switzerland's hamlets and towns consisted of wooden farmhouses generously spaced out. Even where dwellings coalesced into some kind of center, an airy feeling to the layout remained. In Chicago, like most U.S. cities, roads and walkways crossed each other to form perfect claustrophobic squares. Here, the cobbled roads and pavement intertwined like loose spiderwebs.

Despite the pretty view, Jackson's mind turned in dark circles.

"Why didn't they kill me?" he said aloud.

Joe looked up from rubbing Neko.

"Those Hard Living kids in the Jeep," Jackson added. "They had me dead to rights."

"I know," Joe said. "I almost had to shoot 'em."

"They could've hosed me. Why didn't they?" Jackson asked.

Bones shrugged. "Maybe they lost their nerve."

Jackson replayed the scene in his mind—the child soldiers bickering over a tablet with his photo. His stomach tightened as the jet dropped in altitude.

Bones' brow wrinkled and he rubbed his gray stubbled chin.

Jackson narrowed his eyes. "What?"

"Well, now that you mention it." Bones sat more upright in his seat. "What are the chances that we'd run into Elena *and* your uncle in Bitcoin City, of all places?"

"Not very high?"

"Stinks, like a setup." Bones wagged a finger. "Like someone's playing us."

"Svanire?" Jackson asked.

The wheels bumped and squealed on the tarmac.

"Makes sense to me." Bones clutched Neko to his lap. "Those hits on kids, that wasn't the Don. I know it wasn't. Svanire is pulling some shit behind his back, and it's big."

"Perhaps the Don is dead," Jackson said.

A shadow crossed Bones' face.

The jet braked hard, and a dried cat turd rolled down the aisle.

"Gross," Jackson mumbled.

The jet taxied for a few more minutes, then slowly rolled to a stop. The door popped open, and a fresh zephyr blew through that prickled Jackson's skin. The air felt so clean and free of cat shit and pollution that Jackson's first lungful almost burned. Bones stood and handed Neko over.

Jackson took the cat, grabbed his mobile phone from the charging station, then chased after the old gangster. "Hey, wait up!" Jackson said as he stumbled down the jet stairs onto the tarmac. He caught up to Bones and marched alongside, trying to keep pace. "You in a rush?"

OMNIVIOLENCE

Bones nodded, eyebrows raised.

"Oh, right," Jackson said.

A man with a bodybuilder's physique and short blond hair emerged from a two-story square building and crossed the empty airfield toward them.

Jackson's muscles tensed, and he swore he could see Bones coil for a fight. He scanned for more threats. Guys in combat gear, automatic weapons, or a K9 unit, perhaps. Nothing. Just the blond guy.

"Gruezi!" the man said, his voice deep and his smile broad.

"Eh?" Jackson said.

"You are Jackson," the man said. "I'm Christian. Marcel sent word ahead." English rolled off his tongue, the cadence melodic as if he sang the words.

"And Herr Carboni," Christian said, then offered Bones his hand.

Bones shook Christian's thick paw.

Christian peered over Bones' shoulder. "Und Marcel?"

Bones shook his jug-head. "He didn't make it."

"I see," Christian said, hardly phased. "Well, if you don't mind," he said, and raised his arms out to mime being searched.

Jackson frowned.

Christian patted Bones down, head to ankle, taking a damn age around the belt, groin, and thigh area.

"Hey, pal," Bones said, shifting on the spot. "Some of us have been on a long flight with no restroom."

"We gotta *go*," Jackson said. "You feel me?"

Christian plucked the Beretta Tomcat from Bones' pocket and, with a smile, placed it in his own. He turned to Jackson, lightly patted his chest, and felt the kitten beneath, who mewed. Christian let out a light-hearted laugh as Neko poked his head out.

Jackson quickly produced the fur ball from his hoodie. "Just a cat," he said.

Christian examined Neko briefly, then finished his pat down of Jackson.

"We good?" Bones said. "Otherwise, I'm gonna drop my shorts right here."

"Gal, no problem," Christian replied with a chuckle. "Bathrooms are this way."

A fresh breeze at their backs, the broad-chested Swissy led the way across the airstrip and into the main building. Every few feet, someone in an orange vest nodded and exclaimed, "Gruezi mitennan!" while looking so deep into Jackson's eyes, it made him wish for his Lenser mask.

"What the hell are they saying?" Jackson whispered to Bones, who just shrugged.

"It's like a hello," Christian said. "It's polite to say it back."

"They're saying hello to *you?*" Bones chimed in.

"To us all!" Christian said. "*Mitennan* is like saying *To you all.*"

Jackson just glowered.

"Bathroom is in there," Christian said, pointing at two doors.

Jackson headed for the door marked *Herren*, with the universal symbol of a person in pants rather than a skirt. "No need to translate that," he said.

Bones limped after him, but they both froze in the doorway. Two urinals and three stalls left almost no other space to stand in the tiny bathroom. Jackson glanced at Bones, and the two made an unspoken agreement. Jackson headed to the far stall while Bones took the one nearest the door.

Jackson stepped inside the stall, shut the door, and let Neko out onto the tiled floor. The kitten bumbled around in circles as if drunk, never quite making an escape through the gap under the door. Jackson pulled down his jeans and undershorts with a hole in the seam, then rolled up a wad of toilet paper and crammed it between his butt cheeks. The stabbing pain pulsed through his guts until the built-up gases hissed through his anus and over the makeshift muffler.

Bones, however, had clearly not constructed such a device. From two stalls down, a thunderous rumble echoed around the tiled room, so loud and abrupt that Neko skittered out under the door of Jackson's stall.

Jackson blurted out a laugh, then covered his mouth. "Damn, man. Been storing that one up for a while, stake?"

Bones chuckled but said nothing.

Seated on the toilet, Jackson pulled his mobile device, wedged his elbows onto his bare knees, and stared at the screen.

A notification sat at the top of the screen. The Pegasus update Hellcat had promised had come through, which meant his phone was working. "But she hasn't made contact," he whispered. He checked the service, which had connected to a network called SMComm. "Guess that's Scarlett Moon," he said.

"Everything okay over there?" Bones called from his stall.

"No word from Hellcat," Jackson said. "What if Svanire got to her?" He screwed up his face. "And—and don't talk to me, now … it's weird."

With their business concluded, Jackson and Bones emerged from their stalls into the thick air of the restroom. They washed their hands in silence without making eye contact, though each had a dumb smirk on his face.

They dried their hands with the electric blowers then sauntered out. Neko slipped through the bathroom door just before it closed, the pitter-patter of tiny paws barely audible. Another orange vest, perhaps in his mid-twenties, stepped over the kitten and into the bathroom.

Christian stood in the hallway, a brown bag in each hand and a carton of milk tucked under his arm. "Thought you might be hungry." He offered a bag to Jackson.

"That one's always hungry," Bones said, and took the second bag.

"Gipfli," Christian said.

Jackson opened the bag to find a warm pastry inside. "Oh, a croissant."

"Ja." Christian nodded. "That's what I said. Gipfli. And something for your friend." He ripped open the milk carton and poured a little onto the smooth floor. Bones and Jackson stepped away as the milk splattered between them.

Neko waddled over and lapped up the puddle.

"Thanks," Bones said. "What coin do we owe you?"

"No coin," Christian said with a plastic smile. "Only a few francs. But, my treat. I invite you."

"Francs?" Jackson frowned. "Oh man, you still use physical money, right?"

Christian nodded. "Crypto is more like ... shares or bonds, here. Investment opportunities. Trading with foreigners. But the Swiss franc still makes sense within our borders. And the government—well, Scarlett Moon—ensures that it maintains value, no big swings." He swung his hand and smiled. "It stops people suddenly becoming poor ... like when Schmertz Coin crashed and took Greenland's entire government with it." His tone carried an air of pride, perhaps the first real emotion Jackson had registered from the odd Swissy.

Jackson took a bite of gipfli and swept the flakes of pastry from his hoodie as he mused on the idea of real money. He stooped and collected Neko. "But then, Scarlett Moon controls the amount of cash in circulation." He swallowed his mouthful. "And who gets it?"

"It all works out," Christian said with a shrug. "We're pretty fair here in Switzerland."

"I don't know about—my phone!" Jackson blurted out, then stuffed the rest of the gipfli into his mouth and patted himself down with one hand, holding Neko in the other. "Shit, I left it in the bathroom!" he said around the pastry, then shoved the kitten into Bones' arms and ran toward the toilet door.

The orange vest they'd passed at the bathroom door bowled out, Jackson's phone in his hand. "Hoi, du hast dein Handy vergessen!"

Jackson took the phone from the young man, who smiled and went on his way without another word. Jackson inspected his phone for signs of tampering, but found nothing. "Thanks," he said, but the Samaritan had already gone. "Didn't try to steal it ..." Jackson said to himself.

"Why would he?" Christian asked.

"Because he could," Jackson said.

"Not here," Christian replied with a smirk. "No one here is truly poor. He'll get more money from the RAF—still supported by Scarlett Moon—if he loses his job than from selling stolen handies."

"This place is freaking me out," Jackson grumbled as Christian walked away.

"I kind of like it." Bones handed Neko back to Jackson, then tucked into his own savory pastry.

As the trio marched through corridors and along walkways, men and women with luminous vests pulled luggage and greeted them with the same strange words, eye-burning stares, and wide smiles.

"Twenty-one, twenty-two ..." Jackson said through a mouthful of croissant.

Bones frowned.

Jackson crumpled the bag and considered chucking it over his shoulder, but thought better of it. "Counting the number of white faces until I see a brown one," he said, eyeing the pristine corridor, "I haven't seen a single black guy." He stuffed the crumpled bag into his jeans pocket.

Bones opened his mouth to reply, then closed it again.

"We don't have many people of African descent here in the St. Gallen area," Christian piped up.

"I ain't judging, per se. Mom is—uh, was—white," Jackson said, "but it's weird, man."

Christian laughed. "We are a nation of many ethnicities. Czech, Serb, Croat ..."

"Still all white, though, right?" Jackson said. "Twenty-three, twenty-four ..."

"Kid's got a point," Bones said. "It ain't like this over in the States. Least, not in Chicago."

Christian stopped to face Jackson. "I understand, but your position entirely depends on your definition of white."

"My position? I mean white like you or *him*." Jackson jabbed a finger at Bones.

Christian chuckled again, nothing confrontational in his posture. "I'm not white, I'm Romani," he said.

"What the hell is that?" Jackson asked.

"I was born in Switzerland, but I have no ancestral tie to any one country to call home. We don't identify as one particular ethnic group because we are made of many, all mixed together." Christian smiled, then continued down the hall. "Though, I guess if you go back far enough in history, you might suggest the very first Romani came from India."

"Shut up," Jackson said, jogging up to better study Christian's blond hair. "You're Indian?"

"I am many things," Christian said, his mechanical smile never fading. "Just like the ten million Romani on the European continent. Grouping and judging one's fellow man based on the tone of someone's skin seems … offensive, no?"

Jackson stopped, brow lowered, as he processed the thought. Bones shuffled past, a peculiar grin on his face.

"Tarasp is two and half hours' drive from here," Christian announced as they caught up to him in an outdoor parking lot filled with rows of small electric cars.

"Do we, ah …" Bones eyed the sky. "Need to worry about …?"

"Drones? Attacks?" Christian grinned and shook his head. "Scarlett Moon keeps us safe within their cloud-net defense system."

"Oh." Bones continued to search the sky.

"It's a scenic drive along Lake Konstanz," Christian said, "and through the mountains." He opened the back door of a compact cream-colored Volvo and gestured to the seat. "Switzerland is a most beautiful country."

Country? Jackson thought. *More like different planet.*

CHAPTER TWENTY-FIVE
Anja

Anja opened her foldable phone, then the social media application closest to her thumb. It didn't really matter which app—the accounts weren't hers, and the vitriol she found within each of them would be comparable. The desire to engage the net had long since left her, but occasionally—on important milestones in her journey—she plugged into that vapid, insufferable place.

A brief dip into the seedy public consciousness confirmed the validity of Anja's cause. Each spiteful comment, each random, ill-informed judgment, every call to cancel someone or end their life, each bloated, self-important opinion—all of it hammered home Anja's resolve: Humanity could not be trusted to temper its own hatred any longer.

The feed pinged open and she began to scroll. Static images with accompanying reams of text had died as a form of content, replaced by micro clips fifteen seconds long. Post after post, Anja—society—was bombarded with people's thoughts, perspectives, and random musings, all reduced to an out-of-context blip designed to evoke a response. Thumbs up, devil faces, and rainbows littered each post. A ghastly truncation of human emotion. The idea that humans could experience a range of feelings simultaneously—sad but happy, scared yet excited—had dissolved and died long ago. Now a limited number of comical symbols communicated only the most basic emotions and no more. Once, choosing whether to like, heart, or cry in response to a social post about the death of a pet had often plunged Anja into existential crisis.

Now, with a flick of her thumb, yet another ridiculous video scrolled up. A young woman wore a platinum wig and little more than a handkerchief to cover her vulva, sporting a top made entirely of string. She told men to subscribe to her dedicated platform for nudes and self-flagellation with an array of neon-colored toys spread on her mattress in a closet-sized room. Yet her caption read, *Fuck everyone who doesn't feel your vibe, I don't need anyone.*

Anja rolled her eyes at the irony.

"Ms. Kuhn, we have a problem."

She snapped her foldable device closed.

Hans stood by his console, headset pulled down around his fleshy neck.

"We've lost Seoul," he said. "The whole station just went offline."

"Scheisse." Anja threw her head back and stared at the buttressed ceiling, then stuffed her phone into a pocket. "Do we know what happened?"

"North Korea happened." Hans pointed at the twenty-foot screen fixed to the stone wall of the command center. The giant monitor presented an illuminated map of the world, the edges of the continents humming electric blue. Across each land mass, green filaments connected in a web so dense, the Earth appeared to be covered in glowing cotton wool. Within the green haze, strands clustered to form hot spots, each labeled with a number and a window showing a live video feed. Every square feed showed a similar scene: the gray, depressing buildings of a nuclear power plant, a red and white stack stretching to the sky.

Anja made her way to the snack table in the middle of the room. She snatched up an apple and tossed it between her hands. Hans took off his headset and waddled after her.

"As I *told* you it would," Hans said, his voice thin. "The South couldn't hold them off any longer. No international aid, no nothing. Our minimal support wasn't enough. We should have paid for more aid, more weapons. Like Marcel wanted. Instead of your Solution." He shook his head. "It's all over the blog news. China stepped in and wiped out Seoul."

"Sending in our troops just ends in more unnecessary bloodshed," Anja said with a wave of her hand. She nodded toward the monitor. "Can we get the feed back?"

"We got nothing, it went dark," Hans said. "We have to pull out."

She chewed on a fingernail, her gaze flitting from the huge screen to the five or six armed guards along the edge of the room to the rows of her people at their stations.

"Has Marcel even made contact from B.C.?" Hans clamped his hands to his hips. "Do we have the city back?"

Anja cut her eyes at him. "Doesn't matter. I can make it work."

"You can't," he said, then stormed to his station and keyed up a simulation on the main screen. "Without Seoul and B.C., the coverage is sixty-two point three percent." Onscreen, a network of orange lines flashed, then a cloud of a billion fluorescent dots swarmed out from them and around the globe, pushed and pulled by the prevailing weather systems.

"Look, we have all the other sites." Anja pointed at the still-live camera feeds. "And you're using an old model. Latest satellite imagery projects a good weather front passing through the Northern Ferrel airflow cell." She drew an arc with her hand across the Eurasian continent. "Air flows up and to the right in the northern hemisphere due to the Coriolis effect, and that super low pressure over the Korean Peninsula"—she waved her hand at Asia—"will just suck in everything thrown up into the atmosphere in China and Mongolia. Same for Eastern Siberia—it'll all flow from our sites in Kazakhstan."

"If we're lucky. And B.C.?" Hans asked. "El Salvador is still a problem, Anja," he said, directing her to the dead hub between the North and South American continents. "It's in the middle of the doldrums. We couldn't get a toy sailboat to move in there. We need ground-level exposure," he said. "Can't rely on trade winds."

"It'll work," Anja muttered.

"We need to wait." He shook his head. "We get one shot, we—"

"It will work!" Anja yelled, and the urge to hurl the apple at Hans's fat face tingled her fingertips. "We can't wait, Hans. There's no time," she whispered, then recovered her composure. "I have a contingency."

"Nothing happens without Marcel, you know that," Hans said, defiance carved into his pudgy face. "The system needs both his key code and yours to activate."

An uncomfortable quiet settled over the white noise of hundreds of fingers clacking away at the terminals around the room.

"Look, Ms. Kuhn … Anja," Hans said, "we're all with you. We can wait, really." He motioned to the room of people squirreling away at their stations. "Tabea's situation has you spooked, but we'll get another chance."

A middle-aged woman in spectacles glanced up from her post. Anja took in her worried stare. Maybe the woman, maybe all of them, had begun to doubt the plan.

Maybe they've lost faith in me.

The phone in Anja's pocket hummed.

She placed the apple, just one bite taken from it, on the nearest desk, pulled her phone free, and turned toward the balcony.

"Anja—" Hans called after her.

Tabea pushed through the heavy doors, her medical gown flapped open in the back.

Anja spun on a dime.

"Tabea?" Hans took a step toward her.

"Damn," Anja said and lowered the phone to her side. "Tabea, you can't be here."

"I didn't want to be alone," Tabea said, a desperate smile on her lips. She jittered like an ostracized teenager finally invited to the party. "I need to be with people."

"I know," Anja said. The device in her hand buzzed with an incoming video call. "I know, but you have to get back to bed."

"I just want to be with my friends," Tabea pressed, and stumbled drunkenly into the control room. "Hi, everyone," she called out, her smile broadcasting some inner joy.

Hans shot forward and grabbed Tabea by the shoulders. "What's wrong with her?"

Two of the perimeter guards readied their weapons and looked at Anja.

"She's just delirious." Anja gave her soldiers a curt shake of her head. "From the poison. Take her back to her bed." She stormed over to Hans and Tabea.

"Of course," Hans said, "but—"

"Not you," Anja barked. "Not you. Security can do it. I need you here to keep things on track."

Hans pulled a grinning Tabea closer to him, studying her eyes. "You gave her The Solution, didn't you?"

"Yes," Anja said, then slid around Tabea as if touching her might transmit the poison in her system. "We'll all take it in the end." Anja nodded and each guard took one of Tabea's arms.

"Hi, friends," Tabea said with a loving sigh.

Anja hovered for a moment, then whipped the buzzing phone to eye level and unfolded it. The incoming video request had no name, but she knew the number. She stomped down the hallway leaving Hans in control, through the main exit, and made for the red and white guardhouse gate. The phone kept vibrating as she stormed past a set of mounted anti-aircraft turrets, then down the walkway to the outer wall. Two of her mercs in tactical gray and crimson sauntered to the other end of the sand-colored wall to give her privacy.

She stared out over the grassy knolls below, huffed through her nose, and slid her finger across the answer bar of her phone. Onscreen, chaos erupted. The camera view thrashed and wobbled to the sound of gunfire, pained screams, and heavy breathing.

"Elena?" Anja whispered.

"You focked us, you bitch!" Elena bawled, though the video only showed a smoke-filled night sky. More gunfire rattled in the distance.

"Elena, what's going on?" Anja snapped, checking over her shoulder for voyeurs.

"He had help, puta," the woman hacked before angling her device to reveal her bloodied, filthy face, blood in her diamond teeth.

"Marcel had his team with him, I told you that," Anja hissed, trying to keep her voice a whisper. "And probably some local militia."

Elena's ruined face cinched into a hateful mask. "And the mafia, out of Chicago? Or those crazy South African motherfockers?" she spat at the phone. Globs of pink saliva caused the camera's autofocus to struggle.

"Chicago?" Anja glanced at the mercs, who averted their curious gazes. "South Africa? I don't know what you're talking about."

"It's a focking bloodbath, chura!" Elena screamed.

Anja held the device close to her face. "Did you do it or not—is the station online? Is Marcel dead?"

"It's all focked! Traitor bitch!" Elena cried, rocking back and forth behind a stack of wooden pallets. "I'm coming for you, puta, you hear me? I'm—"

A shadow slid over Elena's face. She dropped her phone, which clattered on the ground and settled with the camera pointing straight up. A pair of legs and the muzzle of a very large handgun crossed the video image.

"No. No—!" Elena raised a blood-smeared hand.

"Jou ma se poes," the newcomer said in a deep Afrikaans lilt. The barrel of the weapon lifted and flashed.

The crack made Anja's phone buzz, and her soldiers looked over from the other end of the wall. She waved them away with a weak smile.

Onscreen, the murderer, stepped away from the phone, his large ring glinting in the firelight. Then he came back and brought his heel down on the device.

The feed cut to black.

"Scheisse," Anja muttered. "It's falling apart. It can't fall apart."

From behind, Hans gave an apologetic cough. "Ms. Kuhn."

"For god's sake, Hans!" She whirled on her heel. "It's Anja—can you not just call me Anja?"

The short fat man stuttered, all his courage evaporated. "There's someone coming here to the castle," Hans squeaked, struggling to catch his breath. "To see you."

A crease formed on Anja's porcelain forehead. "Who?"

"Says he's Marcel's nephew." Hans pointed a chubby finger over the outer wall.

Anja whipped back around and leaned over the battlement. Perhaps five kilometers out, a cloud of dust hurtled down the road toward Tarasp Castle. They'd gotten past the barriers and security on the mountain passages. *But ... Marcel's nephew?*

Anja stomped back up to the red and white gate, Hans in tow. "I'll deal with this," Anja said. "You get back to your station. Nothing delays The Solution."

"And Tabea?" Hans asked between wheezed breaths. "She's asking for you."

Anja's shoulders slumped. "I'll go see Tabea, then meet our guests at the gate. Have a security detail join me there."

Hans bobbed his head, then hung back.

Anja stormed through the striped guardhouse gates and marched down the main corridor into the medical bay. The clip of her shoes echoed off the stone walls.

Inside, a barefoot Tabea, her once bright-colored hair now faded ginger, paced in circles. Her medical gown fluttered to reveal graying flesh and black spider veins that crisscrossed her pale legs and buttocks.

"Tabea." Anja grabbed her by the shoulders. Tabea struggled, then locked her glassy stare on some point far beyond Anja's face.

"Tabea, you're sick," Anja said. "You need to come with me." She took Tabea by the hand and led her out of the medical room into the corridor.

"Where are we going?" Tabea asked.

"To be with people, darling," Anja said. "Just like you wanted."

The pallid woman smiled.

As they shuffled along, moisture beaded on the craggy stone walls and the air grew thick. Anja's breath misted the cool air. Tabea hopped from one bare foot to the other as the frigid floor developed a frosty sheen—though she never uttered a complaint.

Ahead, a hefty wooden door with metal banding and heavy studs loomed out of the dark. Anja pulled a substantial brass key from her pants pocket and slid it into the pitch-black lock. With a solid turn, the mechanism clunked.

With great effort, Anja pulled the door open and pushed Tabea inside.

The poorly lit crypt, dank and icy, had rectangular holes cut into the stone walls, each large enough for a human to lie down in—though most already contained hundreds of small, furry corpses. Careful not to linger on the mass rodent grave, Anja led Tabea to the end of the crypt.

"Here." Anja gestured to one of the wall spaces without rats. "You can wait here for me."

"Wh-where are the people?" Tabea said, hugging herself and dancing in place.

Anja forced a smile. "They're coming."

"Oh," Tabea said as she climbed into the mortuary shelf. Her knees scraped on the coarse bricks as she struggled to flip herself onto her back in the coffin-sized space. The flesh of her bare buttocks smooshed onto the frozen ledge. "Will they all come to see me?" she asked. "I miss people."

"I know," Anja said, though the words barely made it past her lips. She backed away, hands outstretched toward the poor woman, then slipped out and shouldered the heavy door closed. She stuck the ancient key into the lock and the mechanism clunked into place.

Tabea's soft moan from deep in the crypt caused Anja to bite her lip and press her forehead to the cold steel rivets.

CHAPTER TWENTY-SIX

Jackson

Jackson lifted his body from the Volvo's seat—careful not to wake Neko, curled up in his lap—and allowed blood to flow back into his muscles. The familiar sensation of pins and needles surged into the backs of his legs. Nearly twenty hours in the jet to Switzerland, and now another three in a car traveling from St. Gallen's tiny airport to their destination—Tarasp Castle—had numbed his body into a near coma.

Bones sat up front, stiff and silent in the passenger seat. Their chauffeur, Christian, tore down Swiss country roads no wider than a Cadillac as if he were clairvoyant and knew if another car would burst from around a blind corner. Each time he slammed on the brakes, Jackson grabbed Neko to prevent the tiny fur ball from launching down to the floorboards.

Ahead in the distance, Tarasp Castle rose from a high outcropping that seemed thrust from the plain. Jackson squinted at the sun and scanned the battlements for the defense turrets he imagined hid there, but the base of the castle hid behind a screen of evergreens. Pockets of strange houses with white walls and black pointed roofs surrounded them. He counted at least three churches in a town that probably held fewer than one hundred people.

Jackson checked his phone again. The screen showed nothing from Hellcat. No contact since Bitcoin City. Perhaps she didn't have cell service in Europe. He pulled the colorful sash up around his face and took a deep breath.

Bones glanced back at him.

"Our guardian angel should've hit me up by now." Jackson waved his phone.

"That one's resourceful," Bones said. "Said she'd meet you here, right?"

Jackson nodded, and nausea swirled in his belly.

"You're missing someone?" Christian asked.

Jackson rolled down his window. Outside, the odd black and white houses whipped by as Christian swerved the electric Volvo down snaky roads and headed for the wall of pines. Jackson ducked and bent his neck at an awkward angle to peer through the windshield at the castle above.

The faint whine of hydraulics floated on the wind. Likely the sound of those hidden defensive turrets. Hopefully Christian's call ahead was enough to prevent them from being blasted into oblivion.

As they entered the shade of Tarasp's forested base, golden daylight fell through needle-covered branches and splattered onto the car's milk-cream hood. Neko climbed up Jackson's shoulder to take a peek at the vernal kaleidoscope outside. Jackson coaxed the kitten back into his lap.

"Almost there," Christian said as he turned the vehicle onto a dirt road that wound around the bluff up toward the fortress.

Bones murmured an acknowledgment and rubbed his thinning scalp.

Jackson poked his nose out of the window. The edge of the road dropped into a sheer cliff just inches from the tires. Vertigo swarmed his brain, and he ducked back inside.

The car lurched to a stop in a claustrophobic lane with a castle wall on its left and a natural wall of rough stone on its right. Christian inched the car, with little room to spare, through the narrow gap and into a slightly wider courtyard.

The doors to the car popped open.

Jackson gathered Neko into his hoodie as the muzzle of a rifle thrust inside the car. A soldier in gray and crimson Scarlett Moon fatigues shouted something that sounded like drunk German.

"Gruezi," Christian said, his palms held up. "Gute morge, mittenan. Alles guet?"

"Wer ish das?" said the merc who'd thrown open Bones' door.

Christian smiled in his robotic way. "Es ish Marcels Neffe und sein Freund Joseph. Sie haben es kaum aus B.C. g'schaft."

The guard's shoulder mic barked the sound of a woman's voice.

Jackson's brain stuttered at hearing English again, but he knew that voice. He'd heard it all across the internet and on every public service announcement that spoke out against omniviolence. "Hey, that's Anja Kuhn," Jackson muttered, but his revelation seemed to go unnoticed.

Christian motioned for the guard's radio and the man passed it into the car.

"Ms. Kuhn, it's Christian." He looked back over the seat, nodded, and smiled at Jackson. "I was supposed to pick up Marcel, but he did not show. Instead, I have his nephew and a man by the name of Joseph Carboni."

Anja's voice crackled over the radio again. "Where *is* Marcel?"

Christian glanced at Jackson, who shook his head and raised his voice. "He didn't make it out of B.C.," Jackson said.

Bones muttered and rolled his shirt sleeves up another fold as the guards trained their rifles on him.

Christian held up a hand and concentrated on the radio.

The car interior seemed to close in, drumming claustrophobia into Jackson's chest. One guard murmured something to the other and they shared a laugh.

"Bring them up," Anja said at last.

Christian handed the radio back to the guard, who waved them through a heavy red and white striped gate. A cannon bigger than the Volvo hung like some sleeping predator atop its tower mount. Past the gate on Jackson's left lay the siege walls of the fortress, and on their right Castle Tarasp itself. Christian parked in the middle of a gravel courtyard. Anja Kuhn stood flanked by guards, her hands pinched to her hips. Christian climbed out of the driver's seat and signaled for his passengers to follow. Joe pulled himself from the vehicle with a grunt. Jackson collected Neko and hopped out, his stiff legs tingling.

Anja examined Jackson head to toe. "Marcel's nephew, I'm told?"

"James was, uh, my dad," Jackson said, distracted by the frigid high-altitude wind that whipped at his neck. "He worked for you too."

She seemed to consider that, then turned her attention to Bones. "And him?"

"Joseph Carboni," Christian said, a smile still plastered on his face. "I think he's looking after young Jackson here."

"Bones," Jackson said. "You call him Bones."

"Is Marcel still alive?" Anja asked.

Christian shook his head.

The woman's posture remained on guard, but something in her demeanor shifted.

"So," Anja said. "Can't have you standing out here all day."

"Good," Jackson said. "I'm starving. And so is Neko." He lifted the little bundle in his sweat-stained, battle-worn hoodie.

Anja's nose wrinkled up.

"Cat," Bones said. "It's a cat."

"This isn't a hotel, *Junge*," Anja said. "And most definitely not a vacation."

"Vacation?" Bones asked.

"Busy day," Anja replied. Without taking her eyes off Bones, she said, "Did you search them for weapons?"

Christian nodded and held up the Beretta Tomcat. "They're clean."

"Good, then come with me," she said.

"Fraulein Kuhn," one of the guards said.

"I'll take them for now. Just give me one of those." Anja motioned to a Sig 220 strapped to the man's thigh.

He looked at his fellow guard, then back to Anja.

"I'm paying you, am I not?" she snapped.

Jackson curled a derisive lip. "Aren't you, like, meant to be all anti-violence and shit?"

Anja took the pistol from the soldier and held it limp-wristed, then used it to shepherd Bones and Jackson in front of her. "Los, bitte."

"You even know how to use that thing?" Bones grumbled as he limped past her.

"Well enough," Anja replied.

Anja poked Jackson in the spine with the muzzle of the pistol to move him along a narrow corridor. They passed by a heavy set of wooden doors that hung open. Inside, a palatial room with a buttressed ceiling housed rows and rows of computers desks, people hurrying from one terminal to the next, and a long table with a spread that made Jackson's family cookouts look like leftover scraps.

"Food!" Jackson darted inside.

"Hey!" Anja barked.

Jackson grabbed a bunch of grapes, two packs of crackers, and a six-inch cervelat sausage. He wolfed down the sausage on the spot. "Bones," he said through a mouthful, "come over here."

Bones grunted, his attention roving the interior of the room.

"Scheisse," said a short man with dark hair, a headset wrapped around his clammy neck. "Ms. Kuhn?"

Beneath an enormous monitor that shone with a map of the world, more Scarlett Moon guards half jerked into action, their hands on pistols at their sides.

"It's fine, Hans," Anja said, then gave a curt shake of her head to the trigger-happy soldiers, who seem disappointed at the lack of real work.

Jackson's fingers danced over a fruit bowl, prawn-filled vol-au-vents, and a plate of cupcakes until he reached a stack of ham. He snatched up a few slices and stuffed them in his hoodie pocket beside Neko. "Got any milk?" he asked. "For my cat?"

"Ms. Kuhn," Hans said. "I'm glad you're here—"

"Not now," Anja snapped. "Junge, follow me." She wagged the Sig at Jackson. "You too, Herr Bones."

Bones had meandered over to a set of doors that opened onto a grand balcony with a dramatic view of the surrounding Swiss countryside.

"Christian," Anja said, and used the pistol to mime her orders, "I need you to stay here in the command center."

"Copy," Christian replied.

"Los, gentlemen," Anja pressed, eyebrows raised. She curled a lock of blond hair behind her ear and pinched her lips.

Jackson stole a cupcake and wandered back through the heavy doors. Bones frowned as Anja urged him on with little flicks of the Sig. He lumbered past and followed Jackson.

Their footsteps echoed down the cold stone corridor. Jackson tucked into the soft cupcake. He wiped away the buttercream swirl that had mashed against his nose and licked his fingers, the whole while making sure to take in as much of their surroundings as possible—every door and window, from the height of the ceilings to the width of the corridors.

He offered Bones half of the cupcake, but Bones just shook his head.

"You know," Jackson whispered, then popped the last piece of cake into his mouth, talking around it, "I've never seen a place I couldn't get into."

Bones furrowed his heavy brow. "Which means?"

"Gun turrets take out anything in the air," Jackson muttered around the sweet bolus, then swallowed. "Walls six feet thick, windows look like they don't open." Hellcat had gotten a camera in here at least once, on the back of a roach or micro-drone. He clucked his tongue. "This place is basically impenetrable."

Bones grunted his agreement.

"What are you whispering, Junge?" Anja caught up just to intrude on Jackson's personal space.

He shot a glare over his shoulder at her. "It's kinda shit," he said, "your castle."

Her expression had soured, and she brandished the gun to hurry him on. "Through there." Anja jerked her head at a set of doors at the end of the corridor. "Then down."

Bones pushed through and the three entered a stone spiral staircase.

"So, like, we needed your help," Jackson said over his shoulder, slowing his descent. "That's why we came all this way …"

Bones limped ahead of him, the echoes of his footsteps fading as he disappeared into the dark.

"Help you?" Anja seemed to consider the thought.

Jackson stopped and turned on the stairs to face her. "I—we—got a psycho mafia assassin on our asses, and a friend of mine told me your network could help us pin him down before he strikes again."

Anja smirked. "This isn't the old Interpol, Junge. We're not here to track down international criminals."

Bones called up from below. "Thought you were here to save the world from violence?"

Anja huffed, checked the small gold watch on her wrist, then jabbed Jackson to continue on. "When I am done, Mr. Carboni," she called out, her voice echoing off the heavy block walls, "I'll save everyone, everywhere. Including you and young Jackson, here."

Jackson clutched Neko close and caught up to Bones, who'd stopped a few feet from the bottom of the stairwell. Anja badgered them through an opening into a long, dark, and very damp corridor. They passed a single door with a white plate screwed into the wood that read *Kein Zutritt*, then they pressed farther into the gloom. The hallway ended at a metal-banded wooden portal.

Anja pulled an oversized brass key from her pocket and handed it to Jackson. "Okay," she said, "open it up."

Jackson studied the key, then the huge studded door. "A fucking dungeon? Are you serious?"

"As I said, Junge, this isn't a hotel." She nodded to the door. "You'll be safe in here until I'm finished."

"Finished with what?" Bones asked.

"It's an important day, Mr. Carboni, for all of humanity," she said. "Now, inside, bitte."

Jackson slid the key into the lock and turned it to the sound of a dull clunk. He leaned back to pull the heavy door open and peered into the murk. A final glance at Bones, then Jackson held Neko close and stepped inside.

Bones didn't budge. "Shoot me, please, Miss Anti-Violence. 'Cause I ain't fuckin' going in there."

Anja set her jaw and raised the Sig to Bones' face. "Go," she said.

His expression gave away nothing. "I don't think you have it in you."

Anja racked the hammer back and shoved the Sig closer to Bones' cheek. Her finger touched the trigger. "I said, go."

Bones looked at Jackson, in the darkness alone. He pinched his lips and stepped inside.

Behind him, the door closed. The lock clunked into place.

"Do you smell that?" Jackson said into the pitch black. Bile tingled the back of his throat.

"Death," Bones said. "Smells like rotting death."

Jackson fumbled around the cold space, shuffling his feet and letting his hands roam across clammy stone walls. Neko mewed in the dark. Jackson's fingers curled around a corner, down into a small cubby-hole, and across a clump of frozen fur.

Jackson shrieked and reeled.

"What?" Bones called out from the dark.

"There's something in here, man," Jackson said, shaking off the cold that seeped through his clothes.

A bright white light burst on.

"Damn, bro!" Jackson said, and covered his face. "Where'd you get a flashlight?"

Bones swung the light around a room too big for the small LED to reach across. "Phone," he said.

Jackson blinked away the spots in his vision. "Oh, she didn't take our phones."

"No need," Bones said, homing in on the alcove in the stone wall Jackson had reached into. "No signal down here."

Jackson pulled his own device out and stared at the screen. Zero signal.

"What the hell?" Bones said, leaning into the recess in the wall.

Jackson peered around Bones' shoulder to the heap of small furry bodies—white, black, and brown—with long hairless tails and yellowed protruding teeth. "Rats?" he said.

Bones grimaced. "I hate rats."

Neko struggled from Jackson's hoodie and plopped onto the ledge with the dead rodents. Bones' phone light cast a long pointy-eared shadow across the stiff, furry cadavers.

Jackson scooped up the kitten. "Gross, Neko."

"We need to find a way out of here." Bones made for the door.

"Like what?"

"This ain't no high-tech prison," Bones said. "It's a fuckin' dungeon with an old-timey lock. The type that can be picked."

"You know how to do that?" Jackson asked.

Bones handed him the phone. The built-in flashlight threw a skinny teen outline onto the back wall.

"For thirty years, I killed people for a living," Bones said.

"Sometimes that means breaking into places."

Jackson hovered the phone light over the keyhole. Bones knelt, rolled up his pant leg, and pulled the stiletto from his sock. He turned to Jackson and grinned.

"Stake," Jackson said with a nod.

Bones' broad shoulders shifted and maneuvered as he worked on the lock.

"So, why didn't you kill her?" Jackson asked.

"What?" Bones said without looking up.

"Anja," Jackson said. "I've seen you disarm a guy with a dick gun and shoot his brains out."

"Haven't I taught you anything?" Bones said with another grunt and a twist of the thin blade. "There are rules. One of 'em is I don't kill women," he said. "Not unless I got no choice."

"Is that why you didn't kill Elena?" Jackson said, moving the light around Bones' thick shoulder. "Back in El Salvador?"

"Gotta have rules," Bones said. "You ain't got rules? Not one? No line you won't cross?"

"Course I do," Jackson said. "Never leave a digital footprint, never let someone see your face …"

Bones stopped his fiddling and looked up. All the cracks in his face, deeper in the harsh phone light, imbued the old gangster with the appearance of ancient wisdom. "Those aren't rules, those are ways not to get caught being a prick." He turned back to the lock. "Rules are what separate you from the animals out there. Rules keep you human."

"Okay, Confucius," Jackson started, "then—"

"Shh." Bones held up a meaty hand.

"You hear something?" Jackson squeaked.

"Shh," Bones hissed. "You hear that?"

Jackson cocked his head and strained his ears. "What?" Neko purred inside his hoodie.

"Listen." Bones got to his feet and turned away from the door.

Jackson closed his eyes and concentrated, his own breath and heartbeat loud in his head. The old man's ragged breaths, the cat. A light breeze seeped through the cracks in the old door, and the hair on his arms stood up.

A faint scrape.

"Another rat?" Jackson said.

"Too big." Bones stepped up behind Jackson, the stiletto held out. "Move, Jack."

Jackson's feet sank roots into the stone.

"Hello," said a child-like voice.

Jackson screamed and fell back against Bones. The phone clattered from Jackson's hand across the stone floor and came to rest with the flashlight pointed up, illuminating one side of the crypt in stark underlight, a slice of alcoves and mounds of dead rats.

Bones fell into the door and the stiletto tinkled away into the dark.

In the middle of the dungeon, the glow of reflected light revealed a woman, unsteady on bare feet, a soiled medical gown hanging off one shoulder. Thin purple veins striated her pallid, almost luminous, swollen skin. Sunken eyes stared out from under lank strands of pale yellow hair.

"Friends!" she squealed, and wavered like a toddler taking its first steps. Then, arms outstretched, she lurched for Jackson.

"No touching!" Jackson scrambled away. Neko hissed and yowled.

Bones picked up the phone and shone it at the woman.

Her maniacal smile widened, pupils locked wide, gums oozing thick black goo.

"Kill it!" Jackson yelled.

"Back up, lady," Bones said as he searched the floor for the stiletto.

"Is this a party? A *slumber* party?" the woman shrieked with glee.

Jackson scrambled and banged against the hard wood with his fists. "Help! Let us out!" Jackson flipped around, shoulders pressed to the wood.

"This ain't no party," Bones said.

"Come sit with me!" The woman's swollen face pulsed, twisting her crazed grin. "We can play music on your phone, right?"

"Got it!" Bones said over a faint metallic scrape.

The heavy door behind Jackson gave way. He tumbled backward into the corridor and crashed again to his rump, but still yelled, "Get me out!" He propped himself on his elbows and squinted into the bright light of a torch shoved inches from his face.

"Khum," a man barked. "Sofort!"

Bones limped into the corridor, clamped onto Jackson's wrist, and jerked him to his feet.

Jackson snatched the stiletto from Bones and jabbed it at the woman in the doorway. "Back off, you fucking geekbag!"

She hobbled out of the darkness, her breathing arduous, her wan skin covered in purple sores.

"Tabea?" the squat, dark-haired man said, training the flashlight on her.

"Hans." Black clotted blood slid down the woman's pallid face. "You're here for the party? Have you met my friends?"

"What did she do to you?" Hans said.

The woman stumbled over her own feet.

Hans caught her and pulled her arm over his shoulder. "Tabea, we must get you out of here." He shuffled her past the two assassins.

Bones stepped into the crypt and, with a groan, scraped up Jackson's phone from the cold floor.

Jackson held the stiletto an inch from Hans's sweaty face. "Not so fast. You got an access key on you—a connected device?" He patted Hans's shirt and trousers. "Marcel said Scarlett Moon could help me."

Hans pulled his focus from the thin blade at his nose to Jackson. "Marcel Cross?"

"Yeah," Jackson said, "my uncle."

Hans's face drew pale. "Your father was ..." He swayed on his feet, then swallowed hard. "You should come with me."

"Hey, you know my dad?" Jackson called after Hans, but the man didn't answer.

Bones peeled the stiletto from Jackson's grip and slapped the phone in its place. He jerked his chin up in the direction of Hans's round-shouldered silhouette.

"Friends ..." Tabea cooed as he led her away.

Less than a hundred feet down the damp corridor, Hans stopped at the large door with the white placard and slipped the same brass key from his pocket. He rammed it into the lock, turned it with a clunk, then shoved the door open.

"What's in here?" Jackson plowed past the pudgy man, who struggled to hold up Tabea.

"Anja's lab." Hans dragged Tabea inside. "She doesn't know I 3-D printed a key."

Bones stepped in and eased the door closed behind them.

Jackson peered inside a transparent vivarium, a microcosm with grass and kudzu and the remnants of burst purple pods. Tabea moaned and reached one black-veined arm toward the greenhouse. Jackson stormed over to the console and a huge rectangular enclosure. He craned his neck to look down into the deep box, covered in straw, rodent food, and hundreds of rat corpses. The pungent stench crawled up his nose and made a home there. He gagged, and bile shot into his throat, hot and acidic.

"Sweet Mary," Bones grimaced and hobbled over. He clapped a meaty hand to his face and backed away. "What is it with you people and rats?"

Neko mewed low from Jackson's hoodie pocket.

"They're the test subjects," Hans said, shifting Tabea's weight beside him. "We have to be quick—you wanted in the mainframe?" he asked Jackson.

Jackson nodded and wiped some spittle with his sleeve.

With a loud grunt, Hans sat Tabea on a stool, waited a moment to be sure she wouldn't topple off, then hurried to ensure the door was locked. He waddled back to Jackson, leaned over a chair at the computer desk, and worked away at the keyboard. The monitor winked on, and after a few keystrokes he was in.

"This is our hub, central surveillance," Hans said, ushering Jackson into the seat. "Should be what you need."

Jackson scanned the configuration. Onscreen, thousands of orbs glowed on a map of the world, each one representing a city thrumming with blue light. "Every damn surveillance camera on Earth?" he asked without looking away.

"It's all part of The Solution," Hans said.

"You keep saying shit like that." Bones folded his arms across his barrel chest. "What are you people doing? And what's with the damn rats?"

Neko poked his bobblehead from Jackson's hoodie. Jackson rattled away at the keyboard.

"It's all the same question and answer." Hans looked upon Tabea with tenderness. "We'll end omniviolence," he said with a sigh. He crouched down by Tabea's black feet and put a hand on her veiny knee. "The rats are the test," he said without looking up. "It worked on them, so it'll work on us."

"Stop talking in riddles," Bones said, his tone hard.

"It's a model. Of every city on every continent." Hans patted Tabea, then slumped to his seat on the stone floor.

Tabea grinned, and black goo squidged thick between her teeth.

"Look," Hans said, the word so heavy in his mouth he seemed unable to lift his head. "Put enough rats ... or people ... in an environment where they have everything they ever wanted ... and society breaks down. There is no hierarchy ... no order anymore."

Bones peeked into the rat enclosure. "No purpose in life," he murmured.

"Correct." Hans shrugged. "No one knows their place, so norms break down until eventually the rats—*we*—turn on each other and destroy ourselves. Evolution is built on war, survival of the fittest, not utopia. We're not *designed* to live in peace."

"So you plan to just kill everyone?" Bones asked.

Hans's head snapped up. "No, no, no," he said, his brow knit. "The Solution is a ... an elegant answer to the problem."

"This one doesn't look real elegant to me," Jackson thumbed at Tabea, his keystrokes now slower and more purposeful as he navigated Scarlett Moon's system.

"Can we play a game now?" Hope shined in Tabea's eyes.

"The Solution—it's a cure for violence," Hans said. "An antidote."

Jackson stopped his typing and looked at Hans, then Bones. "How the hell do you get eight billion people to take a vaccine?"

"You don't *get* them to," Bones said, his tone low, "you *make* them."

Hans swallowed. "People are ... stupid. We had to take control and do what was best for everyone," he said, "for the world."

Bones grit his teeth, and the muscles of his jaw bulged. "How?"

"Plants, pollen," Hans said, his voice excited and more than a little proud. "Easily spread and inhaled without you even noticing. But the pollen is modified." Hans gestured to the vivarium.

Jackson craned his neck to look in the greenhouse. "The kudzu?" he barked. "That shit is everywhere."

Tabea snickered. "I like the purple parts."

"Everywhere," Hans repeated. "Ubiquitous. In just the last five years, in places it had never been seen before. And yet, no one gives it a second look." He shrugged. "We've been seeding this modified strain all over the globe. Once the pods burst, people will inhale the pollen and their brains will be altered. No more evil. No more violence."

Boned limped over to Hans and Tabea and dropped to his haunches. "No more fucking marbles, either." He waved his hand before the dazed woman's face.

Tabea clapped her hands and laughed.

"No," Hans protested, and looked at her with great tenderness. "This is something different. The Solution was—is—perfect. I think. Nature has used this technique for millennia."

Tabea moaned and scratched at her scalp. A handful of hair came away between her fingers.

"Check this crazy shit out." Jackson beckoned to Bones, who groaned to his feet and limped to the computer terminal. "Research files on Anja's computer, here." He double-clicked the mouse on a file called *Diary Entry 46.*

Anja's proud face and short blond hair filled the window.

"The chemicals produced by flukes and hairworms make their hosts climb to the tops of blades of grass or move toward light," Anja said, her expression more energetic and genuine than Jackson had ever seen in her public service announcements. "These have provided the basis for The Solution, however, the inspiration for dispersion has come from plants. Mother Earth is slowly taking back her planet as humans forget to prune back the tendrils of life." The corners of her mouth lifted in a grin. "The results are encouraging. The root system can be activated by a simple electrical signal, causing all pods to explode simultaneously. The last hurdle, though, is to ensure the longevity of the effect."

The recording stopped on her in freeze frame.

Jackson pulled up another—a documentary-style video, this time of a liver fluke traveling to the brain of a cow.

Bones twisted to face Hans. "What does she mean by *longevity*?"

"Well." Hans coughed into his hand. "Even if the pollen reached everyone on Earth, it couldn't affect the next generation, who could just engage in random acts of violence again. The change has to affect the genes that we pass to our offspring."

Tabea dug more hair out. "Itchy ..."

"I don't want to lose my will to fight," Bones snarled. "Fighting keeps me alive. Hell, it's what makes me *feel* alive."

"Isn't that the problem?" Hans pushed back. "You need to be violent to feel alive."

Jackson recoiled from the computer. Was it true? Was he only happy when he hurt people? Onscreen, the liver fluke wiggled its flat body into the bovine brain tissue. Jackson's fingers found Neko's soft fur as a tidal wave of corpses smothered his consciousness—people he'd dispatched with a single keystroke.

"Sounds like you buy into this shit," Bones said.

"Why not?" Hans climbed to his feet. "Scientifically, it's brilliant. Only ... Anja is hiding something from us—about the project," he said. "Some aftereffect, maybe ...?"

Thin strands of pale yellow hair came away in Tabea's bony alabaster fingers. Her scalp bled black as she dug at it with ragged nails.

Jackson peeled his morbid curiosity from the sickly woman and cracked his neck. *No time for this.* He slipped his cell phone out from his hoodie and connected it to the computer with a cable. Once it connected, the Pegasus app launched itself.

"Warning!" the desktop monitor blurted out. Jackson flinched in his chair and almost jerked the phone cord out of the hard drive. Neko cried as Jackson gripped the kitten to his legs.

"Defense system compromised. Anti-aircraft turrets offline," the synthetic voice continued. "Radar offline. Motion sensors offline."

Hans stood bolt upright. He launched over to the computer desk, shouldering Jackson from the chair. "What did you do?"

"Uh, nothing." Jackson held his hands up. "I just plugged in the program so I could … take … over?"

"What?" Hans attacked the keyboard. "Scheisse!"

A single red bulb fixed to the lab wall flashed, reflecting off the vivarium. A well-mounted speaker vibrated with a woman's voice. "We are in lockdown," the voice said. "Everyone, return to your stations. I repeat, everyone return to your stations." An ear-piercing alarm wailed, amplified off the damp stone walls of Anja's lab.

Tabea scrambled to her feet, hands over her ears. "Too loud, it's too loud!"

Bones grabbed Jackson by the sleeve. "We're leaving."

"But, Svanire …" Jackson objected.

"The hell with Svanire," Bones said, and jerked Jackson by the elbow. "Something's wrong. We're leaving now."

Tabea wailed and clutched at her head, tumbling out of the chair into the door. Black goo stained her teeth and her face distorted. "It's too loud!"

"She's blocking the way out!" Jackson yelled over the noise. "Kill her *now*?"

Bones clenched his jaw, indecisiveness fixing him in place.

"Ah, screw this!" Jackson screamed. He shoved both hands into Tabea's flimsy chest and drove her back so hard that she toppled into the vivarium. The wall shattered around her and she tumbled into a mess of shards and wet soil. Neko's claws stung Jackson's belly, tiny needles piercing the cloth.

In the ceiling that still hung above the shattered tank, powerful extraction fans whirred to life. Tabea's thin, straw-colored hair stood on end, flailing in the pull from the fans. She climbed to her knees and covered her ears. "Too loud!" she cried. "Make it stop!" Her eyes screwed shut and her fleshy face pulsed.

"Get back here," Bones rasped, and pulled at Jackson's hoodie.

Tabea, her bloodshot eyes bulging, lurched forward to grab Jackson by his arm.

OMNIVIOLENCE

"I've never kissed a boy," she said, temples throbbing. She groped at his shoulders and leaned forward, lips pursed.

"Get off!" Jackson strained against her arms.

Hans ran for the door, chubby fingers unable to work the key into the lock.

"Kiss me!" Tabea groaned as a black seam peeled open from her forehead down to her chin. Jackson screamed, shrill and high.

"All right, damn it. That's enough." Bones shoved between them and flung her back into the vivarium.

Tabea's skull popped apart with a sound like bedsheets ripping. Her face unzipped down the bloody seam and rent wide open until the two halves of her head sagged against her neck. A cloud of black powder belched from the cavernous wound into the air.

Bones' strong arms lifted Jackson away from the swirling black particles.

"Oh, mein Gott," Hans managed. "Cover your face!"

Tabea's corpse lurched back and forth, arms waving, fingers taut—a human dandelion caught in the glass with its seeds blown away. The extraction fans whipped the pollen into a black tornado, scattering the particles the length of the room.

Bones slipped his sleeve over Jackson's face. "Move!"

Jackson pinned Neko down inside his hoodie as Bones shoved him at the main door.

Hans fiddled with the key in the lock.

Tabea's body, somehow still functioning and spurting out clumps of soot-like pollen, jerked and fumbled about the lab. She took down the remainder of the vivarium wall, then tottered toward the door.

"C'mon! C'mon, man," Jackson said, his voice muffled through Bones' sleeve.

The lock clunked and Hans pulled back the door.

Bones shoved Jackson past him, and Hans screamed as Tabea clamped her arms around him in a bear hug. Her bones audibly snapped, locking them in an awkward embrace, splinters of humerus stretching her gray skin. Hans shrieked and struggled while Tabea's neck vomited up more black dust that drowned him in a sooty cloud.

Bones yanked the heavy door shut with a loud *bang*.

"Holy fuck, man!" Jackson wheezed as he checked the fur ball in his hoodie pouch. "Holy fuck!"

"Yeah," Bones gasped, his back pressed to the damp stone wall.

Behind the door, Hans's cries rose to a falsetto pitch that wavered before turning to a gurgle.

"You get any of that shit on you?" Jackson asked, chest heaving. He looked Bones up and down.

Bones coughed into his fist. "Don't think so."

"You sure?" Jackson whipped the back of his fingers at the old gangster's crotch.

Bones doubled over and cradled his jewels. "You little bastard, I swear to God I'm gonna—"

"Yeah, you're still you," Jackson said. "Let's get the hell out of this creepshow."

Bones grimaced and gave a firm nod, then limped after the teen, who flew up the spiral stone staircase, taking the steps two at a time.

CHAPTER TWENTY-SEVEN
Svanire

The whip and hack of helicopter rotors through the crisp Swiss air echoed across the mountainside and thundered into the distance. Flying at a cruising speed of 155 miles an hour, the quartet of MH-7M Little Bird rapid-assault choppers stayed low against the craggy terrain. Svanire glanced out of the window and studied the staggered formation of his helicopters as they banked back and forth between snowcapped mountain peaks with effortless grace.

The Little Birds burst from the mountains into a narrow valley of green pastures, meandering lanes, and unassuming white and brown wooden abodes. Emerald forests sprawled, dotted with gray patches of stone. Directly ahead, atop a flat mountain encircled by tall pines, Tarasp Castle loomed, foreboding and ancient. Along the castle's flank, six-foot-thick siege walls dated back to the seventeenth century. Yet, on the castle's battlements, leaves gathered on twin-barreled 7.62mm mini-gun turrets and weeds grew up the sides of phallic surface-to-air missiles.

A lurid grin spread across Svanire's lips and heat rose in his chest. Time to play the final gambit. "Defenses are down," he called into the microphone in his headset. "They would've fired on us by now, if they could." He turned to survey his team of mercs, strapped to their seats in full assault gear. "The cropduster delivered its payload?"

Richter leaned forward. "Got confirmation five minutes ago. They dispersed the full load with a focus on the HVAC air intake for the facility. We should have target lock everywhere, by now."

Svanire craned his neck to see the castle grounds below. From the air, the ultra-fine baby-blue UV powder gave the entire place a crystalline, storybook sheen.

The pilot banked hard right and pulled back on the yoke. "We clear?" he shouted.

"Take us around the perimeter. Counterclockwise, if you please,"

Svanire said.

The pilot maneuvered the chopper into a banked three-sixty recon of the castle. The procession of Little Birds followed.

"Two minutes," Svanire said. "Richter, prepare my gift package."

"Copy that, Boss," Richer said.

"Masks stay on unless you want to become a target." Svanire pulled off his headset, then produced the carbon-gray Kevlar skull mask from a duffel bag. He slipped the mask over his head and secured it in place beneath his chin and around his ears. He drew the retention band tight to create a seal and pulled to take in a breath. Like an SCBA, the mask valve gave way and the filter engaged. Svanire breathed deeply and the air hissed through the filter. He took a moment to cycle through the various lenses: ultraviolet, black-hot infrared, and night vision.

His band of hardened killers followed suit, each one fitting an airtight mask to his head. One of the mercs, muscled like a pro wrestler, grabbed the sliding door beside him and jerked it open. Crisp alpine air whipped into the cab.

Richter leaned down to a series of large storage cases at his feet. He opened the first, in which dozens of rows of little golden jewels glistened.

Svanire's testicles and glans tingled at the sight of his MIT bees. He pressed his palms together and roamed over the contents of the second and third cases—compact, square-bodied assassin drones nestled in foam cutouts. Each drone sported a series of quad rotors, a UHD camera, and a payload of IMX-101.

The pilot watched for a moment, then turned back to his controls.

Richter looked up front, but before he could open his mouth, Svanire raised a hand and switched on the mic in his mask.

"My beautiful dancers—first, dear Richter," Svanire said, his voice metallic in his own ears.

Richter reached into the case and extracted the matte black ring, which he slid over his middle finger.

The pilot gawked at Svanire. "Good God," he said, "whatever you do, don't release those things in here."

"Relax," Svanire said. "The UV powder is doing its job on the ground. All is accounted for."

OMNIVIOLENCE

The lead Little Bird banked in a wide counterclockwise turn around Castle Tarasp. The other three followed, mercenary killers anchored in each doorway, their feet on the skids. Below, a scant force of Scarlett Moon's sentries—too few to provide effective security—scrambled this way and that. One soldier raised his rifle and fired off a handful of rounds.

Svanire opened a compartment next to the cockpit and chuckled. "Oh, Anja, your distaste for violence has left you vulnerable, darling." He flipped open a slim Keybook computer and opened a program labeled *Pollination Schedule, Beta 2.0.* His HKT AI accessed the repurposed MIT software and told it to interface with all global social media sites and any online personal identifiers—photos, names, family, DNA testing records—to cross-reference against Scarlett Moon's internal archives.

Ah, the internet, Svanire thought. *So many millions of nobodies, yet each one as unique as a fingerprint and oh-so-easy to find.*

Faces and names began to rapidly fill the fields onscreen.

"Jens Buchi, age thirty-seven, six foot two, ex-soldier turned hired hand," Svanire read with glee. "Likes dogs, long walks, and hentai." He shook his head in disgust. "Carmen Wernli, former environmental scientist at Zurich University and part-time dominatrix for other people's husbands," he said, "now Chief Botanist for our dear Anja Kuhn."

The program rattled along and combined the personal data with satellite information and thermal biosignatures from within the castle. A second window popped up, showing a heat map of Tarasp and a name next to each yellow-orange-red human silhouette.

"There you are, my lovelies," Svanire purred.

A few of the human-shaped blobs on the heat map had no name associated with them.

Svanire tutted. "Last-minute personnel changes, dismissals, or departures," he said to himself. "No matter. My friends will find their way into every host guided by the UV powder you fools are inhaling right now, just like a biological bee to a flower's nectar." He tapped out a paradiddle on the screen. "This mapping exercise is merely to …" His words trailed off as he scrolled through the onscreen names.

"There you are." He unchecked three names on the list: Joseph

Carboni, Jackson Cross, and Anja Kuhn. "Can't have my pretties strip all the fun out of the day, now, can we?"

The helicopters swooped past the northern rim of the castle, past the chapel with its needle-like spire and the gatehouse where three sentries stared up in bewilderment.

"Ready, Boss," Richter said into his mask mic.

Svanire tapped the *Initiate* key on the screen, ensured the program was running, and shut the Keybook. "Send them."

Richter, black ring set on his middle finger, waved his hand over the case. In unison, hundreds of the little oblong creatures shuddered in their foam cutouts. Richter blew out a nervous breath, pushed his mask securely to his face, and eased the mouth of the case to the open bay door. First, just two of the robotic insects crawled to the edge of the case, little translucent wings popping erect from their bodies and lifting the drones into the air. Two became five, became ten, then fifty, until a swarm of hundreds poured from the case and descended on the castle.

"I hate these fuckin' things," Richter said, and pinched his mask close against his face.

"Beautiful, aren't they." Svanire's gaze followed the swarm as they floated down toward the castle, gliding along the crosswinds with ease. "Prep the assassin drones," he said, pulling on a pair of gloves. "Hard points only."

"I'm on it." Richter slipped the Keybook into a backpack and turned to the other cases.

A round pinged off the hull. Then three more. In the open spaces of the castle below, guards screamed and fired randomly into the air as they dropped their weapons to claw at their faces.

"Thirty seconds," Svanire said. "Fan out to your sectors."

The Little Birds broke formation. One banked hard left and dropped inside the walls of the castle just past the gatehouse. Another, loaded with mercs, cut across the compound and dropped fast ropes north of the chapel. Both copters released their men and lifted back up.

A cacophony of gunfire broke the silence below, followed by the harried screams of Scarlett Moon's defenders as Svanire's men stormed across the grounds.

Svanire's Little Bird, followed by a second, looped counterclockwise around the mountaintop fortress, then dropped inside the wall on the east side and touched down outside the castle's last defense—the inner gate.

Four masked killers disembarked, their weapons raised. Shimmering baby-blue UV powder swirled in the air around them. They spread out, and each took a knee outside the wash of the rotors. Richter climbed out, one assassin drone clipped to his gear, another in his hands. Svanire stepped off last and stooped to avoid the spinning chopper blades. With a gust, the Little Birds took flight again.

The whirring of the rotors was replaced with the sounds of battle: the pop of gunfire, the whine of a ricochet, and the muffled *whump* of a grenade exploding somewhere inside the walls.

Outside the gate, a sentry writhed on the ground and clutched at her face. A second guard in crimson and gray stumbled past her, a garbled scream in his throat. His weapon clattered to the concrete as he pushed his fingertips deep into his eyes. One of Svanire's masked killers raised a rifle at him.

Svanire touched the merc's shoulder with a slender, gloved hand. "Let him dance," he said. With a dramatic pirouette, Svanire waved toward the closed gate, a massive, spiked tangle of forged steel. "Richter, knock on the front door, s'il vous plaît."

Richter set the assassin drone on the ground and powered it on. The quad rotors purred to life. The loaded assassin drone hovered off the concrete on auto-pilot. Richter tapped at his smartwatch. "Stand by."

The assassin drone tilted forward and took off at high speed. It skimmed low to the brickwork floor and slammed into the massive inner gate with a rolling blast of fire and the screech of distorted steel.

Svanire stalked into the smoke. "Move."

Richter and the other men took up a spear-tip formation off Svanire's lead. As a unit, they pierced the veil of smoke, white and chalky with dust, and passed through the snarled metal of the inner gate.

"Stop!" A guard in crimson and gray ran at them from deep in the debris cloud. His rifle cracked and a bullet zipped off the stone wall.

Svanire attacked low with a coup d'arret, too fast for the eye to follow. The razor-sharp edge of his blade dragged through the man's stomach. As Svanire rose with the knife, he held it poised in a pakal icepick grip. With a thrust, he punched through the guard's biceps and filleted steel against the bone.

The soldier screamed and fell to his knees in a wash of gore. His rifle clacked against the stone and he used his good arm to clamp fingers against a widening seam of red along his belly.

"Find Joseph Carboni and that lovely boy. Leave no one else alive," Svanire said.

Richter and the other mercs bypassed the moaning soldier, his guts in his hand, and fanned out into the complex.

Svanire flicked his wrist, slung the blood from the talon-shaped knife, and snapped it back into the Kydex sheath at his waist. He stalked through the smoke and smiled as he imagined the horror his skull-faced visage must bestow on the hapless defenders.

An unstoppable messenger of death, Svanire disappeared into the depths of the castle.

CHAPTER TWENTY-EIGHT
Joe

The muted rattle of gunfire from above caused Joe to halt mid step. A deep ache radiated through the back of his heel and into the base of his calf. Joe grit his teeth. When Jackson tried to continue up the twisting stone stairwell, Joe gently pressed him back with a meaty palm.

"Hang on a second, pal," Joe said, more than a little out of breath from the climb out of the dungeon.

"What is it?"

"Gunfire," Joe said.

"You sure?" Jackson asked.

Joe nodded.

"Who would attack Scarlett Moon?" Jackson said, one nostril scrunched up and his brow creased.

For a moment they leaned against the old cream-colored brickwork of the spiral stone staircase, breaths sucking in and huffing out. Another string of gunfire sounded from above. This time Jackson flinched—followed by the thump of a grenade. Then a much larger blast shook the walls of the staircase and rained down mortar dust.

"Definitely an assault." Joe sucked at the air.

Jackson covered his face and coughed. "So, where do we go?"

Joe wrangled their next moves in his mind, the outcome of each possibility murky, at best. "We're stuck in this stairwell. We gotta go where it goes." He turned to Jackson. "Any ideas?"

"These stairs lead up to Anja's command center." Jackson prodded at Neko's little body, curled in the hoodie pouch. "We blow through there pronto, hop a ride in the courtyard, and get the hell out of here."

"Stake." Joe winked at Jackson.

Jackson smirked. "Sounds so stupid when you say it."

"Imagine that." Joe grunted. "Come on."

They trudged up the dizzying loop of the stairwell, and the sounds of war grew louder. Joe's heart, already thumping hard in his chest, ticked up a notch. *The kid's right, Joe. What kind of idiot attacks a place like this?*

As they neared the ancient wooden door that marked the exit to the stairwell, high panicked screams reached down to them.

Joe stopped, his hand on the thick panels. "Ready?" He felt the sounds through the wood.

Jackson nodded, the faint look of fear in his eyes.

Neko mewed.

"I got you, buddy." Joe's jaw muscles flexed. "You stick with me."

Jackson huffed out a breath. "Okay, Bones."

Joe shoved through the heavy door and into the maw. The door to the command center yawned wide as a pair of women dressed like lab techs stumbled over a soldier who writhed on his belly like a snake. The techs scratched at their own faces, digging nails in deep, and horrific screams gargled in their throats.

A chill raked down Joe's spine. He tugged on Jackson's hoodie and they slunk below the enormous monitor toward the command center's massive double doors. All around them, Anja's team continued to scream and claw at their faces. One keyboard jockey smashed his head against the stone wall over and over, his skull smacking with a hollow *thunk*, while others crashed headlong over tabletops and sent computer monitors and keyboards flying.

Something buzzed past Joe's ear, and he flinched.

A deep droning hum swelled like a song in the air.

"What the hell is it?" Jackson shouted over the din.

"Hell, if I know!" Joe watched a skinny young man barely out of his teens careen across the room, wailing and thrashing his arms about his face. The youngster hurtled into a table and bowled it over.

"Let's get the fuck out of here already," Jackson said.

"Follow me!" Joe took off at a hampered run, sidestepping the body of a woman whose eyes remained wide open in death. A thin stream of blood drained from her nostril.

"Whoa!" Jackson swatted at something as it flew past.

Joe held his arm over his nose and mouth. "What is it? Cover your face!"

"Bees." Jackson grabbed Joe's arm. "No, microdrones. And they're not targeting us."

"How the hell do you know?" Joe said, shuffling in a crouch as pain shot up his leg.

"We'd be dead!"

"Why not us?" Joe slowed to watch the drones buzz past.

"Who cares? Let's go!" Jackson tugged on Joe's sleeve.

Joe watched the furious swarms of bee drones encircle everyone but him and Jackson. "We gotta help these people." He limped after a man who'd wrapped his jacket over his head.

"No way, man!" Jackson shouted. "Hey!"

"Help her!" Joe pointed to a full-figured woman with auburn hair in a tangled mess as she writhed against a tabletop. She swatted at the bee drones that bristled across her pretty face.

"What? No!" Jackson turned toward the woman in distress. Neko squirmed in the pocket of his hoodie. "Ah, shit," he said.

Joe snatched the man to his feet without trying to remove the jacket. "Keep your face covered," he said. "Run! Get somewhere safe."

Jackson yanked the Antiguan sash from around his neck. "Back off, you little bastards!" He swung the sash through the swarm around the pretty woman and sent four of them tumbling across the tabletop. Jackson lunged for an empty fruit bowl, grabbed it, and turned it over on top of the buzzing drones.

The bees kept coming, targeting the woman. More circled her head and landed on her cheek.

"Don't just sit there screaming—cover your face, lady!" Jackson thrashed at her face.

But it was too late. Eyes wild, she froze as a microdrone on her cheek lurched into her nostril. The bridge of her nose twisted from a subtle curve into a steep arc as her face distorted. The woman howled a bloodcurdling shriek and clutched at Jackson.

"Help! Me!" Eyes rolled back, she gasped, and blood streamed from her ruined nose.

"I can't!" Jackson pulled away. "I'm sorry!" He ran as the woman broke into convulsions on the floor.

Across the room, Joe shoved the jacketed man through the stairwell door and shouldered it closed. "Sonofabitch," he gasped.

Jackson pointed a finger in Joe's face. "You and me don't help people!" he shouted. "We kill people, okay? Now, let's fucking go! I'm over this!"

Joe held up a hand. "Keep your pants on, Jack—"

The massive double doors exploded in a rolling blast of fire. Splinters rode a billowing cloud of smoke and blue-tinted dust and scattered across the bodies of the hapless dead. Jackson threw himself on the cold stone floor and Joe crouched to cover the teen.

Black clouds and powder rolled over them and dimmed the light. The monitor hung crooked on the wall, still displaying Anja's map of the world.

Joe blew out a breath and stood, ears ringing from the blast, eyes stinging. "Mother of God!" He tried to swallow away the tinnitus.

Jackson scrambled over to a twisted, broad-shouldered corpse with blond hair. "Christian," the teen muttered, groping at his clothes.

Out of the smoke, a specter approached, long and slender and unnatural in the worst way. The figure wore black tactical fatigues and a skull mask. On either side of the tall man, a pair of mercenaries in ghoulish masks of their own appeared, armed with custom weaponry.

"Svanire," Joe growled. "You slippery sonofabitch. I should've known."

Svanire chuckled. "You really should have, Joseph," he said, though the screams of Scarlett Moon's defenders almost drowned out his voice.

"You skinny psycho fuck," Jackson spat. "You killed my mom."

"Now, now, sweet child," Svanire said. "Is that any way to talk to an old friend?"

"You ain't my friend, freakshow," Jackson fired back as he climbed to his feet. From the pouch of his hoodie, Neko's little head poked out.

Svanire waved his hand, and a digital field of pristine green grass and clear blue skies filled the twenty-foot monitor. On that crooked screen, a silhouette approached, hips swaying through pixelated grass.

Jackson squinted. "The hell is this …?"

The curvaceous shadow drew into focus to reveal full lips, shoulder-length hair, and a pinched waist framed by low-cut jeans and a cropped top. She stopped in the tall grass and placed her hands on her hips.

"This, my love, is the endgame," Svanire and the AI avatar said in unison.

Jackson's mouth fell open.

"Is that …?" Joe frowned.

"Hellcat," Jackson said.

"*You're* Hellcat?" Joe turned from Svanire to the female avatar that mimicked the Squid's posture on the screen.

"You're a fucking catfish pedo!" Jackson shouted. "Flirting with me and shit! I should stomp your ass!" He jabbed his finger and took a step forward.

Joe placed his arm across the teen's chest.

"Get off me, Bones," Jackson jerked back.

"Oh, I do love it when they fight," Svanire and Hellcat said, then rubbed their hands together and blew a kiss.

"You played us. The whole damn time," Joe growled.

Svanire in his skull mask and Hellcat in her field of green each took a step closer to Joe. "To bring you here." Each waved a hand, her indicating the grass, while Svanire gestured to a heap of dead techs.

A wandering bumblebee drone with no more targets landed on Svanire's skeletal mask and probed at its fake nostril. Svanire shooed it away and, onscreen, Hellcat mimicked the gesture.

"And those things, with the blue dust." Joe motioned to the swirling bees. "That's you, too," he said, "targeting everyone … but us."

"Can't have my pretties ruining all the fun—not after all you and I have been through," Svanire chuckled. "Just think, Joseph. Every step, every moment has been engineered to bring you to this place. From the hit on Vitale and his daughter, which soured your ties with The Family, to your meeting handsome young Jackson, here, I've given you just enough of a push to keep you moving."

Onscreen, Hellcat covered her mouth with her fingertips and blushed, moving independently of the ghoul.

"The hits on me, my crypto," Jackson said. "The slaysite. That was you."

Svanire gave a dramatic bow and the two skull-faced mercs chuckled.

"Elena ..." Joe said, then let his words trail off.

Svanire near danced on the spot and his voice leveled up an octave. "You had a couple of close calls, there. You, my dears, got a little too popular on the slaysites. And Joseph, I can't take credit for Elena." The ghoul wagged a gloved finger at him. "Who knew you were such the Lothario? Lucky for you, my South African friends arrived to even those odds."

Jackson shook his head. "How'd you even know I'd be able to get in here?" he asked. "Why me, why my ..." He froze, his eyes widening more. "Dad."

Svanire unclipped a long black spearpoint blade from his belt and began to pace. His skull-faced soldiers held their weapons clutched at the ready. "Years ago, a man came to The Family to beg for help," Svanire said, "and I overheard his plea—an earnest plea for his life and the lives of his family." He touched the white chin of his mask. "He worked for Scarlett Moon and his name was James."

Jackson stepped back and his balance faltered.

"I knew this man could be my way into Scarlett Moon's network," Svanire said. With the tip of his knife, he knocked over one of the monitors from a workstation, to which crashed to the floor, raising a cloud of blue dust. "I would have access to everything, everywhere, that I needed to grow my empire. And, of course, I couldn't have Ms. Kuhn unleashing her Solution, could I?" He shook his head. "Take all the spirit out of humanity?"

Joe couldn't see it, but he knew Svanire grinned behind that mask.

"Where *is* our pretty blond host?" Svanire pretended to scan the room.

"Focus, dick face," Jackson spat. "My dad—what happened to my dad?"

"Dear old Dad didn't work out. I thought all was lost," Svanire's cadence rose, and he doodled his fingers in the air. "Until you, my pretty little hacker friend, followed in Daddy's footsteps. You provided my way in—I just had to get you here." He tapped out a rhythm on the stone floor. "Ol' Jojo, grown soft and toothless," he waved a delicate finger at Joe, "was a convenient mechanism to facilitate your safe arrival. Two birds with one stone, as they say."

Joe rolled the sleeves of his shirt tight, hairy forearms bulging. "I'll show you how toothless."

"My dad." Jackson stabbed a finger down into his open palm. "What. Happened. To. Him?"

Svanire let out a whimsical titter. "Such noble devotion!" he said. "Such care for one life, when the fate of the entire world hangs in the balance—"

"Tell me!" Jackson screamed.

Svanire clasped his own wrist and lowered his chin, and onscreen, Hellcat did the same. "I needed to know what he knew about The Solution, Anja's pet project, and how to access the global surveillance network. So, I had a talk with Daddy. I thought a little scare would make him more cooperative … well, maybe I got carried away. Accidents happen, right?" Svanire shrugged. "Lake Michigan is a lot colder than you might think."

Jackson's eyes welled and his body shook. He blew out a breath and spittle clung to his lip. "You drowned him?" He reached into his hoodie pocket where Neko mewed. "You're a fucking dead man!"

"On the contrary, love," Svanire said. "I've never been more alive."

Joe clenched his fists bloodless, an old demon rising inside him. "You murdered my nephew, took everything I ever loved." He cracked his knuckles. "I hope you ate your fuckin' Wheaties today, Squiddy."

"Oh?" Svanire chuckled. "There may be life in the old man yet." He waved a gloved hand at Jackson. "Get the boy," he said, without looking back at his soldiers. "Soften up ol' *Jojo*—but leave him alive for me."

Jackson stepped in front of Joe, pressed his shoulder back into Joe's chest, and discreetly pushed the Beretta Tomcat into his palm. "Give 'em hell, Bones."

"Get behind me," Joe said.

Jackson shuffled back around him. Joe hid the Tomcat behind his thigh.

The two mercs in skull masks stepped forward, both ready with drawn pistols. One aimed at Jackson, the other trained on Joe.

"Sorry Joe, but business is business," said the assassin closest to him.

"Richter?" he said. "That you?"

The assassin nodded. "It ain't personal."

"The hell it ain't," Joe said.

Richter pushed closer and checked the action on his custom Nighthawk Tactical 9mm. "The Squid's money is as good as everyone else's. There's just more of it. A lot more."

Joe sneered. "After all these years, just gonna stab me in the back, huh?" The Tomcat itched against the back of his leg.

"The old ways are dead, Joe," Richter said.

"Well, shit." Joe shrugged, then jerked the Tomcat up and shot Richter square in the face. The .32 caliber round whipped Richter's head back and fractured his skull mask down the middle. Richter stumbled back and his Nighthawk fired into the ceiling, but Joe leaped on him like a tiger and clamped his huge hand around the warm barrel of the weapon.

The other merc wheeled on Joe.

Svanire shouted, "No, he's mine!"

Joe's Tomcat cracked six times as he stitched his one-time friend Richter from knee to groin to a gap in the chest plate. The armored merc gasped and let go of his Nighthawk, but still fought back. Joe shoved the hot barrel of the Tomcat beneath the chin of Richter's mask and fired the seventh and final round through his throat.

Blood poured through Richter's fingers, pinched tight against his neck. He gurgled blood, stumbled back, then crumpled into a heap.

"Gotcha." Svanire's voice whispered close, too close, over Joe's right shoulder.

A flash of pain lanced through Joe's side. He lurched away and tripped over Richter's convulsing body. Joe hissed between his teeth and cupped a hand over the puncture wound below his floating ribs. "Damn it. Damn, you, Squid." He bent and grabbed at his ankle.

Svanire loomed over him like a wraith, the tip of his spearpoint blade red with Joe's blood. The last skull-faced merc swiveled, keeping both Jackson and Joe in his sights.

"Just a little greeting, Joe. Deep, but not too deep," Svanire said. "I want this to last."

Joe secured the switchblade from his sock and flicked it open.

"Yes …" Svanire hissed.

"You're sick," Joe wheezed. "A kid-touching monster. You belong in the ground." His side ran slick with blood.

Svanire made a *tsk* sound through the skull mask. "Joseph, you're such a relic. These are modern times. The term is *minor-attracted person*, and it's perfectly acceptable, just as it was in ancient Rome." He raised an index finger as if starting a lesson. "There's no love like the love of a child."

Joe lunged forward, his elbow tucked, switchblade ready to thrust for the heart.

Svanire sidestepped, executed a beautiful check-parry-pass, and dragged his knife edge beneath Joe's forearm.

Joe grunted and fell against a workstation.

"Death by a thousand cuts is my favorite game." Svanire waggled the tip of his blade. "How much can ol' Jojo take?"

Joe's lungs heaved, his muscles old and tired. His blood-soaked shirt stuck to his side and his forearm burned. He glanced from his adversary to Jackson, who backpedaled, his hands raised, as the last skull-faced merc closed in.

Joe's heart cramped.

For just once in your miserable life, Joe, be the hero.

He gnashed his teeth, then spat on Svanire's boots.

CHAPTER TWENTY-NINE
Jackson

Jackson took another step back and his shoulder blades met the wall. The last skull-faced merc kept his gun trained on Bones, who fought for his life against a terrifyingly fast Svanire.

Jackson's heart banged. A blond bob snatched his attention. Anja shot past the demolished double doors and down the stone hallway.

A heavy fist caught Jackson in the jaw and sent him sprawling to the stone floor. His head spun and his eyes rolled. A kick swept in, fast. "No!" Jackson torqued his body to protect Neko and took the full brunt of the kick in his back. The steel-toed impact tore a hole in him. He gasped, clawing at the floor.

Two blurred silhouettes skittered off past toppled desks. "Neko …" Jackson gasped, trying to reel in his double-vision, but the kitten had vanished.

Jackson rolled to his side and looked up at the swollen profile of his attacker. The skull mask, fixed in a garish grin, stared back. The anonymous killer raised his pistol, silhouetted in front of the huge monitor that hung crooked on the wall.

Jackson covered his face—his gut clenched at the sound of bullets striking meat and shattering bone. He unfolded to see a half dozen bullet holes in the chest plate of his would-be killer's armor. The merc wilted to his knees, then fell back. His head smacked against the stone. A Scarlett Moon soldier with a smoking rifle winked at Jackson as she swatted a passing drone and ran back out the exploded doors toward more gunfire.

Jackson struggled to his feet and searched frantically for Neko, but the little cat was gone. He scrambled away from Bones, locked in mortal combat with the wraith-like Svanire, whose thin arms whipped a blade back and forth with inhuman speed and accuracy. A knot formed in Jackson's gut, and an idiotic notion swelled within him—to help Bones fight the pervert.

"Jack!" Bones yelled from across the command center. "Get out of here!"

Svanire stop-kicked the big gangster's thigh, knocking Bones back. *Anja. The Solution*, Jackson thought. *I have to stop her.*

He shot through the ruined doorway after her.

Out in the corridor, gunshots rang in the distance, but Jackson's own breath seemed deafening. His sweat-soaked hoodie hung heavy on his shoulders like chainmail with none of the protection. He swallowed away the dryness in his throat and stormed down the stony hall toward the spiral staircase. "Her lab," he said aloud. "Has to be going for her lab."

He tumbled down the echoey stone stairs, taking two or three at a time and pinballing off the walls until he reached the familiar dark passage in the bowels of the castle. He crept along, fingers sliding on the cold, damp block. As he approached the door to Anja's lab, now a few inches ajar, a powerful stench wafted out—like mothballs and cabbage. Jackson gagged. Vomit tingled in his throat.

"Oh, hell no," he whispered to himself.

Fighting back the urge to flee, he stole a glimpse through the crack. Tabea's headless corpse lay on the stone floor. Flies buzzed around the open wound that used to be her face. Enveloped in her arms and legs sat Hans, a plastic doll's grin on his face.

A rapid tapping pulled Jackson's attention from the tangled figures. A string of foreign curses drew him to Anja, her face twisted, hunched over her personal terminal.

"*Arschloch!*" she barked, rapping on the keyboard.

Jackson crept in around the door, his sneakers silent on the granite.

Hans looked up, his stupid smirk widening.

Jackson pressed a finger to the poor geekbag's lips and shook his head.

"Sure, yeah," Hans whispered as he picked bits of glass, plaster, and masonry from Tabea's neck stump. "Ssshhhhhhh."

Anja's head snapped up. "You!" she snarled.

"Hans …" Jackson said, and threw his head back. "I thought you had my back, man."

"*Junge!* What did you do?" Anja barked.

"What did *I* do?" he yelled. "What are you doing, you crazy Genial?" He waved his arms at the Tabea-Hans knot of limbs covered in black blood.

Anja frowned and turned her attention back to her monitor. "That … was unfortunate."

The walls shook, crumbs of masonry falling as another grenade detonated somewhere above their heads.

"Unfortunate," Jackson repeated. "So, she's what? A side effect of trying to brainwash everyone?"

Anja continued to type, shoulders back. "She's not a side effect, Junge. Tabea's fate is quite intentional. A means to spread it to places we may have missed. A carrier on the ground with one mission—find a dense population and spread." She nodded to Tabea's mangled body. "I didn't imagine Tabea would be one of the ten percent, but there is no way to predict."

"Ten percent?" Jackson ran the math in his head as he circled Tabea and Hans toward the rat enclosure. "You're willing to pop, like, a billion people across the globe for this batshit crazy plan? Even I'm not that cold."

"You know, your father asked me the same question." Anja tapped a final keystroke. "Didn't think you'd stop years of work so easily, did you?" She cast a satisfied grin at Jackson. "The Solution will be released no matter what you or anyone else does."

Her computer beeped once, and a progress bar inched along.

"Dad …" he said. "Marcel and Svanire, they said he worked for you …"

Anja rose from the desk, her frame now just as thin and malevolent as Svanire's.

Jackson backed over shards of glass toward the broken vivarium.

"Factually correct," Anja said, her tone calm as she stepped toward Jackson. "But, as with all good stories, the devil is in the details. James was low-level." She showed Jackson a tiny gap between her finger and thumb. "Menial job, really. Until he dug a little too deep."

"What the hell does that mean?" Jackson spat back.

"The Solution, Junge. But where to go with such information?" Anja said. "No police. No government to turn to."

Over Anja's shoulder, the computer's progress bar ticked past half full.

"So, he went to people who might have had the means to do something about it." Anja shrugged. "He went to the mob." She shook her head.

"They killed him!" Jackson shouted.

Anja nodded. "Fortune favored me that day, and I didn't have to dirty my own hands." She waggled her fingers at him. "I hoped it would end such nonsense, but you—stupid little arschloch—all these years later, you brought that blade-wielding lunatic right to my door." She raised her eyes to the noise overhead.

"Dad just needed someone's help ..." Jackson whispered.

"Sacrifices must be made," Anja said with a pout, then lunged forward and clasped bony fingers around Jackson's throat.

A surge of adrenaline cranked through his veins and tingled the nape of his neck. He gasped and pulled at the woman's fingers as she drove him back into the shattered vivarium. "Get off!" Jackson jammed his fingers into Anja's eyes.

She grunted and twisted free.

Air rushed back into Jackson's lungs, and he pushed away from the kudzu that climbed the back wall of the vivarium.

Anja pounced on a control panel and slammed her fingers down on the keys.

A whir sounded above Jackson's head. He dropped to the grass and rolled away, barely escaping two multi-jointed arms, each firing arcs of electricity from their ends.

"You're out of your mind, lady!" Jackson yelled. "If anyone needs a lobotomy, it's you, stake!"

"You think I don't know that?" she screamed back.

Under sticky blond tresses, Jackson thought he saw guilt in those glassy eyes.

"None of us are immune," Anja cried. "We're all animals! Willing to kill—to do whatever it takes to survive."

JONES WORTHINGTON

Jackson crawled over the shattered edge of the vivarium and closed his hand on a long shard of glass. "You got that right," he said, and climbed to his feet.

Anja's abdomen expanded and contracted with each breath, the vein in her neck throbbing with each heartbeat.

Jackson looked at the jagged shard of glass in his fist. Joe's voice rang in his ears—*I don't kill women. Not unless I got no choice.*

Anja ran back to her terminal, where the progress bar had filled out. "Yes! Reboot successful." She raised a hand over the keyboard.

"No!" Jackson launched forward and jammed the glass spike as hard as he could into her neck. The sliver popped through her skin, then snagged on the cartilage of her trachea. Anja gasped, and air bubbled around the glass and through the puncture wound in her neck. Jackson forced his weight into her, but his own hand slid, and the edge of the glass sliced his palm. The glass barb cracked and snapped off.

Blood leaked from the puncture in Anja's throat and spattered Jackson's sneakers.

She gagged, grabbed at her neck, at Jackson, at the air. "Please," she gargled, one bloody hand outstretched. "I just …"

Jackson's body refused to budge as warm red life ran down Anja's front and splattered on the stone. "I had no choice," he whispered, and tried to pull the exposed nub of glass out, but it slipped through his wet grasp.

Anja staggered away from him, hands clasped to the wound in her neck, globs of thick dark blood oozing between her digits. She gulped at the air, tripped over her own feet, and crashed into the rat city. There she lay, her ruined breathing like wet hiccups.

Jackson took a few cautious steps and peered down at her.

Anja's sights locked on a single large rat with a white face and dark body, sniffing in her direction.

"Ra … Ral …," she whimpered.

The rat scampered across and bit her on the face.

Anja glugged and choked a scream.

Jackson recoiled. "Holy shit."

The lab spun and Jackson's vision blurred again. His stomach roiled and his brain flooded with both abject disgust at himself and an odd satisfaction with having survived—at any cost. He looked at his hands, then at his blood mixed with hers. The feeling of glass popping through flesh still tingled in his fingertips.

The significant gash in his palm gaped through the blood. "Fuck." He touched for the colorful Antiguan sash around his neck, then thought better of it.

Hans struggled out from Tabea's rigor-mortis embrace and laid her headless corpse on the stone.

"Ah, dammit, forgot about you," Jackson said, his guilt over Anja already slipping away.

"Yep." Hans climbed to his feet. "I'm happy to be here." His stupid smile widened.

"Gonna need your sleeve there, Hans." Jackson stepped over, grabbed one of Hans's ruined shirt sleeves, and tore it free.

"Great!" Hans said.

Jackson bandaged his hand tight, blood soaking the fabric, then marched over to Anja's station. Onscreen, the cursor hovered over a yellow icon with the words *Initiate Protocol*, with one red and one green box below.

"Whoa. That was close," he muttered, then picked up the keyboard from the floor and selected the red box. The screen glitched and came back.

"What exactly *did* I do?" Jackson said.

With Anja's access key still active, Jackson rifled through files and ran searches for a Trojan horse or some embedded virus. He hoisted up a fallen chair and sat in front of the terminal, his brain turning circles. "Down the rabbit hole," he said, and his fingers stroked the keys.

Dozens of windows filled the screen—blog sites and webpages, individual video calls, and chat sections of social apps. Logged in to each site, multiple users had the same line of code running underneath their name—hidden from those on the other end. Within the streaming code, the letters HKT flashed over and over.

Jackson clicked on a blog site where at least six of the HKT bots urged a teenage boy in Italy to kill his mother. Jackson wiped his face with the colorful sash, mind buzzing. The Pegasus program given to him by Hellcat, by Svanire, hadn't just dropped Tarasp's defenses, but unleashed something much worse.

He closed the blog site and opened a live BingOn video where a young girl ranted about some bitch in her neighborhood who'd stolen her boyfriend. HKT-driven bots commented in real time, nagging the girl to disfigure the face of the boyfriend stealer.

Jackson clicked the window closed.

"This is some crazy, next-level shit," he whispered. "Svanire used me to get Hellcat everywhere, like omniviolence on steroids." He huffed out a long breath, his eyes running over the dozens of blog sites, BingOn accounts, video calls, and chat sections. "What the hell am I supposed to do with this shit?"

A single thought caused Jackson to sit bolt upright. He looked at Hans, who fiddled around aimlessly with the loose ends of his shirt. "I could take it all, Hans," Jackson said with a grin. "Dump out Hellcat and put whatever I want in there. Own it all. Not a just cryptokiller—but king of the world!" His grin felt stupid, drunken. Then it slipped away.

Hans giggled and clapped. "King the world!"

Jackson's mother, in her nightgown and fluffy slippers, appeared in his mind's eye. "All I wanted was to get you somewhere safe, Mom," he whispered. He blinked away the last of his doubt. "Just do it, Jackson. Do it for Mom."

He rapped on the keyboard so hard it clattered on the desk.

Hans sang a strange lullaby in German and rocked back and forth in a happy stupor.

"So, Hellcat, or HKT, or whatever the fuck you are," Jackson said. "Your AI protocol is decentralized, which means I can't just shut you down." He kept tapping away. "But ol' Squiddy upstairs is still a Genial and has you running on a total-consensus network." Jackson tutted his disappointment. "Normally, you'd be pretty invulnerable, but," he bobbed his head and smiled to himself, "you already opened your digital legs, didn't you, you little slut." His tapping slowed to meaningful punches of single keys. "Your network inherently requires exchanging packets of info with *all* the other computers in your network. So, all I have to do …"

Jackson leaned back, his finger hovering above the return key. "… is drop a simple virus in and infect at least fifty-one percent of the nodes on your chain." His eyes widened and he stuck out his tongue. "And you *know* I've slapped a few crypto chains off the grid in my time."

He hovered his cursor over the execute button of his go-to malware program. He'd taken down smaller networks before, but the fear that Svanire's bullshit chain was too large niggled at his brain.

"You know, I've never dumped a girl before," Jackson said.

Hellcat didn't respond.

"Silent treatment, eh?" Jackson smirked. "Sayonara, bee-otch."

He jammed his finger on the return key.

The screen went black, and Jackson held his breath.

Hans finished the tune and started another.

Jackson's lungs burned. *C'mon*, he thought.

A single window appeared onscreen. Within its borders, green letters glowed: *HKT program erased.*

"Fuck, yeah!" Jackson whooped, which stopped Hans's off-tune warbling.

A scream pierced the walls from somewhere above.

"Bones," Jackson whispered. "And Neko."

He jumped from his chair and stepped over to Anja's corpse. The rat had all but chewed her face off. Congealed blood coated the metal floor of the rodent city. The lone rat, the one with the white face, twitched its nose, whiskers flecked with blood—quite satisfied with its gory meal.

Jackson squinted at his bandaged palm and at the gash in Anja's throat, then looked back to the rodent. "Perhaps the crazy bitch had a point," he murmured to the creature, whose eyes gleamed. "We're no different than you, are we? But then, in the end, who survived? You and me did, that's who." He pinched up another long shard of glass from the shattered vivarium, careful to nestle the thick flat end in the cloth wrapped around his hand, and made his way to the door, toward the melee of soldiers, mercs, killer bees, and Bones.

CHAPTER THIRTY
Joe

Svanire's stamp kick landed in the center of Joe's chest and flung him back over a table covered in electronics. A computer monitor popped and fluttered black as it struck the cold stone, stirring up a fine haze of baby-blue powder. The old hitman groaned and placed a hand over his sternum where the powerful kick ached. He struggled to his knees. Blood oozed from small cuts up and down his arms, leaving his hands slick and his shirt drenched red. Weaponless, he groped at the corpse of a fallen Scarlett Moon defender.

Svanire laughed—a dry, mirthless sound. He stalked forward, his blood-smeared blade at the ready, his fatigues as clean and unruffled as when he'd put them on. "Finished already, Jojo?"

A trickle of blood ran down Joe's cheek from a nick at his receding hairline. He grabbed at the dead guard's tactical gear and his hand closed on a Glock pistol. "Not just yet." Joe rolled onto his back, ejected the magazine, noted the brass stacked inside, and slapped it back into the mag well.

Svanire holstered his knife. "You're cheating, Joseph. Have you no honor?" He pulled a white smoke canister from a pouch on his belt, removed the wire-like pin, and tossed it on the floor. The smoke grenade hissed a chalk-white stream into the air.

"Hell yeah, I'm cheating. Eat shit." Joe racked the slide and leveled the Glock on a smoke-obscured Svanire.

From his free hand, the long-limbed capo tossed two microdrones into the air, each the size of a golf ball. He tabbed a module on his belt—and his body shuddered and split. Two perfect likenesses pulled away from the central form and stepped away to either side, the forms jittery and broken in the smoke. Each of the three Svanires unclipped a spearpoint knife and a second blade shaped like a talon from their belts. Then they vanished, swallowed by the smoke screen.

"Sweet Mary." Joe squinted through the smoke. He aimed at where the figures had been just moments ago.

"Another gift from my friends at MIT," Svanire said from within the smoke. "Image-refraction technology. Do you like it?"

"Wonderful." Joe's muscles pulled tight. He took a step away from the smoke and something warm, either blood or sweat, trickled down his forehead.

The three perfect likenesses shot from the cloud in unison, the steel of their daggers flashing in the murky half-light. Joe pivoted and fired two rounds from the hip, straight into one skull-masked face. The image shivered and disappeared into the cloud of white, and the bullets zipped off the stone wall beyond.

From somewhere in the gloom, Svanire laughed. "In the game of cat and mouse, deception is king. Is it not?"

A figure pounced from the smoke and slashed Joe deep across the meat of his thigh.

Joe twisted hard and fired at the wraith, but he was gone again. Joe stumbled back—the fresh cut through muscle burned like the touch of frost. "I'll kill you …" Joe murmured, but his movement slowed as a dozen cuts across his heavy frame ran with blood.

"Then do it!" Another wraith-like apparition swiped at him, followed by two more from opposite directions.

Joe reeled back and emptied his magazine.

Two of the figures flickered, but the third caught him in the belly with a shovel-hook punch, followed by four more rapid slashes to his arms and torso. Joe swung hard with his free hand and caught nothing but white smoke. He tripped over the heavy cables from a computer terminal and fell against the wall. Blood smeared the stone and the twenty-foot screen crashed to the floor. His breath came in labored starts and gasps and his heart threatened to tear at the seams. Pain rippled and burned across his body.

He tried to shake the terrible thought, but it lodged in his brain, growing like cancer.

You're gonna die, Joe.

The three Svanires stepped out of the smoke. Joe checked the slide of his Glock, locked to the rear with the empty magazine inside. He let out a defeated sigh and threw the pistol, which clattered to the ground.

"Look at you, Joseph," Svanire said with mock sadness. "So old and pathetic. Such a far cry from the terrifying man of your youth."

"What are you waiting for?" Joe struggled to catch his breath. "Finish it."

"I believe I will," Svanire said.

The three Svanires moved on Joe again, dashing in a fletche attack—but this time, Joe saw the difference in them. Just a shade of the image that was off, but he saw it. One illusion swiped through him and disappeared, then a second.

As the real Svanire lunged in, blade extended, Joe swung down hard with a balled fist and connected with the Squid's wrist. The spearpoint knife clattered to the floor, and Joe kicked it away. When Svanire whipped the second talon-shaped blade at Joe's neck, the capo's wrist smacked into the center of Joe's open palm.

Joe jerked Svanire down by the arm and delivered a crushing headbutt to the skull mask.

Svanire grunted and his knees buckled.

Adrenaline flooded Joe's tissues and tingled down his spine. He bellowed loud and long, scooped his arm between Svanire's bent legs, and lifted him from the floor. Still screaming, Joe took four running steps and flung Svanire sideways through a bank of computer monitors. The equipment shattered, the table toppled, and Svanire rolled on his side across the scattered drives and servers.

A draft from the cracked balcony doors pushed through the room, stirring the thick white smoke and clearing the air. Joe's shoulders heaved from exertion and sweat ran through the blood on his face.

Svanire pushed himself from the stone floor and stood amidst the strewn electronics. He touched his mask and fingered the large fracture that ran down its center. Svanire pulled the mask from his face and appraised its broken form. He pinched his lips into a line, sniffed, and tossed the mask away. A single split on the bridge of his nose bled down his cheek. He wiped it with a gloved hand and smeared the red like a streak of war paint across his alabaster cheek.

"It appears you still have a few surprises in store for me, Joseph." Svanire unclipped another black steel knife from his belt.

"You killed the old man, didn't you?" Joe sucked at the air. "This was all you from the very start. Some kinda twisted game."

"Giordano stood in the way of my ambitions." Svanire touched the knife's razor-sharp point. "Just like you and the rest of the prehistoric relics. Eventually, The Family must evolve."

"After all he did for you … he took you in." Joe spat blood. "I should have choked the life out of you when I had the chance, orphan."

Svanire rolled his eyes. "Even as a child, I could best you, Jojo. You couldn't kill me then, and you can't kill me now." He waggled the knife between his fingers. "And I grow weary of our game. There's so much to do, and my loves await my return." He ran pale, slender fingers in a sensual arc over his crotch.

"You make me sick."

Svanire laughed, absolute focus on his foe as he stepped over Richter's corpse.

Joe stepped back and positioned a long table, topped with computer equipment and scattered snacks, between him and Svanire. A crystalline sheen of baby-blue dust covered its surface. Something hummed beneath an overturned ceramic fruit bowl on the table. Joe dragged a thick finger through the fine layer of powder.

He allowed himself the faintest of smiles.

Svanire stalked forward, knife in hand, and wiped at the trickle of blood on his face. "Time for the end, Joseph."

"For once, we agree," Joe said, and hooked his fingers under the edge of the table.

Svanire's eyes flashed wide.

Joe heaved the entire table over in the capo's direction. The computers crashed and popped, the ceramic bowl shattered, and a cloud of blue powder billowed into the air around Svanire.

The lanky capo coughed and covered his face, then screamed as the three drones whirled around his head. He took off at a blind run, stick-like legs stabbing at the stone. He stumbled over the heavy cable, then crashed to his knees by Richter's dead body. Svanire's slender fingers groped at the dead man's backpack. "No!" he shouted, and swatted a drone away. He yanked the Keybook out and woke it—the profiles of all those to be targeted by the bees filled the screen.

Two more drones landed on Svanire's face. Then another, then five more, and then a swarm. "No!" he screamed.

An odd mix of disgust and gratitude filled Joe's stomach as the drones did his work for him.

Svanire shrieked as the murderous little bees shoved up his nostrils and bored into his brain. He scrambled to his feet, spindly arms flailing, and ran. Joe stepped back as the mad capo streaked past, burst through the balcony doors, and, with a bloody howl, flung himself over the rail. The nightmarish scream, high and feminine, lingered for just a moment. Then it was gone.

Joe sucked at the air and the heaving of his lungs slowed. He sat against the cold stone, his many cuts soaking his clothes red. A lethargy, the likes of which he'd never felt radiated from his head to his toes. He could shut his eyes and sleep for a week—or maybe forever.

The muted rattle of gunfire reached out from somewhere on the castle grounds. Joe searched for a weapon, but found nothing at hand. A ribbon of air whistled over his lips.

Jackson blustered in from the corridor. "Bones?" he called out from the ruined double doors.

"Over here, Jack."

Jackson tossed his glass shank down. It shattered on the stone floor and he sprinted across the command center, where he dropped to the floor beside the old gangster. "Bones!" He hugged Joe hard.

Joe groaned. "Okay, buddy. Easy with the squeezin'."

"Svanire?" Jackson searched the room.

"Dead."

"I wanna hear what happened," Jackson said.

"Arrogant bastard got slayed by his own tech." Joe winced and motioned for Jackson to help him up. "Can never trust that shit."

"Stake." Jackson strained to pull Joe to his feet.

"What about the blond?" Joe asked. He looked down at Jackson's cut hand.

"I, uh …" Jackson touched the bandage.

Joe laid his heavy hands on Jackson's shoulders. "You did what you had to do."

Jackson met his mentor's gaze. "Yeah. I did. It was legit, too. Up close."

"Not so easy?" Joe asked.

Jackson shrugged. "Easier. And …" He lowered his eyes.

"And?" Joe said.

"I kind of got a thrill out of it." He rubbed at the wound in his palm and looked back at Joe. "Does that make me a psycho? Like Svanire?"

Joe cocked his head and tapped the neon green painted #BORNTOSLAY on the back of Jackson's hoodie. "You got rules yet?"

"Rules," Jackson repeated.

He perked up at the faint meow nearby. Jackson stooped and scrambled past electronic debris to find Neko wedged in a corner beside an old chest. He scooped up the little kitten, hugged him beneath his chin, then held him aloft. "I don't kill cats!"

Joe chuckled. "That's a start." He hobbled after him.

Jackson placed Neko on his shoulder and the kitten, shaking after the fury of battle, snuggled down into the colorful sash around Jackson's neck.

"Hey, pal, you see a gun anywhere?" Joe scanned the room. "Just in case."

"No need. Svanire's mercs are bugging out." Jackson thumbed at the sky. "I saw them loading up."

Joe listened as the thump of helicopter rotors grew loud and then faded overhead. He gave a grunt of satisfaction.

The last of the bee drones, their battery life dwindling, skittered around in circles on the blue-dusted stone floor. Around the room, the dead lay jumbled and tossed, as if flung by a tempest.

"So much chaos …" Joe dabbed at the cut on his forehead. "Chaos, original sin," he said, "whatever you wanna call it."

"Huh?" Jackson drew alongside him to look through the open balcony doors at the flawless Swiss countryside bathed in afternoon sun.

"I dunno, maybe my scrape with death made me philosophical." Joe rubbed at his balding crown. "But, think about it—we're animals, just like the rats. Doesn't matter how perfect or safe we try to make the world. Violence is in our DNA. But if we make ourselves passive zombies, then all the best parts of us—the decent parts—those die, too."

Jackson touched the few coarse hairs on his chin and squinted at the majestic snow-capped Alps in the distance. "So, we just gotta make the best of it."

Joe smirked. "I guess so, Jack."

"Is it safe?" A woman in a nurse's uniform poked her head around one ruined wooden door.

"Yeah." Joe motioned with his head. "There's people gonna need your help."

"Like him." Jackson thumbed at Joe.

Mousy and cautious, the woman scanned the bodies, then crossed the room to Joe. He tried to wave her away, but let her give him a once-over.

"You will need stitches," she said in a strong German accent.

"Bastard wanted to bleed me slow," Joe said.

The nurse looked at him with curiosity.

"Fuggetaboutit." Joe waved her away. "Help the others."

She shrugged her thin shoulders and scurried off, checking the bodies as she went.

With Jackson's help, Joe limped out of the fractured double doors into the corridor and toward the courtyard. Finding no one alive in the command center, the nurse scurried off in search of others.

"So, where to next?" Jackson asked as they went down a wide flight of steps.

"I got a few loose ends."

Jackson stopped. "Loose ends?"

Joe stopped to look back up at Jackson. "Svanire kept prisoners." He screwed up his mouth in a deep scowl. "Children. I'm gonna set 'em free."

"A rescue mission?" Jackson waved his hand in front of his face. "Booor-ring."

"You don't gotta come." Joe started limping again.

Jackson strutted to catch up. "Somebody has to keep your old ass in check."

Joe frowned as he pushed through an exterior door.

"And then?" Jackson prodded.

"You're an annoying little prick. You know that?" Joe angled toward an electric Alfa Romeo in the courtyard.

Jackson arched his eyebrows. "C'mon, where do we go catch our breath?"

"You're sayin' I'm stuck with you." Joe shot him a side-eye. "You got someplace in mind?"

Jackson's face glowed with mischief. With his good hand, he pulled up the Antiguan sash from around his neck and smelled it. "Yeah."

The corners of Joe's eyes crinkled. He placed his arm around the teen's shoulders and saw something new in the boy's face. A look of promise, of dreams he once had himself, a belief that one day things would be better.

"Fair enough, pal." Joe rubbed Neko's head, and the little cat mewed a tranquil sound from inside the sash, snuggled against Jackson's neck.

ABOUT THE AUTHOR

Jones Worthington is the pseudonym for Dragon Award Nominees Stu Jones and Gareth Worthington. The best of friends, they technically sit on opposite sides of the political aisle yet leverage their different worldviews to create vivid backdrops and unforgettable protagonists.

Jones works in law enforcement, has served in patrol, narcotics, criminal investigations, and as a team leader of a multi-jurisdictional SWAT team. He is trained and qualified as a SWAT sniper, as well as in hostage rescue and high-risk entry tactics. Recently, Jones served for three years with a U.S. Marshal's Regional Fugitive Task Force—hunting the worst of the worst.

Worthington holds a degree in marine biology, a PhD in Endocrinology, an executive MBA, is Board Certified in Medical Affairs, and currently works for the pharmaceutical industry. He is an authority in ancient history, has hand-tagged sharks in California, and trained in various martial arts, including Jeet Kune Do and Muay Thai at the EVOLVE MMA gym in Singapore. Born in England, Worthington has lived in Asia, Europe, the USA, and currently resides in Switzerland.

www.JonesWorthington.com

Milton Keynes UK
Ingram Content Group UK Ltd.
UKHW031846011224
451858UK00004B/128